Also by
Lizzie Newell

Books

Sappho's Agency

The Fisherman and the Gene Thief

The Return of the Cybernaut Princess

Short Stories

Under an Airless Sky

The Wolves of the Solstice

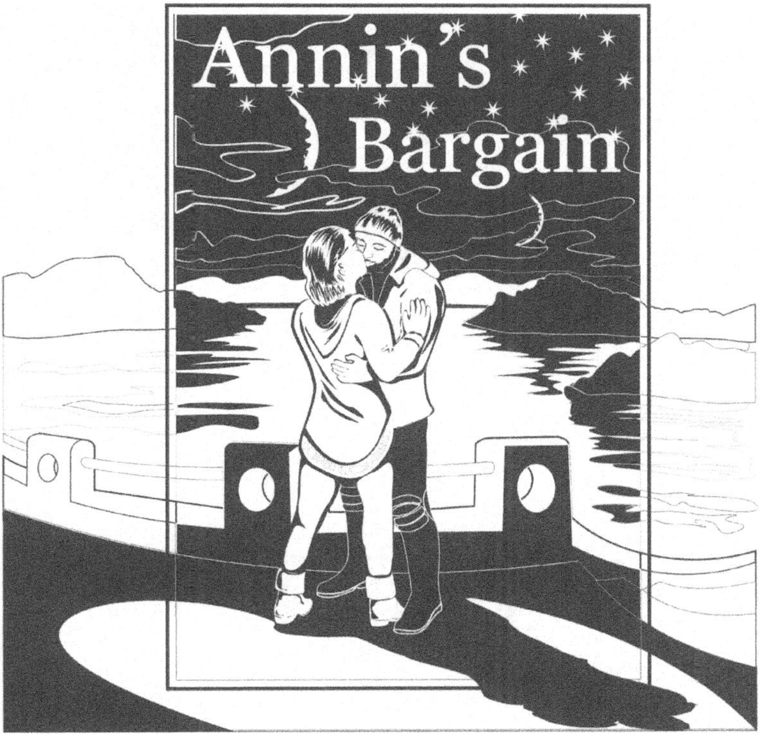

Annin's Bargain

By Lizzie Newell

lizzienewell.com
Anchorage, Alaska

Contents

Chapter 01
Madame X

O N THE WALLS of the waterfront shop, images of naked men gyrated in a shifting mosaic of brawny torsos, rippled abdomens, and muscular shoulders. I gulped. I was fine with naked men but not with the blatant objectification of their bodies. The proprietress of the shop sat on a stool, her long legs encased in black thigh boots. Her vest hung open, barely covering her nipples. Her sexedup interpretation of a Seaguard uniform offended me. I should have just left the shop right away.

"What are you about?" she asked of me, ignoring my brother Teakh. He appeared to be nothing more than a fisherman. His parka and fisherman's bibs smelled of herring but hid his functional Seaguard boots and life vest. Teakh preferred not to flaunt his status and wore both a bandanna and a watchcap over the scars of his implant.

"Just looking," I said. Teakh and I had entered the shop after being intrigued by the sign: "MADAME X'S MANNARY." We were both interested in the economics of the reproductive industry.

Madame X, if that was her name, wore elbow-length lace mitts threaded with electronics. "Look all you want. The question is—what kind of man are you looking for?"

Pretending to be a customer I said, "A father for my child."

"That is what we sell here. Insemination. Either natural or artificial." She glanced toward Teakh with distaste. "A wise choice."

"He's my brother."

"Oh. So sorry. What is your price range?"

"Fratricide!" Teakh swore, using the salty language of a mariner. I winced. To kill a clan member, even unintentionally, was unspeakable. "Why don't you let her decide? Show my sister the best."

"Best depends," Madame X said. "A smart woman picks a sire for the qualities he'll impart to her daughter."

"Boys are just as good as girls," I blurted, stupidly displaying my political views.

Madame X's eyebrows rose. "I still recommend a sire who has talents and interests similar to your own. His genetic contribution should enhance rather than detract from yours. So, Miss? What is your profession?"

"I'm a student," I admitted. I hated that she'd called me Miss instead of Madame, even though I was less than two-dozen years old and so a minor.

She frowned. "What are you studying?"

I'd been studying hospitality, part of social services, but I'd had enough of trying to squeeze enough money from Clan Ralko matriarchs to get through school. "I'm to become a grandmatriarch." I wanted to lead my own clan.

"You?" Madame X oozed incredulity. "You're far too young to be a grandmatriarch."

"I'd best get started then if I'm going to have some grandchildren to lead."

"So you need a man worthy of fathering a clan." She laid on the flattery. "Someone like yourself—a woman of daring, and one who has impeccable genetics. Men like that are difficult to come by, but I know of a stud. Newly available, a rookie." With a ripple of her electronics-clad fingers she signaled to the wall display, bringing up a photo of a naked man. The back of the man's head displayed the scars of a neural implant. The remainder of his hair had been plaited into intricate braids terminating in gold beads. Depths! The stud on display was my very own brother, Teakh, who stood beside me in stained fishing duds.

I was well aware that he'd been auctioning his services as a stud, but I'd never been confronted with the huge, naked reality of the business.

"Yes. Impressive," Madame X said, unaware she praised the very man she'd snubbed or that she was attempting to sell his services to his sister. "He's Seaguard with a genuine neural implant. Those scars aren't just for show."

Between Teakh's fingers, his face shone scarlet.

Madame X continued her spiel. "He's a fisherman. Can you believe it? Risked his life to save a friend from a burning boat. You just don't find genetics like his on the open market."

While in the hospital, recuperating from injuries sustained in the rescue, Teakh had been discovered to have the genetics of the ideal Fenrian man. Supposedly, he was innately altruistic. I knew otherwise but kept my opinions to myself.

"Men of his quality seldom sell for money but for other coin." She stroked her thigh in promise of sleazy payment. "This man's services are up for bid and his price is climbing. If you have enough money you can make an offer for his maiden gig, or I can help you out. Darling, few men can resist me. For a small fee you'll have his child."

I'd had enough. Paying for stud services was one thing. Paying a woman to seduce a man was another.

Madame X turned on her stool, her gaze halting at Teakh. Before either of us could stop her she pushed back Teakh's watchcap and bandanna. Braids tipped with gold beads tumbled out. He shoved her hand away but smiled.

She licked her lips. "Well, this changes everything. Sir, if you'd slip into the back with me I can make you comfortable. We'll help your sister. Any man she wants can be hers. The coin? A trifle from you. No one need know but us."

Good Danna! She considered my brother's semen to be coin, a commodity to be traded as if it were salt cod.

Teakh grasped my elbow. Once outside and away from that hagfish I felt relief. In the lane, we were once again just an ordinary fisherman and a student walking near the waterfront. The breeze blowing from Tristan Bay smelled of the harbor. Houses lined the narrow lane, the ground floors used for businesses, the upper stories reserved for private residences. The digital posters advertising Madame X's Mannary flickered with their promises of sordid wares.

"Succubus," Teakh said.

"You've encountered them before?" Succubi took semen without clan permission, and some men agreed to these under-the-table transactions.

"None as crass as this one." He tipped his thumb to the shop and I noticed that he wore a silver bracelet, a purchase we could not afford out of our shared accounts.

"You won't fall for that, will you?"

"Uh... well. Depends."

His hesitation concerned me. "You wouldn't."

"Depends on how much I like her."

I shivered. "Don't joke about this." If Teakh gave away his semen, the price of his stud services would drop. He was being marketed as having a limited number of children, thus reducing the risk of incest among his descendants while maintaining a premium price. Even worse, if he took part in off-the-record donations, we'd have no way of tracking his children.

"Not joking," he said.

"Seriously, did you like her?"

"That hag eel?"

We continued to our appointment in the capital city as if nothing had happened. We'd had an unsettling experience and walked away. No harm done. Or so I believed.

THE PEDESTRIAN TRAFFIC in the capital city included a surprising number of Seaguardsmen, identifiable by life vests and hip-high boots.

We stopped at our destination, a three-story building with opaque front windows. Dame Bulla, our contact, stood on the stoop. She wrinkled her nose and peered at us as if we were some sort of odious flatworms. Or maybe it was the way Teakh smelled. I didn't mind the odor, but not everyone appreciated the tang of the sea.

The foyer of Dame Bulla's modest office had a row of hooks on one wall but no place to sit. An open door presented a view of gray-green stripes, a wall covering that could be changed on a whim. Dame Bulla's whim today must have been conservative.

Teakh removed his watchcap and bandanna. He stuffed both in his pocket and shook his head, jangling the gold beads in his hair. He hung his parka and fisherman's bibs on the wall hooks. We'd agreed that for the meeting, Teakh would present himself as high-status Seaguard, replete with hip-tall seaboots, their cuffs folded down to display the scarlet band matching the piping on his black life vest. I hadn't designed his clothing and didn't particularly like it.

Dame Bulla served water and a plate of hardtack, minimal tokens of hospitality. The biscuit was tooth-chipping hard, a bit overly traditional in my opinion. Teakh pragmatically dunked his in a glass of water.

Dame Bulla bent over a screen set in her desktop. "You are Annin of Clan Ralko?"

I corrected her. "Currently of Clan Ralko."

She slid her bi-adjustables down her nose. "And this is your brother?"

"Teakh, Noahee Seaguard Chief." I sat up straight.

"I understand you are seeking recognition of a new clan, Clan Noahee."

I attempted a friendly tone. "That's the name we've chosen."

Dame Bulla wasn't moved. "We've considered your petition and have found it lacking. This so-called clan charter contains highly irregular provisions. You intend to allow men to vote? A man may hold the office of grandmatriarch?"

"That's right." I threw down my challenge to matriarchy. "Universal suffrage. My brother's children will be equal to mine."

In most clans, the children of the women became clan members at conception, but not the children of men. That was how matrilineage worked. In our clan, all children would be included regardless of the gender of the parent. Men would also be allowed to vote and to serve on the mothers' council. We would rename it a parental council.

Dame Bulla shook her head. "A man cannot be a matriarch since he cannot, in fact, be a mother."

"He still can be a father," I told her. "We could change the name of clan leader to grandparentiarch." Most clans allowed childless women to vote and hold office. Just because they couldn't get pregnant was no reason to deny voting rights. And men still cared about children.

"Patriarch would be the correct term," Dame Bulla said. "But you have other irregularities here. You have written that your brother will be Seaguard chief, but he is inactive as Seaguard. It appears that, instead of patrolling, he's been working odd jobs."

"I work in investigation." Teakh left out his sideline of training to be a stud. "With proper equipment I can hire myself out as a fisheries detective." Fisheries investigation was a proper occupation for Seaguard.

I yammered on, surely talking too fast. "A failure of Clan Ralko. They haven't provided him with the patrol craft necessary for Seaguard work. On approval of our charter, we'll order a Seaguard esskip. He should receive it in early spring." Paying for the esskip remained a problem that I didn't mention.

Dame Bulla pointed to the screen. "I have here that neither of you are older than two-dozen years of age. You're minors, still requiring parental guidance in signing contracts."

I tried to explain. "Our mother passed away and had no siblings. We're wards of Clan Ralko, but we have no blood relationship to the clan."

Dame Bulla pushed at her spectacles. "Receiving legal emancipation is difficult, nearly impossible. Children can't lead clans."

"I've addressed the issue in our petition. Clan Noahee will be our guardian clan. I've found precedent. In the past, minors have served in clan offices."

Dame Bulla remained unmoved. "You do not meet a single requirement necessary to prove existence of a viable clan. What you have is, in fact, not a clan. Our department has been tasked with registering existing clans, not with establishing new ones."

"But," I objected, "our communication with the Queen indicated our petition would be considered." It was all so unfair.

"It has been considered," she said. "You lack members, territory, and assets. Furthermore you carry significant debt."

I continued to argue what was surely a hopeless cause. "We're not without assets. We have valuable genetics. My brother is a cover stud. He commands some of the highest stud fees in the industry."

Dame Bulla, unimpressed, peered over her bi-adjustables. "Has he received payment for such services?"

He hadn't. Teakh's liaisons, up for bid on Kordelko Auctions, received phenomenally high offers, but bidding hadn't closed, and he hadn't fulfilled any contracts. "A Ralko woman acts as Teakh's manager. She won't allow him to marry or to form a relationship with a woman on his own."

"Ma'am," Teakh said, "we aren't genetically members of Clan Ralko. May I explain?"

She didn't answer him, looking to me instead. I encouraged Teakh with a nod.

He said, "Our genetics are the product of generations of breeding. The Noah Eugenics Project aimed to create the perfect man."

The phenomenal prices for Teakh's services were the result of this failed undertaking. In my view, the project was fundamentally flawed, much like long-ago studies that had attempted to define and identify intelligence as IQ and then sterilized individuals who didn't measure up. Defining altruism was as problematic as defining intelligence.

Dame Bulla wrinkled her nose. "And that is you?"

Teakh said, "Not by a long shot. To achieve their goal, the breeders took as their subjects the descendants of Jamie Noah. They believed him to be the ideal altruistic man. They harvested eggs from our women and bred them with the girls' own fathers: incest. This is how a purebred strain of any species is created. Nearly all the resulting embryos carried harmful combinations of recessive genes. Most but not all of these embryos were identified and destroyed before implantation in surrogate mothers. Some remaining flawed individuals were killed before being carried to term. Despite all this, a number of the resulting infants were born with congenital disabilities. These supposedly defective children were killed or sterilized in the quest for perfect genes."

"We need a clan to protect our children," I said.

Dame Bulla wouldn't budge. "Such genocide couldn't have happened. And if it did it was a long time ago."

Historically, even on Earth, there'd been a link between testing, eugenics, and genocide, along with denial that the link existed or that genocide had occurred.

"It did happen," Teakh said. "If we don't have control of our own marriages and reproductive contracts it could happen again."

If we didn't take care I could be tricked into being inseminated with my brother's semen. I said, "And that's why we need legal status."

As Noahee Grandmatriarch I could wrest control of Teakh's contracts from Clan Ralko, but I had to become grandmatriarch before he produced any children. Ralko had already set the date for his first gig. The timing was critical. If his children were to be born into our clan I needed to have a say in the terms of their conception.

Dame Bulla said, "With only two adult clan members, how can you raise and educate your children? You can't. What happens if you get sick or—Danna forbid—die? What happens to the two of you when you reach retirement age? You're putting an overly heavy burden on your children."

"If this is your answer," I said, "then why have you agreed to meet with us at all? We traveled all the way here from Ralko and Dojko by stratoplane. Your clan, Clan Fennako, paid our airfare."

"If it were up to me you'd have remained in Ralko or wherever you're from. But your petition was seen by the Queen. In her doddering old age she believes your wild proposal has merit. Personally, I'd have tossed this travesty immediately, but the decision wasn't mine to make. She has chosen to grant you clan status on a provisional basis."

The abrupt change of direction left me reeling. If the Queen had approved our clan, why had Dame Bulla withheld the information?

She flicked her screen and read the provisions. "First, Fennako will act as guardian clan. You'll be assigned advisors and accept counsel."

Teakh and I had hoped for sovereignty so that we could make our own decisions. Instead of becoming a sovereign clan, we'd merely swapped oppression by Ralko for the tyranny of Fennako. "Is that counsel? Or do you mean commands?"

Dame Bulla didn't answer. "This is in your own interest. In the eyes of the law you are minors incapable of entering a contract. The Palace has agreed to treat you as emancipated and is offering you exactly what you need: the wisdom and experience of the Queen's own advisors. You'll still have final say."

"But not unless Fennako approves," Teakh said.

"They do approve. Or so it seems. The Palace endorses your unorthodox proposal of extending membership to the children of men. However, they stipulate that membership shall be voluntary."

"That won't work," I said. This stipulation restricted clan revenue. My concern was for our children. "We won't be able to provide health care." They'd be able to opt out, and we could be left with only the sickest as members.

"Maternal clan will provide health care. All members must maintain dual-clan affiliation. Your clan will be supplementary only, a type of club."

"An association," I corrected.

Dame Bulla pointed to her screen. "You may make treaties, engage in bargaining, and sue on behalf of your members."

What I wanted most was to protect Teakh and his children. That could only be done if I were at the table, hammering out his stud contracts.

Dame Bulla went on. "The Palace asks that you accept, as members, patrilineal descendants of Jamie Noah as well as descendants of anyone in the Noah Project. This meets with your stated objectives."

At the time, I'd assumed that only Teakh had need of such advocacy. Fenrian clans were matrilineal, each person remaining in the mother's clan. Thus it had been since the time of Fenna Lee-Smith, founder of clan Fennako, and her husband, Jamie Noah.

Teakh leaned a forearm on the desk. "What about other descendants of Jamie Noah? Matrilineal descendants?"

Teakh and I traced our paternal line to the semi-mythical royal couple. According to tests of Teakh's Y-DNA, his father's father's father had been a descendant of Jamie Noah, although we didn't know the number of generations. In a patrilineal system such as was common on Earth, Teakh might have become king.

Dame Bulla chuckled. "Then I'd be eligible to join your club, not that I want to. Fennako, our clan, consists of the matrilineal descendants of Queen Fenna Lee-Smith and her husband, Jamie Noah. And proud of it."

Her mother's mother's mother had been a descendant Fenna Lee-Smith. Dame Bulla was a cousin of sorts but so distant that the genetic relationship was inconsequential.

She touched her bi-adjustables and read one final provision. "In exchange for clan recognition you, Annin, must bear children. Fennako will choose the sire."

I felt as if the floor had dropped from under me. I'd been asked to have sex with a stranger. I'd wanted sovereignty, not this invasion into my personal life. To gain freedom for my family, I'd have to throw it away for myself.

Teakh reacted faster than I could. He stood up, in scarlet and black, an enraged Seaguardsman. "Unacceptable! That's exactly what we must stop. We must have the right to marry as we please."

"Men are so emotional." Dame Bulla made a patting motion with her hand, signaling that he should sit down. "You still may. Fennako only ask that your sister produce children with a sperm donor of Fennako's choosing. She doesn't even have to see the man. It can be done by artificial insemination. You two are the last of a breed, your genetics a treasure won through the sacrifice of your ancestors. Fennako is cognizant of the difficulty you face in procuring an appropriate sire. Without the backing of Clan Fennako you will be unable to arrange for a sperm donor with genetics of suitable quality. Your line will die out."

So now she admitted that genocide had occurred. Surely Fennako hoped to continue the ill-founded eugenics project. For what? Money? Power? Maybe there was some sort of status to be gained by recreating Jamie Noah. I shook my head.

"Go kill your brother!" Teakh's rage exploded. "You—Fennako—should not benefit from the exploitation of our family. This so-called treasure was produced through incest, abuse, and murder."

Dame Bulla's face reddened, but she remained calm. For that she had my admiration. "You, sir, are benefiting from this treasure," she said with another wave of her hand. "Sit down. I believe you're making money as a cover stud. The proposed arrangement for your sister is little different than the one you enjoy as a stud."

It was different. I would be selling myself in exchange for a clan charter. Teakh was merely selling himself for money.

"She's right." I wasn't being coerced into the contract. "Why is it right for you to sell your genetics but not right for me?"

"Because you're a woman," Teakh said. "The consequences are greater."

Danna! Even my brother Teakh was sexist. "Didn't we agree that men and women should be treated equally?"

"You can't be thinking you'll accept this contract."

Dame Bulla closed the document. "Consider this accord. This decision is not one to rush into. Please take a copy of the provisions and look them over at your leisure."

In the lane, a bird fluttered overhead but was gone before I could determine the species.

"Why did she pretend our proposal had been rejected?" I asked.

"She was softening us up," Teakh said as we walked. "Getting us to accept the terms without question. But we can negotiate, and we will. If Fennako won't accept us as a clan, we'll go elsewhere."

There wasn't anywhere else. Only the Queen had the ability to approve the founding of clans. I kept up with Teakh's long stride. "Fennako is the ruling clan."

"Then we'll take control of our contracts in a different way. We're only cornered if we think we are."

Those who believed Teakh's top stud fees were due purely to his genetics were mistaken. With no training or legal authority to do so, he regularly attempted to dictate the terms of his services. If I could back him as Noahee Grandmatriarch, he'd be more successful. I tucked my hand under his elbow. "So what's the worst that could happen?"

"The worst? Fennako impregnates you with my seed. Our children, the product of incest, are born with congenital disabilities. Then Ralko pulls their support, and so does Fennako. We're left as clanless parents caring for disabled children."

I stepped in front of Teakh, forcing him to a stop. "How would they get your seed? You're a cover stud. Have you donated sperm for artificial insemination?"

"No. But there's this girl I like. And we... uh, well. There's a possibility she took my... uh, stuff... and sold it. I don't think she did. But it's a possibility. And there's Papa."

"Papa? What do you mean?"

"Do we know for sure he never had any other children? Fennako keeps a sperm bank. They just might have some of his seed on deposit. We don't know."

"But Papa loved us and Mama. Why would he have donated sperm?"

"There's a lot of ways for a man to lose control of his seed."

"What are you thinking?" I asked.

"I'm thinking we specify natural insemination. At least then we'll know that neither Papa nor I have fathered your children."

We could forbid incest in our contract with Fennako, but if we accepted artificial insemination, we'd have no way of knowing if they followed the terms. Fennako could slip in unauthorized semen. I shuddered.

As we spoke, a man in a dark parka stepped out of a side street. "A word with you, sailor. Got a lady who wishes to talk with you."

———

Chapter 02
The Alley

MADAME X LEANED against a wall, one knee up, spike heel resting against the masonry. "Darling, we haven't finished our business," she crooned. "My offer still stands. I'll let you know we have complete privacy here." She circled a finger toward a roof cornice and a surveillance camera hanging by a wire. "The security cameras are inoperative. So what do you say we conclude our bargain?"

My gorge rose. How dare this woman make such a crass proposal?

"That's a generous offer," Teakh said. "But we have other plans."

"Do you? We can have a quickie right here up against the wall. You won't regret it. They say my mouth is velvet."

My mind reeled. That anyone should make such an offer and make it in the presence of Teakh's kinswoman—unthinkable!

"I'm sure it is," Teakh said. "But unfortunately, I have difficulty with performance, a bit of a dysfunction. I can't help you. So sorry."

Madame X laughed. "A cover stud with erectile dysfunction. Do you need some pills?"

Teakh steered me toward the end of the alley.

"No need for pills." Madame X tore a package with her teeth. A buzz issued from her hand. "Electro-stimulator."

The man in the dark parka approached. Another stood blocking the alley entrance.

My anger exploded. "You hag!" I knocked the stimulator away, seized a fistful of hair, and yanked. I'd never been in a serious fight before, but by Danna, I'd give her hell. I kicked at her shin and dug my fingernails into her shoulder. She shouted, and I pummeled her head.

Rough hands seized me, and I struggled against my captor.

He spoke to Madame X. "What do you want with her?"

I bit the arm that pinned me against a sweaty chest then stomped on the man's instep.

Teakh yelled, and his fist whistled past my head to strike the goon in the face. The man stumbled and fell. I went down with him. We rolled in cold mud.

Madame X ran, her heels stuttering over cobblestones.

Still on the ground, I seized the ankle of a spike-heeled boot and yanked. Madame X tottered and fell to one knee then recovered and fled.

Other feet pounded the ground. "Peaceweavers! Get down!"

"Do what they say," Teakh said. "And keep mum."

I lay panting on the muddy cobblestones, the smell of clay and piss in my nostrils.

A peaceweaver commanded, "Put your hands on your head!"

Depths! I'd come to Fennako City with such high hopes, and now this.

Booted feet approached—the sturdy footwear of a peaceweaver. The officer stooped and tightened a cuff on my wrist. "Hands behind your back." My hands were cuffed. "You can sit up now."

I rolled, bringing my knees under me. Teakh, also handcuffed, sat nearby. We faced a peaceweaver of substantial build, broad in girth and shoulders. Municipal peaceweavers were invariably women.

A second and more slightly built peaceweaver helped two men who held bloody bandages to their faces. The goons deserved what they'd got. We'd won, if sitting handcuffed on wet cobblestone could be considered victory. I'd meant to tear Madame X apart. No one assaulted my kin and got away with it.

A man moaned. "We were attacked. Lured into the alley and mugged."

The stout peaceweaver said, "By whom?"

"Her." The man pointed to me. "She's crazy. Keep her away from me."

"Her? She doesn't look like much."

"We were the ones attacked," I said.

Teakh shook his head and mouthed, Mum.

The peaceweaver frisked me and found only my comset then told me to sit down again. Next, they had Teakh stand for a pat down. The stout peaceweaver stopped at his chest and pushed open his parka, revealing his black life vest trimmed in scarlet.

She removed the knife from his vest. "Are you Seaguard?"

Teakh responded, "Not saying. We're under hospitality."

"Stranger." The peaceweaver pocketed Teakh's knife. "Don't you pull a fast one on Fennako City Peaceweavers. You can't commit thievery and then claim hospitality to avoid responsibility."

"We aren't thieves."

"Well then, we'll look over the camera records, determine what happened, and let you be on your way. You can sit down now," she said, her phrasing polite but pitched as an order.

With a nod, Teakh complied and squatted beside me.

The other peaceweaver held a handscreen. "We're getting odd error messages from the security cameras. Can't access the records."

"Is this your doing?" asked the stout peaceweaver.

Teakh remained silent, so I followed his example. He had more experience with this sort of thing.

"Let me give you some motherly advice," the peaceweaver said. "Cut the nonsense about claiming hospitality. It just makes it hard on everyone. With that claim, we can't let you go, nor can we arrest you—not technically. So we're all stuck. Son, fess up, identify yourself, and we'll get this over with."

At the end of the alley, two men in Seaguard kit arrived. Just as peaceweavers were invariably women, those in the Seaguard were nearly always men. In her wisdom, or lack of it, the great prophet Catherine Smith had given rule of land to women and rule of ocean to men.

A peaceweaver said, "Harbor Patrol, you boys are a bit late. You missed all the action."

A Harbor Patrolman stepped forward. "We're responding to a Seaguard distress signal."

"Must be him." The peaceweaver stood over Teakh. "Got himself in a brawl, and now he's not providing identification. One of yours it seems, Seaguard. He claims hospitality. Maybe you can talk some sense into the young fool."

One of the Harbor Patrolmen squatted beside Teakh. "I take it you were the source of that distress signal?"

"My kinswoman and I were assaulted."

"And just why were you assaulted?"

Teakh kept his head down. "We're not required to answer."

The Harbor Patrolman turned to me. "Are you the kinswoman in question? Mind explaining what happened?"

"Hospitality," I mumbled. "We're in Fennako City on a matter pertaining to governance. Clan delegates."

"You expect us to believe that?" He shook his head. "You're not matriarchs. Not him, and not at your age."

Just because we were young and Teakh was male, they thought we were unimportant. I nodded to Teakh. "He's clan Seaguard chief. My chosen protector."

"And that makes you a grandmatriarch?" The officer laughed. "Miss, you're a feisty girl and a shiner."

"That might be so." I straightened as best I could while seated on freezing cobblestones with my wrists cuffed. "Under hospitality I could be anyone, even who I claim to be."

"We'll find out about that. Let's see what Tristan Bay Command has on you." The Harbor Patrolman touched a finger to his ear, signaling a hail in progress. Gesturing and grimacing, he communicated silently. "Command doesn't have anything. What's your claim number?"

"What do you mean?"

"When you entered Tristan Bay you either identified yourselves or claimed hospitality. If you claimed hospitality, you were assigned a number to use as identification while in Fennako City. You don't have one, do you?"

"We're guests of Clan Fennako." I'd arrived on a commercial flight. Identification would have been supplied in the passenger manifest.

The stout peaceweaver said, "Then someone must vouch for you."

"We're here to meet with a Fennako representative."

"Who are you meeting with?" she asked.

I didn't want to give out too much information. Most tradeswomen went by last name only or used their professional titles. None of the officers had given out their names—Fenrians avoided using real names in public—but we could assume the officers were all members of Clan Fennako. Teakh lifted his eyebrows and shifted his glance, giving me the go-ahead. I took a breath. "Dame Bulla Fennako with the Department of Clan and Lineage."

The peaceweaver clicked her comset. "Dame Bulla Fennako. Fennako City Peaceweavers here. We have in our custody two individuals claiming hospitality. A man and woman. Young, neither yet in their third dodecade. Seaguard man. Black-and-red kit. Will you vouch for their need to withhold identity?"

Dame Bulla's voice responded: "Possibly. What happened?"

"Some sort of brawl."

"I'll get back to you shortly."

Depths! Dame Bulla would leave us sitting there.

A Harbor Patrolmen stepped forward. "You know, a man who perpetrates a crime is unlikely to call it in."

"We received the call from one of the other two," a peaceweaver said.

"I'm inclined to believe Seaguard regardless of clan."

"You're biased. Look, he doesn't have a scratch on him. He wasn't attacked."

"I'd say the other two took on more than they could handle. They might not have known he was Seaguard. When they realized what they were up against—called in and claimed to be the victims."

The peaceweaver grunted.

The other peaceweaver returned holding forceps and a baggy. "Found these. Looks like a sperm-collection condom—still in the package—an electro-stimulator, and a boot heel, tall." She glanced down.

I turned my toes out, displaying my serviceable but worn flat-heeled shoes.

The peaceweaver's attention shifted to Teakh, and her expression softened. "Victims of sexual assault are often reluctant to report the crime. Son, you can trust us."

Teakh silently returned her gaze.

A comset bleated. "Dame Bulla here. Our young people are indeed under hospitality and should be treated as guests of Her Majesty the Queen, diplomatic immunity. Care should be taken that their privacy is protected from the media and from curious onlookers. Royal Guard is on its way."

The peaceweaver clicked off her unit. "So now we've got the Palace involved. How many agencies do we need here?"

A Harbor Patrolman bowed to Teakh. "Sir, you and your kinswoman sure must be some important people."

Another group of men arrived, also wearing Seaguard kit in gray green but with platinum details.

"Fancy pants over there are Royal Guard," a Harbor Patrolman said. "Supposedly under the direct command of Her Majesty Afra Fennako."

I nodded. Teakh might know the subtleties of Seaguard kit. I did not. Seated on the ground I saw the officers as a forest of green clan legs.

A man with silver swirls on his boot cuffs approached followed by several others. He announced, "Our orders are to protect and give proper hospitality to the guests of Her Majesty. Where are they?"

"A little belated with the protection," a Harbor Patrolman said. "And just what happened to the camera records?"

"We arrived as soon as we were informed."

"Royal Guard is a bit uncertain of their duties."

"Reef it, Harbor Patrol."

With a nod to the peaceweavers, the Harbor Patrolman turned to Teakh. "These ladies answer to the Fennako City Mothers' Council. You don't want to cross them. Harbor Patrol, that's us, answers to Lord Tristan Bay. Our jurisdictions overlap. Royal Guard there"—he lowered his head to the men with platinum spangles—"mostly stands around the Palace looking pretty and bowing with proper etiquette." His smile took on a wicked gleam.

Ignoring the jab, a Royal Guardsman said, "Peaceweavers, release these diplomats immediately."

A peaceweaver knelt to free my hands then did the same for Teakh. I rose and rubbed my sore wrists. Teakh stood beside me.

As one, the Royal Guardsmen bowed, their movements perfectly synchronized. They must have been using neuros to coordinate the action. I nearly laughed.

Their leader said, "Ma'am, sir, our sincerest apologies for any indignities you've suffered at the hands of Tristan Bay Harbor Patrol." He nodded to Harbor Patrol. "Her Majesty has the utmost concern for her guests and has asked that you be provided with bodyguards for the duration of your stay here in Fennako City." He and his fellows again gave a synchronized bow. "Royal Guard will provide security throughout the duration of your stay."

"With all due respect," a Harbor Patrolman said, "requests for hospitality properly go through Tristan Bay Command. Harbor Patrol will provide security."

"When other agencies fail to protect diplomats, Royal Guard may step in," countered a Royal Guardsman.

My mind reeled at the absurdity of law enforcement officers competing to offer hospitality to a ragged student and her odiferous brother.

"Excuse me." A Harbor Patrolman touched his finger to his ear. His face rippled with changing expressions as he transmitted silently. A Royal Guardsman also held hand to ear and carried on a silent dialogue with what must have been his own superiors. The Harbor Patrolman straightened. "I've spoken with his lordship. Tristan Bay will provide a security escort for our guests."

"This is most irregular," a Royal Guardsman said. "However, the palace accept that Tristan Bay must recover honor."

A Harbor Patrolman bowed. "Ma'am, sir, Tristan Bay humbly asks if you'll accept guard provided by Tristan Bay Harbor Patrol."

Teakh's glance engaged with mine then flicked aside. As clan matriarch, the decision was mine.

I cleared my throat. "I must speak with my kinsman in private." We walked away and turned our backs on the assembled officers. "What do you think?"

"I've transmitted to Dame Bulla for instructions," Teakh said. "I have the attack recorded on my neuro, but she recommends we withhold the record. The Palace has asked we attract as little attention as possible and that we avoid involving Tristan Bay. She didn't say why. I don't want peaceweavers involved, and I don't trust the Palace or Royal Guard."

"They're our hosts," I said.

"Madame X knows I'm Seaguard. She spoke of it in her shop, and she claimed the cameras weren't operational in the alley. She didn't think she'd get caught." Teakh tapped his ear. "Recorded by my neuro. So Royal Guard shows up, claiming they're withholding the camera records, and the Palace doesn't want me to release what I have. Seems Madame X and Royal Guard might be in cahoots."

"Do we trust Tristan Bay Harbor Patrol?" We knew next to nothing about the organization.

Teakh grinned "No. But if we accept guard from both, the two agencies will stumble over each other. Should prove entertaining if nothing else."

We returned. With a bow, Teakh said, "My kinswoman is honored, and so accepts guard from both Her Majesty and from Lord Tristan Bay."

"I'm hungry." I also wanted to get cleaned up. We strolled out of the alley. A flurry of activity ensued as uniformed men scrambled after us.

———

Chapter 03
The Diner

THE FARE LISTED by the door to the diner included chowder, whitefish fillets, and braised short ribs. I considered the prices. "A bit over our budget." Nearly everything was over our budget.

Teakh opened the door. "Doesn't matter." We went inside followed by a Harbor Patrolman and a Royal Guardsman. Teakh turned to the men. "Buy you supper?"

"But we don't have much money," I whispered. We didn't have any money.

Teakh lifted an eyebrow.

The Royal Guardsman said, "The Palace will pay."

"The honor belongs to Tristan Bay," the Harbor Patrol officer countered.

"How about you pick up the tab." Teakh nodded to the Royal Guardsman. "And Tristan Bay covers the tip." He whispered to me, "That's going to be a fat tip."

The menu screen set in the tabletop flickered. The upholstery on the chairs was cracked but clean. I left the men and went to freshen up in the washroom, located near the "com-room"—a tattered couch situated in a hallway near the washroom pipes. I cleaned my hands and face and attempted to remove the filth from my leggings.

I returned, and the Royal Guardsman seated me between himself and the Harbor Patrol officer as if I were a fine lady.

Teakh faced me across the table. "Gentlemen, under hospitality, we're prohibited from sharing names. But calling each other hey you is awkward. So what should we call you? Fennako One and Fennako Two?"

"Maybe Harbor," suggested the Harbor Patrolman.

"Guess that makes me Royal," the other said. "Roy is fine."

"Then I'm Harb."

Roy tapped at the most expensive item listed on the tabletop menu. "I'm told the braised beef short-ribs are delicious here."

On a student budget I seldom ate beef. I had pork or chicken occasionally, but mostly ate chowder.

"You fellows have got me baffled." Teakh steered the conversation. "So why are we suddenly important enough to rate guards from both the Palace and Tristan Bay?"

Roy shrugged. "I'm just following orders."

"Honestly?" said Harb. "Because Lord Tristan Bay wants to know why the Palace thinks you're important."

Teakh scratched his head. "We're here on a minor issue regarding clan governance. Not minor to us, of course, but to everyone else."

Harb continued the line of thought. "Possibly the Palace is ashamed that the attacked occurred and is belatedly providing protection." He sneered at Roy. "Or maybe the Palace has other interests."

"I know no more than you do." Roy shrugged. "I was sent by Princess Mareen, Chief of Fennako City Surveillance."

"She's sister to Lord Tristan Bay," Harb said. "They usually cooperate, which is why this situation is so strange."

A waiter arrived at the table, and I knew I was in the big city. Men didn't wait tables in Ralko Village.

Curiosity overcame my manners. "Why aren't you out on the ocean?"

"This is the place to be if you're interested in law," he said. "I help out my aunt and work as a courier."

"Are you a student?" I asked.

"I wish I were. My clan won't pay my tuition. According to them, I'm going to fall off a boat and die before I pay off the cost in clan fees."

"A lot of clans are like that," Harb said. "They think educating men is a waste of money."

"What do you think?" I asked.

He pshawed. "Noah said educate your children. Boys same as girls."

The waiter took our orders and headed to the kitchen.

"We're in Fennako City to petition the Queen for clan recognition." Teakh gave his trust-me glance. "In our clan, we plan to treat men and women as equals."

Harb whistled. "That'll get you in trouble with clan matriarchs. They're not fond of giving up power."

"But men and women aren't equal," Roy said. "Women give birth, and they live longer. They're smarter."

I had come to rely on Teakh's judgment and considered it equal to my own. I said, "With a woman's education you would do just as well intellectually. If you were treated like women, you would live as long."

"No man wants to live like a woman," Roy said. "What man wants to be stuck in a cottage, caring for children, changing diapers, and designing bedspreads?"

I countered, "But if a man wants to, he should be allowed to." Men didn't live as long because they worked in dangerous professions.

"Not me," Harb said. "Patrolling out on the ocean—that's what I want. Exciting work."

"A woman might want that too." Traditional women's work was often tedious.

"What woman would?" Roy asked. "And if she did, who would care for her children?"

Harb asked, "So how much have you been out on the high seas recently?"

"More than you," Roy said. "You know, Fennako is the only clan with women in the Seaguard, and they do a good job of it."

"So now you're claiming women should be Seaguard," Harb responded.

"Women of the royal family. That's different."

My comset bleated at that inopportune moment. "Hailing Annin. Aunt Dyse here."

I went to the com-room for privacy and sat on the tattered couch. "Don't hail me by name."

"Where are you at?" Dyse demanded.

"Send text. This isn't an emergency, and I don't want my name announced in public."

"How am I supposed to hail you, then? Should I address you as Insolent Niece? You haven't been responding to my messages. I am your guardian and responsible for overseeing your education. I trust your symposium is going well. I want a report."

I'd told Dyse that I was in Fennako City for a symposium on clanlessness. I'd left out that Teakh was also in Fennako City. "I assure you that clan funds are being well spent. At the moment, I'm dining with a couple of experts in hospitality." Harb and Roy were experts in hospitality—they were providing it.

"I trust you're learning how to improve the efficiency of the Ralko hospitality program." Dyse's fondest desire was to avoid throwing money at the undeserving poor, and I was among that group. She vetoed nearly every class I wanted to take as being too expensive.

"I believe I am." I signed off and returned to the dining room and a plate mounded with potatoes, short ribs, and mushrooms. I poked at the ribs with a fork. So that was beef. Sampling the meat I savored the sweet, rich fat.

I chastised myself for my lack of charity toward Aunt Ralko. Clan Ralko was locked in an ongoing struggle to balance their budget. Yet oddly, there had been plenty of money for her daughter to study folk festivals of the Fenrian Archipelago. The daughter had returned home with promises of stimulating tourism, but nothing had come of it. Ralko women weren't enthused about parading through the village square, carrying towering puppets. Tourists had difficulty traveling to Ralko to view the spectacle because the Ralko Mothers' Council had refused to extend funding to ferry-dock improvements.

As I ate, Teakh made conversation. "Out our way, we do mostly fisheries enforcement. Small-time stuff—fishermen underreporting their catch, some search and rescue."

"Not much call for that, but we get some," Harb said. "Occasionally, a fellow drops a line off the end of a dock without a fishing permit. Sailors getting drunk and wandering around in the dark. We're mostly traffic cops, so we deal with a lot of vessels failing to yield right of way or speeding in a wake-free zone. We handle port security. Smuggling sometimes. Transport of stolen goods. I worked in the Royal Guard for a while. There's also Fenrian Service. Royal Guard is a prestige assignment, but we're all Fennako, and we transfer between agencies."

"Harb explains it well," Roy said. "More pomp and ceremony within the Royal Guard, but it's a real honor working for Her Majesty."

"How about working for Lord Tristan Bay?" Teakh asked.

"Marsk Fennako?" Harb grinned. "The best there is. He's the Queen's grandson, but he never made a stink about being royal. Things are a bit touchy up in the palace right now. The Queen is getting on in years, and the Princess Royal is lined up as her heir. But it's not a sure thing. Her Majesty could change her mind and go for the second daughter, Marsk's mother. Marsk is the highest-status man in Clan Fennako."

"What about the king?" I asked. Traditionally, the queen appointed her consort to the position of archmagnate, but this queen had chosen her son-in-law. The king was the highest-status man associated with Clan Fennako.

"He's not a member of Fennako," Roy said. "A man can't marry into his own clan. That would be incestuous."

"Marsk is the son of the second princess," Harb said. "It's complicated. That's why I stay away from Palace politics."

"You sure have a lot of opinions for someone who stays away from Palace politics."

Harb squinted. "How does the incident today impinge on royal succession?"

"It's doesn't," Roy said.

Teakh said, "Beats me."

I shrugged.

"If men and women are equal," Roy said with a sly grin, "Marsk becomes queen."

Harb laughed. "Not our chief."

I considered. Suppose that inheritance were patrilineal and traced to Jamie Noah and his wife, Queen Fenna Lee-Smith? As patrilineal descendants of Jamie Noah, Teakh and I would be in line for the throne, or at least competitors. I shook my head. I only intended to protect my brother and had no interest in Palace intrigue.

Roy and Harb accompanied us to our lodging near the waterfront. They argued about the best place to stay. Neither of them approved of our cheap accommodations. I preferred not to have Fennako Seaguard choosing our lodging. They could too easily bug the place. "So nice of you to offer. We're quite comfortable here," I assured them. Teakh and I left the two men in the lobby.

Our small room, similar to steerage quarters, contained two narrow beds, a clothing rod, and a small chest with charging niches. I kicked off my shoes and sat on a bed. "If we'd had clan status, we wouldn't have needed to claim hospitality. Assaulting you would have been punishable as an attack on a sovereign chief."

"Don't rush into this. The whole incident may have been orchestrated by the Palace. How did Madame X know where to find us? Why were the sinking cameras inoperable?"

I was exhausted. "We shouldn't have let on about your value as a cover stud."

"I sure wasn't announcing it. Fennako may have us just where they want us. We need to understand their game. Suppose you go through with having a child then Fennako pulls our clan status. Can we sue the Queen for breach of contract? What if Queen Affra is dead and we face her successor?"

"Her Majesty's protection is better than nothing."

"If today was her style, we'd do better with nothing."

"She did send Roy."

Teakh tossed his head in negation. "That wasn't the Queen. Royal Guard was sent by Princess Mareen. I don't expect help from that quarter. I had that run-in with her over Gull."

Princess Mareen had contacted me to vouch for Teakh. He had been using his drone seagull to do investigative work in Fennako City. I assured her that he was a fisheries detective specializing in identifying illegal catch and that he employed his gull mimic to sample fish fragments as evidence. Oddly, Teakh had been employing his drone to visit art galleries. I'd made excuses to princess Mareen, claiming he had an interest in portraiture and that he'd been helping me with my studies.

He said, "Princess Mareen warned me that if Gull showed up in Fennako City without proper registration, I'd lose my bird to royal override."

The queen reserved access rights to all Seaguard equipment, including artificial seagulls, and she could delegate that right to her agents.

"I'm sure as depths not going to register my equipment as Ralko," Teakh said. "I left Gull in Dojko." He rubbed his shoulder. "I smacked a wing against something, and the joint hasn't healed properly. I need to have an expert look her over. I get over my ankle injury, and then I damage a wing. That's the problem with telechirics— you get twice as many sore body parts."

The telechiric bird was essential for Teakh's work as a detective. Ralko had covered Teakh's medical bills, but they weren't going to pay for repairs of his unregistered equipment. We had pitifully few options. We couldn't continue living on the charity of Clan Ralko, and we were already deep in debt.

Should we accept Her Majesty's offer?

I wrestled with the question.

AT BREAKFAST AT our lodging I told Teakh that I'd decided to go through with the pregnancy contract. I did want to have children, and Dame Bulla was right: without some help, men wouldn't be interested in me and I couldn't afford to hire a high-quality stud.

Teakh wasn't convinced. "Sink genetics! What matters is if you love the guy."

Who was he to talk of love? He'd been selling his services to the highest bidder. "You're the cover stud."

He peeled an egg. "I'm the cover stud who dreams of getting married. At the very least, find yourself a man you like."

The arrangement was for insemination, not a permanent marriage. After I became pregnant, I could marry whomever I wanted. "I will, but later." I sipped my boricha, enjoying the richness of roasted barley.

"Think your husband will like that?" Teakh asked.

The arrangement improved my marriage prospects. I'd be a clan leader, not an impoverished student. The man I married would be senior clan husband, a position of status. "I have to do this. It's the only way to protect ourselves from people like Madame X. We might be minding our own business in Dojko or Ralko, and someone decides to jump you and avail themselves. I'm not counting on Clan Ralko for assistance. If we were a recognized clan, that attack would've been an interclan offense. The Queen would have to step in."

Teakh made a pile of eggshell fragments. "She's not gonna be alive much longer. Will her successor honor the agreement?"

"Her protection is better than nothing."

He pitched his voice low. "We better be damn sure about the terms of the contract. Natural insemination only. Let's make certain the man wasn't jumped in an alley."

I crossed my arms. "This is Fennako we're dealing with, not Madame X. Fennako doesn't assault sperm donors."

"And you don't think that Fennako was cooperating with her?"

I didn't answer. Artificial insemination seemed better to me, more impersonal. "I don't want to meet him. I'm not going to marry the guy."

"What are you afraid of—that you'll fall in love?"

"No. That we'll hate each other."

"If you hate him you shouldn't be bearing his children. Meet with him at least once. We should also get independent lab analysis of his genetics, and we need video records of the act. I'll be your witness."

"I will not have my brother watching."

"It's the only way we can be sure that Fennako acts in good faith. We also need a clause specifying damages if the child has genetic disabilities. Fennako might attempt something genetically risky."

"You mean incest?"

"Aye. Deceit happens all the time with breeding programs. It goes all the way back to a fellow on Earth named Plato. He proposed breeding humans as if they were hunting dogs."

"We're not dogs."

"We just might be to Fennako."

"What do you think Mama would say about all this?" I asked.

"Same thing I'm saying: only do this if it's what you truly want. I've met a girl and I'd like to marry her if she asks, but not at this cost. We can have a relationship on the sly. I don't believe Mama and Papa had clan approval of their marriage." He twisted his silver bracelet.

I said, "And you know how hard that was on Mama." She'd lived as an outcast, never quite accepted by Clan Ralko. I'd never known what she'd done for work over the network. I now had an opportunity to improve our lot. I could live differently, a clan leader, not a strange woman living in the marsh.

The hotel clerk entered the breakfast room. "There's a courier here with a package for Annin Noahee."

I went out to the front desk where a Royal Guardsman waited. He set a parcel on the counter and bowed. "A gift from Her Majesty."

"Uhh, thank you."

"What is it?" the clerk asked.

"I don't know." I took the package to our room and tore open the paper. Out spilled a new tunic, a pair of leggings, and an envelope bearing a clot of pale-green wax imprinted with a fanciful wolf with the tail of a fish. I broke the seal and removed a sheet of thick, creamy paper inked in an elegant hand.

Please accept this token of our hospitality.

The signature was illegible chicken scratch.

I set the note aside and shook out the hooded tunic. It was traditional and tasteful with a brocade front panel concealing numerous pockets supplied with a rattle, teething ring, and soft cloths. The panel also concealed cleverly placed openings for nursing, and expansion pleats over the belly. The leggings had a waistband cut low enough to pass under the bulge of pregnancy.

The message from Her Majesty was quite clear: she looked forward to my pregnancy.

—

Chapter 04
Negotiations

TEAKH ACCOMPANIED ME to a meeting with Dame Bulla although, like me, he remained suspicious. I wore the gifts sent by Her Majesty but was uncertain as to what acceptance of them signified.

"I am so distressed by that attack," Dame Bulla exclaimed. "Dreadful! You poor boy. And Annin, so brave. Fortunately, Fennako responded quickly."

"How do you know what happened?" Teakh asked.

"The Palace is withholding the record to protect your privacy."

"What about the woman who assaulted my brother?" I asked. "Are you protecting her privacy?"

Dame Bulla hustled us into her office and pulled out chairs. "The Palace is taking care of everything."

"What about that woman?" Teakh wouldn't be appeased or silenced. "I believe she was sent to steal my seed so that it could be used to impregnate my sister."

"That's disgusting," Dame Bulla said.

"It is. We'd better make sure it doesn't happen, so we'll make changes to this contract of yours." He nodded, giving me the go-ahead.

I opened my handscreen for notes. "I shall be required to produce only one child with the specified man."

"Fennako proposes three—" Dame Bulla began.

"No!" Teakh interrupted. "If my sister produces only one child and is unable to continue with the arrangement, Fennako cannot abandon her and the child. The terms of the contract must go into effect after one pregnancy."

"I will convey your wishes to my superiors." Dame Bulla folded her hands.

"Insemination must be done by natural means."

Teakh and I had argued about this, and I'd conceded. By meeting the man once, I'd know at least something about him, and I'd be able to tell my child about his or her father.

Dame Bulla looked over the top of her bi-adjustables. "Are you sure?"

Teakh said, "If insemination is by direct cover, we can be certain, or somewhat certain, that my seed hasn't been used. We would like there to be a witness, chosen by my sister, and for video records to be made to ensure that the act has been performed according to the contract. We also ask for independent lab analysis of the man's genetics."

Dame Bulla objected. "Fennako understands your concern, but the man's privacy is of utmost importance. Fennako will provide analysis and certification of compatibility, but you will not be provided the details of his genetic profile."

"When my child is tested after birth," I said, "I will know quite a bit about the father's genetic profile."

Dame Bulla looked over her spectacles. "But not all."

"What detail wouldn't I know?"

"Clan," Teakh said. "Mitochondrial DNA is inherited only from the mother. With matrilineage, mitochondrial DNA indicates clan."

"Not always," Dame Bulla said. "But that is the concern."

"Our concern is the man's Y chromosome," Teakh said, "We must be certain he's not a close relative."

"Be assured," Dame Bulla said. "He is not of your close kin."

"Is he my distant kin?" I asked.

"Everyone on Fenria is kin," Dame Bulla responded. "We descended from only five men."

"Plenty of women, though," Teakh said.

"Aye," Dame Bulla said. "In the dark ages, we had a severe shortage of men."

"The Five Forefathers." Teakh snorted. "They just might be mythical."

"Jamie Noah wasn't," said Dame Bulla.

"Ah, yes," Teakh said. "Our common ancestor."

I'd never been sure how much about Jamie Noah was myth and how much was historical. He'd brought life from Earth aboard an ark, written the Noah Code, founded the Seaguard, became the first king of Fenria, and left his Y-DNA to Teakh. It all seemed a bit much for one man to have done. "Let's leave Jamie Noah out of the discussion," I said. "I fear that the proposed man might be a descendant of those in the Noah Eugenics Project. If he is, then according to our charter, he's a member of Clan Noahee, and the relationship is incestuous."

"Only if he chooses to be a Noahee member," Dame Bulla said. "But this man is not directly the product of that eugenics program."

"Then he could be Noahee?" I asked.

Dame Bulla danced around the issue. "Given the quality of his genetics, there's likely some correspondence between his profile and the genetic ideal. The relationship is not close enough to cause problems. Fennako views this as an advantageous cross."

Given that convoluted answer, the man was surely kin of some sort. Was clan incorporation worth the risk of recessive disorders?

I said, "We're going to need child support. I haven't yet finished my studies and am not financially prepared for motherhood."

"Fennako is aware of the difficulty of caring for a child while completing your education," Dame Bulla said. I was unsure if she knew I wore maternity clothing given to me by the Queen. "They propose treating you and your children as Fennako sept. Fennako will provide health care. You may share childcare with Fennako women while completing your studies in Fennako City."

Surely there was a hitch. The proposal gave me everything I needed with the exception of the man's identity. As sept, my child and I would have all the benefits of Fennako membership without being genetically related to the clan.

Teakh voiced my own misgivings. "Your offer is suspiciously generous."

"Queen Affra favors the two of you." Dame Bulla peered over her bi-adjustables. "As unlikely as it seems."

It did seem unlikely. Affra Fennako was the most powerful person on the planet. We'd never met her, and I had no idea why she had an interest in several nearly clanless orphans and was so keen on pregnancy for me.

———

Chapter 05
Justice Poker

S INCE AUNT DYSE believed I was in Fennako City for a conference on clanlessness, I had to make it true. Using information sent out by symposium organizers I located the building containing multiple hexagonal auditoriums, a veritable honeycomb of meeting rooms. I entered a hallway that ringed the specified auditorium and served as a foyer. Here attendees could draw apart and discuss issues in small groups. Inside the auditorium proper, folding chairs had been placed in a circle. Overhead screens displayed relevant graphs and requests to speak.

Trying not to disturb proceedings I located an empty seat and opened my handscreen.

A woman in academic robes addressed the ring of listeners. "Contrary to popular views, the majority of clanless haven't been banished for criminal behavior." The attendees tittered, and the speaker continued. "A significant number are members of bankrupt clans. Generally, these clans have become too small or poor to absorb the cost of medical procedures. However"—a bar graph shifted to become a pie chart—"the largest slice is made up of men who are clanless by choice. These men claim clanless status to avoid paying taxes and to receive free food, shelter, and healthcare." The expert raised her voice. "And why should they pay clan fees? They're young and healthy and don't have children of their own." Another chart flashed on the screen. "Here we have the life expectancy of men and women. Due to fishing accidents, men frequently do not live long enough to receive the retirement benefits they've worked for. They may not be entirely shortsighted, but when they do become ill or if they survive the nearly inevitable fishing accident, their only recourse is hospitality."

Teakh had broken his ankle while working aboard a fishing vessel and resorted to hospitality for his medical care. A lab technician had run blood tests and discovered his valuable DNA. This technician contacted Aunt Dyse, who arrived to claim Teakh and induce him to become a stud for hire. Odd how quickly Aunt Dyse had acknowledged us as kin when there was money to be made.

On the central screens, requests to speak and numbers of supporters flickered and rolled. A topic moved to the top of the list, and a woman came forward. "We must have safeguards to ensure that those who claim hospitality have legitimate needs and haven't merely failed to plan ahead or attempted to dodge clan fees."

Teakh and I weren't lazy or shortsighted. Ralko held a grudge against our mother and so wouldn't extend the funds we needed for education. I transmitted a request to speak. My topic languished near the bottom of the listing as other attendees spoke of the strain placed on society by the clanless, then I heard my name called by the moderator.

"We have an unusual view. Annin Ralko reports that she and her brother are among those regularly claiming clanless status. Perhaps she can shed light on our dilemma."

With fear in my belly and my heart pounding I stood, then I gulped and spoke clearly:

"Here's how it is: my brother and I are members of a clan in name only. My brother, a Seaguardsman, doesn't have an esskip. He can't go on patrol, so he works as a common laborer or as a fisherman."

A woman raised her hand. "You say he's Seaguard working as a fisherman? I find that hard to believe. No Seaguardsman would fish for a living."

"My brother works a variety of jobs." I glossed over his planned gig as a stud and his hopes of becoming a detective. "For low pay. He can be fired for any reason or no reason at all. Our clan won't do anything to help him"

"I see. But you aren't actually clanless."

"We might as well be," I said.

"That doesn't make sense," the woman said. "Surely it's in a clan's best interest to educate its daughters and to provide equipment to its Seaguard."

"That's what I've told them. They won't listen, so I'm starting a new clan. To the depths with them. Men are equal to women, and that's how it's going to be in our clan."

"Surely this is a sick joke." Disgust contorted her face

"It's not. We've written up articles of incorporation. All we need is the queen's approval."

Discord erupted. Women abandoned procedure and shouted their opinions. The moderator in academic robes blew on a whistle repeatedly. The next speaker stepped forward. "I cannot believe such a proposal would ever pass. It would destroy—yes, destroy—our most sacred institutions. Motherhood itself."

The next speaker said, "If people are allowed to choose between mother's and father's clans, they'll abandon the lesser clan, forcing smaller clans into bankruptcy. This will swell the ranks of the clanless, exacerbating rather than solving the problem of filthy vagrants infesting our docks."

The din swelled and ebbed, swirling through the room.

"Silence!" shouted the moderator. "Let her speak."

I stood in the midst of the chaos and spoke the truth, "Men must be allowed to support their own children. They should be allowed to vote in clan elections and hold matriarchal offices. If their children are clan members men will have a vested interest in their clans. They will be full members with the same rights and responsibilities as their sisters."

Women again shouted out of turn. "Already vested in their sisters' children."

"Sisters' children aren't the same as your own children," I shouted back.

"No man can be sure his wife's children are his own."

The argument slipped beyond my control. "He can be sure. What about paternity tests?" I shouted, my voice drowned by the din.

"Sit down!" ordered the moderator. "You've had your say."

I yielded the floor to another who declared, "Men are selfish. They'll never voluntarily contribute to childcare. The long challenge of woman has been to civilize man. On ancient Earth, women made a sad bargain to remain in oppressive and stultifying marriages in exchange for men taking responsibility for children. I tell you it did not work. Men abandoned any children they considered to be bastards and punished any women they even suspected of adultery. This is a slippery slope. If we give rights to men they'll subjugate women. Even if men grind us into the mud, they'll still refuse to take responsibility for childrearing. They will not do it."

Someone shouted, "They'll vote for whoever buys them beer."

In having my say, I'd kicked over a hornet's nest. I could only imagine what these women would have done if Teakh had asked to speak.

As I departed, a woman stepped across my path. "Men are inherently selfish. If you think otherwise you have sphagnum for brains. I take it you've never had children. You're no true mother."

"All men and women are inherently selfish. Some more than others." My head held high I walked past her into the foyer.

"Lubber!" shouted another. "You must be so proud of taking the hard-earned money from other women."

I didn't answer. I wouldn't be further drawn into fruitless and irrational arguments. Yet, uncertainty seized me. I was shivering. Had I jeopardized our clan charter?

Maybe I was wrong about men. If given the chance to vote and support their children, would they? Would they be willing to pay clan fees for this privilege? If they did vote, would they choose to fund education? Or would they squirm out of paying clan fees, and use the money to buy ever-larger boats with powerful engines?

I exited the building to confront Harb and Roy in the lane.

"Why are you following me?" I thrust my hands in my pockets.

"At your service." Roy bowed. "We are to protect you."

"I don't need protection."

"I'm sorry, madame. According to the Palace you do."

I stopped. "Do you know what I said in there?"

"It's on record," Roy said. "Every woman is allowed to speak her mind."

"What about men?"

"We keep our opinions to ourselves. I'm Royal Guard. Despite what Harb thinks, we do more than stand around looking pretty. We safeguard civil discussion, regardless of our personal opinions. We step in when disputes become violent. Women tend to calm down around men, especially around men believed to be neutral."

"I think it is your business. I said that men should be allowed to vote. We shouldn't have symposiums attended only by women. It's wrong."

"Men too often speak with their fists," Roy said.

"Peaceweavers are the most effective with combative men," Harb contributed. "We could bring them in as Royal Guard."

My simple idea of protecting Teakh and his children propagated like waves from a seismic event to engulf the boundaries between genders. Harb had taken the idea and immediately proposed acceptance of women as his colleagues. I shook my head. To tell the truth, none of this made sense anymore.

WE CLIMBED THE steps to the Zenhedron Plaza. Teakh had joined us for a tour of Fennako City with Roy and Harb acting as tour guides. They'd suggested it.

Atop Lawrock, I stopped to catch my breath. Tristan Bay spread below us, an expanse of bright water nearly the same shade as the blue sky. Behind us, the green copper dome of the Zenhedron rose from the high plateau.

We stood as if on a rampart. Harb pointed out and named the islands. including Tristan Head. "Harbor Patrol headquarters are there," he said.

Roy took over, conducting us across the plaza and inside the courthouse. The vast amphitheater resembled the discussion hall but on a giant scale, big enough for nearly a grand of spectators. The dome arched over a speaker's arena ringed not by a rail but by a parapet surround by four quadrants of banked seats. A jade compass-rose marked the center of the arena directly below the oculus of the dome.

Roy explained that the amphitheater wasn't actually big enough for a representative from every clan. Most meetings and voting happened by remote teleconference. "This place is a theater as much as anything. People get hopping mad and need a place to yell at each other and throw rotten foodstuffs. Royal Guard gets to sort everyone out and clean up the mess. Clan matriarchs can be vicious barracudas. As a grandmatriarch, you'll be in the thick of it."

I was struck by a premonition, a double vision with the future superimposed on the present. Someday I'd stand in the Zenhedron, speaking for the rights of men.

"There's an excellent pub over this way. How about if we treat you two? We can relax." Roy set off down the steps from the Zenhedron's heights.

"He's a smooth one," Harb said.

Teakh took Roy up on the offer. He never passed up a chance to schmooze.

THE PUB HAD dark paneling and a comfortable scattering of armchairs. After a meal of fish and chips washed down with cranberry seltzer, we played justice poker. The goal of justice poker was to achieve balance. Or to appear to achieve balance while cleaning out everyone else. The game was traditionally played for chores or small items and could be a convenient method of getting rid of unwanted Solstice gifts. Lacking items we were willing to part with, we agreed to play for questions—a popular way to get to know people.

Roy called for the waitress, who brought cards, chits, and pencils.

I touched a pencil to the smooth ivory of the chit and

considered my question. I wanted to know why Harb and Roy were so solicitous of my opinions. I wanted to know if they agreed with me regarding suffrage or if they were merely humoring me. Most of all I wanted to know the identity of the man who would father my child. In the end I wrote: "Would you vote if you could?"

Roy glanced my way. He cupped his hand around his chit as he jotted. After he shuffled and dealt, I fanned my hand and glanced over the top at Teakh. Part of the fun of the game was deciphering what people actually wanted. Both Harb and Roy were bent, studying their cards.

"How do we know you aren't cheating?" I asked. Seaguard could use their neural implants to communicate during the game, putting me at a disadvantage.

"We wouldn't do that," Roy said. "I wouldn't, anyway. I don't know about Harbor Patrol."

We played. Harb won and collected the chits. He thumbed through them. "A question from Roy. I believe he intended this for our radical grandmatriarch. Describe your ideal man." He grinned and held up the chit. "Roy, what business is that of yours?"

"I thought it was worth asking," he mumbled.

Harb cleared his throat. "I'm not such a cad. I'm directing Roy's question to our visiting Seaguard."

"And why would you want to know his ideal man?" Roy asked. "I thought you went for girls."

"Honestly, Roy, that's a juvenile question. We'll change the wording for the gentleman," Harb said. "Sir, describe your ideal mate."

Teakh had the look of someone backed into a corner. "A woman, not a man." In all-male company, he probably would have described breasts, hips, and legs. I have a good idea of how men talk, so what he said took me by surprise. "She has brown eyes and auburn hair. I like her smile and the way she laughs." By the North Star—my brother had described a specific woman. Then I recalled that he had mentioned a girlfriend. The silver bracelet he wore had the look of a love token. So my brother was sweet on someone. Odd that I find this out by playing Justice Poker.

Roy toyed with a chit. "So here's a question for the lady. Who do you support as the next princess royal of Fenria?"

"I don't even know the candidates. Why does it matter anyway? The queen appoints her successor."

"Not exactly." Roy set the chit aside. "Grandmatriachs and Seaguard lords vote to approve her choice. The royal family would like the next queen to begin her rule with a significant mandate."

Harb broke in. "Here's how it is—if clan matriarchs refuse to pay banking fees, Fennako cannot collect revenue. They blackball the queen, a vote of no confidence. And Seaguard lord can refuse to yield administrative access, no royal overide. Same thing. Blackball her. She might be queen in name, but she'd have no revenue and no power."

"Let me get this straight," I said. "Once we're a clan, my brother may remove royal override from his equipment?" The queen and her appointees had the ability to lock equipment used by Seaguard. They could even do so midflight, causing an aircraft to crash. Princess Mareen had threatened to do so if she sighted Teakh's drone in Fennako City.

"Yes but it's a vote against the Queen," Roy said.

What difference would one small drone make to the Queen? I thought. I asked a more practical question; "Are you acting as an agent of the royal family in seeking my view?" Roy could be a member of the royal family himself, but then again, those wearing the kit of the Royal Guardsmen might not even be members of Clan Fennako.

"I'm playing cards," Roy said, his answer evasive.

———

Chapter 06
Princess Mareen

ROY ESCORTED ME to the Palace. A postern gate unlocked to his touch and he ushered me into a walled garden. Yellow leaves littered the pathway and gave off the sharp incense of autumn. A woman, presumably Princess Mareen, stepped forward to greet me. She wore Seaguard kit, but her boots and vest, both in the muted green of Clan Fennako, bore no decoration or badge. Her dark hair was plaited in a single braid, but the temples and sides of her head had been shaved and displayed the intricate welts of a Seaguard neural implant. Kicking through leaves I followed her across the garden and into an office.

The place wasn't what I expected from a room in the Palace. Robotic parts cluttered a desk and workbench. An entire wall was covered with niches filled with equipment. Each cubicle contained one, two, or three drones, robots, and cameras. Under the high ceiling of the office, the equipment storage was stacked far higher than a woman could reach. In fact, the shelving resembled nesting boxes for birds. A crimson drone fluttered from a cubicle and flew toward a wall panel, which opened, allowing the craft to exit. Such a rookery would be the envy of Teakh or any other enthusiast of remote-control devices.

Mareen cleared part of the desk by pushing aside a heap of parts. "Pull up a chair. I'll be right back." She went through a door, and I caught a glimpse of a kitchen beyond. She returned with an elegant tea set painted with zoomorphic patterns—creatures with fish tails but the head and forepaws of wolves.

She closed her eyes, and the wall panel slid open. A gray drone flitted from the garden into the room. The device had wings like a bird but spindly wire legs. Its oversized eyes were surely camera lenses. It settled into a cubby. Mareen's shoulders moved as the drone folded its wings.

Inviting me to sit at her desk she said, "Let's discuss that incident down by the waterfront."

So this meeting was to be an interrogation. Arms crossed I prepared for her accusations. "We claim hospitality."

"Your claim is on record." From a drawer she removed a stack of graph film. With a glance I saw it was a hard copy of the Noahee clan charter. She dropped our charter on the desk. "We need to talk without our brothers or their agents listening in. My brother is Lord Tristan Bay, Tristan Bay Harbor Patrol Chief, and I have it that your brother is Teakh Noahee, né Ralko. He currently resides in Dojko."

I blanched. She had accurate information about us. I spoke of Harb and Roy. "Your brother has a man following us. So do you, I understand."

"I've asked a kinsman to look after you. I trust there have been no additional problems." Mareen poured tea. "You and your brother present a tangled skein. As Chief of Fennako City Surveillance, I'm responsible for security cameras in Fennako City. Peaceweavers received a distress call and responded first. They're with Fennako City Social Services."

"Harbor Patrol showed up and then Royal Guard." I nodded.

She set a cup and saucer before me. "I sent the Royal Guardsmen. I serve as the liaison between Seaguard and Fennako Social Services. It's part of my job. I'm considered to be both Seaguard and a peaceweaver."

I flat-out asked her, "Are you in line to become queen?"

She scowled at the heap of parts on her desk. "That depends on my grandmother's mood. In the line of succession I rank somewhere between third and not at all. I mostly supervise camera repair. Kids with rocks? The bane of my existence."

"You were the one who withheld video records."

Mareen placed her hand on our charter. "You should be grateful I did. You don't need a dispute with a sucky right now."

Sucky, a crude term for succubus, wasn't the type of language I expected from a princess.

"The records won't become public. As surveillance chief I consider privacy to be of high importance. The Fennako mothers prefer that I operate underfunded and understaffed—until a robbery occurs, and then there's Poseidon to pay. Sweetener?" She offered me a bowl of sugar lumps and leaned back in her chair, legs outstretched. "I often leak rumors about inoperable equipment. It makes my job easier. Everyone with something to hide descends on the blind spot. It can become crowded with couples making out, fistfights, and people engaged in heated arguments. I'm not going to interfere with lovebirds or with drinking buddies raring to fight, but if I see a pattern emerging I contact Fennako Social Services to arrange for counseling and treatment. If there's an immediate danger I bring in the peaceweavers. In your case I didn't have to. Both peaceweavers and Harbor Patrol received calls."

"Teakh made the hail to Harbor Patrol. He'd been assaulted." I crossed my arms and set my lips, challenging her.

Mareen set her cup aside. "I've reviewed the video records and it appears that you could have walked away. Your brother attempted to do so. You unnecessarily escalated the situation and then failed to comply with police instructions."

"I did what I was told."

"You didn't comply immediately."

I rose to my feet. "I am grandmatriarch of Clan Noahee, a sovereign clan. We have no territory or resources other than ourselves. You've read our charter. The theft of semen from my brother is tantamount to kidnapping. His semen could be used to impregnate me, leaving generations of our descendants at risk for recessive disorders. Maybe we could have talked our way out of the situation. Maybe we could have walked away. Maybe peaceweavers would have arrived to protect us. I couldn't take that chance."

"I must understand your reasoning if I'm to work with you." Mareen spoke mildly despite my outburst. "That is if the arrangement is acceptable to you."

As with Dame Bulla, the abrupt change from interrogation to solicitation unhinged me.

At that moment, the door banged open and in flew a crimson drone. A child in a pink-and-orange tunic followed close behind. She had a gap-toothed smile, her front baby teeth missing.

The drone alighted on the desk, landing on four legs, then flapped and folded its wings. The device was a perfect miniature dragon replete with gold whiskers and claws. It lashed its tail then tipped its head sideways in an attitude of curiosity. The girl stood with eyes closed, the angle of her head mirroring that of the small dragon.

Lids over the dragonette's camera-lens eyes blinked. I smiled at the device, one of the finest telechiric toys I'd ever encountered. It must have cost a fortune.

Gold whiskers quivering, the dragonette reached out its neck and sniffed my arm. The creature lightly scrambled to my shoulder, and its whiskers tickled my cheek.

Mareen admonished the girl, and the dragonette leapt from my shoulder. Its claws clattered as it landed on the desk.

"It's all right," I said, charmed by the girl and her miniature dragon. "Does it breathe fire?"

The creature coughed, and a glittering filament of tinsel licked from its mouth. The girl pouted. "Mom thinks I'd burn down the Palace. She's no fun." With her dragonette on her shoulder, the girl went through the inner door.

Mareen sighed and shook her head. "Girls with neural implants."

A child's telechiric could be made in any form he or she wished. Teakh had owned a number of them.

"I'm only surprised she didn't want a unicorn," I said.

"Unicorn for my daughter? Only a fire-breathing dragon will do for her. My apologies for her behavior. I've explained to her that most people don't like to be sniffed by a drone."

"My brother does have that robot seagull," I said. Teakh had programmed Gull to delight in sampling rotten fish.

"There is that. Do you think you can work with us? I'd like to go over your charter and contract carefully, make sure everything is in order for when you have children."

"I might not have children," I said.

"Not according to this contract."

I pondered her proposal. No need to rush into it, but she was right. If I went through with the agreement, I'd be bound to the queen and her heir. "We can work with you if you can work with us," I said.

"Good." Mareen smiled. "I'd like to keep Harbor Patrol out of this. Getting pregnant and raising a child is a woman thing. If you want Seaguard as an escort, I'll send someone from the Palace, but I can assure you I have security in hand." Mareen waved toward her cubbies filled with equipment. "Just don't go down any alleys where the cameras are inoperable. It puts us in a bind."

We stood for the traditional touching of hands to conclude the bargain, yet I felt a sense of foreboding, as if I'd made a deal with Poseidon.

AFTER DAYS OF negotiation and multiple meetings, Teakh and I waited in Her Majesty's antechamber. Sunlight streamed through roundels of colored glass, casting jewel tones on the polished wooden floor. We'd dressed in our best. Teakh had left his watchcap and stained parka behind. I fidgeted with the hem of my smock, a gift from Her Majesty.

Fennako had conceded to only one child, but they'd refused to yield on any issue related to privacy. No video documentation, no independent genetic analysis, and no witnesses. To my surprise and delight they'd ask that I attend law school, and they'd agreed to pay my tuition, room, and board as well as a stipend.

A Royal Guardsman bowed. "Her Majesty Queen Affra Fennako will receive you."

Teakh removed his bandanna and his gold beads tinkled and flashed. The doors swung open, most likely triggered by wireless.

The chamber beyond resembled a well-appointed captain's office. Curvilinear carvings graced the walls, the shapes suggestive of nautilus shells and flowing water. A thick area rug cushioned the floor, vibrant wool against planking which resembled that of an ancient ship. In an armchair, a frail woman sat hunched, her back stooped with age, her slipper-covered feet on a hassock. An attendant adjusted the Queen's lap robe.

A Royal Guardsman announced us. "Your Majesty, Annin of Clan Ralko and her brother Teakh."

I genuflected and lowered my head in the royal presence, the great-grandmother to all of Fenria. A half step behind, Teakh did as well.

"Enough of all that." The Queen dismissively flicked her blanket, her bony hand marked with dark blotches. "Come here, child."

I knelt beside the chair. The Queen touched my cheek. "So this is Annin. Of course you are." Keen eyes peered from her crinkled face. "And this must be your brother. Let me see you."

Teakh knelt on the other side of the Queen. She kissed him on the cheek. "So handsome. They tell me the two of you are founding your own clan. Imagine that."

"Aye, Grandmother," Teakh said.

The Queen patted my hand. "A patrilineal clan. They read me your charter. My dear, you are a radical. Both of you are. I like it."

"Technically, our clan will be ambilineal," I corrected. "We will treat everyone as equals. All of our children. The gender of the parent doesn't matter."

"The idealism of youth." She sighed. Her eyes became dreamy, and her head nodded. She woke with a start. "Oh my. Where were we? We must have our agreement witnessed. The notary camera."

Attendants rolled forward a camera mounted on a tripod and offered a document screen.

"Now, dear, if you would be so kind, read our agreement and stop at the places indicated. We'll nod and say, Yes, we agree—that whole rigmarole. We can dispense with all the hand touching."

I read the document. When they got to the part about only one child, the Queen pouted, her expression surprisingly like that of her granddaughter, the girl with the red dragon drone. "We were hoping for more. Enough to found a clan."

Teakh said, "Just one to fulfill the contract."

"Oh, Posii," she said primly.

I continued reading. She smiled and nodded at the part about Fennako providing education and childcare. "Now, understand. If you choose to give me more great-grandchildren, the offer stands for them as well." She again patted my hand, the touch of her fingers dry.

As we left the Palace, Teakh said, "What did she mean by great-grandchildren? Does she think we're her grandchildren?"

"We're all her grandchildren. Or maybe shes' confused."

The ways of royalty were inscrutable.

———

Chapter 07
Ralko Village

I HOISTED MY DUFFLE and walked up from the dock. I was back in Ralko Village and the tedium of living as a poor relation. The shuttle boat sped away, the wake washing against the dock pylons. I'd flown from Fennako City by stratoplane. Teakh had departed on a different flight bound for Dojko. Ralko didn't even have proper facilities to handle stratoplanes, so my trip had required multiple layovers, the final leg taken on the bi-twelvenight ferry shuttle.

By the entrance to the clanless shelter, a man in tattered clothing slumped on a bench, a cane in his hand. Nearby, two other men loitered in grimy parkas, waterproof boots, and grease-streaked bib overalls. The reek of dead herring wafted from both of them. Most likely they'd been chopping chum for bait.

The man on the bench glanced up, and his expression brightened. "What are you about?"

I offered the traditional response. "Observing the tide." I knew the fellow but not his name. Noah had taught that charity given to strangers was of the highest honor. "I've been traveling."

He placed hands shaking with palsy on the top of his cane. "A young journeywyv. Traveling around, seeing the sights, learning how the world works. That's the life."

"Yes, Grandfather." I addressed him respectfully as was the due of an older man from a different clan. Marriage was always to someone outside the clan, so it was possible, although unlikely, that he was my grandfather.

He beamed. "You're a good girl."

"I'm working on my thesis." I should have been working on a thesis, but Aunt Dyes and the Ralko Education board had rejected all of my proposals.

"There you go. Teach your children well," he said, citing the Code of Noah.

I shifted the strap on my baggage. "I'd best be making lunch."

"You do that." The man flicked his thumb toward the other men. "They're mighty hungry, and—if you don't mind me saying—you cook better than Auntie in there."

The two others nodded in agreement. Likely, Aunt Trudia had been scrimping on the groceries again.

In the kitchen, Aunt Trudia stirred a pot, both the spoon and her stroke nearly worthy of a rowboat. "Where you been?"

I told her I'd been attending a symposium on clanlessness.

"Don't know why you waste your time. We've got plenty of that here, and we got soup to make. Those potatoes need peeling."

In the women's bunkroom I dropped my bag and parka on a cot. The hostel served as cheap or free accommodations for travelers according to the second precept of Noah: assist the stranger in need. In actuality, no one paid. It was a clanless shelter for strangers. I was a clan member but happened to live at the shelter, working for my room and board such that it was.

I rolled up my sleeves and returned to the kitchen.

"You were due back days ago." Aunt Trudia pointed to the wall clock-calendar with the butt of her spoon.

Mildly I smiled and nodded. In Ralko I did my best to disappear or at least to blend in and avoid conflict. I rinsed my hands and dried them. I added potatoes to the broth then chopped and sautéed onions. While the vegetables cooked, I heated oil and flour in a pan for roux to thicken the chowder. When the clock hand neared noon I combined ingredients and tasted the result. It needed a bit more of something. From a canister I sprinkled in herbs—dried, not fresh, but they'd do.

Aunt Trudia stirred the soup, grimaced, and filled a pitcher to add water. "We'll just stretch it out a bit."

I stopped her. "There's enough." If we needed more, the freezer contained leftovers from previous meals.

At noon, we carried the soup into the dining room where a half-dozen men waited. Sure, on Fenria, women outnumbered men, but men were more likely to seek free lodging while traveling. Young women did travel as students, but Ralko had nothing worth studying. Of the boarders, no one was paying. They rarely did.

"Lazy, good-for-nothing freeloaders." Aunt Trudia placed the soup on a serving table. "Think they can get a free meal by claiming hospitality."

The men politely ignored her. Everyone knew that listening to Aunt Trudia's complaints was the price of a meal at the Ralko Village shelter, so in a sense it wasn't free.

I whispered, "You're being rude." I placed a basket of hardtack beside the soup pot. Those men were her kindred. Before the discovery of his valuable genetic code, my own brother had lived as they did.

"I speak the truth like I see it," Aunt Trudia said. "None of these men are clanless, and some of them, like Grandfather over there, have been doing this for years. His shaky hands? Fake. Those two"—she flicked her thumb toward the men in coveralls—"had good work until a day ago, then they had a disagreement with their captain, didn't want to buckle down and take directions. The others..." She shook her head. "That one is a drunkard. The runty one's a runaway. The rest are too lazy to cook for themselves."

"Mama Ralko, you're as full of pickled herring as ever," Grandfather said.

"None of that, old man."

"Old? Who are you calling old?" He gave me a sly grin. I passed him a bowl of chowder. He accepted it with leathery hands and spoke the traditional words of thanks: "Honor is yours."

"Honor." I always suspected Grandfather had a soft spot for Trudia Ralko. Why else would he keep coming back for watery soup?

Aunt Trudia thrust an elbow into my side. "Don't encourage them. You're too nice. Word will get out and we'll have more tramps like him arriving. We'll have to feed them all."

Grandfather said, "Tramp?"

"It's fishbone soup," I said. Feeding the guests cost very little. We'd made it out of remnants left after the valuable fillets were removed from fish carcasses. The chowder was wholesome, nutritious and, if I could manage it, tasty, but it wasn't expensive.

Aunt Trudia, fists on her stout hips said, "Noah commanded that we feed these people, and that's what we'll do.""But no smiling." I kept my sarcasm sweet.

Grandfather winked.

When the men had been served, I filled my own bowl and sat at the common table. Aunt Trudia went back into the kitchen to eat a sandwich alone.

Grandfather gazed fondly after her ample form as she

barged through the kitchen door and let it swing shut behind her. "She's quite a gal."

"Why don't you go sit with her?" I said.

Grandfather shook his head. "She won't have me."

As we ate in companionable silence, I thought about how my dining companions wouldn't have been allowed to speak at the symposium. What would Grandfather have to say if he'd been there?

I broached the topic. "I've been considering the problem of clanlessness. Seems if you're clanless you'd be experts."

"Maybe we have clans. Maybe we don't." This was said by one of the men in greasy coveralls.

I said, "I'm thinking that if you can't vote, then you're not really part of a clan."

"Vote for what?"

"For clan government. You pay clan fees. Surely you should have a say in how the money is spent. You could vote for grandmatriarch, the school board, and the mothers' council. Or maybe serve on the mothers' council."

"Our boat is a cooperative, so I vote my share. I don't care about the clan. That's women's business."

"What if your own children were clan members? Everyone would be a member of two clans: their mother's clan and their father's clan. You'd be a parent, so the education board would be your business."

"There's one thing I've learned." He dipped a spoon in his soup. "When it comes to kids, women are always right. And with two clans, I'd have to pay clan fees to both of them. I hate to say it, but that's a bad idea, a real stinker."

Revenue again appeared to be a problem for our clan.

I GATHERED BEDDING and towels and took my load

to the village laundry. While the machine went through its cycle I sat on a bench and caught up on my studies. Words coalesced on the taut fabric of the screen.

> *The great prophet Catherine Smith instituted base-twelve numbering and designed her calendar to calculate both ovulation and high tide. Taking advantage of the effect of moonlight and pheromones on ovulation, she brought the human fertility cycle in phase with the period of Luna Majora, making ovulation predictable. In her system, all cycles—year, month, and day—are represented on a dial divided into twelve units. Like ancient clocks of Earth, each cycle is divided into two-dozen units, two rotations of the dial representing one cycle. Both menstruation and ovulation occur at twelve of the month.*

I glanced at a dial on the washing machine—also divided into twelve units—and, above the machines, a calendar clock with the time and date. Sometimes I hated Catherine Smith. No woman on Fenria could escape knowing when she would ovulate and menstruate. Every clock, every date on a document contained this information. I sighed. To resent Catherine Smith's calendar was heresy. To do so was to question the first precept of the Noah Code: Observe the tide, and you shall survive. Traditionally, tide meant the flux of estrogen within women's bodies as well as the rise and fall of the ocean.

Two Ralko women walked in, carrying baskets of laundry. I couldn't keep from overhearing their discussion.

"She doesn't want to share her husband."

"So what is her sister going to do for the Spawning Moons?"

"I don't know. Maybe she'll go down to the docks."

Ralko women gossiped endlessly about the spawning season. The Noah Code also prohibited gossiping and boasting. Idle talk was considered shine, and the superstitious believed it drew shipwreck and infertility.

Attempting to make myself inconspicuous I focused on reading, but even the history text blathered on about the spawning tide.

> *With the moons in phase, all went well, and Fenria resembled Earth. However, with the moons in opposition, women lived in constant light, ovulating unpredictably. Luna Minora became known as the moon of chaos. Always in a rush she laps her sibling moon every six years. A baby boom of planned births occurs roughly nine months after Minora laps Majora. A shadow baby boom of unplanned births occurs nine months after Minora opposes Majora. These two demographic bulges occur three years apart. Clan planners came to count on the effect and employed additional methods to reinforce the pattern. Soon, planned pregnancies were as likely to occur under the shadow of Minora as they were under the brightness of both moons.*

The Ralko women continued gossiping, and my concentration slipped.

"... Cousin Rilla and Fimbie's husband. You know they're interested in each other. So Rilla's going to ask Cousin Fimbie if he can father her child. What do you think? If my husband were running after my cousin, I wouldn't let him father a child on her. No, ma'am."

Avoiding eye contact with the gossiping women I glanced at the clock. The hands tracking the phases of the moons had yet to align.

"Then there's Cousin Starna," said the other woman.

"Her?"

"She's listed for pregnancy."

"Who's going to father her child?"

"She'll apply to the clan sperm bank. Can't get a man on her own. Can't borrow a man either."

One of them turned toward me. "There's always a lot of men around down at the shelter. But a girl must be very desperate to do that. You just don't know what kind of genes your children will have."

If she believed I planned to get pregnant using a random man I met at the shelter, she was seriously mistaken. Then I realized she was implying my mother had availed herself of the services of such a random traveler. I straightened, snapped shut my handscreen, and gave the two women a silent stare.

"My sweet child." She shook her head. "Dear, dear. Poor girl. We of course don't hold you accountable for the indiscretions of your mother."

I lifted my chin. "My paternity is not your territory, and discussing such issues in a public washhouse is generally considered shine." Good Danna. Ralko women sure hoarded their grudges. Years after my mother's death they still resented my unauthorized conception. Every trip I took, pursuing my education, put me further in debt, but no, that wasn't enough for them. They had to insult my entire family.

"So what do you think I can find on your genetics?" I asked, my tone mild.

The two women gaped at me in surprised disgust. I gathered laundry and stalked out, head held high. If I'd had my way, men would live longer and there'd be plenty of high-quality males around, no fussing about swapping husbands. Ah, but that would leave Ralko women with nothing to gossip about. Founder them!

In the lane, Aunt Dyse bore down on me. If it wasn't

one overbearing Ralko woman, it was another. Ralko was supposed to pay for my education, and the clan had a say in what I studied. Theoretically, this ensured that my education would be used productively in service to the clan. In actuality, daughters of important clan members got their pick of careers. Girls such as me took the leavings. Dyse had been assigned as my advocate in place of my mother, but she'd rebuffed nearly all my career plans, claiming they were too expensive or unworkable. I'd given up on support from Dyse.

She shook an accusing finger. "You haven't checked in with the education board for months. Just where have you been?"

I put on a smile. "Helping out at the shelter. You know where I've been—Fennako City at a symposium."

The two other Ralko women watched from the doorway of the laundry.

Dyse took my arm. "I must talk with you about your brother."

I shifted my basket. "I've got to get this laundry back to the shelter."

"Not right away. We'll have a cup of tea at my place." Dyse left it unstated that she wanted privacy for the discussion, which would surely get personal and accusatory.

———

Chapter 08
Aunt Dyse

I DROPPED MY BASKET in Dyse's foyer. She hung her coat and slipped on house slippers.

"You know you're welcome to stay with me," she said. "I am your assigned guardian."

I kicked off my shoes. "I appreciate your offer. It means so much to me, but I don't want to inconvenience you." In truth I didn't want Dyse aware of my activities or that I was plotting to leave Clan Ralko.

"Oh it's nothing. Do sit down." Dyse indicated a chair upholstered with large pink flowers. She settled herself on a companion chair, a bag of knitting at her feet. "Now tell me about your idea to reduce the cost of providing hospitality." She scooped up a partly knitted project, a lumpy strip of wool.

I explained my plan for reducing costs. "Men, not just women, should take responsibility for their children. If the mother's clan won't take responsibility for their members, then father's clan should do so."

Dyes thrust a knitting needle for emphasis. "Quite right. Those deadbeats should pay."

I kept a straight face. Ralko itself might have counted as one of those deadbeat clans. With my proposal, Ralko was likely to pay out more than it saved. I hoped Dyse wouldn't figure this out until after we'd left Clan Ralko.

AFTER DROPPING OFF the laundry at the shelter, I walked along the waterfront to the Mermaid Tavern. I'd often passed the place but seldom went inside. In the interest of research I needed to interview mariners.

I spoke with Cousin Treena. She and her mother ran the tavern, the favorite gathering place of sailors and sea captains. Inside, men drank beer or played pool.

"Hey, Skipper Shanny," shouted Treena. "My cousin is looking for opinions. Got any?"

"I might," Shanny set aside a pool cue and plunked down on a bar stool.

I explained that I was researching men's suffrage.

"What the depths is that?"

"Voting rights for men."

"But we do vote," Shanny said. "And the boys keep electing me as captain. Of course I've got the captain's share, and I vote for myself. That always helps with getting elected."

"I'm considering clan votes."

Shanny scowled. "That ain't a good thing. On some boats, the clan has the biggest share. That's trouble because women don't know nothing about fishing. I bought out the clan shares of my boat, so now I'm captain free and clear. I only got to convince the boys, not some screen watchers back in the village. Anyway, man is a hunter. We're good at killing things and not much else. Now woman. She's creative. She's smart, and she's a weaver. She makes stuff, and she gives birth. What is man to that? We can only destroy."

"Would you be more willing to pay clan fees, if you could vote for mother's council and school board?" I asked my question.

"Clan fees! I tell you I haven't paid clan fees for three conjunctions of the moon."

"You could take part in your children's education."

He barked a laugh. "No, thank you. I ain't seen the inside of a classroom since I was a dozen years old. I know how to figure and how to read a weather report. No need for art appreciation or governmental theory. I'm a hell of a lot smarter than most Seaguard enforcers."

"How do you avoid paying clan fees?" I asked, genuinely curious.

"It's easy enough. My clan is way across the Western Ocean. They don't know what I do."

"What about retirement?" This topic had come up at the symposium.

"I'm not going to retire. I'll die on the sea as a man. That's our lot."

From Dyse's perspective of reducing costs, my plans had been shot down. If these men were typical, men's suffrage wouldn't increase clan revenues or decrease the cost of caring for the clanless.

A MEETING WITH Aunt Dyse was akin to a game of justice poker. Neither of us fully let on what cards we held as we pretended amicable friendship. I'd returned to her parlor for another round of the game. I resented her maybe more than I should have, but she was not my mother, and she seemed to care more about money for herself than she cared about me or Teakh.

Dyse leaned toward me. "You do know that Teakh is innately monogamous?"

She looped yarn over a needle. "It's a problem. The very characteristic which makes him valuable as a stud interferes with his—" she cleared her throat. "Sexual performance."

"I have no interest in discussing my brother's 'performance,'" I said.

70

"You should. He's functionally impotent, but selling his services for a high price. He may not be able to follow through."

"That's his business."

"It's our business." Dyse looped yarn around a needle. "I have a proposal for you. How about a gift for Teakh to sweeten the pot? I know about this Clan Noahee thing."

My stomach dropped.

"Don't give me that sour look," she said. "I applaud your idealism. It's nice to dream of being grandmatriarch with your brother a Seaguard lord."

How much did Dyse know? I couldn't ask without giving away more information.

Dyse went on, "Personally I think Teakh is stubborn, not monogamous. His impotence is all in his head."

"That's generally the case with sexual attraction." I said. "The brain is the most important sexual organ."

"If we give Teakh a gift he'll be happier with his career." So that was her scheme.

"So expensive gifts are now a treatment for impotence?"

"Haven't gifts always been part of sexual coercion? It'll make him more cooperative."

"Teakh! Cooperative?"

"I feel for him," Dyse said. "By rights he should have an esskip. I've tried to speak about it with the mothers' council, but they won't release the funds. They're still upset with me for giving your cousin Gorby an esskip."

Traditionally, each Seaguard flew his own ground-effect aircraft, a flying boat. The craft were either handed down from an uncle, or provided by the man's female relatives. "We can't afford an esskip," I said.

"But you can," Dyse inspected her yarn. "Or, should I say, 'we can.' We'll take out a loan. With my approval, Ralko will provide backing. Teakh is pulling in amazingly high bids for his services. If he follows through, we'll have plenty of money, and we'll spend it on him. He deserves an esskip."

Dyse's plans always came with a price. "What if he doesn't follow through?"

"Well then he'll have to pay off the loan."

"I will have to pay the loan," I said.

"Then make sure he follows through. He will with this incentive. What is it about men and their boats?"

Dyse had offered a tricky balance. An esskip was essential if Teakh was to work as a fisheries detective, regardless of if he continued with his stud career. Ralko would absorb the cost if we couldn't pay. Reneging on a loan could seriously impact a woman's status within a clan.

———

Chapter 09
Esskip

THE RIPRAP EMBANKMENT held the water of the Ralko esskip lagoon at a level higher than the tide. Dyse and I walked along the shore. An esskip flew towards us, skimming above the ocean. The craft bore directly toward the men's house then rose to clear the embankment and land in the lagoon. It taxied toward the hangar. A door opened, and the esskip glided inside.

At the door to the Seaguard men's house, Dyse announced our arrival. The door swung open, and we entered a cavernous room lit by high windows. Rows of esskips hung from gantries for storage. Other craft lay on blocks, some partly disassembled. Dyse bustled off to find Gorby.

A group of older men, great uncles, lounged in chairs, seemingly snoozing but first one then the others opened their eyes. A great uncle smiled. "Well if it isn't Annin. I hear you've been gallivanting in Fennako City."

"Yes, Uncle." I returned the smile. "I even saw the Queen. And now we're going to order an esskip for Teakh." I was already nearly an outcast. What did I have to lose by taking on a loan which I might not be able to repay?

"It's about time," an uncle said. "I was flying an esskip when I was only dozen years old."

"I was nine," another old fellow said.

"That wasn't an esskip. It was a drone aircraft. I recall that little airplane of yours. You'd fly it behind the clan hall. Those aunties were livid, I tell you."

"Pull up a chair and sit awhile," a great uncle said. "I tell you, nothing is duller then auditing catch records alone. You close your eyes and watch videos of fish being loaded into holds. So we sit down here and talk or maybe keep an ear out for the nephews. Maybe one of our nieces wanders in on the way to purchase an esskip for her brother. Much more interesting."

"Your brother has a good eye for auditing," a great uncle said. "We got him started. Yes ma'am. His lordship wouldn't follow up on minor poaching so Teakhy goes off and blackmails the fishermen." The uncle guffawed. "They had no idea they were being blackmailed by a kid. That's our boy! We'd let on to Teakh about who to blackmail just to watch the fun. It's gotten mighty slow around here since he's been in other parts."

Ralko great uncles may have been a good influence or a bad one on Teakh. I said, "He'd going to be a Seaguard chief,"

"Our Teakh?"

"We petitioned the Queen," I said. "I'm to be grandmatriarch, and he'll be chief."

"Well, fancy that."

"Tell me something. If you fellows could vote, would you?"

"Vote for what?"

"Vote for grandmatriarch, mother's council, heir to the Seaguard lord."

"Vote for the Seaguard lord? I sure would. I've got some ideas about how things should be run. "

"Would you like to run for mother's council? Or maybe school board?"

"My kids aren't in Ralko."

"What if your grandkids were here?"

"That's an interesting idea you got. I like to have the grandkids around. Was that your idea or Teakh's?"

"Mostly his."

"Figured it was." He chuckled. "That boy is always up to something. He does us proud."

I thanked the great uncles, and caught up with Dyse. Gorby had lowered his esskip into a docking bay and assisted Dyse in stepping aboard. I scrambled in after her and slid into the back seat. Dyse announced that she'd forgotten her knitting and she went back to get it.

While we waited, I asked Gorby why he was always flying Dyse around as if he were her lackey.

"I'm an orphan, same as you and Teakh," he said. "I do stuff for her, and she does stuff for me.

"I don't think I ever met your mother. What happened to her?"

"I don't have a one." He shrugged. "I'm just Ralko. I'll give you some advice. You and your brother would have it easier if you tried to get along with them."

"You aren't Ralko any more than I am. Ralko bought you. Probably one of Dyse's failed money-making schemes. "

"If my mother sold me," Gorby said. "I want nothing to do with her or her clan."

"What will happen to you? Will you be allowed to marry?"

"Dyse says I can."

Dyse might not make good on the promise. She'd have to give up her chauffeur often enough that he could have conjugal visits. Or maybe she'd sell Gorby's stud services. "What about when you're old? You'll have no close relatives, no nieces or nephews looking in on you." I imagined him as one of the great uncles jawing in the men's house and keeping tabs on nephews who weren't really kin and who didn't care about him. He'd have a lonely life, always be chosen last for the plum assignments and first for jobs which were dirty, tedious, or dangerous.

"With luck I won't live that long," he said.

He gave the same fatalistic answer I'd heard in the Mermaid Tavern. I felt for him. He was a slave and didn't even know it. "If you ever need help, let me know."

When Dyse had returned, we glided out of the hangar and onto the lagoon. The esskip came up to speed, racing along on hydrofoil struts before it leapt the seawall. We flew over the ocean, waves blurring beneath us.

"Auntie, you've been carrying that bag of yarn around for months and you hardly ever actually knit. What are you making?" I asked.

She said, "Knitting makes the right impression. A true woman is a weaver. You don't actually have to make anything, just have knitting needles and some yarn. If you actually produce something it's even better, but I don't have the patience for it."

The word for weaver, woman, and craftsperson were identical in our language.

"I do," Gorby said. "It passes the time."

So who was the true weaver here? What could Gorby do if he were allowed to reach his full potential?

At the Wilberko dock, Gorby waited in his esskip while Dyse and I met with the Shipwright Wilberko in her studio. She wore gloves threaded with electronics. She cupped her hands, and a holographic image of an esskip formed above a gleaming black table. "What is your price range?" she asked.

I hated that question. "My brother is in the Seaguard and needs a craft for patrol work."

With a rounding of her fingers, Wilberko produced a fuselage with stubby wings and a high tail stabilizer. "Will he be flying in coastal areas or over blue ocean?" The deep ocean was called blue. It could be miles deep.

"What does it matter?" Dyse asked.

"For lakes or coastal he'll want a small maneuverable craft, but it won't be as stable in high seas. No craft can do everything well, but we can try." The stubby holographic wings elongated. "Here's a floatplane with dihedral wings. With anhedral wings, the craft is for ground effect, an esskip." The wings shortened and drooped. "We can make modifications which allow the craft to travel submarine. But truly, a flying submarine is nearly as awkward as a submersible airplane." Wilberko showed a dizzying array of options accompanied by rapid-fire technical terminology.

I'd been studying clan structure, not aeronautical design. I suggested that we ask Teakh what he wanted.

"This should be a surprise," Dyse said.

"It may be more important that he gets the type of craft he needs. Let's get Gorby to help out. He actually flies an esskip, and he knows Teakh. I'll give him a hail." I activated my comset before Dyse could stop me.

Gorby joined us. He and Wilberko went into a complex discussion of handling characteristics. Dyse fidgeted and actually pulled out her knitting.

"My brother does a lot of work with drones," I said. "He specializes in surveillance." I envisioned Mareen's office with its wall of niches. Teakh's operation should be mobile. "He needs storage and charging for his equipment." Depths! I couldn't freely discuss Teakh's needs with Dyse listening in.

The discussion again became technical. Dyse yawned, and I took my chance. "Auntie, if you want, maybe step out for some fresh air. Gorby and I can work out the details." Leave. Just leave. If I couldn't get rid of Dyse, I'd have to arrange to get to Wilberko later without her.

After I'd hustled her out, I set to work on Gorby. "I'd like to talk to Wilberko alone. I'd be appreciative if you could step out as well. You know how my brother is, a bit shady in his dealings."

"Oh yeah." Gorby accepted the explaintion and went out the door.

Alone with Wilberko I spoke freely. "I'm concerned about confidentiality and security. The woman I've come with isn't my aunt. She's my guardian assigned by Clan Ralko. There are a number of things which I'm unable to discuss in her presence."

"If she is your guardian and Ralko is paying for the esskip," Wilberko said, "then I must share information with her."

"That's just it. Ralko is securing the loan, but won't be paying it. My brother and I are founding a new clan. The Queen has approved our charter on a provisional basis. We wish to withhold the details of the agreement from Ralko while we're still in negotiations. I'd like confidentiality in this matter."

"We can't grant confidentiality to a minor without approval and assurance of Fennako," Wilberko said.

"For assurance you can speak with Dame Bulla Fennako of Fennako Clan and lineage."

Wilberko stepped into the private part of her house for a muffled conversation. She emerged pocketing her comset. "Well, young lady. Fennako assures me that you're telling the truth." She sat and arranged the apron panel of her gown. "Although I don't know how this relates to aeronautical design."

"My brother will be Noahee clan chief, and his esskip will be the start of our fleet. I'd like removal of royal override. My brother doesn't want to lose control of his fleet to the Queen."

"That's not recommended," Wilberko said. "It's a safety issue. Suppose your brother was in a crash and was knocked unconscious. He could die before rescuers freed him from his craft."

"But invoking royal override could cause a crash. My brother nearly lost his one telechiric to royal override. He was let go with a warning."

"Fennako might bluster, but they wouldn't have done it, not unless the device posed a verifiable danger," Wilberko said. "Clans most commonly assign administrative access to their Seaguard chief. This is the most secure since he can carry the codes in his implant without writing them down. The Queen holds backup access in case something happens to the chief. There have been occasions of malfunctioning implants, which have necessitated action by Her Majesty."

"What if the Queen causes an implant to malfunction?" I asked

"There's still another reason to give access to the Queen," Wilberko said. "Your brother's esskip can't be registered to a clan which doesn't exist. Once approval of your clan goes through, the Queen can use royal override to change the registration. If we don't grant royal access, the esskip will remain registered to Ralko."

"Okay. Then we'll register it to Ralko for now and give the Queen override."

We returned to Ralko Village. The days shortened with the approach of winter. My grand plans stagnated. Fennako wouldn't accept me as a law student until I'd fulfilled my side of the bargain, and that waited on alignment of the moons. Impatient with waiting I composed a message.

Hailing Dame Bulla. Annin Noahee here.

I am eager to start my study of law. The autumn semester has commenced, yet I am prevented in enrolling until after fulfillment of the contract. I await a communique from Fennako regarding an appointment with my assigned man. I would be most pleased if this appointment could be arranged as soon as possible.

Annin Noahee signing off.

———

Hailing Annin Noahee. Dame Bulla here.

We understand your impatience. However, we believe that it is your best interest and the best interest of your child to delay conception until the moons align. This will ensure that your child has friends and classmates of the same age and that you will form bonds of sharing motherhood with Fennako women who will be giving birth at the same time.

Dame Bulla signing off

Depths! If I waited on the conjunction of the moons I'd miss both the autumn and winter semesters.

Hailing Dame Bulla. Annin Noahee here.

If it is at all possible, I'd like to commence with my studies before fulfilling the stipulation that I become pregnant. I am concerned that I will be suffering morning sickness during the start of my studies. I can assure you that I have every intention of following through.

Dame Bulla signing off

———

Hailing Annin Noahee. Dame Bulla here.

We appreciate your patience.

Our debts were still rising. I didn't give a kinkill if Luna Minora wasn't yet in the proper position. If my child were to be the oldest in a birth cohort, so be it. My own brother had been conceived out of season. The only resulting bad fortune had been Ralko's ongoing resentment.

———

Chapter 10
Solstice

EXITING A STRATOPLANE I searched for Teakh on the dock. I'd flown to Shelliko to spend the Solstice holidays with him and his girlfriend. He waved, one arm around a woman wearing a fur-trimmed parka. I walked up the dock ramp. The woman pushed back her hood, revealing a rich cascade of auburn hair and skin of creamy freshness. She wore soft knee boots and her parka was a subtle shade of chestnut. I felt dowdy in comparison. My own shoes scuffed and worn, my hair a drab brown. In Ralko Village, unremarkable was good, particularly for a poor relation of dubious conception who might be getting above her station. Still, confronted by such a beauty, I wished I'd taken more care with my appearance.

"Sis, meet my sweetheart, Marjoram Shelliko." Teakh gave the woman a squeeze.

I would have bowed, but Marjoram touched my hands and gave the greeting of friendship. "Amatha." We stood for a moment, foreheads nearly touching, then Marjoram stepped back. She wore a narrow silver bracelet, similar to the one worn by Teakh.

"I'm so pleased to meet you. Your brother talks about you. His big sister." She grinned, her cinnamon eyes bright with welcome. "Do call me Angel. I never liked being an herb."

The three of us walked up from the waterfront to Angel's place, a large cottage with the front workroom converted into an art studio and smelling of turpentine. Easels held partly finished paintings. Panels and stretched canvas leaned against an artist's bench while charcoal sketches of nudes covered the walls.

I approached a painting of a man, his musculature and skin tones carefully rendered in transparent layers, his genitalia depicted briefly and honestly. The face, however, remained incomplete.

"Who is this?" I asked.

"One of my clients," Angel said. "Well, that's not quite right. Actually, the husband of one of my clients. But you know who this is." Smiling she rested her hand on Teakh's arm and pointed to another painting, this one of Teakh reclining on a divan. "My grand odalisque."

Chagrined by my ignorance I asked, "What's an odalisque?"

"A painting of a love slave," Angel said.

His arm around Angel, Teakh grinned.

"He's my brother." I diverted my gaze to a sketch on the wall. That was a naked man as well. I refused to gawk at men while with my brother. I resolutely focused on the props and backdrops, a brown couch, the same divan shown in the painting.

"He's also the best model I've ever worked with," Angel said. "He's got great muscle definition, and can hold these amazing poses for a long time."

I glanced at Teakh, my eyebrows raised. "You're full of talent."

"I do what I can."

I shook my head. Teakh's talents—gathering information from seemingly casual conversations, nude modeling, and impregnating women with his supposedly superior genetics—weren't exactly the skills of a Seaguard chief.

Angel squeezed Teakh's hand. He seemed happy with the artist, and her paintings, style, and bearing did have some refinement, despite the subject matter. At any rate, they were superior to the imaged displayed in Madame Xs shop.

I ACCOMPANIED THE lovebirds as they joined the traditional festivities in the village square. Bonfires blazed, sending vermillion sparks soaring into the night sky. Tree trunks thrown into the fire burned to glowing coals, spidery arms of ocean-silvered roots collapsing into the flames. Around Solstice bonfires, couples, threesomes, and foursomes gyrated to pounding rhythms.

A cup of hot spiced cider was pressed into my hands. Angel and Teakh whisked past, joining the dance, eyes only for each other, leaving me alone at the edge of the firelight.

The song ended, and the traditional Solstice countdown boomed over the square: "Lord of Tristan Bay here with his Royal Highness, Archmagnate of all Fenria, our Supreme Seaguard Chief. We observe the tide, bringing together data gathered from around the world, broadcasting from Fennako City."

The banter had been nearly the same as far back as I could recall. The King and Lord Tristan Bay never gave their names, only their titles. When king or lord passed away, his heir slipped into the role, and the tradition continued unbroken. The impression was, or was supposed to be, off immortal oceans and seas, the planet itself conversing about the tide, identity submerged in tradition.

"One hour remains until the illustrious moment of solstice," announced the King.

The previous year, Teakh and I had celebrated Solstice in Ralko Village, both of us lurking around the edge of the festivities. Here in Shelliko, Teakh, who had always stood beside me, had been swept into the dance, together with his beloved, leaving me happy for him but alone.

The King began chanting in the old language. Lord Tristan Bay joined him in harmony. The revelers picked up the chant, stomping with the beat until the rhythm reached a crescendo and unraveled into cheering.

Another tune played, this one a carol. Teakh and Angel danced slow and close.

I cradled my cup of cider, warming my hands. The swaying dancers included plenty of men, but most were accompanied by at least two women, and none were alone. I shifted my feet, attempting to move heat into my cold toes. Surely in that crowd, one man remained unattached.

Tristan Bay spoke again. "We approach the Danna Solstice as one, all of Fenria celebrating at the same moment. Making observations, we have the Seaguard magnates—the coastal lords of fjords and bays, the river lords, the deep sea lords, and the ice lords. This tide of Solstice, all of Fenria is kinfolk. All are family."

Family? I had no kinship to the disembodied voices over the address system. I'd lost my one kinsman to a beautiful painter of nudes.

"It's a lovely evening here in the Fenrian Archipelago," Tristan Bay announced, "but for those of you over in the Andean Ocean it's morning. Let's have a report from the North Pole. We bring you Lord Borealis. Sir, how's the weather up there?"

"Dark and clear with the north star Danna glittering in the night. We're observing to see how low she's going to sweep toward the horizon."

"Thank you, Lord Borealis," Tristan Bay said.

A man in tan pants and waterproof boots danced in the firelight, a woman on each side of him. In the smoke of the fire, a single glowing ember rose above the others and continued to waft upward.

In the entire crowd, every man had a woman beside him. Only the men speaking over the address system could possibly be unaccompanied. The King was married to the Princess Royal, but the others—Lord Austrialis, Lord Borealis, and Lord Tristan Bay—What of them? I refilled my cup from a steaming kettle.

"It's a bright day here at the South Pole," Lord Austrialis said. "The sun has been circling around for quite a while. Solstice means sun-stop. Folks call it that because the sun doesn't seem to move much higher at all. Around the time of the equinox he's charging along, changing every day, but not now during Solstice. It's a bit tricky to determine the exact moment of sun-stop, but we've done our observation, and we've got that old sun pegged."

As far back as I could recall, Lord Austrialis had repeated the same inanities. Surely, pedantry wasn't inherited with lordship of the South Pole, which indicated that this Lord Austrialis was significantly older than I was.

What about Lord Tristan Bay? His voice was pleasant and, in Fennako City, Harb had spoken well of him. Lord Tristan Bay was now a person to me, Harb's boss and Mareen's brother.

I shook my head. Setting my sights on Lord Tristan Bay wasn't just going above my station, but going for the very best, the top man in Clan Fennako. I sipped my spiced drink and shifted my feet to warm them.

As the moment of solstice neared, the dancers paused and chanted the countdown from two-dozen together with the King. "Twozen. Eloze. Teoze. Noze. Octoze." I joined in. "Sevoze. Sioze. Fizz. Foze. Throze. Twoze." The crowd and indeed all of Fenria chanted together. "Edooze. Dozen. Eleven. Ten. Nine. Eight."

On the count of one, dancers swung their partners and kissed, and the crowd cheered. I raised my cup and drained it. As the revelry settled, Tristan Bay spoke. "To folks in the northern hemisphere, we wish you a joyous winter. And to you in the south, here's wishing you a bountiful summer. Until we swap winter for summer at the Poseidon Solstice, tide carry us all to good fortune."

Aye. To the tide. And to whatever it might bring in the new year; a new clan I hoped.

———

Chapter 11
Clinic

I STOOD ON THE dock in Kasaanko harbor. Frost glinted on the planking of the pier. I shoved my hands deeper into the warmth of my pockets. With Solstice over, we were now in the depth of winter. Small airplanes and esskips splashed down, none of them seemed to be the craft sent to take me to my insemination appointment. A green and white esskip skidded across the harbor, water spraying from around the hull. The tail bore a Fennako call sign and the wolf face logo of the ferry system. The wings folded and the craft glided to the floating pier below me. A line handler assisted in mooring the esskip as another craft came in.

The pilot climbed out and walked up the ramp. The wolf face and compass-rose of Fennako ferries was emblazoned on his parka as it was on the esskip. I waved. Was this my ride?

It seemed so. He greeted me with a bow. "In the service of Her Majesty Fenna. I take it that you're my passenger."

"I have an appointment," I said.

He hefted my bag, and I followed him down the ramp to his craft. "Do you know who I'm meeting?" I asked.

The canopy of the craft opened. "Madame, I've been instructed to respect your privacy."

I settled into my seat in the cockpit and he handed me my bag. I tucked it beside my seat atop a lazarette. He took the pilot seat and the canopy closed. I rubbed my gloved hands together waiting for the cockpit to warm.

I allowed him silence as the esskip taxied from the dock and went airborne. Most likely he was in communication with Kasaanko command. Our flight steadied out about a meter above the water.

"Where are we going?" I asked.

"I'm sorry. I've been instructed not to discuss it with you."

I made another attempt at a conversation. "So you're with Fennako Ferries.

"Aye."

"Have you been with the ferry system for long?"

"I'm truly sorry. I've been instructed not give you any information or to ask for any."

Mist obscured dark timber on the mountainsides. The craft's flight was nearly silent, only the wash of air over canopy and wings as the engines pulsed, an action more felt than heard. The overcast sky cast no shadows on the gray ocean. I didn't even know what direction we headed.

I'd been up since before dawn. Lulled by the swaying of the esskip I dozed and awoke with no idea of my location or the direction of our travel. The ocean remained the color of slate, the mountains obscure hulks of blue-gray and white. We rounded a headland. Houses and buildings clustered along a waterfront.

I didn't pester the pilot by asking the name of the village. Instead, I noted tails, bows, transoms for vessel names, and call numbers. The most common call sign prefix, Gulf Lima Victor, most likely indicated local clan.

If all went as planned, Noahee would soon have our own call sign prefix, November Ophelia Alpha Alpha. If only that tide would come. The call sign had orginally belonged to Jamie Noah, or so some believed. Others claimed it had been the anacronym of an agency on Earth. The esskip splashed down and docked. A woman was waiting for me. "Miss, I'll accompany you to the clinic."

The pilot passed me my bag. "Tide carry you."

I wondered what he thought I'd be doing.

At the clinic, the receptionist glanced up from her planning screen. "Biometric identification please."

I touched my thumb to the proffered pad.

"We've received your records. Please look them over to make sure they're correct." She handed me a screen.

I sat on a chair upholstered in muted foliage patterns, and flicked the device. My medical records came up; immunizations, childhood illnesses, dental work, exercise and eating habits, my age at the time of my first menstrual period, pages of genetic analysis, everything but my name and the names of my parents.

I handed the screen back and the receptionist gave me a medical identification bracelet. "Our intake counselor will be with you in a moment."

I was led into an office to face the counselor seated at a desk and flanked by two notary cameras.

As I sat before the cameras, the counselor gave me a standard spiel. "We are required by law to inform you that your confidentiality will be respected. Your records, including notary video records, will not be shared with anyone without your express consent. Please show agreement by saying aye and touching your thumb to this pad."

I complied, the pad slick, cool, and slightly greasy.

"The law also requires us to ensure informed consent. You have requested insemination for the purpose of conceiving a child. Please indicate agreement."

I touched my thumb to the pad. "Aye."

"We have that you have requested natural insemination. We must inform you of the risks of this procedure. We recommend against it. Natural insemination carries multiple risks. Standard practice for achieving pregnancy is to undergo artificial insemination. We have made every effort to protect against transmission of diseases. However, with this procedure, the risk of pathogens cannot be completely eliminated. Do you still wish to proceed with natural insemination?"

"Since when is artificial insemination the normal procedure?" I asked. "Haven't people and animals always had natural sex?"

"Merely indicate that you agree or disagree. Do you wish to proceed with natural insemination?"

"Aye." I again touched thumb to pad.

"Natural insemination can be painful or even traumatic for a patient. If you wish, you may be anesthetized for the procedure."

"No."

"Do we have that you decline anesthesia?"

"Aye."

"Do you understand that you will not know the identity of the sperm donor nor will he know yours? You will not speak to him nor see his face? This is triple blind privacy. We at the clinic also know neither his identity nor yours."

It seemed likely to me that we might encounter each other afterwards while we waited for transport. Possibly, the man could have been at the harbor before me and had watched me walk to the clinic.

After I'd agreed that I understood the risks of natural sex, a woman dressed in scrubs entered the room. "I'll be your attendant throughout this procedure," she said.

Feelings of stillness settled over me as if I were buried under a great weight of clay. She led me into another room. "You may undress here and put your clothing in this locker. Please wash in the shower bath. When you're finished, put the towels in the hamper. You may use this garment." A hospital gown had been placed on a bench along with towel and washcloth.

I undressed and took a shower, giving myself over to needle sharp spray. Finished, I donned the gown which reached to mid-thigh and fastened with a string. I placed my folded clothing, along with my bag, my comset and reading screen, in the locker.

The attendant stood at a doorway. "Let's get you prepped."

In the next room, this one with a counter and sink— sat on a bench. The attendant brought out a mechanical razor. "Now, if you'd be so kind, pull your gown aside and lift your arm."

I allowed the attendant to shave the hair from my underarms. "What's this for?" I asked. I'd discussed insemination procedures with Teakh, not in detail of course, but enough to get an idea of what to expect. He'd given the impression that insemination was usually arranged according to a woman's preferences.

"Cleanliness. Bacteria like to hide out in hair."

"Oh really? And how does that interfere with conception?"

"The smell. And now for the important part. Lie back and I'll shave the site of the operation."

I supposed if I smelled bad the man might find me unattractive. I opened my legs and the attendant moved the buzzing razor over my skin. She set aside the device for a smaller razor and moved, shaving the area around my anus. I became rock still, fearful of a slip of the attendant's hand.

"This probably isn't necessary, but it's standard procedure." With a cloth she cleaned away remaining hair fragments. "You can sit up now."

What was the real reason for shaving? I rubbed my thighs together, my skin oddly smooth. I knew adult body hair disseminated pheromones, and the most expensive perfumes either imitated or enhanced these natural scents.

The attendant covered my head with a cap. "Can't be shaving your head. This will have to do. How are you feeling?"

As near as I could tell, they aimed to dehumanize me. "All right," I lied. I'd agreed to the procedure and planned to go through with it.

"It's normal to feel nervous." The attendant opened a door. "But the procedure will soon be over. Into the insemination room with you."

The room contained what looked like an examination table with stirrups and a disposable covering. The attendant touched a foot pedal and the table lowered. The covering crinkled as I sat down.

"Feet up," the attendant said cheerfully.

I allowed my ankles to be strapped in place. "What's this for?"

"Safety. Sometimes a patient thrashes around during the procedure. You could kick the donor. We wouldn't want that happening, now, would we?"

Why would they think I'd kick the man? I had no intention of doing such a thing unless he attacked me first. Did that mean he would be violent?

"Now lie back. We'll secure your hands."

I reminded myself that this operation was a normal procedure, no different from getting a cavity filled. My wrists fit into cuffs at the side of the table and my head was fastened down well. These people had been professional and had shown concern for my comfort and safety.

I was now completely immobilized. Founder it all! I should have specified dim lights and soft music. I'd been warned by the counselor and by Teakh, but I'd been too stubborn. I'd been anxious about the well-being of my baby and my family, and hadn't given much thought to the experience of getting pregnant. I'd heard only what I'd wanted to hear. Panic washed over me. I jerked my wrist against a restraint. I calmed myself. I'd agreed to this and would go through with it.

The attendant placed a drape over me and fixed a screen blocking my view. I wouldn't even to able to see the man. I might have just as well gone with artificial insemination.

The attendant spread the stirrups apart, spreading my legs with them. "Comfy? I can raise your head up a bit."

"Please do. I have an itch. Forehead. Along the edge of the cap."

Cool fingers adjusted the elastic and tucked a lock of my hair. "Better?"

Danna! If only this would be over with. I'd have my clan designation, my baby, and my entry into law school.

I tried to keep my panic under control. "Stay with me," I pleaded.

"If you don't mind me watching."

Far worse to be helpless and alone with a man they thought I'd kick if I had the chance. I drove my fingernails into my palms, the tiny bite of pain reassuring.

A door clicked open. Footsteps crossed the floor and the man spoke. "What in Poseidon is this?" He had a pleasant voice, deep and commanding.

"Sir, please refrain from talking."

"You expect me to...Good Danna!"

Blood roared in my ears. He stepped between my legs, the fabric of his hospital gown tickling my thighs. He rested his hand over my vagina. He could do anything to me. Anything.

I jerked. I couldn't help it. My hands shook even my legs.

He stepped back. "She's terrified."

"Sir, no speaking."

"Do you know who I am?"

"Sir, I do not. And neither should she."

"Get out of my way."

"Sir! Sir!"

He jerked the screen out of the way, and his gaze met mine. "What did they do to you?"

I attempted a smile. "Nothing. I'm fine. We're not supposed to talk."

He smiled back. "Rules. What are they to us?" He freed my head and pushed back my cap. "Who are you?"

I liked his eyes. The color was unusual, gold-brown flecks floating in gray, the glint of sunlight on water, but there was something else. He had a neatly trimmed beard, and his hairstyle was simple. I glanced again at his eyes and saw a generous spirit. Maybe the impression was because his interest seemed so genuine or maybe I was mistaken.

He released my hands and my feet, then covered me with the drape.

I sat up. Tears started in my eyes. I brushed them away, furious with myself for crying. I did not need sympathy. "Who are you?"

"I asked first."

"We're not supposed to say."

"Oh, that's right. Pesky rules. I can't perform with you trussed up this way. Call it a quirk of mine."

"There, there. " He stroked my hair. He smelled good—musky, spicy.

The attendant came through the door. "Stop that. You're violating privacy."

"What about our privacy? Now if you'd pipe down, the lady and I will have a talk. We'd be much obliged if you'd step out of the room."

"Go ahead," I said. "Just go!"

The attendant glowered at the man before she exited, closing the door behind her. The man seated himself on a stool. "Now then, why do you want to bear my child?"

"My child," I corrected.

"Ours," he agreed.

"I have an agreement with the Queen. If I let you father my child, she'll recognize me as a clan leader."

"I don't understand."

I wiped my face. "I wrote up a clan charter. My brother and I petitioned the Queen for clan recognition. She agreed to grant my petition if I accepted her choice of father for my baby."

"Are you sure of this?"

"I've been working on this for years and we spent months negotiating the terms. My brother and I met with her in the Palace. It's all notarized."

His brow furrowed. "There must be more going on."

"My brother thinks we might be kin. Do you know anything about the Noah Eugenics Project?"

"Wasn't that some crazy idea about recreating Jamie Noah?"

"His genetics anyway. Do you have any connection to that project?"

"Not that I know of."

"Well, that's good. Because then you probably aren't my uncle or my brother."

"Why would I be your brother?"

"Your father could be my father. Or they could be brothers."

"They aren't."

"How do you know?"

"They just aren't."

I said, "I'm concerned that someone, the Queen maybe, might be trying to produce a purebred strain."

"What's wrong with good breeding?"

"Producing a purebred strain requires incest," I said. "Tell me, are you a cover stud?"

"A what?"

"A cover stud, a man who inseminates women for money."

"I wouldn't do this for money. "

"Then why are you here? You asked me first."

"Someone I care about asked me to, and I was curious."

"Someone you care about?"

"We're not kin," he insisted without answering my question.

"So how much do you trust Her Majesty?"

"She is the queen," he said. "I need to think about this."

"After we finish."

"Let's not rush this. We can meet again in a more conducive setting." He turned his head to glance around the sterile room. "I told the truth. I can't do it in these circumstances. But I'd like to kiss you."

"I'd like that too."

I closed my eyes and we kissed. I savored the softness of his lips and the scratch of his beard against my face. I inhaled his smell, unfamiliar and musky. A lump under the drape gave lie to his claims about performance. Poseidon! I reminded myself that just because a man was aroused didn't mean he wanted to father a child.

We parted and he left the room, but his words came through the closed door. "Poseidon damn! She's not out of her second dodecade. What the hell is going on?"

———

Chapter 12
Shelliko

I WIPED MY FACE with the drape, tossed it aside along with the cap, and squared my shoulders. I wouldn't be defeated.

The attendant waited in the next room.

"He left," I said.

"And the procedure?" she asked.

"Didn't happen."

"How about artificial insemination? Much more reliable."

"Poseidon take you!" I flung off the hospital gown. The attendant fluttering after me I fingered open the lock on the cupboard. My crotch was starting to itch.

Fully dressed, I exited through the receiving area. "When's my transport coming?" I stalked out of the clinic and to the waterfront. I hoped to catch the man before he left. A muted green esskip moored at a pier bore a Fennako tail-number and the twelve-point badge of Tristan Bay Harbor Patrol.

I touched the comset at my shoulder. "Teakh. What do you have on this call sign?" I read the designation.

"Tristan Bay Harbor Patrol. Where are you at?"

"I know it's Tristan Bay Harbor Patrol. But I'm not in Tristan Bay. Who owns this esskip?"

"I can't tell you. Fennako is tight with information."

Use of a Fennako esskip might not mean anything.

Fennako had provided transport and might have sent Harbor Patrol instead of Fennako Ferries for the man.

"How about clan designation Gulf Lima Victor?" I asked.

"Galvako."

"That's where I'm at. My appointment flopped. He told me he couldn't perform, and made promises to meet with me. He's lying. I'm sure of it."

I signed off and located a café. There I ordered a sandwich and began running searches through stud catalogues. I entered SEAGUARD and HAZEL EYES. The few resulting men didn't look anything like my man, so I tried the same search but with GRAY EYES and GREEN EYES. No luck. I barely tasted my meal as I worked through all Seaguard studs available in the Fenrian Archipelago. Teakh, of course, came up

I hailed him. "Not finding him in Dale's Men. He's Seaguard. I'm sure of that as well."

"Seaguard studs don't usually advertise," Teakh said.

I was at a loss. I'd planned to go to Fennako City for prenatal care and to meet with my academic advisor, but I wasn't pregnant, not unless a miracle had occurred. "Drop in on Angel," Teakh suggested. "She might have some ideas."

"I can't."

"Why not? You liked her at Solstice Tide."

"That was a holiday visit. And you were there. She's your girl."

"So? If all goes well, she'll be my wife."

After signing off I composed a message on my tambour screen.

Hailing Dyse, Annin here.

An opportunity has come up. I won't be returning home for several days.

THE SUN HAD set by the time I stumbled up the covered dock ramp and into the Shelliko terminal. Angel met me, her hood thrown back from glossy auburn hair, stunning even in twilight. I accepted her embrace, fur and hair silky against my cheek. We sat together on a bench, holding hands, heads bowed. The few other passengers went on their way.

"I did agree," I said. "It's notarized and everything. But then he didn't...he didn't..."

Angel handed me a handkerchief. "We'll go up to my place. Do you have any baggage?"

I held up my bag. "Didn't think I'd be gone for more than a night."

We left the terminal. A single silver-edged cloud drifted over the face of the full moon. A few stars twinkled from a sky not yet fully dark, a delicate shade of dark blue.

Angel's front porch gleamed with the rosy glow of night lights. I followed her through the studio, the details of her paintings indistinguishable in the dimness. She turned up the kitchen light, shaded ruby in accordance with the taboo against shine. But what did it matter with Luna Majora full? What did it matter anyway? I wasn't pregnant regardless of if I'd ovulated or not.

I slumped on a stool in her kitchen. "Horrible. The whole thing. They shaved me and made me wear one of those miserable hospital robes. This guy came in to get me pregnant. He wouldn't do it. He refused!" I hated myself for sniveling, but I was tired and disappointed. "He told me. He told me he couldn't perform, and that we'd try again another time. But he lied. I'll never see him again."

Angel opened her cold cupboard and brought out a bowl of noodles garnished with chopped herbs and lumps of goat cheese. "Then you do want to see him again?"

"If he'll see me. I...I had my legs open like a cheap whore, all for a deal I'd made."

"Don't be ridiculous." She set a bowl before me. "I've seen your clan charter and the contract you did. You're brilliant and daring. You went right to the Queen to present your idea, and she approves."

"But the man doesn't." I prodded at the noodles with a fork. "And now you and Teakh can't get married."

Angel dished up a bowl of pasta for herself. "Marriage isn't essential to love. And consider that your man just might have been telling the truth."

"But he—"

"Sometimes a man gets an erection, but can't ejaculate. Your brother is like that."

I didn't particularly want to know this about Teakh.

"A characteristic of Noah men." She twirled noodles around her fork. "It takes them a bit longer to do it, and that keeps women happy."

I sampled the pasta, the herbs fresh, a nice change from chowder. "I thought that kind of thing only happened with older men."

"Mmm." Angel's eyes sparkled. "They do get better with age. But think. What would Teakh do in such circumstances? If you were a man, what would you do? Maybe he knew you weren't ready. If you're not ready, especially if you've never done it before, sex hurts. Honestly, were you ready for him?"

"I'd been prepped."

"Teakh tells me every animal species has innate courtship behaviors. You can't suddenly fling aside eons of evolution to fulfill a contract."

"He'd say that sort of thing." Teakh often displayed odd combination of biological knowledge and romanticism.

"Maybe Fernako can come up with a different man."

"But I don't want a different man."

"You're just like your brother." Angel sighed. "Do it once and you're in love."

"But I didn't do it, and I'm not in love." My life was a mess. I'd have to go back to Ralko and wash sheets for the rest of my life. I'd grow old and become Aunt Trudia, stretching fish bone soup to feed crowds of vagrants.

In the morning I felt somewhat better. Angel was in her studio, a long-handled paintbrush balanced in her hand. She daubed color on a nude of Teakh, building paint in rich, delicate layers. I checked my comset. A message waited and it was from the man.

"He wants to meet with me," I said. "Next full moon. At the Havi Resort in Hanalee."

Angel dropped her paintbrush in turpentine. "Hanalee! Why that's wonderful. The tropics!"

"But it doesn't matter. I'm not going." That one experience had been enough. I didn't want to go through it again.

"You can't turn down a date to Hanalee," Angel said.

"Oh yes I can."

"Who do you think he is?" she asked.

"It doesn't matter."

"I think it does. Consider. Not many men could arrange a trip to Hanalee overnight. Not for a Full Moon in spawning season. They're likely to be booked years in advance."

"But it's not fully spawning seasons and it won't be for months."

"Go to Hanalee. Have a good time."

"And get pregnant?" I asked.

"Wasn't that your plan?"

She was partly right. Considering the timing, he had to be a man of importance, but that didn't make my situation any better. He had all the power. "He's probably a Seaguard lord," I said.

"Nothing probably about it. To arrange your holiday trip he must have contacted important people. Likely hailed them in the middle of the night. Only a Seaguard lord can pull that off."

"He could be anyone," I said.

"Then you are going to follow through?"

I had no desire to repeat my foolishness and humiliation. I thrust my jaw forward. He would have to come begging.

———

Chapter 13
Shopping

IN THE OBSERVATION lounge of the ferry, I'd given up my attempts to read. Fennako City slipped past the windows in a lacework of buildings, bridges, and stone—some of the islands connected by high spans, others reachable only by boat. Gantry cranes, overhanging shipping docks, loaded and unloaded goods. Aircraft buzzed overhead, coming in to splash down and dock at airports. Water taxies and small ferries shuttled across Tristan Bay, linking Fennako City together, a bay constantly in motion.

I'd softened my stance toward the man. Angel had convinced me to travel to Fennako City to purchase clothing for my next rendezvous. According to her, if I dressed well, I could meet him eye-to-eye as his equal or better. "You'll be his goddess," she'd promised.

Angel's elbow jostled me as she sketched, her stylus recording impressions: a tower jutting above an island, at the top a glass-sided, hexagonal viewing station.

I leaned, watching her shade the tower. "So now you're drawing something besides men."

She selected a new color, and her stylus continued moving. "Not really. I'm drawing Marsk Fennako."

"He sure looks like a traffic control tower," I said.

She chuckled. "Very large. Very erect. Wouldn't you say?"

"Be serious."

"I am." She gestured to the view beyond the window. "There's not much difference between a magnate and his territory. Or so he tells me." She leaned back, holding the sketch at arm's length.

Each lord had underwater sensors which linked to his neural implant making him inseparable from his territory. Even if Angel had met Lord Tristan Bay, a respectable woman wouldn't ask a Seaguard magnate about the details of his underwater network. "Oh come on."

"It's true." Angel placed her pad in her lap. "You know your brother and that gull of his?"

"Always off flying." Teakh used his robotic gull for investigations but maybe that was only an excuse. He liked flying.

"Give him some credit. He's good at it. The point is, when he flies, he thinks he's a seagull. I mean, he knows he's a man but, at the same time he's a bird. They tell me that's the way it feels for all of them."

I stared at her. Apparently Angel had spoken with a number of Seaguard men about such intimate matters.

"Men in the Seaguard all use telechiric devices. It's the way it is." She twiddled her stylus. "The ones who are really good at it are selected as magnates. Seaguard lords make really good artist models, and they make good lovers. I like their feet. The best of the Seaguard can move each toe individually."

"Teakh can't."

"Actually he can. He's magnate quality. The best thing though is that magnates tend to be both respectful and direct about what they want. They have to be. They're constantly dealing with boats moving in and out of their territory as if traveling on the man's back. They mean what they say."

Beyond the window, waves rippled and surged in ever-changing patterns, brocade and satin. "About Lord Tristan Bay. What part of him are we looking at? A gull makes sense. It's got two feet, two arms—well, wings— and a head, just like a person. But a bay?"

She agreed. "No bilateral symmetry. They tell me it's not really a problem. It's easy to imagine being a starfish or even an amorphous blob. If you can imagine it, you can be it. Marsk Fennako is rather reserved and hasn't told me much. I'm certainly not going to ask, but consider the names of the islands." She pointed with her stylus. "That one back there with the tower. Tristan Head. I'm not sure which of his heads."

"What man has two heads?"

Angel laughed. "Every man. One of those heads is near two rocks. I've always wondered about Lawrock."

My face heated. I didn't want to discuss the neurological connection between a Seaguard lord and his rocks.

She elbowed me. "But don't worry. Considering the islands with 'hold' in their name, I'd say Tristan Bay holds Fennako City in his arms. That's the difficulty with loving a magnate, or any man for that matter. You'll always have to share him with the sea."

I folded my tambour screen in preparation for debarking. Angel stowed her pad and stylus. We walked down the gangway to stand once again on Lawrock Island. Last time here I'd been a student. After Angel's explanation I now saw it differently.

Under the shelter of a pitched roof, a panel displayed a schedule of local ferry routes, predictions for high and low tide, and weather advisories. Angel glanced at the timetable, then we strolled along the waterfront.

If we'd turned right instead of left and taken an alley between shop fronts, we'd have arrived at Madame X's Mannary, maybe even have seen Madame X seated on her tall stool and fencing pilfered semen. Walking farther would've brought us to a lane hemmed in by governmental offices and to Dame Bulla bent over a planning screen, approving or rejecting petitions.

I had no wish to repeat the path taken in that direction. Instead, we caught a ferry shuttle to Icehold Island. There, we climbed uphill along narrow, brick-paved lanes. A sign, hand painted on a driftwood board, pointed the way to Pennyroyal's Bed and Breakfast. Angel opened a gate made of what looked to be gaff spars. Sculptures filled the courtyard: large birds constructed from fuel tanks, anchors, and masts, and an assemblage of junk resembling a giant mechanical man.

Penny stepped into the yard and waved. Angel dropped her bags, and they greeted each other, hands touching and repeated a traditional greeting between friends. "Amatha."

Penny stepped back. "What are you about? More painting?"

"Helping a friend." Angel placed a hand on my shoulder. And I see you've added to your sculpture collection."

"I just love frequenting junk barges." Penny laughed. "I assume you've been adding to your man collection."

Angel dropped her hand from my shoulder. "Only their images."

Penny welcomed us into her parlor. On the wall, a structure resembling a huge handfan reached from floor to ceiling, most likely the pinion plates of an esskip. A plate of butter cookies topped with jam waited on a glass-topped table. The pedestal supporting the glass had frayed cables.

Penny noticed my interest in the table pedestal. "That's the atlas coupler off a Seaguard weather buoy. I'm told the part corresponds to a man's neck."

"So this is a decapitated Seaguard holding up your table?" I asked.

"When the bearings on a coupler wear out, a Seaguard lord replaces it, no harm done," Penny explained. "Still it's quite a find, rather like finding a vertebra of a giant. Fancy being able to change out body parts when they wear out."

"That's for deep sea lords," Angel said. "They think they're standing on the ocean floor. Coastal lords are prone, supine, or reclining. "

I imagined the entire ocean full of giant men linked together to form the Sense-net. In the deep water they stood with only their heads above the seas. Along the shores and on icefields they lounged like beach goers or seals hauled out on icebergs for a snooze. I imagined the giants calling to each other electronically, shouting warnings about predators, big waves, and bad weather.

Angel, seated in a rocking chair made largely of knotted and spliced cord, bantered, "Are you saying coastal lords are shallow?"

"I didn't say it." Penny disappeared through the door into her kitchen.

A nearby shelf displayed a mechanical hand, the fingers bright yellow and the sensor pads black. Such a device must have been scavenged from a submarine repair bot. The yellow color would appear white in the dim blue light of the ocean depths, if there was light at all. Some lords served as guardians of rivers, each man a watershed.

"If coastal lords are shallow, what about river lords?" I asked.

"Turbid and shallow," Angel said, with a gleam in her eye. "Ice lords are frigid. Brrr!"

108

Penny returned with tea service and placed the tray beside the cookies. I sampled a delicate pastry topped with raspberry jam and washed it down with the sweet but faintly astringent tea. "We're shopping for a trousseau," Angel supplied.

"Did you pop the question?" Penny asked, all eagerness. "Is it for that Noah stud you've been raving about? Her latest interest," she said as an aside to me.

Angel plunked a lump of barley sugar into her tea. "My only interest."

"Marj has a thing for Seaguard lords," Penny poured a cup for herself. "And cover studs, any man trapped by status."

Teakh's girlfriend had a dizzying number of monikers. "Marj" must have been another of her nicknames. Angel, come Marj, stirred her tea. "This one is the man for me."

"She rescues them," Penny said.

"I do not," Angel protested. "I paint portraits. The trousseau is for Annin."

"I set my net there's a Seaguard lord involved," Penny shook her finger. "I know you, Marj. People exist more deserving of your pity than rich, handsome men."

Angel selected a cookie. "But those other people aren't as rich or handsome."

Penny flopped against the cushions beside me. "Poor fellows, too powerful, too much money, too much sex. What are they to do?"

"They don't actually have all that much sex," Angel said. "Conjugal relations every few years. They get lonely. It's sad, and they're some of the nicest men around."

"They still have money and power," Penny scolded.

"Not much of those either. Without freedom, what is power worth?"

"Money. Pity the man who has too much. I notice you don't feel pity for the women." Penny peered over the rim of her teacup.

"But I do. My paintings are for them, something to keep in their bedrooms while the men are gone." Angel cleared her throat. "Excuse me. Annin is my fiancé's sister."

"Your fiancé?" exclaimed Penny. "Would that be Stud Wonderful the Noah man?"

"My brother. Teakh Noahee." I blushed.

"Is he going to give up the profession?" Penny asked bluntly.

"We weren't planning on it," Angel said, then mercifully changed the subject. The new topic wasn't much better. "Annin has a rendezvous with a Seaguard lord."

"A little early for a trousseau," Penny said.

"The rendezvous is for the Full Moon," Angel said.

"Oooh. A baby then. How exciting. Who's the lucky man?" Penny put a hand to her mouth.

"Well..." I began. Angel gave me no guidance. I went on, "He's Seaguard, tall, hazel eyes. I don't know if he's actually a lord, and I don't know if I'm going to follow through with it, so that doesn't matter."

Penny leaned forward, cup in hand. "How did you two meet?"

"A blind date." I left out the details.

"And you hit it off? How romantic."

"The Queen set them up," Angel said.

"Her Majesty a matchmaker? I want to hear all about it. Do you have this fellow's name?"

"It's supposed to be anonymous." I explained that my clan charter was dependent my pregnancy.

"If it goes through," Angel supplied, "Annin will be Noahee grandmatriarch. She'll give permission for me to marry Teakh."

110

"Grandmatriarch? At your age?"

"It's an amazing charter." Angel gestured excitedly, nearly dropping her cookie. "The children of men are included as members, and they'll have dual clan membership. When Teakh and I have children, they'll be members of Clan Noahee as well as mine."

Penny frowned. "The Queen approved this?"

"Only if Annin agrees to the Queen's choice of man," Angel repeated.

"He seemed nice enough," I said.

"Then you like him?"

"I suppose I do."

"Of course you do." Penny nibbled a cookie. "He's one of those noble, self-sacrificing Seaguard lords."

"I don't know that."

"I'm certain he is," Angel said. "We're going to buy a trousseau so that Annin can rescue her handsome Seaguard man from loneliness. See, I'm not the only girl who cares about such men."

"Surely he's already married?" Penny said, with a nod of certainty.

"He probably visits his wife once every three years," Angel said. "He needs rescuing."

"Do you really think he's already married?" I asked. I'd hoped to have a man of my own, not a sneaky one-time liaison.

"Given his age, his quality, and the shortage of men it's nearly a sure thing. But if it remains anonymous, there'll be no impact on his marriage. He might even have his wife's permission. Smooth sailing. What more could you ask for?"

What more? How about a promise that he'd stick around? How about assurances that he wasn't a monster?

WE SET OUT for Trader's Wharf for an early start on shopping. Gallery owners and shop keepers addressed Angel by a variety of nicknames and brought out their best. The cost of custom-made clothing shocked me, but Angel confided that such expenses were necessary. "That understated difference whispers quality. Besides it fits better." She smiled. "Seaguard lords wear bespoke, so we do the same."

"Who do you mean by we?" I asked.

"Those of us who service Seaguard lords."

This was as close as Angel had come to calling herself a prostitute, but she wasn't. For one thing, Teakh didn't have any money and couldn't pay her. Maybe courtesan was the best label for her combination of artistry and allure.

As we left a beauty salon, I caught sight of our reflections in a window. In a new, royal blue parka and boots trimmed in fur I looked as much a courtesan as Angel. Who would have thought it of me? Less than a twelvenight ago, I'd been serving soup to the clanless.

IN THE AFTERNOON, we attended a soirée—artists, poets, and writers eating canapés and discussing aesthetics.

"You must be a painter." A woman sipped from a fluted glass. "Mata Carrie does such beautiful work."

"I'm unfamiliar with the artist." My face heated. I might have looked like a courtesan but felt myself a fraud.

"You seem to know her quite well." The woman extended a slim finger to Angel. "They say you're her protégée."

"You mean Angel?"

"Her nom d'artiste is so evocative. Mata Carrie, the legendary siren. She seduces with paint rather than song. So profound."

Profound? Angel painted naked men. "I'm sorry," I said. "I admire art, but I'm not an artist myself."

"Everyone is an artist."

"I write legal contracts and articles of incorporation." I'd authored two such documents, anyway.

"Legal poetry," she suggested.

"Hardly. Work with reproductive contracts."

The woman's eyes lit "So that's the connection. It's so intriguing how Mata Carrie's paintings both exploit male sexuality and simultaneously expose exploitation, the naked truth."

To me the painting was my little brother in the buff, something kinky he did with his girlfriend. "I suppose so."

After sunset, we returned to the ferry under the rosy glow of streetlights. Snowflakes swirling in the red light resembled sparks, embers of cold.

WITH DAYLIGHT STREAMING through the windows, I sat reading. Angel walked in holding a handscreen. "We've got an invitation. Sarana Comryez."

I set aside my screen. "Sarana? Isn't that the flower that smells like manure?"

"Stink Lily. Comryez clan leader always pin that delightful moniker on the granddaughter designated as her heir."

There was a song about greedy Blackmouth Comryez and how he swallowed boats. I hummed the tune, one I'd learned as a child.

"That's the one. Lord Comryez is actually a pleasant gentleman. His sister though—" Angel glanced skyward. Figures that she'd have met Lord Comryez. "Stink Lily just might swallow an entire fleet. She wants to meet with us. You specifically."

Since childhood I'd been told stories of how Comryez lurked in the shadows, ready to eat misbehaving children. "What for?"

"Who knows. Comryez might not be the most powerful clan on Fenria, but they are odd." Angel dropped her screen on the bed. "Possibly it's about portraits of her sons."

"But I'm not a painter."

"Maybe because of your brother. Comryez trains their sons as Seaguard and marries them off well. It's a way of forming allegiances." Angel turned her stylus end over end. "Honestly? I fear you'll arrange a marriage between Teakh and Comryez, and they won't want me in the bargain."

"You told me Comryez sells men. Now you are saying they're buying?"

"Their business is producing top quality men. To do that they need a top quality sire. I'm just an artist. I can't match an offer made by Comryez."

I tried to make sense of my brother's dealings with Angel. Was it personal or a business relationship? "I'm not selling. You're family, and he's family."

What a tangle our lives had become. I didn't know which was worse, my brother's interaction with his girlfriend or my own impending liaison.

———

Chapter 14
Stink Lily

THE FERRY SHUTTLE glided across Tristan Bay, foam churning in its wake, a double streak of white across gray. I stood at the rail, cold wind buffeting my hood, blowing it back, whipping my hair. Snow had dusted Lawrock Island and was now melting. Accretions of houses, law offices, palace complex, and courts mounted upward, culminating in the green, snow-crusted dome of the Zenhedron courthouse.

On Lawrock Island, we climbed stairways that served as lanes between the dense buildings. A hotel reached upward with a full six-story facade made of blue-green glass set between white columns. We would call on Stink Lily Comryez at her temporary place of lodging. Above the doorway, a bas relief depicted a bowhead whale, its mouth a comb-work of stone baleen. We trod up the wide steps and through a set of double doors. The foyer lounge contained wing chairs and potted plants in groupings on patterned rugs. The concierge welcomed us with a smile and a bow.

Sunburst patterned transoms topped each doorway, opening onto a central hall lit by light shafts piercing the center of the building. In the parlor of a luxury suite, a middle-aged woman greeted us. Her black hair, streaked with white, was plaited into a single braid.

Her hooded, calf-length black robe had a front panel displaying horned puffins in flight, their beaks golden yellow and red. The horned eyes, which gave that species of puffin its name, resembled the exaggerated black and white makeup of a clown. Under the robe, her legs were encased in tomato-red, waterproof thighboots! Fully functional, seaboots! So, this was Stink Lily Comryez. She smiled, her dark eyes lined with black. Was it makeup?

I glanced away, trying not to stare. Stink Lily licked her upper lip with a tongue as black as her eyes and gave a predatory smile. Her gaze traveled hungrily over my body, seemingly undressing me, assessing the potential of plunder. Danna! The song had named the chief as Blackmouth Comryez. I hadn't thought of the coloration or behavior as literal.

Belying her fearsome demeanor and reputation, Stink Lily passed around a plate of oatmeal cookies and served chamomile tea with lumps of barley sugar and dollops of goat milk. Stink Lily set the milk pitcher aside and gestured with one hand. "Let's have a look at you."

Instead of directly refusing I raised my eyebrows.

Stink Lily twirled a finger. "Stand up would you, dear. And turn around. I like to see how the genes actually express."

"This is uncalled for," Angel said.

"Noahee has burst onto the scene with a revolutionary clan charter and stunning genetics," Stink Lily said. "I would very much like confirmation that this phenomenon is for real."

I did my best to stare her down. "Are you assessing me as breeding stock?"

"Yes," Stink Lily said, her honesty disarming. "I'd like a demonstration of your balance and coordination. Go on. Show me. I've heard you're good, you and your brother both."

How would Comryez know anything about us? Teakh's genetic profile could be found in a number of stud catalogs, but not his name. I kept information about myself strictly private.

"It isn't all that important." Stink Lily patted a chair beside her. "Sit with me. How you think. Now that's vital."

Her predatory honesty both intrigued and repelled me, so I accepted the seat. "Whatever for?"

"Survival," Stink Lily said. "Our clan, Comryez, has only one thing going for us. We're ruthless. Other clans have deep-water harbors, bountiful fisheries, arable lands. Not us. We're pirates. Oh, we make our living by charging pilotage, but it's about the same thing. We have the most treacherous strait on Fenria. If we cannot hold the Pass, someone will take it from us, someone even more ruthless than we are."

"Why hold it at all?" I asked. I had no desire for such real-estate.

"The Pass is the portion of the ocean allotted to us, our home. To hold what we have, my kin must be smart, coordinated, and above all, driven. The most important decisions a woman ever makes are those regarding the well-being of her children and grandchildren. We need men and women with daring and initiative." She tapped my knee. "You have plenty of both. If you think you can do a superior job of holding the Pass. If you think you're more ruthless than we are, we'll co-opt you."

I washed down a cookie with chamomile tea. "I'm not selling, and I don't want your Pass."

Stink Lily smiled, her teeth gleaming in her black gums. "I'm not buying. But possibly your grandchildren will marry my grandchildren and we will find ourselves allies. Dual clan membership. Isn't that your idea?"

"This is a bit early. I don't have any children."

"Never mind that. Your clan is Noahee. Yes? The patrilineal descendants of Jamie Noah?"

"Actually, ambilineal. The children of both men and women. This doesn't bother you? We're giving equal membership to men."

"I love my sons as much as my daughter," said Stink Lily.

"But you're a hereditary matriarch. Your sons might take over."

"They'd do a good job of it too. Anyway, you have it wrong. I'm not grandmatriarch. That's my mother, and even she doesn't have absolute power. The Comryez Mothers' Council can oust her if they so please. You're one up on me or better. You're grandmatriarch. And with no mothers' council putting a check on your authority. Go ahead. Put men in charge. They can't do any worse than clan matriarchs. Who needs Fennako? Seize what you may." Lily took a bite of a cookie. "I always like oatmeal. So hearty. That Fennako woman is sharp for an old biddy."

"Who?"

"The Queen, or so she styles herself, but we've never given her royal override. She snapped you right up. I'll tell you, if she lets you down, come to Comryez." Stink Lily licked her fingers. "Comryez can always use a good lawyer."

"I'm not a lawyer yet." This Comryez woman was presumptuous, planning on marriages of children not yet born, in a clan not yet approved, to a mother who had yet to be accepted as a law student.

"The bar was cooked up by cowards. I like you, girl. You'll make a fine matriarch. Let me be the first to welcome you into the club." She smirked. "We're a feisty bunch of old hags. Best be on your toes."

118

ANGEL AND I descended the steps of the lane shoulder-to-shoulder, close enough that others walking nearby wouldn't overhear.

She said, "With enough bald courage, a woman can do anything. Even wear red seaboots under matriarchal robes. That name Stink Lily fits her, an oxymoron if ever there was one."

"Her kin does gobble down ships and spit them out in splinters." I pretended to chew and push out ship parts as if they were cherry pits.

"Pull that off, and you can wear anything you want. But she has me worried. Comryez has a way of twisting things around. I've heard the Seaguard was founded as an educational cadre. They inspected boats, put out weather reports, and taught fishermen about safety. Along comes Comryez. Their Seaguard is armed, a navy. Other clans followed their lead."

Water safety instructors at war would be funny if it weren't so serious. "Do you trust her?" I asked.

"Poseidon no! Playing games with people's lives is her little hobby. You noticed her eyes and tongue. Comryez bred it into themselves. Most likely just to shock people. Maybe they spliced in genes from fish or birds. Comryez will stop at nothing."

I tapped my forehead. "Are they insane?"

"They'd like us to think so. Truly, they may be belligerent, proud, and inbred, but they're fully aware of the tide. "

"She was certainly upfront about her intentions."

"And what did she tell you? That Comryez can't be trusted." Angel rubbed her cuticles with her thumb. "Teakh is the sort of man they like, loyal, daring, and a bit loose with legal niceties."

"I'm not selling anyone." I'd had enough talk of buying and selling. "Certainly not my ethically flawed brother."

"It's not a flaw. To him, law is plastic. Same with you."

"Only Comryez would see it that way. Poseidon take it! Lawlessness isn't genetic." I halted on the steps of the lane. "My brother is my equal. I don't own him. If he wants to impregnate every woman in Clan Comryez I won't stop him. But I won't sell him either. It's his choice."

I TRAILED AFTER Angel as she met with a framing specialist and purchased supplies. In a shop as we looked over paint and canvas Angel said, "You've created a buzz, and it's good for business. My patrons are eager to meet my mysterious assistant." She held up a tube of paint, burnt umber.

"I didn't give you permission to spread my name around."

"I haven't, but Penny adores gossip." Angel dropped the tube in her basket. "You can set your net, rumors are flying. We can't stop the shine. There's no reason to. It benefits both of us."

The shop proprietress bundled Angel's purchases and we arranged to have them delivered.

We left the shop. Angel had a meeting with a client and I again tagged along. We sipped the usual mint tea as Angel and the client chatted about portraits. Bored, I gazed out the front window at people passing in the street. Again I noticed Seaguard men carrying satchels as they hurried past.

"How much do you want for her?" The client asked. My attention jolted back to the client. Was she talking about me?

Angel recovered first. "Now then, about a portrait. What size were you considering? Small can be intimate, but large has a particular impact."

"I'm interested in her," the client insisted.

"We're friends. I'm not her manager or her handler," Angel said.

"But you are a handler."

"I'm a painter. So, about that portrait—" Angel arched her eyebrows.

"Of her."

"She doesn't model." Angel's expression became icy, the skin around her mouth and eyes fixed in smooth perfection.

The client snorted and rolled a bill cylinder in her hands. "So young lady, how much for a baby? You're a surrogate mother, I understand."

I hadn't expected being dickered over like a barrel of cod. I seized my parka, and left. In the lane, I shook with anger. If I were as mercenary as Comryez, I'd have shopped around, accepted bids for my services, compared offers. I wasn't selling my baby to Clan Fennako. It might seem that way, but I wasn't.

Angel caught up with me and tried to apologize. "She's a new patron. I had no idea."

We turned the corner of the lane, and I stopped. "She called you a handler."

"I'm a painter."

"You know too much about...about everything. You're Teakh's handler, aren't you?"

"He's not the sort of man who can have sex with strangers. For him a stable relationship is essential. I provide that for him."

"Does he pay you? Does anyone pay you?"

"Your brother models for me, and I sell the paintings. It's a fair exchange, mutually enjoyable and one which supports both our careers."

"You're selling more than paintings."

"Art is always more than paintings. It's the experience, the interaction with models and patrons. I paint male nudes for women who share my interest in men. Your brother happens to be the best there is."

"He's a smelly fisherman trying to pass himself off as a detective."

"A diamond in the rough," Angel said.

"Does your interest extend to selling women? To selling their babies?" I crossed my arms.

"Nothing of the sort!" She grasped my shoulders. "I consider you a colleague, a fellow connoisseur. Do you intend to be the handler for your man?"

I jerked away and continued walking toward the ferry stop.

Angel ran to catch up. "You just might have to be. He most likely has obligations to other women. He may need your assistance in meeting those obligations. Nothing shameful about it. Most grandmatriachs act as handlers of sorts for their husbands. Or they arrange for such assistance."

I faced Angel. "Husbands? Plural?"

"When a grandmatriarch outlives her first husband her second marriage is usually to a younger man who serves as clan stud. She coordinates the services of all men married into her clan or delegates the duty. A man with valuable genetics can have any woman he wants— or man for that matter. His handler collects the sperm for distribution. He doesn't need to have sex with anyone besides his chosen partner."

I reached the ferry dock and the screen displaying the constantly updating schedule. I'd catch the Icehold ferry shuttle. "Why did that hag think you're my handler? We're both girls."

"Clans prefer same-sex handlers for surrogate mothers. Less chance of contamination, so to speak."

My fury rose. "There's a market for this?"

"For the genetics. It's the same as the stud market. Only—"

"Only the female carries the child for nine months and gives birth."

"A woman could sell her ovum—"

"And the purchasing clan could buy a stud as well, so the baby has no blood relationship to the clan. A commodity." Was this how my own mother had been conceived, purchased by Clan Ralko?

The years of isolation weighed down on me, the sense of never truly belonging.

"You're the lawyer," she said.

"Not yet," I turned along the harbor front and increased my speed, outpacing her. Had Ralko purchased her mother then discovered Noah characteristics to be more than they could handle?

Drive, initiative, and a willingness to break, bend, or change laws might be valuable in a king or a pirate chief, but not in a poor relative.

AFTER OUR BUSINESS in Fennako City was complete, we sailed from Tristan Bay. My purchases, crammed in a stateroom, included a new luggage set now neatly packed with custom-made clothing. According to Angel, the styles and colors of the trousseau complemented my figure and complexion. In the observation lounge Angel once again sketched, this time designing clothing. I regarded my brother's girlfriend with new wariness. Despite Teakh's romantic attachment, their relationship carried more than a tint of shadiness.

My reading had taken on a renewed sense of purpose. What happened to children who had a surrogate for a mother and a stud for a father? How extensive was the practice? And how did the purchasing clans treat their adopted members?

Reading, I uncovered what must surely be the horrors and complications of my own ancestry. Most of those purchased children were Seaguard and considered of high status, but they had little control of their own lives and were allotted high-risk assignments. For such "guard dogs," as they were sometimes termed, breeders preferred characteristics of loyalty and willingness to make sacrifices for adoptive clans. I considered it possible that cousin Gorby was such a guard dog.

Damn that client who'd so cavalierly offered me money. For the descendants of Noah, loyalty trumped legality. If Ralko had treated us well, or even welcomed us as kin, this loyalty would have been expended on Ralko, but Ralko had thrown us away. Or had they?

My mother, by raising children in a remote estuary and seldom visiting the village, may have intentionally isolated us from Ralko, directing our loyalty to each other and ultimately to our true kin, the guard dogs.

I'd never developed emotional closeness to Ralko, surely not to Dyse, despite her cloying concern. Surely the guard dogs were our cousins and kin in a way that Ralko could never be. My charted course stretched before me. We would not be treated as a commodity.

But first I had to get pregnant.

———

Chapter 15
Hanalee

IN SHELLIKO, ANGEL and I waited for my ride to Hanalee, and my long-awaited vacation with my man. An aqua-gray stratoplane splashed in ice-flecked waters of the harbor. By tail number and insignia, the craft belonged to Her Majesty.

The otter fur of my hood tickled my face. I adjusted my scarf. Only a month had passed since my first meeting with the man. Winter had taken a firm hold on the north.

"Still thinking your man could be just anyone?" Angel said with her hood pulled forward against the cold and the wind ruffling the fur.

A man in parka and seaboots exited the craft, his chin smooth shaven, his kit the aqua-gray and platinum of the Royal Guard. My heart sank. He wasn't my man.

Behind him another man exited. He wore a cream-colored parka partly open over a sweater, tan pants, waterproof boots and, on his head, a knit watchcap. He met my assessing gaze, his smile kind and unmistakable.

I smiled back, ticking off the fine points I'd learned from Angel. My man's beard was neatly trimmed, his neck shaved smooth. He grinned, his teeth bright, the hair of his mustache cut precisely above his top lip. His clothing fit him smartly, the sleeves and pant legs neither too long nor too short, the hem of the parka even. The natural wool sweater, knitted in a traditional cable pattern, showed no hint of pilling. His boots lacked scuff marks. The parka, although nearly white, remained pristine.

He walked up the dock ramp and bowed. His imitation of a mariner wouldn't fool anyone. Even Teakh did a better job of passing himself off as ordinary, but he looked nowhere near as good as my man, nor was he as gallant.

Giddy I stifled a giggle.

Angel's glance, gleaming with amusement, shifted slyly from the man to me. Mouth dry, I blushed, overwhelmed by his presence, though both of us were standing and dressed, not only decently but well.

The warmth of his smile radiated from his eyes. "Two lovely ladies."

I attempted an introduction without using names. "My brother's fiancée."

"Pleasure." He nodded to Angel, but his gaze flicked to me.

My face heated yet again. Last he'd seen me, I'd been naked below the waist, and he'd been between my legs. He gestured a Royal Guardsman forward, and my baggage was whisked from the dock and stowed aboard the plane.

Angel embraced me. "Tide carry you. Now remember, enjoy yourself."

Inside the cabin of the stratoplane I pocketed my gloves then removed my hat and scarf, both made of qiviut, the soft under-fur of musk oxen, hand gathered and spun into yarn.

He assisted me with my parka. Underneath I wore knee boots, buff leggings, and a tunic knitted from tan qiviut and white silk. He smiled appreciatively—or so I hoped—then hung our parkas in a cupboard seemingly built for such a purpose. I sank into rich upholstery and fastened my seat harness.

Two Royal Guardsmen cast off the lines from the stratoplane, then climbed aboard and secured the hatch. They seated themselves in a compartment just aft of the cockpit. Imagine Royal Guardsmen serving as flight attendants!

My man shut the dividing curtain. We were together with only a small table between us in a cabin appointed more like a sitting room than the interior of a stratoplane. He offered an apricot from a basket, the fruit fragile and out of season.

I bit into the tangy flesh of the fruit and considered him. His style, despite casual pretense, displayed care. His belt buckle was unadorned, so was the case knife attached to his belt. I enjoyed the angles of his face, so masculine. If I had Angel's talent, I'd have sketched his likeness, trace his brow and the bridge of his nose. I glanced away. With my tongue I separated fruit from pit. Was he married?

Most men wore some sign of clan affiliation, a badge on a hat, the style of a vest, but his clothing was strikingly neutral with no sign of clan whatsoever. Even the cables in his sweater which were often knitted in patterns indicative of region could have been knitted by anyone. He retained an air of easy command, his gaze intent, a smile on his lips and in his eyes, a nice smile, but then sometimes even crooks had gentle eyes. Seductive eyes.

I spit the pit into my hand. "What?"

"Nothing." He accepted the pit and deposited it in a waste receptacle built into the paneling of the cabin.

The plane took off. I caught sight of Angel on the dock, then we banked and rose, my ears popping with the altitude change. Our flight leveled out.

He rested his hands on the table. His nails were clean. "So tell me about yourself."

I faced a moment of panic. Generally people responded well to me initially, but I hated being told what to do, especially by people who were wrong. I'd been naked before him physically, but to reveal my mind stripped bare with all its imperfections? That frightened me more.

He spoke gently, his voice pleasant. "Her Majesty calls you a visionary and compares you to the prophet Catherine Smith."

"The first queen of Fenria?" I'd never considered myself anything like the founder of Fenrian civilization.

"That was her daughter, Fenna Lee-Smith. Great-grandmother Catherine was a statistician and a social engineer."

I withheld my opinion. Catherine the Prophet had instituted rigid conventions regarding proper occupations for men and women. The restrictions chafed, especially when I knew the reason: males were expendable. I'd have preferred comparison to Jamie Noah, who'd taught that no one was expendable and had attempted to make work at sea safe.

"You're similar to her, a social engineer." He reached for my hand. I let him hold it and squeezed back. "The Queen thinks we'd be good for each other." A smile flickered on his lips and the corners of his eyes crinkled.

I took my hand away. "Then why all the hush-hush and anonymity?"

"Political reasons," he said without further explanation.

When he looked up, I met his gaze, challenging him. "Tell me about them."

"I can't." He leaned back into his seat, the gray-green upholstery contrasting subtly with the natural wool of his sweater, and more strongly with his brown hair and beard. "Let's leave out our names. They're just incidentals anyway. I want to know about you. Who you are on the inside?"

I rubbed my fingertips on the soft wool of my sweater. What if he didn't like who I was?

The upholstery rustled as he shifted his weight. "The Queen told me about your mother. Apparently she operated a sort of underground network for the clanless and indigent."

Mama had been zealous regarding the Noah Code, particularly about treating strangers well, but I'd never known exactly what she did for work.

"Tell me of your family," he said. "From your perspective."

He already knew some things about me. Maybe more than I knew about him. "There's only me and my brother. We grew up in a bog. Well, technically a fen, saltwater marsh. We had a little cabin. My mother did her work over the network. My brother and I ran wild. We were homeschooled and didn't see other people often. Papa visited us every now and then. And that was always good."

"You knew your father?" he asked, only a little surprised. Paternity was considered private. Clan members often maintained a fiction that they'd all been sired by the grandmatriarch's husband. I wouldn't accept the usual pretense that all members of a clan shared paternity. "Not his name or his clan. We called him Papa and he was Seaguard."

My man grinned. "Then an anonymous relationship isn't new for you."

"I suppose not." I recalled running to meet Papa after he'd landed his esskip. "But then he died." Mostly likely Papa had been a guard dog. "I don't know the details. Later, Mama died too, a sudden illness. My brother and I moved into—" I almost named Ralko Village. "Into the village. The clan took care of us, and we went to school with the rest of them. They didn't like us very well. My brother got into trouble a lot. He wanted everything to be fair. If a classmate cheated on a test he'd tattle. If he disagreed with a teacher, he'd tell her loudly and vehemently."

"And you?"

"I knew when to remain silent." Teakh eventually had learned the same discretion, maybe learned it overly well. His activity as a fisheries detective more closely resembled blackmail than anything else. I hoped once we were a clan he'd accept only legitimate investigative work.

I changed the subject. "What about your family?"

"We're close with lots of cousins, aunts, and uncles, and my aunt's husband. The man leaned on an armrest. "My sister—" He paused as if changing his mind about what to say. "We get along well. She helps me out."

What had he left out in that pause?

"Then you're like me," I said. "One sibling?"

"One maternal sister," he corrected. "I have some paternal half-siblings but that's about the same as cousins."

"Older or younger?"

"My big sister who looks out for me. Like you with your brother."

"How do you know I look out for my brother?"

"Didn't I hear something about a clan in the works in order to protect your brother's children?"

I smiled and nodded as Teakh would have, encouraging the man to continue spilling information.

"My mother was often away or busy," he said, "but my sister was around. My grandmother always had time for me. She didn't have any sons, so I was her boy. Spent time with my great uncle too before he passed away. He could be hard at times, but he was fair, a strong sense of justice, like your brother. I always knew I'd follow in my great uncle's wake, being Seaguard and all."

Lordship was inherited through maternal lines, passing from uncle to nephew. I locked the information in the secret of my heart. He'd very nearly admitted being a Seaguard lord.

I asked, "If you weren't Seaguard, what would you do?"

"I don't know. Maybe live in a bog and raise children. Chop driftwood."

"You wouldn't like it," I said. "No running water."

"I enjoy camping," he said.

"Fun for a few days, not for twelvenights on end without bathing. Not for using an outhouse while the wind is blowing, and there's freezing rain. It was as if we lived in the dark ages before Catherine Smith taught women to raise children cooperatively. Her greatest innovation? Not base-twelve numbering or the calendar. Village sanitation—running water, hot showers, and flush toilets. In a village, even if you detest your clan members, you can bathe and wash away your own stink."

"But you have a clan. Yes?"

"They're a greedy lot of selfish hags and no kin to me." Danna! Surely my vehemence would push him away. "They're selling my brother's children, auctioning his seed to the highest bidder. I want my own clan." I glanced up. He was smiling and nodding, as if I'd said something extraordinary. As if...as if he shared my feelings. "I'm sorry." Why had this handsome Seaguard lord agreed to anonymous paternity? And most importantly, why did he seem to like me?

"For what? Judging from what the Queen tells me, you're quite a woman. She'd like us together."

Maybe he was a stud to Clan Fennako and I was intended as a gift to Her Majesty's favorite. Not likely. I might have been considered pretty, but I wasn't gorgeous like Angel. Maybe Fennako had designs on my genetics and planned for her child to become a stud in, oh, a few dozen years. The second possibility made more sense. Inexplicably, the man seemed to both like me and agree with my agenda. That didn't fit either explanation.

And what do I think? I asked myself.

Honestly, he was too good to be true. There had to be a hidden reef under that warm smile and the sincere interest.

THE PLANE TRAVELED above the clouds with the sky arching above, flawlessly blue. The clouds thinned until I glimpsed steel-blue water far below. The man had his eyes closed, either sleeping or maybe transmitting.

With my screen open I read history, this time about Clan Habsburg, a royal family of ancient Earth, who repeatedly practiced inbreeding, niece to uncle. They'd even outlawed exogenous marriage. The Habsburgs by law had to marry into their own clan.

I didn't understand the arcane technicalities of inheritance on ancient Earth, but I did understand the tragic results, a scion, the last of his line, so crippled by disabilities that he couldn't care for himself or even properly chew his food. I pondered my own choices and the unforeseen risks of mixing genetics and politics.

With sunlight through the starboard windows, the stratoplane descended toward verdant cliffs rising from the sea. Then we splashed down and coasted to a dock.

The air seemed to press down, heavy with humidity. Sweat gathered on my back. I fanned myself.

"A nice thing about the tropics." The man smiled slyly. "We'll be more comfortable if we remove some clothing.

"Is that what you think? You first."

Crossing his arms he grasped the sweater ribbing. Slowly, he removed the sweater revealing a close-fitting shirt that clung to his muscular chest.

As he watched, I shimmied out of my own sweater, struggling to keep my silk chemise from lifting along with the wool. He stroked my shoulder, tracing the embroidery of the shirt and through it, my skin.

A Royal Guard opened the hatch and fixed the ladder in place. My man tossed aside his own pullover. We left our clothing in the aircraft since it would remain in Hannako until we returned.

My man offered his hand and we descended to the dock. The breeze smelled of luxuriant greenery. A power-cart waited under a strange looking tree, not quite spruce or fur, its needles short and lush. I strolled to the hotel arm-in-arm with my man, stealing glances at him. His shirt hugged his shoulders and chest. He smiled back and squeezed my hand.

In the hotel lobby, the receptionist greeted us, but no names were mentioned. We were shown to a spacious suite with a balcony overlooking a sandy beach and an azure bay. The receptionist left and the two of us were alone together.

From a bag, my man removed a folio and presented it to me. "I thought you might like to see this."

I opened the folio which contained a certificate of health.

"Inspections all up to date," he said with a grin. The certification was required for studs and prostitutes. Often for their clients as well. Teakh had one.

"Excuse me." The man turned away, a hand to his ear, surely in communication with someone.

I exchanged my boots and thick leggings for sandals and a pair of sheer stockings. My man reclined in the sitting room, hand to ear, face mobile with expression. Teakh sat that why when he flew his gull.

My man's bags remained packed. Curious, I opened the slider. He just might have seaboots and vest hidden inside. From color and style I'd then know if he were Fennako or from a clan associated with Fennako. Quickly I shut the bag and turned my head away. I wouldn't peek. I'd given my word, but by Danna it was difficult not knowing his identity for sure.

———

Chapter 16
Beach

I LEANED ON THE balcony balustrade beside my man. Below us, white sand sloped to a turquoise ocean where surf broke, waves crashing only to coast up the beach, then retreat, leaving behind shimmering smoothness. Scantily clad couples, threesomes, and parties of four cavorted, some wearing nothing at all. Clothing, it seemed, was optional. Touching his hand I imagined our entire bodies in contact, skin-to-skin.

"The tropics are always a nice change in the winter," he said, as if he weren't tracing my knuckles with his fingertip.

"I've never been much beyond... Beyond my village. I've been to Fennako City, of course. And you?"

His hand covered mine. "Actually I've travelled quite a bit, part of my work."

"Have you ever seen the Southern Trident?" I kept my voice cool despite the electric thrill of his touch.

"We can view it tonight, if you wish. It'll be over on the southern horizon. I once travelled on an icebreaker on the Antarctic Ocean, but I haven't been to the South Pole. No one goes there. The ice lords do all observations and repairs by remote and can live wherever they want. Sure would be nice."

"Then you aren't an ice lord?"

"Coastal," he said.

"Ah. You slipped up."

"I suppose so. How many coastal magnates do you think there are?"

"I've never thought about it."

"About nine grand-gross, give or take a few grand. We aren't particularly rare."

I leaned against the cool balustrade. He was older than me, but his face remained unlined, his hair dark and thick. He was fit with a lean, muscular body, and he'd had time to prove himself as Seaguard. If he were in the business of selling stud services he'd be at the peak of his career.

"You're young for a magnate," I said. Seaguard lords tended to be middle aged or elderly. A lord held the position for life and inherited it only after his predecessor had passed away.

"My grandmother had no sons, so when my great uncle died, I was next in line," he said. It seemed that in his case, inheritance had skipped a generation, passing from great uncle to nephew instead of the usual uncle to nephew.

We descended a stairway to the beach, then strolled along a walkway between well-tended palm trees and spiky shrubs. The pathway ended in a patio and an outdoor bar under the shade of a shaggy roof.

I ordered a lemon and papaya smoothie. How exotic! What was papaya anyway?

"A gin and tonic," my man said.

"It's the full moon. No alcohol," the bar mistress admonished.

He whispered to me, "They're sticklers here about alcohol and the tide." He ordered a tonic with juniper. The bar mistress filled a tumbler with bubbling water and added a sprig of juniper, complete with pale blueish seeds.

While the blender whirred with my smoothie, we sat at a table. Along the shore couples, threesomes, and foursomes continued to cavort. A couple, both women, lay entwined on a blanket. Three laughing women tackled a man in the surf, playfully taking him prisoner. A pair of women snuggled with a man. My own man twiddled his juniper twig, watching the activities.

Inclining my head I cleared my throat.

"I'm observing. My duty as Seaguard. Got to make sure no one drowns. Habits die hard. Even if Hanalee Seaguard has this beach covered. Take a look over there. One of the lifeguards."

The lifeguard wasn't dressed like Seaguard. Instead of a life vest, he sported a deep tan. He also wore sandals, skimpy bathing trunks, sunglasses, and a broad-brimmed hat.

"Tough job for those boys. Gotta make sure no one has a heart attack while getting it on. Our own boys are around too, trying to keep their eyes from bugging out I'm sure."

The lifeguard climbed a ladder into a hut on stilts, one of a row of huts set along the beach. From what I could see, no Royal Guardsmen lurked among the palm trees or lolled on the beach.

The bar mistress brought my smoothie to the table. I sampled the odd flavor.

"Being a coastal lord is pretty much the same as being a lifeguard," he said. "You gotta watch your part of the coast. Only difference, I'm on the lookout for ships, not drowning victims. Got to make sure vessels don't run into each other."

With his broad shoulders, rugged features, and the warmth in his expression, my man was nice on the eyes. He sipped slowly, gazing back at me. He drained his drink then touched finger to ear. "You'll have to excuse me for an hour or so. I've been asked to visit with Lord Hanalee. It's an obligation I can't get out of. I'd like you to come along, but there's that pesky anonymity thing."

He squeezed my hand and promised to return. At the entrance into the hotel he glanced back then departed.

I continued to sip my smoothie, enjoying the combination of sour and sweet. A breeze blew in from the ocean. The surf purled, much bigger waves than I was accustomed to in the cold fjords of the north. The bright sails of small boats flitted across the bay. Swimmers played in the surf. Some stood on boards, riding the curlers into shore.

A man came my way, white pants clinging to his lean hips. The apparently blond hair atop his head must have been bleached.

He rested a foot up on the rung of a chair. "I see you're alone."

"Uh…No," I stammered. "My…boyfriend…" Was that the right word? "…will be back soon."

He cocked an eyebrow. "Why would he leave such a beauty?"

I leaned away from him. "Sir?"

He straddled the chair. "My woman saw you alone and was concerned." He nodded to a woman seated across the patio. She smiled back. "Many couples come to Hanalee without much previous experience. My woman and I make a business of helping out, smoothing relationships, greasing the rails, so to speak."

"Then you're teasers," I said casually, not as naïve as I appeared to be. In the reproductive industry, the distinction between teasers, handlers, and prostitutes was often academic.

"We prefer to call ourselves facilitators of affection. I go by Sal. My woman goes by Coco."

The polite thing was to offer information in kind, but my man and I had agreed to remain anonymous to each other and to those around us. "We're under hospitality," I said.

"Well there." He laughed. "We'll assist for the honor of it."

"No, that's all right. I meant...I meant..."

Sal leaned forward. "We understand. These arranged liaisons can be dicey. Men often have odd tastes—cuffs, chains, whips, cutting. That's where we come in." He patted my leg. "We can fulfill his desires while protecting you. My girl and I have medical training. If you or he has a taste for pain, we can arrange it so there is no lasting harm." He touched the open collar of his shirt. "Threesomes, foursomes. Maybe you'd like two men at once. They say a pregnancy is more likely to take if the girl enjoys herself. We can bring you to a long, satisfying orgasm."

I stood, leaving my half-drained glass on the table. "That won't be necessary."

"If you need any assistance, our address codes." Sal held out a comset. "Or just give a shout. We're in the suite below yours."

I smiled frigidly, picked up my hat and left the patio. Free of the "love facilitator" I kicked off my sandals and walked along the shore, feet sinking into the sand, roughness delicious. The breaking surf foamed as it flowed back from whence it had come, the rhythm persistent and perpetual.

Walking on the wet sand I considered my future. My Fennako advisors had recommended I become a lawyer specializing in reproductive law. Truly, this future seemed to best encapsulate my interests and talents. I cared about my kin and others like me. If I continued on this course, I'd be working with people like Sal and Coco, maybe representing them in court.

Maybe all people should have monogamous marriages. If a woman or her partner were incapable of conceiving a child they should go without. I shook my head. Every woman had a right to at least one child if she chose. Strict monogamy wouldn't work on Fenria, not with the death rates for young men. And what about same-sex couples. Were they to remain childless?

Who was I to speak out against the entire reproductive industry or to condemn Sal and Coco? My own brother was poised to command some of the highest payment in the industry, and his fiancée, Angel, was in the thick of it.

Jagged stone interrupted the beach and held a tangle of silver-bleached driftwood and red-brown bull kelp, tubular stems bulbous. I set my back against a log and wiggled my toes in the sand.

What was my man doing right now? I touched my comset tucked into a delicately embroidered pocket at my shoulder. But no. He was meeting with Lord Hanalee. He'd hail when the meeting was over.

I was returning along the shore when he hailed. "Where are you at?" he asked.

I turned my back to the breeze, my tunic fluttering. "On the beach."

"You're beautiful like that." He came across the sand still clad in close-fitting shirt and tan pants.

I waved. He ran, sand kicking up under his feet. He'd removed his boots and now wore a bandanna in place of his watchcap.

"Lord Hanalee is a nice old fellow, full of advice though." My man entwined his fingers in mine.

"You told him about me?" I asked.

"A little. He approves. Hanalee is all set to offer a romantic cruise, a private beach, anything we want." My man shrugged. "I turned him down. The beach and cruise might seem private, but every man in Hanalee

Seaguard would know what we're doing. They'd talk to wives and girlfriends. In less than a quarter of an hour we'd be news, planet-wide." He held out his arms. "Plenty of reason to dress as a common mariner."

I slid a finger under his belt. "Or in nothing at all."

He removed his shirt. I peeled off my leggings and panties. I wore only a tunic of fluttering silk. He stripped down to shorts. We left our excess clothing in a heap.

He caressed my leg, his hand sliding over my hip and teasing open the split side of my tunic. He slipped his hand under the fabric and settled his palm against inside of my thigh. I leaned into him, and he lifted ever so slightly. This was it. I was going to get pregnant and become a lawyer.

He released his grip and smoothed the fabric of my tunic. We walked along the shore, the surf booming beside us and foaming around our feet. A gull cried overhead. I bumped him toward deeper water. He returned the bump. The waves rose now to our knees. With another bump I fell into the waves. I came up sputtering. I tackled him, and he let himself be taken down.

Laughing, we swam into the rising and falling water, diving under a breaking wave. I stood, my feet gaining purchase on the sand. As the trough passed, I became aware of my wet tunic clinging to the curves of my body. The tunic floated where it met the water, leaving me naked below a swirl of periwinkle. Then he was beside me, embracing me, the bulge under his shorts pressing against my thigh. We collapsed into the next wave riding it up the shore to be deposited on the beach. As water and sand rushed away, he straddled me.

He pinned my wrists into the sand and planted kisses on my chin, cheeks, and lips. I pressed upward. He lay on top of me, his nose against my ear, the fabric of his bandanna against my cheek. Was this what I wanted? To be fucked by a stranger!?

"You don't know me," he said as if reading my thoughts.

"I know you enough." Blood pounded between my legs I tipped my head back. "I want your child."

"My child or all of me?"

"You."

"Then I want all of you." His hand was now under me, pressing into the small of my back, while his other hand fondled my breast through wet silk.

A shudder went through me as another wave caught us and lifted the hem of my tunic. His hand was between my thighs, rubbing and touching. A fleshy tip jutted through a slit in his shorts. Creamy fluid splattered over my belly. Then a wave broke behind him, and the foaming backwash sluiced the fluid away.

I sat up, sand sticking to my tunic. He held me, his skin slick with water. Overwhelmed by clashing fear and desire, hope and disappointment I wept, my tears mingling with brine. He touched my cheek.

I wiped my face and smiled. "I'm happy. But...but I wanted...I hoped..."

He squeezed my shoulder. "We'll do it again." He scooped up a handful of sand. "But without the grit."

IN OUR SUITE he sat with his hands on knees. He opened his eyes. "I tried to delegate and left instructions, but some things came up."

Angel had warned me that I'd have to share. "It's all right."

When Teakh flew his gull, his consciousness far away, he usually twitched. That my man didn't was due to either excellent genetics or training.

142

I went out to the balcony and inhaled the moist tropical breeze. The surf broke on the shore, the perpetual dance of waves throwing themselves on the beach, the love between ocean and land.

From the patio below Coco called out. "Ahoy! What are you about?"

"The tide. The sea is beautiful today," I said, giving customary praise of the weather.

She held up an ovoid fruit with pale-green skin mottled with yellow. "We have papayas. Have you ever tried one?" In her other hand she held a knife.

"I'm not sure." Was that maybe the exotic ingredient in the smoothie?

"Well then, come taste it."

I descended to the paved patio enclosed by a low wall. Coco set the fruit on a table and lifted the knife. She wore a rectangle of fabric wrapped around her body, seeming held there only by her full breasts. A shell necklace nestled against her tan skin, and a creamy flower had been tucked in her black hair. "Papaya is very rare, a taste of old Earth. It's a delicate plant. It can't survive freezing temperatures and must be protected in a greenhouse." She drew the knife against the papaya, the blade piercing the dappled skin, cutting into succulent orange flesh. Split open, the fruit revealed a hollow filled with dark, juicy seeds. The breeze blew back Coco's wrap, exposing a bronzed hip and thigh. With two fingers, Coco scooped out the seeds, then licked the dripping juice from her hand. I turned my head away. In the distance, Sal swam in the waves.

I accepted a slice of papaya and tasted it, the flavor sweet but with overripe undertones, trashy almost. Coco reclined on a net hammock held open with broad stretcher bars. I sat beside her.

"Sal is a good partner, sensitive, courteous." Papaya juice dripped down Coco's chin. She wiped it away with the back of her hand. "He knows how to please either a man or a woman. We work mostly in Hanalee, but I've been around. I'm concerned about you and that man you're with. I've seen him with another girl. He passed himself off as a Seaguard lord and made all sorts of promises. He said he'd set her up in style, get her with child, and that the baby would have top genetics. But now he's here with you."

"He never claimed to be a Seaguard lord," I said, which wasn't quite true.

"If he is a lord," Coco swung the hammock, "he can do as he pleases. Women throw themselves at his feet. He uses them and tosses them aside when he tires of the game. If a girl has no connections, no one will object."

She put her bare foot beside me, only a single layer of fabric spilling between her open legs. "Sweetie, if you need any help just let me know."

What would it feel like to kiss Coco? I shuddered. I shouldn't have even considered it. Yet, to lie against Coco's soft body and kiss that generous mouth...

That might be nice. I shook myself. No, maybe I would have my man and Coco at the same time, to be pressed between them, both making love to her. And Sal? Maybe Sal would watch.

What was I thinking? I turned toward the ocean, letting the cool breeze bathe my face. "I'll be all right."

Naked, Sal walked up the beach toward us, sand clinging to his calves. I looked no higher than his knees.

"Darling," Coco called out. "We have company."

Sal entered the patio and embraced Coco. His hand slid down her back. She rotated her hips, rolling them against his groin. Coco stepped back. "He's quite good. You're welcome to try him."

"That's okay." Not daring to look directly at Sal I stood and straightened my tunic. "The fruit was delicious."

I ran up the stairs to the balcony and went inside. I wouldn't speak of Coco or Sal to my man. I was too embarrassed by my illicit desire to lay naked with Coco, caught up in the net of the hammock, limbs entangled, Sal gloating over his catch. My face heated yet again.

In the bathroom, I bypassed the sunken tub and stepped into a shower lined with polished stone. The spray cascaded over my shoulders and breasts. My skin tingling, I toweled off and slipped on a dressing gown.

While my man took his turn in the bathroom I waited on the bed. He came out wearing nothing at all. His shoulders were straight, his belly pleasingly flat. I swallowed. My eyes skimmed over his male equipment, not quite acknowledging it. His thighs were long, his calves nicely defined. He splayed his toes, then crossed his pinky toe over the fourth, the display as impressive as it was subtle. If his toes were so nimble, what about the rest of him?

The bed yielded to his weight. He caressed my shoulders through silk. I leaned into him, and his strong hands stroked my hair. His hands on either side of my face he kissed me, his tongue probing between my lips.

His hand slipped under my robe, and I let him unwrap me. My robe lay pooled around my waist, the satin cool and smooth, the sash still tied. I gasped, fear at war with desire. He was beautiful, his movement, his strength, and his gentleness. Yet, for all I knew he could turn on me, in an instant, his gentleness becoming cruelty.

His gaze on my breasts, his eyes became dreamy. He eased me against a mound of pillows, and his hands moved lower. He bent his head and his lips gliding over my belly. Slowly he untied my sash. I lay exposed before him.

"Let me please you," he whispered, his fingers between my legs, his touch delicate. "What do you like?"

I had no idea. "You."

"May I?" he asked.

"Oh yes."

His head descended between my legs, his mouth moist and soft.

"I want you," I opened farther for him, welcoming him. "Your baby."

"Not until you love me." He sucked, his mouth now open, tongue flicking. I gasped, and my back arched, but he held me fast, one of his fingers resting on my anus, probing. "Not until you can't live without me."

I tightened against his finger.

"Yes?" he asked.

I tossed my head. I wasn't ready for anal sex.

"All right." With only a light touch from behind he drove into my other opening with his tongue. Excruciating pleasure radiating from his touch, then he withdrew.

My breath came is gasps. My body bucked.

Danna! He was good.

He hummed, his touch gentle again. He lay on top of me, licking and biting my ear, his shaft now hard between my legs, driving downward, thrusting against me but not entering. He slid forward now, straddling my back, his balls soft against my buttocks, his penis sandwiched against the base of my spine. He groaned, his hips working, his hand twisted in my hair. With a shudder he gasped and warm fluid splattering on my back.

Sink it all! On my back!

I turned. "What was that about?"

"Uhh."

"We're supposed to produce a child. That was our agreement."

"We'll do that." He grinned. "Didn't you enjoy yourself?"

"We keep almost doing it and then..." I flopped on the pillows. "Let's do it over."

"I can't. We men are like that. Takes a bit of time to reload."

"Oh. I wanted...why didn't..."

His grin was endearingly sheepish, apologetic. Yet, he hadn't made any effort to insert his tool in the correct slot, and he did seem to know where all the slots were.

"No rush," he said. "Might as well enjoy it."

"We should have done it the first time."

"I told you the truth. I couldn't perform."

"But now you can, and you haven't."

He touched my nose. "We'll do it again. But not right now."

His apology seemed sincere and what option did I have anyway?

I rolled away. He spooned against me, and I tried to relax. Dozing I entered wild dreams. I was an esskip or maybe a bird flying through the corridors of a palace, and then out along a lane, my flight uncontrollable as I careened, nearly knocking the cornices from buildings. People in the lane glanced up in surprise. I awoke to the heady tingling of his body pressed against mine, effervescence in my veins.

———

Chapter 17
Suspicions

I DREW MY KNEES to my chest. He still slept, rumpled bedclothes thrown aside, his breathing even, eyelashes soft against his cheeks. At Teakh's gym, the studs thought nothing of lifting weights while in the buff. Truly, my man wasn't as honed as most studs, but his body pleased me; his limbs long and cleanly muscled. Best of all he was mine, a wonder which the tide had washed up on my shore. But then, was he mine?

He reached out an arm. When it encountered empty sheets, he opened an eye. I rolled against him, my arm across his chest. He pushed it aside and straddled my hips. I lay belly down. His firm hands smoothed my shoulders.

"I'll be honest with you," he said. "I don't intend for you to get pregnant immediately."

I nearly pushed him off me.

"Here's the situation." His fingers worked into the muscles along my spine. "There are parties who do not wish us together, but the Queen has commanded that I get you with child. They can't openly oppose her." His hands continued kneading. "Once you're pregnant, these parties won't be restrained. We'll string them along. I'll claim erectile dysfunction, difficulty ejaculating, that I need more time to get comfortable with you."

My heart sank. I'd hoped to start law school months ago. "For how long?"

"Until I'm sure about us and we make arrangements. I must know that you and our child will be safe."

"What if I don't want you in my life?" I caught myself only after the words came out. Ah well I was a lawyer to the core, considering all ramifications and eventualities.

"Then I won't be getting you with child, but I hope you'll accept me." His hands now cupped my buttocks. "Have you ever done this before?"

"Well, no. But I'm not ignorant or inexperienced. I read." I'd been pouring over texts related to the reproductive industry including sex manuals. I'd studied the diagrams.

He laughed "Reading? Is that what it takes?"

"Reading is safer," I said, although seeing diagrams of labeled parts had little resemblance to laying beside a living man, his body warm and slightly sweaty.

He chuckled. "Promise me you won't let anyone else in. This is mine." He grasped my mound.

"Will you promise me the same?"

"I wish I could." His mouth descended, distracting me.

I collapsed on the bed. "That's hardly fair."

"I know, but I can't make that promise. Roll over. I want your other side."

At least he was honest. I turned to lie against pillows, knees up and his head between my legs. I stroked his head, fingering the scars at the base of his skull. His teeth were now lightly on my labia. I recognized experience when I saw it. No, when I felt it. He was good, too good.

WE RESTED FOR a while, nestled together, his hand on my breast.

What if he were a con-man?

Maybe he'd slipped into the clinic in place of the man specified. Or more likely, as Coco had suggested, Fennako had set me up as his sexual toy. An old woman might be easily manipulated and, as Coco had reminded me, I had no importance.

Think girl. What's the worst that can happen?

Get pregnant and fall in love with the man, then get dumped, dumped by him and dumped by the Queen.

I sat up.

Well, if I was going to be dumped it would be better not to have the responsibility of a child. Without a law degree I couldn't even support myself. He was just too good. A man with his skill at pleasing a woman, his ability to tease and coax, to dominate without being overbearing couldn't possibly be the result of naivety.

He smiled at me, relaxed and confident, his hands behind his head. I turned my back on him. He behaved like someone in the business. A stud learned those skills, a teaser maybe. The most horrifying possibility again reared up. Someone intended our baby as breeding stock. I closed my eyes, pursuing my thoughts, closing out the gorgeous man beside me. I had to examine the consequences.

After my baby's birth I might be declared unfit as a mother and my baby taken from me to be reared for the purpose of sexual servitude. Even if he were a Seaguard lord, my man could have been born and bred for the profession, a sort of private reserve stud, a man who serviced only to the elite.

"My love, what's wrong?" he asked.

I shook my head. It was likely Coco had seen him with one of his clients. Being a Seaguard lord didn't preclude him from offering services to women. Matriarchs ruled, and they told men, even magnates, what to do.

I opened my eyes. He was at my shoulder, his brow furrowed.

Getting pregnant according to the contract had seemed simple, purely a matter of bringing sperm and ovum together. Complications sprawled in a tangled net. He wanted an ongoing relationship.

Did I want him in my child's life? Did I want him in my life?

"You're right," I said. "We shouldn't get pregnant yet. I want to, but what if I fall in love with you and you leave me?"

He put his arm around me. "I haven't left you."

"You might. If I love you and you leave me....I can't bear it."

His beard pressed warm and rough against my face. "What makes you think I'll leave you?"

"It's part of the agreement. I thought I'd be okay with it. I'd get pregnant and never see you again. But now it's not okay. It just isn't."

His soft mouth touched mine. I nibbled his lower lip. He whispered, "As soon as I can get you settled where you're safe, where we can be together whenever we want, we'll do something about a family."

I nodded. Delaying pregnancy would give me time to determine if Fennako would hold up their end of the bargain. "Are you genuine?"

He shrugged "What else would I be?"

"Someone told me that you pursue women. After they fall in love with you you leave them."

"Who told you that?" he asked.

"Coco. Our neighbor."

He pressed his lips together, frowning.

I forged ahead. "She said that you only pretend to be a Seaguard magnate so that you can do whatever you want with girls."

He pointed to the scars on his head. "Do you think this is pretend?"

"I've seen you transmitting, and you've let things drop, little things that would be impossible to fake." Like the way Royal Guard deferred to him. He called them boys for Danna's sake. "But maybe you're so important that I don't matter at all. Coco told me you were here on Hanalee with another girl."

"That's a lie."

I buried my nose in his shoulder, inhaling his musk. "How can I trust you?" Secure in his solid arms I said, "The more time I'm with you, the more I'll love you. And the more it'll hurt when you leave. I won't know if I can trust you until after I love you, and then it will be too late."

"If you already love me, there's nothing to lose."

I squeezed my eyes shut.

"Take the risk," he said.

I thought I should say that I loved him, but was that the truth? Was it a promise I could keep?

I SAT ON a blanket on the beach. My man had gone for a swim. In the distance, his arm rose as he stroked through the water, a strong crawl. I wasn't a good swimmer. Ralko lacked a swimming pool and the waters of Ralko Sound were cold with strong currents. Still, I appreciated watching him.

Sunlight glinted off the water. A pair of legs draped in white pants approached. Sal smiled down at me. "A word with you?"

I adjusted my hat. "What is it?"

Sal crouched beside me on the sand, polite enough not to sit on my blanket, not yet. "I've been asking around, finding out about that gentleman you're with. I feel I should warn you about him."

I tugged on the brim of my hat. "Go on."

"He strings women along. When he tires of the game, he tosses them aside. He might pretend to be a big man in the Seaguard, but I have it on good authority that he's not. It's all in the conquest for him, anything to get at a girl. He may never have claimed to be a magnate." Sal repeated Coco's warning nearly word for word. "But he leads you to make your own assumptions. That makes his deceit all the more insidious."

"I find it unlikely that he is lying. He has three Royal Guard stationed nearby and he's on good terms with Lord Hanalee."

Sal toyed with the fringe of the blanket. "I understand you have an important agreement riding on the outcome of this rendezvous." He pursed his lips and looked skyward. "If you don't mind me saying; I found out that you're obligated to bear a child. That scoundrel has you up against a wall." Sal sat on my blanket. "I can help you out. Paternity can be difficult to prove."

"You are suggesting?" I raised my eyebrows.

"I'm offering."

"Well then. I'd best be going." I seized the blanket and gave it a smart tug. "Get off my blanket!" Blanket over my shoulder I set out along the shore, watching for my man.

He strode out of the surf, waves breaking behind him, water streaming from his chest and arms. I ran down to meet him, careless of my wrap flapping in the waves.

"Dearest, what's wrong?"

"Someone told me terrible things about you. Sal, Coco's partner. They're teasers. He said that you've had other women here, and you made promises to them, promises you didn't keep."

The surf lapped my feet sucking the sand out from under my toes.

"Who is this Sal fellow? What exactly did he say?"

"He told me that you make a habit of seducing women, that it's all a game to you. He repeated what Coco told me, that you were here with another woman, and that you promised to get her pregnant but didn't."

He frowned. "Remember what I told you. Some parties will try anything to keep us apart."

"Why?" I asked. "Explain it."

He looked away. "That's something I can't discuss with you."

"Then why should I trust you?"

"Because..." He touched a finger behind an ear. Maybe he was transmitting or maybe the gesture was purely habit. "Here's what I think happened. Now this is just a theory. Those people who don't want us together found out about our travel plans. They contacted teasers working in Hanalee—"

"Sal and Coco."

"—and hired them to scuttle our relationship."

"Coco seemed sincere."

"She may be," my man said. "But they've been hired to do a job. Did you notice they're never with clients? They're circling like sharks. Every time I leave you alone for even a moment they move in for the kill. Coco waits on that patio. Whenever I come out, she dodges inside."

"And Sal..." I took a breath, not wanting to say what happened, but if I expected honesty I had to be honest myself. "He offered to get me pregnant if you wouldn't."

My man's face darkened. "What did you do?"

"I didn't slug him in the face."

The corner of my man's lips quirked with a hint of a smile. "You could have taken him apart."

"Why do you say that?"

"Uh. I know that it's a bad idea to cross you. That's why you can trust me. I'll take care of this." He placed a finger just behind his ear, and his face once again became stern as he transmitted.

We walked from wet sand to dry.

"Done," he said. "I spoke with the hotel management and with Hanalee Seaguard. Those two will be escorted from Hanalee Island."

His actions had been quick. With a single transmission Sal and Coco had been banished. My man clearly had authority. I should have felt relieved. Instead, I felt trapped. If he could get rid of Sal and Coco so easily, and on so little evidence, what might he do to me?

That he'd reacted so swiftly suggested their accusations had merit.

Think. Think like a lawyer. No, I needed to think like a detective, or else hire a detective. I'd have to talk to Teakh, but his expertise was in fisheries, not sexual fidelity. Once we were in our suite, I messaged Teakh anyway.

Hailing Little brother, Sis here.

I hadn't wanted Teakh witnessing my liaison with my man, but I was driven to ask his advice.

I met a couple, Sal and Coco, who told me that my man makes a habit of seducing women. They claim he pretends to be important and makes promises that he doesn't follow up on. When I confronted him about this he denied it. He then contacted local Seaguard and had the couple banished from the island. My man thinks this couple was hired to scuttle our relationship. I'd like to know who is telling the truth.

Signing off.

Sis

―――

Chapter 18
Return to Ralko

I STOOD AT THE rail of a ferry that cruised toward Ralko under a gray sky, the frigid north still in the grip of winter. Warm memories still enfolded me: dancing on the beach by torchlight, laying together on a blanket while gazing up at the stars, snorkeling side by side above an underwater landscape of anemones and waving fronds of seaweed. Despite the warmth of my feeling, suspicions lingered.

My man's voice issued from the comset at my shoulder as he hailed me.

"What are you about?" I asked.

He laughed. "The tide as always. Just the tide. And you?"

The dark shoreline slipped past with its steep spruce covered slopes jutting from gray water, beached cakes of ice, and snow-dusted cabins huddled in the cold.

"I'm almost home. Such that it is. I'd rather be with you."

"It won't be for long. I promise. I've already talked to...taken the appropriate channels. I'll get this worked out, and we can be together."

A gust of wind carried icy snowflakes pattering across the deck.

"I'd like that. Do you know my name?"

"Well, yes. I did a bit of research and contract doesn't bind me. Still, to be fair, let's keep this as if on hospitality."

"On hospitality then." The ferry bumped the dock, deckhands standing at the ready with mooring lines. A gate in the gunwale opened and a deckhand heaved my luggage on the dock. I clambered off the ferry, then stood by my pile of baggage as the ferry pulled away.

Walking the length of the pier I searched for the cart normally left near the landing. A camera mounted on a pylon followed my movement, dock security. I hunted along the shoreline, clambering over grubby snowbanks studded with bare branches, but the battered cart was gone. I returned to my baggage and pushed back my hood.

If I relayed gear in multiple trips, my belongings would be left unattended, and Ralko layabouts, even if they claimed to be my kin, might rifle through them for valuables.

I addressed the watching camera. "Ralko Command. Annin here."

"What do you want?" The voice issued from a speaker.

"Just got in. I was hoping you could keep an eye on my bags while I run up to the shelter."

"Girl, I'm not a porter."

I smiled up at the camera. "Well. It wouldn't be much trouble for you."

"We can't be responsible for your belongings."

"Honor." My frustration shaded the words as sarcasm, but he'd already given his attention to something else.

My comset activated, a hail from my man. I walked well away from the camera for privacy to speak with him. "I'm stuck down by the dock with more baggage than I can carry. I hailed our Seaguard, but they won't help me out."

Had I become so accustomed to service that I expected Ralko Seaguard to wait on me?

"I'll talk to them," he said.

"You'd better not. They'll know that you know who I am. One of my aunts might help me out." I signed off and contacted Aunt Trudia. "I'm down at the dock. Could you send someone down to help me carry some baggage?"

She shouted, "Hey, you louts! Give Annin a hand with some bags. She just got off the ferry."

"I don't want to be any trouble," I said.

"Freeloaders," Trudia muttered, then shouted loudly, "You heard that, you're lazy!"

A man I knew as Grandfather and a younger man soon sauntered down from the shelter. At the dock, Grandfather commented on my appearance. "That's some get-up. What have you been doin'?"

"Shopping."

Grandfather hefted a bag. "You sure have."

"Are you going to be all right carrying this?" I asked.

"I've hauled around heavier. I remember the time I was working as a stevedore out at..." He commenced into a rambling tale of his prowess in his younger days. "We were down on pier six offloading fish when the webbing split wide open, and the fish came pouring on out right on top of me. I'm telling you, Mama wouldn't let me in the house for days. And Trudia...well, she's Trudia."

The three of us walked to the shelter and into the common room. Trudia stepped out of the kitchen, wiping her hands. She flicked the towel toward my boots.

Grandfather set down my largest bag. "She went shopping."

"Whatever for?" Trudia wiped the serving table with a rag. "And where did you get the money?"

158

"I took out a loan."

Trudia spun around. "A loan for clothing?"

"A professional wardrobe. An investment."

"And what profession would that be? Store mannequin?"

Such clothing wasn't ordinarily a necessity of law school. That I'd purchased the trousseau to impress a coastal lord only made me a gold digger. I had no intention of telling Trudia my plans.

I seized a case and stalked into the women's bunk room. There, I changed into my oldest tunic and leggings. I stowed my baggage before helping Trudia in the kitchen, heating soup and warming bread.

In the dying light of a winter evening I served supper to only three men. This time Trudia ate with us in the dining room. When the meal was finished, I swept the floor while Aunt Trudia washed dishes. Beyond the dining room window, Luna Minor, the little moon, rose full and yellow. I pulled the blinds, protecting myself from bad luck. It might be a silly superstition, yet the light of the little moon affected women's hormones.

In the rosy glow of a nightlight I stole pillows from other bunks and piled them on my own. Might as well. I was the sole female guest. I changed into a silk slip. When I'd last worn it, I'd been beside my man

The high windows of the bunkroom faced north, allowing not even a gleam of moonlight. Laying against the pillows I slid the strap off my shoulder, longing for his touch.

I hailed him. "I wish you were with me." I scooped my hand around one of my breasts, imagining that he held it.

"Why don't you come to my place?"

"Right now?"

"Sure. I'll fly over and pick you up. I'll get in at about midnight. Is that too late? How about if stay with you."

I sat up. "Aunt Trudia will kick up a storm." Men weren't allowed in the women's bunk room. "But maybe I can sneak you in. Or we can meet..." Where could we meet? Certainly not down by the docks or at the village laundry. "We'll have to get around Seaguard."

He'd have to file a last-minute flight plan and receive permission from the local Seaguard to enter Ralko waters. No sovereign clan liked a sudden and inexplicable intrusion by a foreign aircraft, an intrusion which too closely resembled a raid.

"This isn't going to work." For one thing I was exhausted.

"How about tomorrow then? You can come to my place."

"You can't pick me up here. Local Seaguard will be suspicious, and everyone here gossips. Maybe meet me in Kassanko." This was the third day of the waning moon. The ferry wasn't scheduled until the seventh day. "But it can't be tomorrow because the ferry doesn't run."

"I've got the schedule up. Hmm. Looks like you've got ferry service only three times a twelvenight."

"They don't like visitors here, and they figure if a man doesn't have a boat he should stay put. As for women— we can beg rides from the men."

"Your clan is difficult."

"I want to be done with them."

"We'll get that taken care of," he said. "The Fennako Education Board is considering approving your application and grant regardless of the contract."

My head seemed to float. I could become a lawyer without getting pregnant.

"Do you still want to come to my place?"

"Yes! Oh yes!" My excitement bubbled.

"Then it's settled. Meet me in Kassanko on the seventh at five pm."

I settled against the pillows. I'd have a bit of time to do laundry both my own and bedding and towels from the shelter. Trudia probably hadn't bothered. "Kassanko on the seventh," I agreed. My eagerness kept me awake for much of the night.

As WE WERE serving breakfast, Dyse stormed into the dining room. "Just where have you been? You haven't responded to any of my messages."

"I've been busy with my studies." I kept my voice down so as not to involve Grandfather or the others.

Dyse reproached me. "I'll remind you that I'm responsible for overseeing your education. You must inform me of where you are going and why."

I stirred a pot of oatmeal. "I was on a field trip arranged by Clan Fennako." I'd been gone for a month, so it had been a long field trip.

"She's been shopping," Trudia said.

"Our girl has style," offered Grandfather.

"Shopping? With your income?" exclaimed Dyse.

"What does it matter to you? I'll be paying the bills."

"You can't be running up debt that way," Dyse said.

"I thought you wanted me in debt." I kept my voice sweet. "Because if I'm in debt, Teakh will have to work as a stud to pay it off. He'll be your indentured servant." Teakh and I had linked accounts, so our debts were shared.

"That isn't my wish at all. Why under Danna are you doing this to him?"

"Because I'm selfish and greedy," I responded. That's what she thought, so why even try to change her mind. My trousseau cost quite a bit less than the esskip we'd ordered for Teakh.

"You're impossible. I have it on good authority that you were in Hanalee with a man of dubious reputation. You've been duped. And you're not the first young woman who's been so used."

"Where did you hear that?"

"I have my sources," Dyse said smugly.

Had she been contacted by Coco and Sal? Or maybe by whomever had hired them?

Teakh hadn't gotten back to me and I needed to speak with him. We had to know what we were up against.

BEYOND THE WINDOWS, frost encrusted the trees as if with glittering lace, the result of warm ocean air encountered by a cold front.

If I hailed from the clanless shelter I could be overheard. If I went down to the waterfront, I'd be in view of dock surveillance. I pulled on my parka and hat and went outside to trudge uphill through the village. In these temperatures, the snow squeaked under my boots. Women seated in their front rooms glanced up to watch me pass. In the village square, children were sledding under the vigilant eye of mothers and aunties.

Ralko watched me. What did it matter? Regardless of where I was, Ralko Seaguard could tap my communications. Maybe they already had.

Standing on the hill behind the village I hailed Teakh. My distance from the waterfront and village square would have to do for privacy. "Auntie knows about my trip south. She gave me that same warning about being duped. I don't know how she got the information or who's telling the truth."

"The couple is reputable," Teakh said, not mentioning Coco and Sal's names. "I did some asking around. I'm not so sure of your date. Give me some idea of his identity."

"I can't discuss it. This channel isn't secure." If my man were Lord Tristan Bay, Fennako would have good reason to monitor my communication. "Ask your girlfriend," I left out Angel's real name. She'd left broad hints about the identity of my man, and she'd be able to speak freely. The stipulation of anonymity did not extend to Teakh and Angel.

I headed down the hill toward the waterfront, my numb fingers balled in my pockets. Many women fell in love only to be trapped in an abusive relationship. Maybe the start of all relationships had such uncertainty.

What woman truly knew what she was getting into?

Normally, a woman's clan could enforce a restraining order, but if my relationship didn't work out, no one would protect me, surely not Dyse.

———

Chapter 19
His Castle

As I waited at the Kassanko aircraft dock, the light of sunset tinged the water pink with the reflection of sunset sky.

I was determined to follow through with meeting with my man for what would be our third date. This time I wouldn't become pregnant. It was the wrong time of the month for that. My man's esskip skimmed over the glinting water and dipped a wing. The craft wasn't the gray-green of Fennako, but blue-and-white, the colors darkened by the twilight. He splashed down, water spraying from his skis. The tail number wasn't from a clan I recognized. Not that it meant much. A powerful lord could borrow any craft he liked.

The canopy slid back, and he stood with the glow of the setting sun on his face. His craft bumped the dock, and he leapt ashore, wearing a dark-blue parka. His trousers covered the tops of fisherman's knee boots.

I reached up to kiss the softness of his lips. His mustache tickled my nose as he enfolded me in an embrace. "Fly away with me to my castle."

I giggled. "You don't have a castle."

His lips brushed my cold cheek, his breath warm. "It's secure anyway." He lifted my valise and secured it in the back of the craft, then held out both hands. "My lady, welcome aboard."

He assisted me into the cockpit. The canopy closed, and the glazing took on the opacity of milk, diffusing the light of the setting sun and concealing the surrounding harbor. "I want to surprise you," he said. "No peeking."

"How can you see?" I asked.

He put a hand to the back of his head and nodded to the dash and opaque windshield. "Neural implant and cameras in the prow."

Water slapped the hull, the sound magnified in the enclosed space. The lapping changed to a hiss as the jets pulsed, driving the craft from the dock. We picked up speed, the hull vibrating, the acceleration pressing me into the seat. The sound quieted as we went airborne. Knowing that the craft was an extension of his body I felt safe, as if I were riding on his back. That was probably what it seemed like to him.

"I can play music if you'd like," he offered, and I accepted. Music throbbed softly, violins and flutes.

We approached our destination after maybe three hours of travel. We dropped and slowed, water rushing around the hull, then we turned, slowed further, the hiss of spray gentling to lapping.

The canopy cleared and I blinked in dim red light. Overhead, beams supported a high ceiling, as if in a warehouse. The ruby light glinted off rows of suspended esskips.

He fastened a silk scarf over my eyes, even in the darkness his hands sure as he knotted the fabric.

"I promised that you wouldn't know who I am, and I keep my promises," he said.

The craft swayed. He steadied me then helped me to the wing, and then lifted me down from the craft.

An arm around my shoulders, he drew me along as if in a dance promenade. "Let's go on up." The words were swallowed in the cavernous hangar.

A door whooshed open, then he nudged me forward. The door shut, and we stood together while the elevator floor rose.

I pressed against him enjoying his solidity. We exited the elevator, our feet tapping against hard flooring, the building solid and otherwise silent. How thick were the walls?

A door clicked open, we stepped through.

He pulled off the scarf, and I blinked in soft candlelight. Tapers in cut-glass holders shed warm light on a table set for two. Heavy drapes hung over tall, opaque windows. Burnished molding gleamed in rich shadows. Beyond double doors, a bed frame towered with a superstructure of green cast bronze. Matching green velvet padded the headboard behind mounded pillows of the same shade.

His eyes sparkled. "My castle."

I removed my boots and doffed parka, hat, and gloves. He hung our parkas near the door. Then popped opened a bottle. "Blackberry sherry? I trust you're not pregnant."

I'd already ovulated and nothing had come of it. "No thanks to you."

He splashed the dark liquid into a stem glass.

I sipped the liquor, sweet and strong. Behind him, candlelight flickered on the polished sheen of cupboards set flush with wall paneling.

He unlatched a door to a dumbwaiter. From the recess he removed a covered dish and lifted the lid to reveal mounds of glistening caviar on toast accompanied by white cheese and chopped herbs. He offered me a round of toast topped with caviar. I rolled the fish eggs between tongue and palate, breaking them on my teeth. He gazed at me, his liquor-filled glass dark between his fingers, bliss on his lips. I enjoyed the crunch of the toast, the salty tang of caviar, but most of all him, the rugged angles of his face, and that impish grin.

"How did you manage all this?" I asked. The candles would have burned down if he'd lit them before flying away, not to mention creating a fire hazard.

"An uncle helped me out. He runs the kitchen here."

Customarily men cooked only on shipboard or in Seaguard facilities, no surprise there. After we had enjoyed the canapés, my man returned the plate and cover to the dumbwaiter. The door closed and the dumbwaiter silently descended. He again opened the door to reveal a steaming tureen along with soup plates and a ladle. He filled the plates with a bouillabaisse rich with cockles, mussels, and shrimp.

He offered me a fragment of mussel, and I nibbled it off his fingers, glancing at his eyes, watching him smile. We enjoyed the shellfish then tipped the bowls to drink the last of the broth. Empty dishes disappeared into the dumbwaiter, and the next course arrived, steaming paper packages.

He dropped a package on my plate and blew on his fingers. "Watch out! They're hot." He tore open the bundle to reveal halibut cooked with lovage, scallions, and fingerling potatoes. The salad course included sea vegetables: wakame, dulse, and pickled kelp. For dessert, we had blackberry tarts and a rich soft cheese.

With the dishes loaded in the dumbwaiter, he picked up a candle and led me into the bedroom, dominated by the massive bronze superstructure of a bed. Base relief fantasies of wolf-headed dolphins, their teeth, fins, and snouts jutted from the patina.

Luna Majora hadn't yet risen, so the lights in the apartment were dim, only the rose-colored lights which didn't disturb night vision and the flicker of candlelight reflecting from burnished bronze.

On the wall, a giant clock calendar reached from floor to ceiling. The dial was in the form of a globe viewed from the South Pole. The hour hand, a huge arrow, pierced the globe and pointed to eleven. Its tail, feathered in bronze, touched the eleven at the bottom of the dial. The numbers glowed softly. The month hand pointed to seven waning; Luna Majora would reach her apex at seven am. She wouldn't rise yet for two hours.

I reclined against the pillows. Standing in front of the sculptural clock he removed his vest and shirt. Candlelight softened his lean musculature. When he knelt on the bed, I tucked my fingers under the waistband of his trousers and eased them down. The coverage of his hair narrowed as it descended his belly, becoming dense and luxuriant as it met and surrounded his penis.

He stood and removed the trousers. His smiling eyes gleamed in the flickering light. He put a knee on the bed then unfolded his long body beside me. I rolled toward him and put a stocking-covered leg over his. I stroked his back, my hands skimming his lumbar.

He kissed my forehead.

I pressed against him. "Give."

"Not yet."

"But...But...." If I didn't fulfill the contract, I couldn't become a legal intern, couldn't even take a class in law. Angel and Teakh wouldn't be able to marry, and I would have no say in Teakh's stud contracts.

"The moon is waning," I said. "I'm not going to get pregnant."

He leaned back. "I've studied up on the Noah Project. Did you know we're prone to hostage syndrome?"

"What do you mean we?"

"I happen to have Noah characteristics myself. We like being held prisoner."

"Are you going to take me prisoner?"

"I was thinking about it. Or you could take me prisoner? Which do you prefer?"

A jolt of alarm went through me. The walls were thick, and no one knew where I was. If I shouted, I couldn't be heard. What if he happened to be a monster, as if from a fairytale, with mangled corpses in his locked closets?

I had no way of knowing. A woman was supposed to find out about a man first, then fall in love, then have his child. For me, it was happening backwards. No, I hadn't fallen in love. If I did, I'd truly be stuck.

Get out! Get out before it's too late!

———

Chapter 20
Escape

MY MAN LEANED languidly against the pillows, his eyes following me as I touched my shoulder comset and hailed Teakh.

Turning my back on my man I whispered into it. "I'm with that man, the one assigned by Fennako. Everything is okay. Only—want you to know I'm with him. Just in case."

"Good Danna! What happened?"

"If I don't call, and you can't hail me then..."

"Let me talk to that lubber."

"He's listening in."

Teakh's words burst from my comset. "I'm warning you, lubber! You harm my sister, and I'll smear you from here to the Andean Ocean. No hiding behind your rich mommy's skirts. Your reputation won't be worth mud when I get through with you."

"Do you know who I am?" my man asked, still leaning against the pillow, his words casual, a request for information.

"Maybe I do. Don't toy with my sister."

My man sat up, the blankets falling from his torso. He said, "I happen to know you're a cover stud. You get women pregnant for money then leave. Well, I'm not that kind of man. If your sister wants my baby, she gets me as well."

"The deal is for an anonymous liaison. Get her pregnant then get out. You have no claim on my sister."

"I didn't sign that contract." My man now stood. "And before I stick a woman with a baby, I'm going to be sinking sure she wants me as part of the bargain, because that's what she's going to get. Your sister is free to leave at any time. She gives the word, and I'll fly her anywhere she wants."

"Prove it," Teakh said.

"Let's take this to a private channel," my man said. "Dearest, do you mind?"

"Go ahead."

My comset went silent. He paced, head nodding, lips contorting as he carried on a transmitted conversation. He finished with a shake of his head then sat beside me. "Your brother basically told me I was the no-good remains of a rotting fish carcass, and then catalogued everything he knew about my identity. He didn't miss much. Quite impressive." He lifted a strand of hair from my forehead. "It seems your brother is a detective. Or so he told me. What do you want? I'd fly you home, but the time is rather late, and we'd arrive in the wee hours. Or you can have my bed, and I'll sleep in another room. Fly you home in the morning. What do you say?"

"Take me home." If he couldn't accept no for an answer, he wasn't the man for me.

"Are you sure?" He asked. "I'd planned on waffles for breakfast."

"I'm sure."

He dressed and then held out the silk scarf. "If you don't care about fulfilling the contract there's no need to maintain anonymity. We can dispense with this blindfold thing."

I accepted it. "It's just..." I didn't know if loving him was a good idea. My feelings were tangled. "The tide isn't right."

He nudged my hand, directing it to his arm.

We descended in the elevator to the coolness of the esskip hangar. I followed closely, unsure of the location of the docking bays. One misstep could plunge me into a watery abyss. He clasped my hand to guide me into the cockpit. With the rustle of his parka he was in the pilot seat. The canopy shut, enclosing the two of us.

"You can peek now," he said.

I did and again faced blackness. "Too dark."

A soft rosy light glowed from under the gunwales of the craft. "This better?"

"A little."

"When we get out a way, I'll clear the canopy."

The craft moved, backing from the dock.

Once airborne he asked me where to go.

"Kassanko. The place where you picked me up."

No, that wasn't right. I knew no one in Kassanko and securing lodging in the middle of the night would be difficult. Arriving in Ralko in the middle of the night with a strange man would be even worse. Dojko?

Teakh was likely to be awake already and worrying, but he lived at Pretty Boy's Gym and shared quarters with Keno, his trainer. In the morning I'd face the studs who lived there, all of them curious about my nighttime arrival.

That left Angel. I rejected that idea as well. She'd also want an explanation.

"If I go home my kin will know about you. They'll try to keep us apart."

The esskip slowed, and water again hissed against the hull. The canopy cleared. "We don't have to go anywhere," he said. "It's a beautiful night."

Overhead the sky glittered with stars. Luna Majora shone so bright that the color of my gloves was distinctly blue. Snowy mountainsides of peninsula and island nearly glowed. "The seats recline. We can sleep in the cockpit under the stars. I'll set autopilot to bivouac."

"Then I'd truly be your prisoner."

"Or I'm yours." With a squeak, the back of the pilot chair reclined until his head lay in my lap.

I smoothed his hair. "I want to control my own life. No one telling me what I can or can't do."

"What about children?" he asked.

"I want the same for them."

"Is that what a mother should do? Give her children complete freedom?"

"Well, I don't want other clans telling them what to do."

"Maybe you want, not freedom, but power. Freedom is the ability to do anything, no constraints. Power, the ability to do what one believes is best. Sometimes a person has to give up freedom for power. It's a good bargain I think."

"Have you made that bargain?"

He tensed, his head lifting from my lap. "Seaguard lords have neither. Our lives are constrained by duty. A clanless dock rat has more freedom than a Seaguard lord. As for power; I cannot take what I most want." The touch on my face was gentle.

"Why me? I'm nobody of importance. I'm at odds with my clan. They aren't even blood kin. I'm in debt. And I have no marketable skills."

"You are somebody. That first time I met you I was angry, furious about what had been done to you. And to me. I was once married to a woman dodecades my senior, a marriage of convenience. My duty was to impregnate my wife's kinswomen as she commanded, all strangers to me."

"I thought you were the one who asked for anonymity," I said.

"Well, yes. I want to be loved for myself. Is that so wrong?"

"Nothing wrong with that. But that clinic meeting didn't help with either love or lust."

"My intent was twisted weirdly," he said. "Maybe by those who wish to keep us apart. They allowed us to meet, but made sure the experience was unpleasant."

I wondered what sort of negotiations had gone on behind the scenes. Above us a cloud drifted over the face of the moon.

He said, "I spoke with the Queen after that time in the clinic. And I asked around, checking records. You were in a fight on Lawrock Island. You and your brother. Took some arm twisting, but I viewed the camera records."

Humiliated I covered my face. "Danna, no!"

"It's all right." His touch on my wrist was gentle. "You're fierce. No technique but fierce. Match your passion with legal knowledge and you'll be a force to contend with. The Queen is counting on it. She figured you'd come through despite the nastiness at the clinic."

"It was horrible," I said.

"I know." He reached up to stroke my cheek. "It was the only way she could gain approval for our meeting. If we're together, you'll have my backing. We can put an end to coerced liaisons."

"Do you know of the guard dogs?"

"We're all guard dogs," he said. "I'm not the one coercing you. I just want to be on your boat when the blast hits the rigging. If I take advantage of you, get you pregnant and leave, sure as Poseidon, either you or your brother will come after me. And even if you don't, I'll still regret it for the rest of my life. I read your charter. Any descendant of Jamie Noah can be considered a member of your clan. That's a lot of powerful men and women. If I father your children and back you, you'll be untouchable. My mother will back you as well. She won't abandon the mother of her grandchildren, not if I love you. And I do. Danna! I didn't intend to tell you all that."

"I'm afraid to love you," I said. "To trust you without knowing you."

"When can one truly know a person?" he asked.

I combed through my memory of our encounters, searching for any knot of betrayal.

"Let's go home. I promise you waffles and clotted cream for breakfast. Allow me to prove myself trustworthy."

I stooped to kiss his lips, an awkward position, our faces turned chin to nose.

Then, with the seats again upright and the canopy clear, he scooted across the moonlit waves, extended wings, and leapt to the air. Our ink-black shadow zoomed with us across the glimmering water. As if he were a bird, he skimmed above the seas in the light of Luna Majora, the moon of fertility and rightness. As we drew near our destination, he offered to darken the canopy. "Unless you want to give up on this anonymity thing. How long do you think we can maintain it?"

"Until the contract is fulfilled," I said. "As long as necessary."

The canopy blackened again plunging the cockpit into darkness. This time it didn't bother me. The esskip moved in time with my man's breath, gathering itself with his inhale, soaring on his exhale.

When we'd returned to his place, we rode the elevator up to his suite with me once again blindfolded. I removed the scarf and nightlights glowed in the room. He offered me the bed.

"Where will you sleep?"

"Where do you want me to sleep?"

I pulled him close. "With me."

"But you don't trust me."
"Maybe I do."

IN THE MORNING, sunlight filling the room, the tall windows now frosted translucent, and the drapes pulled back, but he was gone. I threw back the velvet cover and swung my feet to the floor, expecting the shock of cold stone on my bare feet, but the mosaic of what appeared to be light and dark jade had the warmth of a hearth facing.

I padded to the window and examined the glazing, adjusted to the opacity of frost.

Where was the window control pad?

The bronze armature holding back a curtain seemed odd as well. I'd initially taken it for a rope, but it seemed to be a jointed robotic arm.

I felt along the frame. Sometimes windows had a remote pad. I searched the bedside table, pulling out drawers stuffed with electronic devices and small multi-legged robots, but no window controls. What would I see if the windows were clear?

I moved my examination to the headboard, feeling the polished smoothness of a bronze wolf's teeth.

"Good morning." His voice boomed from speakers hidden in the walls. "I'll be down in a moment. By the way you're looking quite nice."

"I'm not wearing anything."

From the ceiling coping, a dual-lens camera pivoted my way. "I can see that. Very nice."

He returned, and we sat down to breakfast. I'd dressed. He cut a waffle with the side of his fork. "I spoke with Dame Bulla and the Fennako Education Board this morning. You can start your studies."

I put my hand to my mouth. It was all too simple. He'd given the word, and I had what I wanted.

———

Chapter 21
Law Student

WE FLEW FOR over an hour with the esskip canopy opaque. Leaving his place, we'd encountered no one in the corridor or hangar, which seemed odd given the number of esskips I'd glimpsed earlier. When the canopy cleared, my eyes adjusted to the glare of daylight. We skimmed over ocean bounded by steep mountainsides which could have been nearly anywhere on Fenria. Occasionally, a cabin peered out from between dark spruce and fir, or a dock hugged the shore.

The density of houses and docks steadily increased until we passed islands fully encrusted with buildings and structures. Gantry cranes reared up. Long fingers of breakwaters and piers reached out into the water to hold boats and ships. Such a density of human habitation could only be Fennako City. We passed Tristan Head and approached Lawrock Island, unmistakable with its extensive harbor and, above it, the palace complex surmounted by the green dome of the Zenhedron.

We skimmed past the municipal harbor, banked and came in behind the palace complex. His esskip leapt the lagoon breakwater, and we splashed down. The barest huff of the propulsors brought us to an embankment. The canopy drew back, and he stepped from cockpit to wing-shoulder, then offered his hand to me. We left the lagoon behind and entered a gated passageway.

In a flutter of crimson wings, a tanager landed on the gate, or what I took to be a tanager. My man enfolded me in an embrace, and we kissed, his lips gentle. He pulled back, his eyes searching. "Do you know how to get to student housing?"

"I've got the address. I'm to stay in Lee-Smith Hall." I'd received a confirmation message that morning.

"That's up on Lawyer Roost as we call it around here. I'd come with you, but we'd be seen together. Do you have the address codes for your academic advisor?"

"Don't worry. I'll be fine."

"Hail me as soon as you have your room." He opened the gate. On the other side, stairs led upward. "Tide carry you," he called after me.

Valise in hand, I set a foot on the steps, then looked back. He stood at the gate still watching. Squaring my shoulders I set off and ascended the stairs to emmerge from the passage beside the palace complex. I took a breath and followed a lane which intersected with another. I was lost already. The map provided by student housing with directions to Lee-Smith Hall made no sense. They'd assumed I'd be arriving from the municipal harbor.

I hailed my man. "I'm lost," I admitted.

"Try this." A map appeared on my handscreen, actually a chart so detailed and complete that it must have been compiled for the Fennako City peaceweavers. A line glowed on the map.

"Head northeast," he said.

"Which way is north?" I asked.

"I see you. Go uphill."

I glanced around at the buildings and didn't see him, but at the intersection, a security camera had turned toward me. I waved.

I set off again, following his directions through the narrow lanes so steep that they had stairs.

"How do you do deliveries here?" I asked. Hauling groceries or carts up and down the stairs would be exhausting.

"There's a utilidor for freight. Also elevators. Lawyers Roost is just a little farther."

My path ended in a courtyard enclosed by a gray building. I panted, winded from the steep climb. Vines, leafless in this season, clambered up the building's sides. A skiff of snow lay on the ground and capped the statue of a woman at the center of a courtyard. Surely the statue depicted Fenna Lee-Smith, the first queen and namesake of the student hall. She'd been sculptured stepping forward, a child astride her hip and three clinging to her skirt, only one of them a boy—my ancestor? In her free hand she held a planning screen.

I set my valise on the snowy flagstone and considered this woman who in all likelihood was my forebear; Fenna Lee-Smith, foundress of Clan Fennako. She'd declined to give her children her husband's surname and in doing so, had set the precedent for matrilineal clan names. What had Queen Fenna's feelings been toward her husband, Jamie Noah? And what would the great queen feel toward me? Her descendent, standing in slushy snow and bent on reversing her precedent, or at least modifying it.

The lobby contained potted plants, puffy upholstered chairs, and bright rugs. The housemother stepped forward and introduced herself.

"Annin. Annin Noahee," I said, naming my male forebearer.

She smiled. "We've been expecting you. Will your partner be joining us soon? I'm sorry, we don't have her name."

"I don't have a partner," I said. My anonymous relationship was private.

"Please excuse my assumptions. The room you requested is furnished for a couple. It's the oldest part of the hall. It was once part of the office of Fenna herself."

I hadn't specified the room, but I said, "I greatly admire Fenna Lee-Smith. To have the privilege of rooming in her former office, I am beyond honored." The housemother might as well believe I had asked for the room myself.

My upstairs quarters seemed small in comparison to my man's apartment, but larger than what I'd glimpsed of the other student rooms. A woman's moon clock hung on the wall. Traditionally, such clocks glowed when Luna Majora was full helping to regulate ovulatory cycles. The clock hands were the same as those on the oversized clock in my man's apartment.

The antique heating system kicked on with a hum. I stooped to look at the grate. Seemingly as old as the building itself, the system had a motor-driven fan.

I unpacked the minimal clothing from my valise and hung the garments in one of the two closets. I hailed my man, "I've got an appointment with attorney Myrtle Gratianiko. I'm going there now."

"She's a bulldog," he said. "Which is good."

Next, I hailed Teakh.

"Are you okay? Where are you?" he asked.

"Fennako City. I'm in! He got me into law school."

"He better have," Teakh said.

I LEFT LEE-SMITH Hall and went up a steep lane to the address given by my advisor. I hailed her.

"Come on up." The front door opened. A woman greeted me at the top of a flight of stairs. "Myrtle Gratianiko here. You already know that. Call me Gratia."

180

We went into her office, and she removed a stack of legal volumes from a chair beside a square table. "Mint tea?"

I sat on the edge of the chair. "No, thank you."

"Can't abide the stuff myself. Heard back on Earth they had some really good steeping herbs, black tea, and something called coffee." Gratia filled cups anyway and sat across the table. "Now then. You're wanting to go into interclan law. Just why is that?"

I twisted the hem of my smock. "The Queen asked me to."

"Not good enough," Gratia said.

What was good enough?

"It's because of my brother. Last time we were in Fennako City, someone assaulted him for his semen. We've founded our own clan so I can protect him and negotiate his stud contracts. That's why I'm studying law."

"I suppose that's as good a reason as any." She leaned back. "Girl, you've got a step up on most women entering this field. What most folks don't know is that interclan law is all marriage contracts. The bulk of our business is writing and negotiating the things. Nearly the entire remainder of our business is mopping up marriages gone bad. Occasionally clans get into a dispute which amazingly doesn't involve sex or marriage. But dig deep enough and every conflict and every treaty involves men. Yep, we got ourselves a shortage of males here on Fenria. That's all politics is, fighting about who gets the beefcake." Gratia flipped open a folding screen. "I've got your contract and clan charter here. Nice work by the way. Your contract has precedents. Your charter though, now there's a hot one. Men and women treated as equal, and this part about membership open to all Noah descendants." She tapped the screen.

"Not all," I corrected her. "It's patrilineal descendants of Noah and survivors of the Noah eugenics project."

"When it comes to proving Noah descent, the distinction is moot. For practical purposes you can have anyone in your clan you want."

"That was a stipulation requested by Fennako," I said. "And I have to convince people to join up and volunteerily pay clan fees."

"Her Majesty's idea, surely, the old girl making one last mark. Are you ready to carry that legacy forward? You'll have to work for it."

"I suppose so." I was only a dozen-four and ready to challenge the entire matriarchy, but I knew enough to present myself as respectful and unassuming.

"A lot of my colleagues wouldn't touch your education with a six-meter spar," Gratia said. "There's sure to be trouble. But girl, you got talent and you got mettle. Not many women could write a charter like that and get it before the Queen. By the way, how is it going with fulfilling the contract?"

"We've decided to take it slow. We're getting to know each other. Not our names. Other stuff."

"Wise of you." Gratia moved a legal volume. "If more young people did that, we'd have fewer problems on the other end. You know, I've never previously encountered a young woman required to get pregnant before starting her education. Plenty of girls face the opposite problem."

"When do I start?"

"You've already started, but I have some materials for you." Gratia shoved the volume toward me with a list of recommended course work put out by the bar association, along with schedules of lectures, seminars, and symposiums offered in Fennako City. "I've arranged for you to join a study group. They'll be your best teachers. Keep me abreast of your progress. Understand you're responsible for your own studies. You have no education board looking over your shoulder, offering either reprimand or guidance."

"I'm to report to the Fennako Education Board," I reminded her.

"Ah yes. But they have many students. Your education is far more important to you than it is to anyone else. Take whatever tests you deem necessary to prove yourself competent. I recommend you prepare a thesis for peer review and approval. You can use your charter and contract as a basis. You've got a lot of work ahead of you. Your clan reputation rides on you and you alone."

I collected the volume and list feeling the weight of responsibility. Was I up to the task I'd agreed to take on?

AT SUPPER IN Lee-Smith Hall, students sat talking and enjoying their meal. I went through the buffet line.

A student looked up with a smile. "Welcome. What are you about?"

I balanced my tray. "Studying law."

"Aren't we all? Who's your advisor?"

"Attorney Myrtle Gratianiko."

"Judge Gratia?" The girl shouted, "Hey, Rayleen, she's one of yours. That's your study group over there."

The group made room for me at their table. "We're Gratia's Bleeding Hearts," announced a student. "That's what the others call us. We're studying human rights law. Those over there, the Fish Mongers. They get excited about fisheries treaties." She rolled her eyes. "Those—the Pirates, crime on the high seas. Of course, a lot of our interests overlap, depends on if criminals are abducting people or abducting fish."

My future colleagues introduced themselves and I struggled to remember names. They knew of my clan charter and that I planned to represent the clanless in court. That's how they understood it, anyway.

Rayleen, the most senior of the group had a narrow face. Her straight black hair was pulled back into a queue and tied with a velvet ribbon.

"She's nearly a full-fledged lawyer, specializing in human rights," Zelta said.

Rayleen shrugged. "My thesis should be completed by autumn, but you know how it goes. Until then I'm working as a paralegal. Your charter meshes with my thesis. I've proposed making a clan of the clanless. The Queen incorporated my suggestions in your charter. I am pleased to finally meet you."

"Are you planning to apply for territory?" Gale asked. Later I learned she was from a deep-sea clan. They specialized in selling insurance and didn't live in their territory. They maintained Seaguard equipment in a section of the Andean Ocean. In return, her clan received voting rights and representation in the House of Water.

"Go for riparian territory," Rose said. Her clan controlled the Wasatch watershed. "Orchards, gardens. Little danger of tsunamis."

I hadn't thought much about it. Maintaining valuable waterways could give a clan significant power, but if all went as planned Noahee would have members all over the planet, so a watershed probably wouldn't suit us.

"River and coastal territories are hard to come by," Gale said. "Apply for polar or deep ocean. You can live wherever you want."

"There's always atmospheric and orbital," someone said.

Rayleen shook her head. "Noahee's mandate is protecting the descendants of Noah. It's an entirely new concept, not even a true clan."

Discussion flew so fast that I couldn't track who was talking.

"Matriarchs tell people who can and can't have children. It's not right," someone said.

"But clans must be able to control the size of their populations. If they didn't, people would have too many children, overrun their resources, and then invade other clans."

"They might starve first."

"One woman! One vote!"

"That's a recipe for disaster. A clan can set up explosive population growth to take over territory from another clan who has limited its growth in order to conserve resources."

"But people produce ideas. Having more people leads to more innovation."

"They need education, or they can't develop those ideas."

Dizzied by the discussion, I cut in, "Surely clans can control population size without dictating women's sex lives."

"Just how are they going to do that?"

"Offer incentives," I said. When clans needed to raise the birthrate they offered mothers their pick of housing. When a lower birthrate was necessary, women who delayed childbearing were given preferential placement in childcare programs. No one was forced to either bear children or forgo children."

"So a woman's only child gets to be treated as special and a fifth child is a second-class citizen?" Rose asked

"That's not what I meant," I said.

"What will you do if a member of your clan refuses to control her family size? Suppose she's constantly pregnant and has five children with less than a year between births. Will you force sterilization? Will you refuse to pay for the education of her children?"

"But what about accidental births?" I asked. "What about a woman who has only two children, but without clan permission? What if the woman has three children and then twins?"

Rayleen clapped me on the back. "That's our job. The rights of the individual."

Hailing Annin Noahee,

Please attend a meeting in my office, 2 pm. We will be discussing the genetic implications of men's suffrage.

Attorney Gratianiko signing off

I WALKED UP the hill to Gratia's place. I didn't feel much like a law student or look like one. I hadn't slept well in the drafty former office of Queen Fenna, which was cold despite the noisy heating system. The tunic I'd brought along to my tryst was now rumpled and in need of being laundered. But there hadn't been time, and I was due at my advisor's office.

I hailed and ran up the steps to her upstairs room. Two additional women dressed in somber robes were seated in the office. Gratia introduced them as Valarin Hellenboreko and Cordalis Sibriko of the Fenrian Eugenic Council. I nearly bolted for the door.

"Annin," Gratia stopped me. "If you're going to be a lawyer you must hear all sides and listen to those who oppose you."

"And those who attack my kin?" I demanded. "My brother was assaulted in Fennako City in broad daylight."

"These women weren't responsible," Gratia said.

"What's to prevent them from abducting me or chopping out my ovaries? What about their eugenics project?"

The Hellenboreko woman got huffy. "The Noah Eugenics Project was one of the most ill-founded studies ever undertaken."

"Come now," said Sibriko. "There have been worse. We're indeed representatives of the Eugenics Council, but we strongly condemn the Noah Project. Our concern is with the evolutionary fitness of the Fenrian gene pool. Current studies are subjected to rigorous review. All of our subjects are treated humanely and ethically."

"No assaulting your subjects in alleys then?" I asked, not keeping the bitterness out of my tone.

Hellenboreko said, "It would be counterproductive. We seek to reduce violence within our population. We nudge the gene pool by advising clan leaders such as yourself in regard to the impact of policy on genetics."

"Excuse me," Gratia said. "May I introduce Annin Noahee, foundress of Clan Noahee?"

"Using the name already?" Sibriko said. "I understand she's of Ralko extraction."

"I'm not related to Ralko," I said.

"You're certainly not," Valarin said. "We've been given to understand that you've proposed extending full suffrage to men. Is that right?"

"It's written in the Noahee clan charter," I said.

"And you plan to treat your brother's children as fully equal to your own?"

"Aye."

"Regardless of the number of children he fathers?"

"Of course. Why is that important?"

Valarin nodded to Sibriko. "That is what we've come to speak about. We view all human behavior as the result of evolution."

I cloaked my disgust in curiosity. "The survival of the fittest?"

"If only it were so. In actuality it's often survival of the most promiscuous. If you produce enough offspring fast enough then it doesn't matter if you or most of your offspring die, your genes will still become dominant. Evolution isn't about survival of the individual but about survival of genes. Genes that increase the number of descendants proliferate within the gene pool at the expense of other, possibly superior, genes."

"And Noah genes are the fittest?" I asked, barely hiding my skepticism.

"On the contrary. Noah genes aren't aggressive enough. They tend to lose out to stronger strains. Thus, the Noah Eugenics Project. It's controversial, but we're here to speak with you about policies, not your genetics."

Sibriko glared at me. "Allowing men to vote!"

I returned her gaze without flinching. "And what's wrong with that?"

"Men are genetically over aggressive. They're driven to produce high numbers of offspring regardless of infant mortality. None of this is conscious. They're randy and don't recognize their lust and bravado as instinct."

"Male competition isn't all bad," Sibriko butted in. "For evolution to occur, some offspring are going to die. Males thin the herd." Sibriko and Hellenboreko went at each other with arguments and counter-arguments.

"Not necessarily," Hellenboreko said. "During an epidemic, a high number of offspring is advantageous, but without such pressure, evolution devolves into male head-butting. The biggest rooster wins and forces his offspring on the females. Clans lose. They have the burden of supporting excess offspring through pregnancy, childbirth, and early childhood. Only to have them starve to death or die due to lack of resources. The result is survival of the lucky, not the fittest."

"Survival of the most prolific actually, like chickweed and dandelions," said Sibriko. "Women aim for something which grows slower and doesn't take over. Roses. Women's genetic goals of offspring survival more closely align with the good of the clan. They vote to provide for children. Men, if given the chance, try to increase the status of themselves or their clan at the expense of children. Women support school athletics for all. Men support the winning team."

"That's shine," I said. "A lot of men support children." Teakh was the assistant swim coach in Dojko. "My brother for example—"

"Your brother has Noah genetics."

Hellenboreko said, "It's merely evolutionary pressure and not true of all men or all women. If men are given unbridled access to sex and power, the genes of a few big roosters will flood the gene pool. Genes for sexual aggression will crowd out other genes and so decrease evolutionary fitness of the entire population."

Sibriko said, "On Fenria, we've given men all the sex they want, but limited their access to power and money, so that they can't divert clan resources into displays of prowess. By giving men the vote, you'll throw all of that out. Your brother could father grosses of children who will take over and outvote your descendants. In generations to come, we will have bloody warfare as aggressive men vie against each other for the right to spread their genes."

"Teakh is providing limited edition stud service," I said. "He's not going to father grosses of children."

"What about his grandchildren and yours? If a son can produce more offspring than his sister, there's pressure for the mother to prefer the son. You may think that men's suffrage is a step toward equality but, in evolutionary terms, it denigrates women."

Sibriko interrupted again. "The fact is, a man can produce more children than a woman can. Chickweed and roses. It's biology."

My anger sizzled. "Men and women are equal. Our charter has checks and balances in place. We ensure that all purchasing clans have the resources to support my brother's children. No one is forced to bear Clan Noahee children or to join Clan Noahee."

"We have our doubts," Sibriko said. "What will you do when your brother's children outnumber your own? Be warned: they'll control your clan. They'll vote their own into office, replacing you with someone who isn't as scrupulous."

Was the dig about scrupulousness a backhanded compliment? Or a suggestion that I was naïve?

STILL ANGRY, I descended the steps from Lawrock as I returned to Lee-Smith. A woman called out a greeting. I turned to see Coco who I'd last seen in Hanalee.

"Fancy seeing you in Fennako City," she said.

"I'm a student here." I hid my irritation. "And you. How is your business? I was concerned when you left so suddenly."

"Nothing to worry about," she said. "That sort of thing happens. Has that gentleman followed through? I told you the truth. He's married to multiple women."

"Who paid you to say that?" I asked.

"Does it matter?" she asked with a pasted-on smile.

IN MY QUARTERS I hailed Teakh with an update. "I met with women from the Eugenics Council."

"Hags!" Teakh said. "What did they want?"

"They warned that you'll take over Clan Noahee and kill babies."

"That bad?"

"Actually, they think Clan Noahee men will have more children than can be supported, and so children will starve. It all amounts to dead babies." I told him about meeting Coco. "Who is paying her?"

"Maybe the Eugenics Council," he said.

"That's my suspicion."

He said, "I'm still thinking we should get independent genetic tests on that man."

"That's not the agreement, and it's not necessary." I'd undergone a complete physical exam and provided blood and saliva for comprehensive genetic analysis, both requested by Clan Fennako.

"Founder the agreement. All you need is a strand of hair."

"And what good will those do? If all goes as planned, I'll be pregnant."

"You won't be pregnant at first," Teakh said. "It takes a while for the ovum to implant."

"What are you suggesting?"

"If the guy is too closely related then take some pills so that you don't ovulate."

"No," I said.

"Don't you want to know who he is?"

"Unlike some people, I don't stick my beak into other people's gut piles."

"I have a friend who's a lab technician," Teakh offered. "She can do the tests and analysis."

"What's her fee?"

"Nothing. I told you she's a friend."

We signed off and I went to the window. The light of Luna Majora spilled across the courtyard, throwing the inky shadow of Fenna Lee-Smith long across the foot-muddled snow. Judging from the direction of the shadow, my window faced north. Observe the tide. I drew thick curtains across the window, no self-darkening glass in this old building.

My man might as well have been way off in the Andean Ocean. How would we manage to meet? Despite the circuitous route from his place, I already suspected he lived just across the bay. Public ferries didn't go to Tristan Head Island. I'd checked.

I lay on the bed, my comset charging in a wall niche. Loneliness washed across me. My bed felt empty and cold on this winter night. I pulled the blanket closer around me. Staring up at the dark ceiling I listened to the odd creaks and clicks of the venerable heating system expanding or contracting in its struggle against the chill. The fan clicked on and began its infernal hum. The grating rattled in counterpoint to the fan.

I rolled to my stomach. A new sound joined the others, a squeak behind the wall. Something or someone was there. I reached for my comset.

———

Chapter 22
Midnight

IADJUSTED THE BLANKET and lay convinced that the rustling in the walls was merely the building settling or the heating fan continuing to rattle and hum.

But my comset crackled.

"May I come in? I'm in a narrow and very dusty passageway. "

"Hurry up."

A rosy beam of light punctured the darkness.

A panel clicked and scrapped. The light shut off.

"How did you get here?" I asked.

The mattress sunk under his weight. "The city utilidor from the tanker dock, as if I were a delivery of hydrogen for the city fuel cells. All to keep my favorite matriarch warm."

I put my arms around my man's waist. "But how did you know about the passageway?"

"An old family secret."

I gave him a squeeze. "Was there a hidden meaning in the room assignment?"

"Aye. I want to be with you."

Before dawn I reached for the pocket of warmth where he'd been, but it was empty. "Don't leave me," I said.

He hadn't left yet but stood in the dimness wearing only his skivvies. "Need to take my morning constitutional. Can you direct me to the facility?" he said, with mock formality.

He opened the door. From the hallway, ruby nightlights threw a bar of light across the floor.

"Aren't you cold?" I asked.

Backlit he shrugged. "Cold water is my thing."

When he returned, we snuggled under the warm blankets.

Then he said, "I've got morning watch."

He left my side to dress. The door to the hidden passageway creaked open, the mechanism seemly as ancient as the heating system. He stepped into the dark cavity, and the panel shut behind him. I was alone again. The wall clock glowed with the hands at four am.

RAYLEEN AND I looked down on the courtroom arena, a stone floor marked with a jade compass rose. The layout and proceedings resembled a game of justice poker. We'd taken seats in the northern quadrant behind the judges.

"It's a murder case," whispered Rayleen. "A man killed aboard a multi-clan fish-processing ship. It's complicated. The victim's clan is seated over there." She flicked a thumb toward the nearly empty southern quadrant.

Empty except for two women with four children neatly dressed and arranged by size, the smallest child on a woman's lap. They reminded me of the statue of Fenna-Lee Smith, sculptured holding a planning screen and an infant while caring for three other children.

The modern-day Fenna-Lee Smith stood and delivered the child to the other women, then entered the speaker's ring. At the center of the compass rose she faced the judges and proclaimed:

We demand justice. Justice for my son, my only son. I am Silvi. These are my grandchildren. My clan." She opened her arms in the children's direction, then straightened. *"We are not recognized as such.*

Rayleen whispered. "I told you this was complicated."

"We have recorded your name as Silvi Clanless," said a judge. "Is this correct?"

"It's Silvi Silviko," the woman insisted. "We are Silviko. We may be a small clan, but we take good care of our children. My daughter works as a cleaning woman. She doesn't make enough to pay for my grandchildren's education, so I'm their teacher. My health is not good." She coughed, a hand to her chest. "I fear what will happen when I am gone. We relied on my son, their uncle, to bring in additional money, but he was brutally murdered, leaving my grandchildren bereft and destitute. A man's life has no price, but justice demands that my grandchildren are given the money my son would have earned if he'd lived."

A shout came from the western quadrant. "He was a hag-sucking lubber and deserved what he got."

Silviko ignored the heckler. "We place ourselves at the mercy of the court." She bowed before returning to the south and accepted the smallest child from her daughter.

The courtroom rustled. A representative from the eastern quadrant took the floor and testified: "My nephew and this man had a dispute. This man fell down a shipboard ladder and died. But it was not a result of blows delivered by my nephew. The man's death was due to Dusko negligence. It was their ship. Dusko hired a clanless man with a history of careless, violent, and ungovernable behavior."

Angry shouts arose from the west. Dusko, accused of negligence, urged a representative forward. She took to the floor:

> *Who is this who accuses my client? The man who passed away claimed to have a clan. He lied. Is this who speaks for him? We have a clanless woman who, for some unknown reason, chose to produce two children when she lacked the means to support them. Her daughter even more irresponsibly produced four children. Silvi, I call on you to explain. What led you and your children onto such an irresponsible path?*

Carrying the youngest child, Silvi entered the ring to face Dusko. "I am not clanless by choice. Years ago, when I was a student, I became pregnant. I love my daughter, but her conception was an accident that occurred during a waning moon. I am a good woman. I observe the tide, but ovulation isn't always predictable. Since I had not received permission from my clan to have a child, and because I refused to have an abortion, they struck my name from the clan rolls."

"But then why?" Dusko asked. "After being burdened with one child did you choose to bring another into the world? And why did you allow your daughter to have four children when you lacked the means to support even one?"

"We could support them and did, until my son was murdered. You, Dusko, by your negligence, and you, Hiltiko, have killed one-third of our adult membership. My grandchildren's only beloved uncle." Silvi swayed, comforting the child.

"This is no clan," Dusko said, "but a thoughtless pair of women. They parade children in an obscene play for sympathy, but these two have never given much thought to the future. We ask that this case be dismissed."

"Hear us," Silviko pleaded.

"You may return to your places," a judge said. "We will consider."

The three judges drew together in a discussion and made a decision delivered by one of them:

"Although we feel sympathy for the plight of these children, this family does not constitute a clan and lacks the authority to negotiate in court."

"What?" I sprang to my feet. I shook and my heart pounded. Marching down the aisle, I pushed past the bailiff into the speaker's ring. "I, Annin Noahee, Grandmatriarch of Clan Noahee speak for Silvi! Silvi and her family are members of my clan!" Kinkill, I should have said our, not my. "Noahee demands justice."

A bailiff stepped forward. "Ma'am, please leave the speakers ring. You haven't been called."

"Let her speak," the judge said.

"I am Annin Noahee, Grandmatriarch of Clan Noahee. I speak for Silvi."

The judge asked. "On what basis do you represent this family?"

I swallowed. "According to the Clan Noahee charter, our membership includes descendants of Jamie Noah. Silvi, her daughter, and grandchildren are descendants of Noah, so they are members of Clan Noahee."

Dusko came forward. "Is that so? Tell me, Silvi, have you ever met this woman before."

Silvi tossed her head in negation.

"And Noahee, or whoever you are, has Silvi every paid clan fees?"

"No," I admitted.

"What proof do you have that these are descendants of Jamie Noah."

"It's likely," I said. "He has a lot of descendants."

The courtroom laughed.

"But this is wrong!" I shouted. "What about the children?"

"You're out of order," the judge said.

"Their uncle was murdered and you aren't going to do anything?" I demanded.

The bailiff grasped my arm. "Please leave the speakers ring."

"Do you think this is right?" I asked.

He didn't answer as he escorted me from the floor.

Rayleen met us at the bottom of the aisle. "She's with me."

The bailiff let me go. People were leaving the courtroom, the case dismissed.

"Come on," said Rayleen. "It's a sad situation, but it's not the only one."

I followed her up the aisle.

"When my clan is approved, I'll have the case reopened," I promised to her back.

Rayleen turned to look at me. "The murder happened before incorporation of your clan. You can't."

"I have to do something."

"Right now your charter isn't worth the data space it uses. You must have real authority to back it up—members, territory, and allegiances. If you had these, you could pressure other clans to take up the lawsuit. Silvi's children and grandchildren had fathers. And those fathers have clans."

"Why don't they do something? Why doesn't the Queen do something?"

"She has." Rayleen mounted the steps. "She approved your charter."

I felt like I was shouting at the wind. I couldn't do a damn thing.

———

Chapter 23
Spitfire

Hailing Annin.

Mareen here.

I'd be delighted if you'd stop by for a chat at your convenience. We can catch up on news. Let me know of a good time.

Best regards.

Mareen sending

WHAT WAS THIS about?

I hadn't seen Princess Mareen since my last visit to Fennako City. Now she was messaging me as if the were best friends.

I hailed her as I paced in my room.

"What do you think of stopping by?" she asked casually. Too casually. Anxiety clutched at my throat. Maybe Mareen had seen my outburst in court.

I calmed myself. Keeping my tone neutral I asked, "What's this about?"

She said, "I heard that you've entered law school and are now living in Fennako City. Staying in Lee-Smith Hall even. I've spent some time there. I did most of my studies outside of Tristan Bay waters. Travel gives a woman perspective. I was a Pirate, by the way."

"Pirate?" I imagined Mareen, cutlass in hand, striding across the deck of a ship.

She laughed. "Student slang for high seas law, my field of study. I understand that you've got my old room in Lee-Smith Hall. Burr, that place was drafty. I hope you have a lot of blankets."

"Uh..." So this had been her room. Words jostled in my mind. I wasn't cold because my man was hot. Couldn't say that. I blundered along. "I have enough."

"Do come on up to my place. It's warmer here."

I gulped. "Right away. I mean if that's okay with you."

"How about this afternoon, three-ish?"

I HURRIED UP the steep lane to Mareen's place. I glanced at each woman I passed wondering if she were a lawyer and if she were the person I would meet. Or maybe I'd be meeting a man. Fewer of them traveled here near Lawyers Roost, as they called it.

I located her garden terrace. Beyond the bars of the gate, red wings flickered—the tanager I'd seen earlier? More likely it was one of Mareen's drones.

The gate swung open and a crimson creature screeched and plummeted toward me. I shied from a perfect miniature dragon. She pulled up, then circled, glinting scarlet and gold.

The dragonette delicately landed on my shoulder. Intrigued, I craned my neck to look into the lenses of the robotic creature. It bobbed its head in a semblance of a bow, then took off, swooping and dipping.

A girl—surely the dragon operator—scampered toward me.

Behind her, Mareen stood in the open doorway to her office.

The girl skidded to a halt. "Greetings. What are you about?"

"Observing the tide." I gave the customary response as I glanced past the girl to Mareen.

She made introductions: "Daughter, this is Auntie Annin. Kinswoman, this is my daughter Reena." The dragonette landed and flapped its wings, the sound so loud and furious that distinguishing words was difficult. Mareen continued, "She's been most eager to meet you and to play the hostess. I hope you don't mind."

Reena bowed, her decorum perfect, but her eyes mischievous. The dragonette streaked through the open door.

Crayons and graph film littered Mareen's desk. The dragonette landed and skittered to a stop, sending graph sheets flying and crayons rolling. I stooped to pick up a sheet and smoothed it on the desk. The drawing showed a row of three people amidst a perfusion of winged creatures.

"That's Vunk, Mama, and me," Reena pointed to each. "These are our telechirics: Scorch, Vunk's esskip. And these are Mama's drones."

"Is Scorch the name of your dragon?" I asked.

"Uh-huh." Reena put a hand to her ear. "Mama says I'm supposed to invite you into the kitchen for fish fingers."

"She's offering hospitality," Mareen explained. "Breaded pollock prepared by the palace kitchen. They're better than you'd expect."

Reena opened a door leading from the office to a dining room. Soft music played from hidden speakers. Scorch the dragon landed on the table, gold toenails clattering on the laminate. With a delicate gold claw, Scorch pushed cloth napkins into place.

Reena pulled out a chair. "You sit here," she said.

Seated, I spread a napkin on my lap. Reena left the room.

Mareen was seated across the table said, "I asked you here to meet my daughter. As you might have gathered, she already knows about you."

Reena carried a tea service to the table. Mer-wolves depicted in green glaze cavorted on the teapot.

With dimpled hands, Reena poured hot water through an herb strainer set in a pot, her mother watching with approval. Reena covered the pot with a tea cozy then went to a dumbwaiter for the promised fish fingers.

I dipped one in the tartar sauce. Reena held hers out for Scorch to sniff then took a bite—the two of them functioning together with smooth precision.

"How do you manage it?" I asked. "Scorch has four legs and two wings. Which are your hands?"

Scorch tapped front feet on the table. "Easy," said Reena. "These are my hands, so are these." The dragonette flapped her wings, crimson membrane stretched over delicate pinion struts. "I switch between them."

"She's working on the landings," Mareen supplied. "That's when she transitions from wings to forelimbs."

Reena poured tea first for me then Mareen before pouring one for herself.

"Do you like Vunk?" she asked then sipped, peering slyly over the rim of her cup.

"Your uncle?" I asked as I realized she spoke of my man.

"Uh-huh. Mama's brother. He's in love with you." She set the cup down.

Mareen frowned. "They're both under hospitality. We should not speak of it."

"But I saw them kissing. Eww. "

"Auntie is not supposed to know who he is."

Reena pouted. "That's silly. Everyone knows who Vunk is. And I wasn't looking through windows. They were by the esskip lagoon."

"I don't know his name." I smiled to reassure the girl. "But I do like him. Were you using Scorch?" I recalled seeing that flash of wings that I'd taken for a tanager.

"Uh hu. She saw you." Reena held another fish finger to Scorch before eating it herself.

"Very good," I said as I finished my portion.

Mareen nodded to her daughter. "Auntie and I must talk without Scorch looking on. You may work at my desk as surveillance chief."

Reena left the dining room, her dragonette on her shoulder. The door shut.

Mareen pushed aside plates and utensils. Her gaze met mine. "First, I must warn you. Very few places are secure against eavesdropping as you found out with my daughter."

"I didn't realize she was watching. Mixing children's telechirics with aircraft seems inadvisable. "

"We do not. I monitor her usage. Assume everything is monitored." Mareen placed a palm to the back of her head. "My neural implant links me to the Sense-net, the same for all Seaguard members. Our sensors lace the entire ocean. We have cameras on docks and in ferry terminals. We even provide surveillance in urban areas, as you have found out."

"I have nothing to hide," I said.

"You do now." She stretched out her booted feet. "Get accustomed to it. Be extremely careful with names. The Sense-net is crawling with spy algorithms. Use nicknames and oblique references. Fingerspelling may be useful. When discussing sensitive information, use background noise as a mask, like this." The music faded to be replaced by an audio drama, two sisters vying for a position on a mother's council. "The voices are similar to ours. You may have noticed all that wing-flapping while I made introductions. My daughter has been schooled from birth on techniques for confounding spies. You'll have to quickly learn such methods. Let's talk privately. No use of names. Do you understand?"

"Aye." I nodded and swallowed.

With her lips nearly touching my ear she whispered, "We've had your brother under surveillance for years. At the tender age of a dozen-one he commenced on a career of blackmail. His actions weren't initially illegal, but when authorities didn't follow up his reports, he took matters into his own hands. Ever since, we've kept a watch on him."

"Why did you let him continue if you knew what he was doing?"

"He went after petty crime." Mareen shrugged. "His work saved everyone a lot of bother, including the poachers. They'd pay him, and word of their criminal activity never reached the ears of their clan mothers."

"But now he's a stud for hire," I pointed out.

"Aye, one with phenomenal genetics! We should have seen it coming, but we didn't. How many twelve-year-olds have the boldness to confront fishing captains and ask for money?"

"A dozen-and-one," I corrected.

"There you go. The same sort of mettle. You would stand up to the queen herself. I saw your performance in court the other day."

I put my hands over my face, recalling the Bailiff escorting me off the floor, "What performance?"

"You demonstrated passion for defending the clanless. You'll make a fine lawyer."

My voice rose. "If Fennako doesn't stick to their bargains, I'll be a clanless mother just like Silvi."

Mareen touched a finger to her lips. "Remember, keep it soft and no names."

"Right," I whispered. "If you don't stick to your bargains, I'll be clanless just like those women."

"We will. I'll stand by you and your man, but be prepared. You have enemies. You're going to have more of them. We must keep quiet about your relationship until it's secure."

"You mean until I'm pregnant?"

"Secure enough that it can't be scuttled. Your agreement with my grandmother gives you authority. Once your relationship is solid, you'll be able to speak in court and people will listen."

"You seem to know quite a bit about this relationship of mine."

"I do. I'm sorry about that first meeting at the clinic. It was necessary."

"Truly?" I asked.

"The...man was previously widowed. He refused to take another bride from his wife's clan. That clan opposes your relationship. The eugenics council also opposes you. They both agreed to your insemination, provided it was anonymous and clinical."

"I take it we're talking about your brother."

"Our brothers. My brother the deadbeat widower and your brother the blackmail artist cum stud. Neither do what they're told."

"Your brother could have married Silvi's daughter. Why did your grandmother approve Noahee but not Silviko?"

"Mostly because of your brother, strange as it may seem. He's Seaguard and that makes a difference. He's also willing to disregard rules when he sees fit."

"You don't think that's a problem?"

"Well, my brother doesn't do what he's told any more than yours does. We know laws are little more than agreements. If Noahee and Fennako agree, then we've made new laws." Mareen held out her hands. "Will you accept me as your sister-in-law? I'm sorry we're a difficult family."

"Of course." We touched palm to palm, but I wondered. What agreement with royalty truly was binding? If they didn't follow through, I had no recourse.

I HUDDLED UNDER blankets and listened for the sounds in the passageway. Maybe he would come again tonight.

The wind whistled as it tore at the corners of the building and the fan rattled.

The latch rasped and he entered, this time without hailing. In the dimness he was an inky shadow.

"Quick, get in bed with me," I said.

His vest fasteners clicked, and the vest dropped to the floor with a clank. I curled around his back as he removed his boots. He stretched out and I pulled the blankets over both of us, making a cocoon of warmth. The fan continued to hum.

"I met with your..." I paused remembering the warning against names. "The surveillance chief and her daughter."

"What did you think of them?" He nuzzled my back.

"The daughter is a spitfire. She showed off her dragon."

He laughed. "Isn't she? And a bit spoiled I'm sorry to say. The dragon was a Solstice gift. Her first flying telechiric. She crashes a lot."

"She did rather well. But your...uh... the chief told me to be careful about surveillance. The spitfire has been spying on us. She saw us kissing behind the esskip house."

"That scamp. She must have seen me arrive."

"The chief also told me that any place might be bugged."

"This room is as secure as we can make it," he whispered. "The chief cleared it. And the place has the noise generator."

"The what?"

"The heating fan. It also generates electronic noise. Anyone who snoops on us will think it's old and poorly maintained. If we keep our voices down, we can say anything we want."

"The chief told me that your grandmother set up our horrible first date to please the eugenics council and the clan which thinks they own you."

"They don't, and that wasn't a date. I didn't like it and still don't."

I touched his face in the darkness. "Do you want to be my consort?"

"I'm sure of it. If I couldn't have you, I'd want someone exactly like you, but there isn't anyone like you. I'm glad the spitfire didn't turn you off by whining."

"She was charming and very proper. She served me tea and fish fingers."

His fingers caressed my shoulder. "When I became magnate, we conceded that my sister would have only one child. That was the deal. The spitfire is in line to the throne, but she has no siblings or near cousins. The royal family is like any other clan, only worse. If we have too many children, princesses squabble for power. The spitfire might become queen, but only after she's past childbearing age because she won't get permission to marry or bear a child. Our relationship, you and me, changes that. We may be able to apply enough pressure that she can marry whomever she wants and have a normal family life. My sister and I never had that."

I rested my head on his shoulder. "Is that what you want? A normal family?"

"I want children who help each other as brothers and sisters and who can choose who they love."

"That's what I want as well."

"It's the royal family who needs your help, not the clanless. I need your help the most." He enfolded me in an embrace. I didn't care who he was as long as we were together.

Chapter 24
Royal Trafficking

BEYOND MY WINDOW, a young woman tramped past the statue of Fenna Lee-Smith under an overcast sky. My comset bleated, "You have a visitor."

Maybe this had something to do with my contract. I closed my screen and went down to the front lobby. A girl my age waited. She was pretty and wore high heels, fishnet stockings, and a smock that hugged her curves. She'd removed her coat.

I asked the traditional question "What are you about?"

She smiled. "The tide. And I aim to bring a lawsuit against my own clan. I understand you can help someone do that."

I invited her into a meeting room off the lobby where we settled into chairs. She crossed one leg over the other.

She studied me then said, "You went up against your own clan, yes? I want to do the same thing. They want me to study medicine, and I don't want to."

Clans paid for education and so had a say in what a girl studied. "You should take it up with your clan education board," I advised, feeling like an adult for once.

"I've chosen my career. They don't like it," she said. "I'm already making money doing work I enjoy."

"What's your profession?"

"I'm a prostitute," she said without hesitation.

"And you like this work?" I asked. I'd never considered such a career.

"I do. My clients, mostly men, are appreciative and pay me well."

"But what about diseases and getting pregnant?"

"I take precautions. My clan wants me to become an andrologist and give men prostate exams." She grimaced. "What man wants a prostate exam when he could have fellatio? I like making people happy."

"There are other ways to please men. You could be an insemination assistant. Or maybe a dancer, or an artist. I have a good friend who specializes in painting male nudes."

"I can't paint, and I'm not very good at dancing. No sense of rhythm. My clan says I have to be at least two-dozen one to work as either a prostitute or insemination assistant."

"I can't help you," I said. "I'm not a lawyer yet and my clan charter hasn't been approved."

She sat dejected, her hands on her lap. "What can I do? There must be a way."

"Keep studying andrology and try to work with your education board," I suggested. "Do you mind if I speak with my academic advisor about your problem? I'd also like to enlist the help of my study group."

"Anything to get out of prostate exams. I detest the procedure."

A RUBY LIGHT glowed in my man's hand as we crept down a narrow stairway. A second panel slid open to a wider corridor. He shone the light on pipes and tubing as we walked. The utilidor branched, one passage blocked by a wall that was pierced by pipes, conduit, and tubing. He opened a door through the wall, and we continued through a maze of corridors and stairways until we stepped out of a closet into a wide, well-lit hallway with a polished floor. He knocked and entered a sitting room. Chairs were arranged near broad windows which looked out over the roofs of Fennako City.

Reena bowled into him. "Vunk!"

He picked her up. "How's my big girl?"

I could no longer pretend otherwise. My man could be none other than Reena's uncle, Marsk Fennako.

Reena rattled on. "We played make-believe at school. And knitting. I'm going to try knitting with my dragon. She can make herself socks."

"That might get in the way of landing," Marsk winked at me.

"Okay, a hat for Scorch."

"What about your letters?" I asked.

"Oh, I know the alphabet. "Alpha, Ace, Bravo, Charlie, Delta, Echo—" she said, fingerspelling the letters.

I stopped the girl before she went through all two-dozen-eleven letters.

"It's easy because they are the same as on the tails of esskips." She danced around the room. "Our clan designation is Foxtrot, Echo, November. That's the same as the start of my clan name. What's your clan designation?"

"You're not supposed to ask." Marsk tickled Reena. She squealed and Scorch flew across the room.

"Reena, where're your manners?" Mareen went to a wet bar for a pitcher of juice and filled four glasses.

"Oh sorry. Greetings Auntie, Vunk."

Reena arranged her dragon in her lap, a knitting needle in each forepaw. Maureen passed out drinks and asked about my studies.

"I'm mostly attending court," I said. "I'm following a difficult case of a surrogate mother who died in childbirth, and several cases of men seeking release from their marriages so that they can marry women in different clans."

Marsk looked away "There is that."

"I saw someone." I said. When he looked towards me, I finger spelled Coco. "She told me you're married."

"Someone we met down south," Marsk explained to Mareen. "She warned this gal away from me." He put his arm around my shoulder.

"I asked who was paying her, but she wouldn't answer. Why did she say you're married?"

"Because it's partly true," Marsk said. "My wife died. She was an elderly grandmatriarch. It wasn't the best of marriages. I was her third husband and was expected to produce children with other women in the clan. I didn't like it. I'm Seaguard, not a stud."

"What's a stud?" Reena asked, and the dragon dropped a needle. It clattered to the floor.

"Someone who helps women make babies," Mareen said smoothly.

Marsk said, "I'm still technically married to her clan, so that woman is right, but I never chose those women and never promised them anything."

"Have you considered taking this to court?" His case was similar to one's I'd been studying.

"That clan will fight hard," he said, "and I haven't wanted to until now."

"So here we are," I said. "All of us wanting to choose our own lives."

"Except for Spitfire," Marsk said. "She's making hats for dragons."

Reena now had yarn tangled around her starboard wing. That day in the palace she was knitting, but surely someday the girl would want more.

IN THE AFTERNOON I explained the prostitute's predicament to my study group.

Zelta said, "It would be human trafficking only if she were being forced into prostitution. She could choose another branch of medicine and doesn't have to be an andrologist."

"But if education funding is dependent on her compliance it's coercion into bodily penetration," Rose said. "In short, it's rape."

"But in giving prostate exams she's doing the penetrating," Zelta said.

What an odd game of logic. Should a surgeon be allowed to refuse a patient? "I'm in nearly the same bind," I said. "My clan wants me to run the clanless shelter. I don't mind the work, but it doesn't actually help the clanless. So I've applied to found a clan instead."

"Ah yes," Rayleen said. "And in exchange you agree to produce a child. That's not much different from prostitution. You're still a minor like this girl who prefers working as a prostitute. The truth is, your contract is on very shaky ground. Fennako could be held accountable for human trafficking."

I frowned. If coercion were the measure, Fennako was systematically engaged in human trafficking by victimizing members of the royal family. But how could you sue people for trafficking themselves? The tangle seemed to have no end. It just looped back on itself. Who was coercing whom?

———

Chapter 25
Man on the Floor

M Y MAN WENT into the hallway. I dozed, catching a bit more sleep. The door remained ajar. A shadow passed the doorway, and footsteps receded. A woman screamed. I sprang from bed and seized my robe. Still belting it, I ran into the hallway. Other doors opened. Bleary-eyed students in pajamas, nightshirts, and robes peered out.

"A man," someone exclaimed. "Naked. Bare ass naked."

My man burst through a gaggle of excited students. He was not entirely naked, but wore skivvies. "Excuse me ma'am. I'll be on my way." With dignity he joined me, and we returned to our room.

"One of your fellow students walked in on me," he said. She seemed to think I get my jollies from sneaking into women's dormitories."

"But you do."

"Only from sneaking in on you."

AT BREAKFAST, THE dining room was abuzz with talk of the mysterious man, "Stark naked and taking a leak."

The house mother approached me as I sat with Rayleen and Zelta.

"I understand there was a man in your room last night. Is this true?" she asked.

"Yes ma'am."

"What was he doing there?"

I gave what I hoped was an innocent smile. "Sleeping."

"That is strictly against house policy. Men are not allowed overnight. They're not allowed at all unless they're kinsmen or husbands. Do you happen to be married to that man?"

I could have truthfully answered in the affirmative. Our relationship was clan sanctioned and bounded by a contract, but I merely said, "That's under the strictures of hospitality."

The house mother glowered. "Do you expect me to believe that?"

"You may contact Fennako authorities for verification." I gave my claim number. "I might point out that we are paying for a couple's room, and if my partner were female, his presence wouldn't be questioned."

"We don't have facilities for men," she said. "Walking in on a naked man in the bathroom can be traumatic for a young woman. He might—"

"Find the woman attractive? Or is it that she might be traumatized by witnessing a good-looking man?"

"Male energy is disruptive," the house mother said.

"My fiancé was minding his own business. What would you do if a man wanted to study law? The Noah Code says educate your children and doesn't distinguish between male and female. The man who wrote that code must have visited his wife Fenna Lee-Smith." I was sure of it. The hidden passageway into her converted office had two possible uses—escape or covert visits. I gestured toward the courtyard and the statue beyond the window. "Their children are depicted in that statue."

"Why I never." The house mother put her hand to her chest. "To suggest that Fenna Lee-Smith and Jamie Noah—"

Zelta snickered.

"Virgin birth." Rose rolled her eyes. "Artificial insemination, each of Queen Fenna's four children was sired by one of the great studs."

I had evidence that Jamie Noah had sired at least one of those children, but that evidence was my brother's DNA. I said, "Fenna Lee-Smith slept with Jamie Noah. I follow precedents." In our case, I was Noahee sleeping with Fennako.

"Their relationship is purely allegorical," sputtered the housemother, "a representation of law and code."

"Is it?" I asked. "Who are your ancestors?"

She retreated to her office.

Zelta whooped. "You're a born lawyer. What a shiner."

"Precedents set by Fenna Lee-Smith." Rayleen laughed. "Never heard a better defense of making out with a boyfriend. Good-looking guy, too."

"Believe what you will."

"Do you actually have a hospitality claim number?" Rayleen asked.

"Find out for yourself. Tristan Bay Seaguard processes the claims."

As they left the dining room, Rayleen said, "I've seen your contract. Is that the man?"

"I'm not saying."

———

Chapter 26
Exposé

O N A BALCONY, I sipped fizzy drinks with Zelta and Rayleen. All of Fenria seemed to pass below, ascending or descending the city steps: fishermen in coveralls and parkas, businesswomen, financiers, shoppers, emissaries from distant clans. Zelta enjoyed watching the Seaguard couriers, mostly young men carrying important legal documents too sensitive to be entrusted to the network.

Seaguard couriers remained the favorite topic of speculation for law students.

"Take a look at him," Zelta said. "I wonder what he's carrying."

"In his satchel or his 'satchel'?" Rayleen asked.

Zelta set down her glass. "Why, over there. I think that's the King."

The middle-aged man in the plaza had a bit of a paunch and wore the kit of Royal Guard, aqua-gray with details in bright platinum. The Seaguard with him, also wearing aqua-gray, was younger—Marsk. I didn't wave or acknowledge him.

"He's probably coming from court," Rayleen said. "Or maybe from the Palace."

"That man beside him must be Lord Tristan Bay," Zelta said. "He's as handsome as Poseidon himself."

Rayleen lifted her glass to me. "Even better looking with his clothing off, aye?"

"Why would I know?" I said.

"Why shouldn't you know?"

"You know."

Rayleen set down her drink. "Aye, avoiding any news. Unwise for someone who works in law."

"I wasn't even supposed to see his face," I said.

"Well, you did," Rayleen countered.

"What are you talking about?" Zelta asked.

"Annin's sweetheart. She's pretending not to know just who sneaks into her bedroom every night."

"He's right up there with the King," Zelta sipped her fizzy.

"But the King is a geezer," Rayleen said. "And he's married to the Princess Royal. Nay, Annin here has gone for the best."

RETURNING TO LEE-SMITH Hall, we passed through the courtyard under the frozen gaze of my ancestress and her four children immortalized in stone.

The house mother greeted us and handed me my mail: a flyer, a formal envelope, and a small parcel. I swiftly pocketed all of it, refusing to ease the curiosity of either the housemother or my fellow law students.

Once in the privacy of my quarters I looked over the parcel, sent by Jeena Idylko, Teahk's lab technician friend. It contained rows of tiny glass tubes packed in foam—a DNA test kit. I closed the box. Would testing Marsk's DNA negate the contract? What if I were found out?

I hid it in the drawer of my desk.

The flyer displayed a detail of a painting, the torsos of two men, and advertised an art exposition titled NOAH DISROBED. Of course Angel's show would be of male nudes. But the title had me worried. As a direct descendent of Fenna Lee-Smith and Jamie Noah I had much to keep hidden. Disrobing either of them disturbed me.

The envelope contained a paper invitation, creamy parchment with gold lettering. I seldom received mail and had never received a formal invitation. It announced the time and place for the exposition and included a handwritten message:

> *Dearest Sis,*
>
> *Please come to our show. It would mean a lot to your brother and to me. Bring your student friends. They may be interested in meeting the other guests which will include prominent members of Clan Fennako.*
>
> *Best wishes.*
>
> *Matta Carrie—that's my artist name.*

That she mentioned Fennako while avoiding all other true names hinted at exactly who would attend. That unnerved me as much as the title of the exposition. She struck too close to the truth.

THAT EVENING, WHEN my man had emerged from the wall, I showed him the flyer and invitation. "This has me worried. What do you think?"

"I got those as well." He produced a similar flyer and invitation from his pocket.

"I take it that your one of those 'prominent' members. Maybe the only one. Do you know what's in the show?"

He shrugged. "Paintings I assume,"

"Of my brother?"

In the dim light, my man squinted at the nude torsos on the flyer. "Does that look like him?" He turned it toward me.

"Hard to tell," I said.

He set the flyer and invitation aside. "The artist is known for discretion."

"Do you know her?"

"Aye. I've sat for her. Not much came of it."

"We shouldn't be seen together," I said, realizing that I did in fact plan on going.

"If we arrive at different times, no one will think of us as together."

"There's something else." I opened the draw for the package of test tubes. "My brother is worried that you and I might be first cousins. He had this kit sent. If I see the results of your DNA test it will violate the contract. But then, I already am in your clan, so maybe it doesn't."

"My family doesn't want anyone to see my DNA test results. If people knew of the details of my maternal DNA, they could make counterfeit evidence and claim royal blood."

"It seems to me that a person could swipe royal hair from a royal comb, or spit from a toothbrush."

"They can't get into my bathroom or be sure that it's mine."

"We only need to know if you and I share a grandfather. That will satisfy my brother. We only need paternal DNA." I handed him the kit.

Marsk turned on a light. "Sorry to violate the codes against artificial light, but you're not testing my DNA in the dark." He spilled out the contents of a kit: vials, antiseptic swabs, adhesive bandages, and a lancet in sterile packaging. He held up the lancet. "You are after royal blood. Why not a cheek swab?"

"This is what the lab sent. It shouldn't hurt much. About like a paper cut."

"That hurts. Do my left hand."

I held his finger and stroked it against my cheek.

"What will you do if the test comes back positive for grandfather?" Marsk asked.

I kissed his fingertip. "Consider our chances. Our marriage might increase the risk of recessive disorders in our children."

"I'm considering that you're going to stab my finger." He pulled his finger within my grip.

I brought his hand to my mouth to kiss his fingers, one by one, cradling each one with my tongue.

"How about we skip the tests. Get down to other business."

"This won't take long. Which finger?"

"This one?" He offered his ring finger.

I cleaned the finger with a sanitary wipe. He kissed the top of my head. I tore open the package. I poised the sharp slip of metal against his skin and jabbed.

He pulled back. "Kinkill!"

I squeezed the finger, milking it, turning it purple. On the pad, a red bead of blood glistened. With my other hand, I removed a glass tube from its case and touched the glass tip to the ruby sphere. The blood raced into the capillary.

He took the tube from me. Working together we placed his blood in each of the tubes, then bandaged his finger.

"Now it's your turn." He opened the second kit and we took samples of my blood. We sealed both packages.

He set the kits aside. "Now let's get down to other business."

We shut off the light and tumbled onto the bed.

MY FELLOW STUDENTS giggled about the flyer. They took to the idea of the art show with great enthusiasm.

Rayleen laughed. "We're offing moral support."

"It's an art show, not a peep show." I corrected. "And it's relevant to our work as lawyers. Clans use paintings like this as part of marriage arrangements."

The house mother wasn't as excited. "I expect better from future lawyers," she scolded, and I agreed with her for once. "

I ATTENDED THE gallery opening along with a mob of law students. Angel welcomed us.

As my fellow students collected drinks and canapés, Angel whispered, "You-know-who hasn't arrived yet."

I smiled and nodded, acknowledging that I'd heard her, nothing more. I wandered casually about the gallery—tried to anyway—as I viewed floor-to-ceiling canvases of Teakh and another man. The nude paintings had a sense of grandeur as if the two men were larger than life, not just my brother and his friend, Keno, the one who ran a gym.

An alcove contained two paintings, one of Teakh, the other of Keno. Candlelight gleamed on a reliquary displayed in a locked case. The small gold box revealed a used condom, the detritus of sex displayed as if it were a precious object of religious devotion.

An art patron commented. "What a profound criticism of the cult of Noah."

"It's trash," another said. "I have an idea. Let's display used snot rags and call it art. How about ear wax?"

The first patron commented, "Semen, blood, and tears. Sacred or merely disgusting?"

While I was contemplating the strangeness of art, and weathering the storm of my emotions, two women in conservative robes came toward me.

222

Good Danna! The women were Valarin Hellenboreko and Cordalis Sibriko of the Eugenics Council. The last people I wanted to see.

I pasted on a smile and politely asked, "What are you about?"

"Interesting show you have here." Hellenboreko raised her eyebrows in a question.

I tried for intellectual sounding words. "Why, yes. Matta Carrie is a fine painter. So evocative."

"And you gave permission for this?" Hellenboreko demanded.

"My brother can do as he pleases," I said.

"Men need guidance," Sibriko added. "A firm hand."

"Take care. He will throw you off," said Hellenboreko.

How could I get out of this discussion smoothly?

I waved to Rayleen. "I have someone you might like to meet."

Rayleen came our way. I longed for a neural implant to warn her about these women. I made the introductions. "This is Rayleen. Senior in my study group."

"We're pursuing human rights law," she said.

"Oh, one of Gratia's brood?"

"I take it you're eugenics spawn?" Rayleen asked slyly.

"No need for that," Hellenboreko said. "The eugenics council takes a broad view. We all work toward the common good. The individual cannot exist without society."

"Or society without the individual," Rayleen said. "But come. Matta Carrie does gorgeous paintings."

"A provocative show," said Hellenboreko. She and Rayleen headed back toward the paintings. I'd have to thank Rayleen later for taking the woman off my hands, if only temporarily. Oh, they would be back. This I knew.

———

Chapter 27
Full Moon

G LOSSY, DARK WATER flashed with silver moonlight. In the cool evening, my man and I walked the waterfront. Nearby, spherical hydrogen tanks gleamed white. Luna Majora, nearly as round as the tanks, rose over the skyline of Fennako City.

My man opened a shed door and flashed a ruby light inside, illuminating an esskip on davits, its wings folded close against the fuselage. We scrambled inside and the canopy closed. "All set?" he asked.

"Aye"

The davits extended and we hung over the silky blackness of the water. With the release of the davits we plummeted.

A single flap of wings hauled our descent. He shifted in his seat, then with a sharp exhale he spread the wings and soared toward Tristan Head. The hydrogen tank farm on Lawrock Island receding to our stern. Nimbly, he jetted his craft over the seawall, and we coasted through an open hangar door.

OVERLOOKED BY THE bronze wolves of his bed, my man and I cuddled until I fell asleep. I awoke, and he was gone.

But his voice issued from room speakers, "A problem came up."

"Where are you?" I spoke to the ceiling molding with its hidden mircrophones and cameras.

"Upstairs in the Command Center."

I sighed. "I wish you were here."

"Same," he said.

After a shower and a change of clothing, I approached an opaque window. Robotic hands opened the curtains and the panes cleared to transparency revealing the sun rising over Tristan Bay. Both water and distant buildings sparkled in the morning light.

He hailed, his voice issuing from the ceiling. "On my way down. Breakfast is on its way from the kitchen."

When he returned he was wearing Tristan Bay Seaguard kit. In gray-green life vest and seaboots he strode to the dumbwaiter.

"The kitchen doesn't know you're here, but I claimed to be particularly hungry." He removed a plate filled with kippers, scramble eggs, fried potatoes, crisp bread, and cloudberry jelly followed by a single steaming mug of barley tea, boricha.

He handed me the mug before fetching another from a cupboard and filling it with water for himself. But we ended up sharing the beverage, both sipping out of the same mug.

"Tough morning. Everyone traveling." He reached across the table and squeezed my hand. "Thank you for being here. Full moon holidays are the worst. That time in Hanalee, I swear I wasn't trying to ignore you. I'm sorry I couldn't give you my full attention."

"It's alright," I said. "I'm used to it. My dad and all."

"Seaguard?"

"I assume so. He didn't visit often. During grand tides, the ocean flooded in under our cabin and we couldn't go anywhere. Sometimes he came..." I recalled his esskip skimming over brown water. He would tie up under the house and climb up through a trap door. "He brought gifts. We were happy then, a family."

"What about at low tide?"

"You can take an esskip over tidal flats."

"True," said my man.

"How would you spend the holiday," I asked. "if you could spend it anyway you wanted?"

"Honestly? With you. We'd go sailing. No ferry schedules, no air traffic control, just you and me on a boat."

"I'd love that. If only we could."

He sighed. "That's the way of things for Seaguard. All clan duty. No time for family."

"I always thought clan and family were the same."

He shook his head. "Far from it. We work so that others can be with their families for the grand tides."

"Well. Let's have a good time Even if we can't go sailing, let's have a good time. Anything you want." I lifted a shoulder and glanced through my eyelashes, my attempt at being sultry.

He licked his lips, his eyes gleamed.

What did he have in mind?

I'd read about the odd tastes of some men, bondage, whips and chains. If that's what he liked, I'd give it a try.

"Anything, except let's not get pregnant yet. No work. Just fun."

His eyes sparkeled, the gleam becoming a grin.

Hand-in-hand, we escaped into the bedroom, dishes left on the table.

"I've got some toys I'd like to try out," he said. "Lay down."

I stretched out on the velvet coverlet giving myself over to him, trusting him.

I unbuckled his vest. "Now close your eyes. May I hold your arms?"

"Please." I nodded, eager for whatever he had in mind.

His touch on my arm was cool and soft, not human skin. I peeped. A velvet-covered manacle encircled my wrist.

"It's a telechiric extension." He wiggled his fingers. "I can hold you in place and make love to you all at the same time. "Wanna try it?"

"Uh huh. Sure do." Velvet hands grasped my ankles and wrists, the grip responsive and not at all mechanical—a living touch.

The restraints released as he let go. "Depths! I'm needed in the command center. It's that damn grounded vessel. Kinkill!"

When he'd gone, I despondently loaded the dishes in the dumbwaiter and sent them down to the kitchen. Would the dishwashers notice the extra mug and fork?

Most likely the work was being done by adolescent boys, their first part-time jobs in the Seaguard. Teakh had done that job. Besides getting room and board, he'd been paid. My stale resentment resurfaced. The unfairness cut both ways. Usually girls had it better, but not always.

I adjusted the setting on the window glazing to gaze on the boats moving across the bay. I envied the boats moving freely over my beloved.

On the sculptural wall clock, the hour and tri-minute hands moved slowly, two-dozen tri-minutes to an hour, two-dozen hours to a day. I felt my heartbeat, three beats to a tri-minute.

Seated on the bed, I opened my screen for a sex manual with diagrams of various positions. The manual emphasized attention to one's lover as of utmost importance, far more important than technique.

The hour hand crept downward to noon and still he hadn't returned. The tri-minute hand began its descent from straight up before he again hailed.

We kissed at the door. I savored his touch, the scatch of his beard and the softness of his lips, all over too quickly.

I served dinner from the dumbwaiter, then we sat side-by-side dining on pork tenderloin and roast vegetables from the same plates.

"I've gotten a lot done," I told him, hoping to ease his regret. "It's been quiet."

He covered his ears. "The radio chatter is deafening. Good Danna! What a din." He stretched out his boot encased legs. "Let's go for a swim this evening. I'll sneak you into the Tristan Head gym and pool. That's where Harbor Patrol works out."

"I didn't know you had a swimming pool here," I said.

"Sure do. Teaching swimming is part of our job."

"I don't know how to swim."

"What! How can that be? You lived on a tidal flat that flood once a month."

"Yeah. I lived on a tidal flat with mud and swift currents. And I don't' have a swimsuit."

"No one will see you except me," he chuckled. "We can reserve the entire facility at five o'clock. That's when the evening watch is at supper. And day watch is still on duty."

"What about the night and morning watches?" I asked. "No need to disrupt the routine of the entire harbor patrol force."

"Rank has few enough privileges. I can't make love without getting Poseidon-damned authorization. I can't show you a good time. Good Danna I've left you alone all day. My kinsmen can sure as depths delay weightlifting for an hour."

228

He went to the dumb-waiter for dessert, bread pudding with clotted cream.

"A vessel ran aground last night during low tide," he mumbled. "My mistake. We had to divert seaplane landings to avoid the grounded vessel. Ferries and air flights are running behind schedule. Mechanical breakdowns in the Western Ocean. We're prioritizing travelers who are planning to conceive, and I have to follow up with clan breeding councils to make sure insemination has been approved."

"That's not always fair. What about couples who haven't registered a request with their clans?" I asked.

"There's nothing I can do anything about that. Those folks should plan ahead so that they don't get stranded. Some travelers claim they intend conception when they don't. I understand that, but it's not fair to travelers who get bumped. Nothing I can do about that either. What I can do is show you a good time, for a few moments anyway." He set the bread putting before me, and we took turns feeding it to each other.

"You're the one who's supposed to have a good time," I said as I fed him the last of the clotted cream.

In his chamber, my man stripped off life vest and shirt and sat on the edge of his bed. I stepped into his embrace.

He rested his chin on my head "You smell good." His breath stirring my hair

I snuggled in closer and he sighed, his tension releasing under my touch. "I may not be good for much. There's flooding near Trader's Wharf. And I've got seaplanes stacked up waiting to splash down. I didn't get much sleep last night."

"Do you do all of that?" I asked rubbing his shoulders.

"No, but I supervise those who do.

"I'll make you comfortable."

My man reached to open a drawer, which contained tubes, packages, and a number of unrecognizable devices. "I'm prepared," he said with a grin.

I looked over the selection and chose a bottle of oil."I'm your masseuse then."

My man was exhausted. He lay face down on the green velvet of the bed, his pants and boots still on. I straddled him and applied oil to my hands.

I should have studied up more on massage and less on bondage.

I smoothed my hands over his back, feeling his bunched muscles, and set to work kneading his tension away. As his muscles softened, his breathing became even until he drew in a snoring breath.

Taking care not to wake him. I opened cupboards and drawers until I found a blanket. I covered him and then slipped underneath the blanket beside him.

He shifted in his sleep then awoke with a start. "How long?"

"Only a few tri-minutes," I said.

He bolted upright. "The tide is ebbing, and the currents will be bad for small boats."

I touched my lips to his cheek. "Tide carry you."

"Aye. Tide carry."

WE RODE A freight elevator to the level of the weight room, gym, and pool. He apologized for the lack of a woman's locker room.

He changed into swim trunks then dove into the pool and swam with long, smooth strokes. I stripped down to my chemise and panties. Cautiously, I lowered myself into the water. Ralko Village didn't have a swimming pool, not even in the Seaguard men's house. And I'd been raised on that tidal flat—muddy water rushing in and out below or cabin. I went ahead with a dog-paddle.

My man finished a lap. His head came up. He hoisted himself out of the pool and returned with a foam board. "Try a kickboard. I'd give you lessons, but playing around is better. That's how people best learn."

Holding the floatation device by both edges, I set out across the pool. My man continued his laps. After swimming, we sat in the hot tub and relaxed in the bubbles.

"We'd better get going," he warned. "The afternoon watch will be here soon. They like the six o'clock slot. Workout before supper."

We showered, dressed, and dumped wet towels in a hamper. I carried my sopping underwear as we slipped into the passageway and returned up the freight elevator to his apartment.

We shared a bowl of smoked halibut chowder, savory with herbs and perfectly seasoned. Whoever was in the kitchen could do wonders with something as common as chowder. My man and I fed each other steamed crab buns, and finished off with a confection of raspberries and meringue. Twilight now filled the room and silver nightlights came on, the color appropriate to the full moon.

He stood. "I'd better make a showing in the dining room. The fellows will be wondering why I'm holed up in my quarters."

I tidied up then waited in the bedroom. Our relationship was proving to be extremely frustrating.

The lunar hand glowed bright as it pointed straight up to twelve. I opened the drawer beside the bed and looked over the contents, easily identifying condoms, lubricant, and sanitary gloves. Other items remained a mystery.

The hour hand had risen to seven before he hailed. "I'll be out a bit longer."

He hailed again at two-dozen after. "I've got a situation near Traders Wharf. I'll be with you as soon as we get it resolved."

"I'm tired of waiting." I spoke to the ceiling molding. "You make promises and never follow through."

"Good Danna. I'm sorry. I swear I'll make it up to you."

"When?" I demanded.

"When... when the tide is right. . . I'm sorry that sounds so weak. I shouldn't have invited you here. I'm sorry."

"No that's alright," I said, but I wasn't sure.

ALONE IN HIS apartment, I spread study materials and notes on the table. I tried to read and then gave up and paced.

Did I want this relationship?

We would never have much time together. Angel had warned me that I'd have to share him with the sea, and maybe with other women. I would become like my mother, living apart in hopes of seeing my father on the sly, and only occasionally at that. I had no idea if my father had another wife and other children.

The moon rose higher. I could tell him it was over. We could conceive a child as originally planned and end the relationship. If he'd agree to it. He might.

Realistically it wouldn't be over. My feelings for him wouldn't end. We'd come in contact with each other—awkward encounters. We would pretend we hadn't met—pretend that we didn't care for each other. We would ignore that we had a child together. Try to ignore this. What would I say to our child?

I shook my head.

What if I stayed in the relationship? I would be with him some of the time—time that he could spare. I glanced down at my study materials open on the table.

As a lawyer, I could advocate for him. I could make the time.

I dropped down on my chair at the table, my resolution made. I would stay.

AT NEARLY TEN o'clock he returned, haggard. He stripped off his vest and boots then said, "We should be good until the morning watch change. Danna providing nothing happens at high tide this midnight. Good Danna! We get these high tides every three years. You'd think merchants would plan."

I gathered and stowed my study materials.

In the bedroom he pulled off the rest of his clothing and leaned back on the mound of pillows. Silver light from the wall clock limned his profile.

"So tell me, what would make you happy?" I sat on the bed beside him. I now wore a silk chemise that didn't hide much. I'd bought it with Angel. Blue embroidery circled the neckline. "I've been doing some reading," I said. "I'm willing to try about anything."

"Whatever you want to try."

I admired his long, lean body. He didn't have the heavy musculature of some men, but he was fit, a swimmer's body. His penis lay in a nest of dark hair. I stroked his chest and then lifted his penis, naming the parts.

Lightly I wrapped my finger and thumb around the shaft of his penis and stroked from base to tip. He sighed and settled into the pillows. His penis rose in my hand, and the glans pushed past the foreskin. I flicked the tip with my tongue. I kissed it, then slid the head into my mouth.

"Oh Danna," he whispered.

So this was the way to help him relax.

"Turn around," he said, his voice husky.

I turned so that I faced his feet. His tongue licked into me.

I was confused. Should I try to please him? Or should I think about how he was pleasing me?

I moaned appreciatively then inhaled, bringing the tip of his penis against the back of my throat. With each rock of his hips I opened to him. What did seminal fluid taste like?

I'd soon find out. My lips reached the base of his penis, my nose against the suede soft skin of his scrotum.

Fluid filled my mouth. My throat constricting, ejecting him from my mouth. I licked my lips, sampling the flavor, not all that sweet and somewhat tannic. "I gagged," I said.

"Nothing wrong with that." He rolled me over. "Your turn."

"But you're spent."

"You aren't." He reached for an object in the drawer.

HE STIRRED, THE velvet coverlet shifting.The clock hour hand pointed to four. He dressed in the dimness then stooped to kiss my cheek.

"Breakfast is in the dumbwaiter," he said. "And there's tea in the cupboard. See you at noon. Earlier I hope."

When I awoke again, sunlight filled the room. Wearing my robe, I opened the dumbwaiter for breakfast, now cold.

After eating I cleared the table, showered, dressed, and straightened the bedding. Then I sat again at the table and wrote up a report on life in a Seaguard men's house, leaving out my research into sexual technique.

Legalities? Legalities.

In the grand political scheme, what did it matter that powerful men weren't getting enough sleep?

Yet, possibly my man had grounded a vessel because he was tired. And he wasn't the only Seaguardsman with such a brutal schedule. Surely my father had attempted the same precarious balance between family and clan.

We departed in the morning between changes of watch, avoiding patrols men coming and going.

We sped toward Lawrock Island and splashed down in the palace lagoon and coasted into the palace esskip hangar. Anyone who was watching would have thought he was visiting his sister.

"Will you stay with me during the new moon?" he asked.

"I'll be with you." I squeezed his hand.

Together, we entered the underground utility corridors.

I SAT WITH my study group in a Lee-Smith Hall meeting room. When my turn to share came, I stood and announced: "I have a report on problematic labor practices within the Seaguard."

"This is a change," Rayleen said. "Last we spoke you were advocating for the clanless."

"I'll still advocate for the clanless. But, in a Seaguard men's house, I've noted work shifts exceeding sixteen hours, and Seaguardsmen deprived of sleep. "

"It's a full moon holiday during the conjunction of the moons." Rayleen shrugged. "It happens only every six years."

"Every three years," I corrected. "For Danna sake! It's during spawning tides. When are these men to have families?"

"I don't see the problem. Fishermen have similar work patterns, periods of intense work followed by downtime."

"Aren't you listening? It's during the spawning tides,"

I repeated my voice rising. "All of us women have three days to ourselves once a month. Seaguard lords are always on call. They don't have time off. And they don't have time for family. It's a brutal, lonely life."

"Whoa!" exclaimed Rayleen. "You've come a long way."

"I have." I lifted my chin.

———

Chapter 28
Royal Tanistry

NEARLY A TWELVENIGHT later, the waning moon had shrunk to a sliver visible only at dawn. I packed my valise for the New Moon holiday, the tide of reflection and meditation—for women anyway. Fittingly, I included my oldest and most comfortable tunics along with extra panties. And of course, menstrual pads.

On my way out, the house mother stopped me beside the front desk. "Dear, do let me know where you'll be staying. I only ask for safety's sake."

"So kind of you," I said with a sincere smile, despite my irritation. Depths! I hadn't prepared an answer. "I'm not going far," I said quite honestly. "An acquaintance knows where I am and has given me leave to stay in their cabin."

Honest, except that the suite of Lord Tristan Bay wasn't in any way a remote cabin.

I left by way of the courtyard, passing before the stony gaze of Fenna Lee-Smith with her clinging children. I traveled alone to the ferry terminal as if I were leaving Tristan Bay. Inside a door to the utilidor, my man waited. I slipped inside with him and the door shut, closing off the passengers waiting to board ships.

His embrace enfolded me with comfort and a sense of home.

We set off along the utilidor.

"What about the spitfire?" I asked.

"What about her?"

"It's the new moon. Don't you want to be with your niece?"

He sighed. "She'll be with the other palace children. Too much work for me with the new moon tides. Not as bad as full moons, but still too much for me to spend time with her."

"I know how it is," I said. "I don't have an uncle. Not a real uncle. My brother and I tried to be quiet and take care of ourselves during the new moon."

"No big team games? No swimming or sailing?"

"We didn't have a place to swim and lived by ourselves. So no. Not until we moved into the village. But we didn't know how to play the games."

We hiked underground to the palace lagoon for his esskip then flew to his place. At about half-past eight we glided into a docking bay in his place.

"Depths!" My man swore. "One of my cousins is over there." He jerked his head to the side. "Get down."

Harness unbuckled, I crouched in the cockpit.

The canopy opened briefly, and my man scrambled out.

He was gone.

I gazed upward through the glazing at the tracks and gantries crossing the ceiling. A nearby door opened onto the lagoon. The door slid upward, blocking the window above, and an esskip exited.

My man hailed. "All clear. Go quick."

The canopy opened.

I grabbed my valise, scrambled out of the cockpit, and made for the elevator. My man waited at the top.

THE SOLITUDE HAD a familiarity—that of my childhood spent on the tidal flats with brown water rushing below our house and no place to go.

I settled into the apartment for a comfortable stay—no place I'd rather be.

My man went to work in the command center while I reviewed my notes, jotted while court was in session.

At noon he joined me and had lunch: sole with mushrooms and sunchokes.

He paused mid-bite. He set down his fork and put a hand to his head.

"Are you transmitting?" I asked.

He nodded then said, "My mother would like to meet you. She's on her way here."

"Here?" I asked. "Now?" My voice rose to a squeak. "The princess Mar..." Then I recalled not to use names. She was none other than Princess Mareen Fennako Senior.

I wore an old, favorite smock with frayed cuffs and multiple repairs. My laundry was soaking in the bathroom. If I'd sent panties, pads, and linens through the men's house laundry, the Seaguard men would know a woman was in the house. Bedsheets might be passed off as stained by a nosebleed, but not pads and panties.

"Aye. She's an excellent pilot and often drops in. She makes sure I'm taking good care of myself: making my bed, that sort of thing."

"Or who is in your bed?" I asked.

"She approves. We wouldn't have gotten together otherwise."

WE GREETED HIS mother in the esskip hangar, cleared of all personnel. Her gray-green esskip glided into a docking bay, and the canopy retracted. The sides of her head had been shaved to display intricate implant scars. Her remaining gray hair had been pulled into a queue and tied with a silk ribbon.

My man assisted her in stepping ashore and made the introductions; "Dearest, this is my mother. Mother, please met my fiancée."

Other than her implant scars, she didn't appear to be Seaguard. She wore neither life vest nor boots. Her hooded robe had strands of aqua-gray woven into the fabric. It wouldn't have been out of place on a lawyer or judge.

She held out her arms showing off her robe. "I came from work, entertaining visiting dignitaries."

We went up to the apartment. She entered with her shoes on as if they were Seaguard boots.

The door closed.

"It's safe to use names here," said my man. " The room has a faraday cage built into the walls. I keep a watch for electronic bugs. My mother, Mareen Fennako." He nodded to her and then to me. "Annin Noahee né Ralko."

"There are a lot of Mareens in the family," she said. "A political move. I go by Big Mareen if that helps."

"And 'Marsk?'" I asked.

"Aye, similar. You're observant. It's a reminder that we're a family. To business. I came to warn you. Take action with the next Full Moon. That's unless there's something you haven't told me."

"What kind of action? I don't understand?"

"Fulfill the contract," she said. "Have you done so?"

I understood her drift. "I'm not pregnant yet."

"It might be wise to behave as if you are. Since you're sequestered here, no one will know if you've menstruated or not."

"Unless I sent clothing through the laundry," I said. "I have not. What's going on?"

"Your relationship threatens my sister. If she gets the chance, she'll scuttle it. She's already tried."

"You mean in Hannalee with the love facilitators?" I asked.

"Aye. And before that. Let me explain."

We went to the sitting area. My man and I sat on the sofa. Big Mareen remained standing near the window. She said, "Our disagreement started with the birth of my daughter, Mareen. She was supposed to be a boy, but I refused to use gender selection procedures. My sister has never forgiven me for that. Even after I bore a son."

"A matriarchy which prefers boys? That's odd." I squeezed my man's hand.

She glanced our way. "Not odd at all. Every girl in the royal family could ascend the throne. We practice tanistry. The queen chooses her heir from amoung them. When I gave birth to a girl I produced yet another contender. Better to have boys. They aren't in competition. "

"But your son isn't a contender. What difference does it make who he loves?"

"A big difference. Your relationship represents an alliance between Noahee and Fennako. With Noahee support, my daughter could supplant my sister as heir. This my sister won't allow."

I asked, "Was all of our trouble her doing? The love handlers? The clinic in Galvanko?"

"Aye. She insisted that the liaison remain clinical. She oversteps her authority. Always has. I was also supposed to be a boy. My family was disappointed, but my sister and I initially made a pact. I'd still become Lord Tristan Bay regardless of my gender. After the birth of my daughter, my sister went back on our agreement."

My man said, "She would have done well as Lord Tristan Bay. Maybe better than me."

She said, "You do an excellent job of it. I'm proud of you, and I support your choice of fiancée." She turned to me. "My sister has done everything in her power to neutralize me and my children. I wasn't allowed to marry. Her husband sired my children. My daughter was restricted to only one child and forbidden a relationship of her own. My son—" her gaze softened.

My man put his arm around me. "I was given in a marriage of convenience."

"It seemed like a good arrangement," she said. "He married a woman past childbearing age and so could choose his own relationship, provided it was in the same clan."

"Do you mean a handler?"

"To put it bluntly, but he never bonded."

"I couldn't." He passed a hand over his forehead. "I visited only during the full moon, often for only a few hours. They tried to have me impregnate one woman after another until I finally refused."

"I'll never be a lord and I'll never be queen. I have no designs on the throne for myself or my family," Big Mareen said. "I want my sister to stay away from us. I can accept that. I cannot accept her interference with my children and grandchildren. We must be allowed to choose our own relationships. I hope you can help us with this. We need you as a lawyer. I pushed to get you into law school. I hope you'll be patient with us. We're a small family and have no experience with monogamous marriage."

"I thank you," I bobbed my head in a semblance of a bow.

"Don't thank me yet. You're bound to have a tough time of it. I suggest making an appointment for a prenatal exam but go on a honeymoon instead. Anyone snooping will expect you to be in town for the appointment. Cut all communication while you're gone. Return prepared to look like and act as the leader of a clan. Even if the pregnancy doesn't take, you'll have a stronger case."

"We can't leave immediately," my man said. "I'll have to make arrangements."

"So do I. My brother is scheduled for a liaison. As a stud. I promised to stay in communication with him. In this, I'm acting as both his lawyer and clan matriarch."

"I understand you have an esskip on order for your brother. I'll expedite the process. Make sure you're incommunicado during the full moon holiday."

"I do have a responsibility to him."

"You can trust me to look in on him and make sure all goes smoothly. We have been monitoring him for years. We need you safe and ready to be a clan leader."

"You mean pregnant."

"Aye. Secure in your contract. My sister fears Noahee will support nomination of Mareen as royal heir, my tanist, with the rest of the Seaguard lords following the Noahee lead. They will force my sister's hand. You are a queen maker. What you do in the next month will determine royal succession."

———

Chapter 29
Royal Kin

MY MAN GAVE me a lift back to Lawrock Island. As we hiked amid the pipes and conduits of the utilidor, I said, "If I lived at your place you wouldn't have to fly over to visit me."

"I'd have to give you a ride to Lawrock to meet with your study group. It's about the same either way."

We walked farther. A relationship with a Seaguard lord was proving difficult. Angel had warned me that I'd have to share him with the sea. I was determined to make it work. It was mostly a matter of scheduling.

"I'm sorry about how I was in Hanalee," I said. I hadn't known about his disastrous marriage and had been pushing hard for immediate pregnancy. "I didn't realize how it was for you."

"You couldn't have known. I was still angry, but I shouldn't have taken it out on you."

We reached the door into the ferry terminal and his hand crept to mine. He said, "What I like best? Sleeping beside you. No pressure. Just being together. When you told me you didn't want to get pregnant it meant a lot to me. I knew you cared about me for myself, not for what I could give you. Or I hope that's what it meant."

"It is." There was no denying that he could give me a lot, but he was a good man, one I could love. I did love him.

IN LEE-SMITH HALL, I unpacked and checked my messages.

> *Hailing Annin, Jeena Idylko here.*
>
> *I have the results of your tests. Please let me know how you'd like to receive them.*
>
> *Jeena sending*

I went downstairs to the laundry in the basement. I had to wait my turn. This always happened after the New Moon. Standing with the other students, I considered how to respond to Jeena, keeping in mind that my communications were most likely be monitored and that correspondence with Jeena could put me at risk. My turn came up. I loaded the machine and adjusted the cycle for cold soak followed by a hot wash. I realize that the tests mentioned could just have easily been for pregnancy, not necessarily on the genetics of the father. Other girls studied while waiting on the machines. I sat as if studying and wrote:

> *Hailing concerned friend*
>
> *Confidentiality is of utmost concern. Please avoid using names in all forms of communication. Neither the mail nor Network communications are secure. We must meet in person as soon as possible.*
>
> *Your friend sending*

When the laundry was clean and dry, I gathered it in a sack and returned upstairs to my quarters. Again I checked my messages.

Hailing my friend.

I understand. I can arrange to meet you in the next few days where you live and will provide my own travel.

Concerned friend sending

Amazed at Jeena's generosity, I stared at the screen. Travel from Idylko to Fennako City would cost money and take time. Why would she agree to such extravagance for a woman she'd never met?

TWO DAYS HAD passed since Big Mareen had given the warning. I'd set up a prenatal exam for the ninth of the month. At night Marsk and I slept together in Lee-Smith Hall. Under the covering noise of the aged fan, we whispered our plans to go sailing. I packed my valise.

My comset bleated with an announcement of a visitor. I went down to the lobby. A woman waved and smiled. She had chestnut hair, smooth skin, and large brown eyes.

"Greetings my friend," she said, her words repeated a line from the message and so established her identity as Jeena.

I repeated the closure of the letter, confirming my own identity. "Your concern means so much to me."

"Your brother borrowed your tea set," Jeena said. "He hopes you don't mind."

It had been a toy tea set borrowed years ago in one of his childhood schemes. "That scoundrel."

Our identities established, I suggested a visit to a place called Aristotle's Coffee House. Rayleen had assured me that the place had enough background noise to mask conversation.

"What is coffee?" Jeena asked.

"Some sort of drink. On Earth, students drank a lot of it, or so I'm told. This place serves baricha." Apparently, roasted barley was the best substitute for some sort of plant which grew only on Earth.

At the coffee house, I opened the door and was hit by a blast of music, conversation, and the promised milk-heating machine. We ordered two barichas with steamed milk and choose a table near the back of the room. The trick was finding a place with enough cover noise, but not too much.

I blew at the foam on top of my drink. The milk heating machine made a satisfactory whooshing sound.

Jeena unfolded a reader screen. "He's not your brother," she announced. "At least not your paternal brother."

"Are you saying he could be my mother's son?" I shook my head. Big Mareen wasn't my mother unless maybe Marsk or I had been adopted. That wasn't likely.

"All I'm saying is that his Y DNA is different from your brother's, so they had different fathers. The strange thing is this—" Jeena paused, and the milk machine whooshed. "Their mitochondrial DNA is identical. So is yours"

"That can't be." Marsk's mother was Princess Mareen Fennako Senior, Royal Minister of Finance and Banking. My mother had lived in a salt marsh, and no one seemed to know what she'd done for a living.

"I'm only saying what the tests show. You're not siblings. The rest of the genetics aren't that close, but have a shared female ancestor."

"He's Fennako royalty." My perception abruptly shifted. I'd been concerned about Marsk's grandfather when I should have been worried about his grandmother. Oh, one should never underestimate the queen.

If Jeena was telling the truth, and she had no reason to lie, my grandmother had been a member of the royal family. What if my mother had a neural implant? She could have been a Seaguard lord monitoring Arctic or Antarctic weather, an ice lord. But if so, surely Teakh would have been her heir.

Jeena leaned forward. "Here's what I think. The Noah Eugenics Project concentrated the genes of Jamie Noah. So where did they get the original material? The project harvested eggs from royal women and put them in surrogate mothers. Your grandmother escaped from that project."

Maybe. But there was another possibility nearly as dark. My grandmother had been yet another Fennako princess who'd given birth to a girl instead of a boy. The Royal family may have had too many girls competing for the throne. In order to protect her daughter she'd gone into hiding.

I didn't recall neuro scars on my mother's scalp. Surely as a child I would have noticed something like that. "Do you know if everyone with a Seaguard implant has scars?"

"I don't know. Why do you ask?"

The milk machine didn't seem load enough to protect me. How had my mother and grandmother died? I asked. "So should I marry this man?" I'd meant to say have children with him.

Jeena closed her screen. "It's up to you. Your genes suggest you share a common female ancestor, so you're cousins, but not close cousins."

By marrying, Marsk and I would gain much for ourselves and for our families. "What do you recommend?" The risk of recessive disorders might be acceptable. Was this how it felt to be queen, balancing genetics, and politics against personal feelings? What right did I have to risk the health of future generations?

Jeena set her cup aside. "Our ability to choose mates

has evolved over time, same as our ability to breathe and to eat. If you like the man, bear his children. If you dislike him, stay away. You be the judge. Trust your intuition."

"One more thing," I said. "Please destroy this information. I don't want it falling into the wrong hands." The caution might be too late. I'd given Fennako samples for genetic tests. They already had evidence that Teakh and I were members of the royal family. Jeena agreed easily, as if such a request was routine, and maybe it was which was disturbing in and of itself.

———

Chapter 30
Honeymoon

MY MAN AND I had agreed to tell no one other than his sister and his mother of our honeymoon plans. In the dark of early morning I passed the statue of Fenna Lee-Smith. I remained tense. My ancestress loomed dark against glittering stars, the milk of Danna splashing the night sky.

My man traveled through the city utilidors while I tread the steep lanes descending Lawrock. The tang of kelp drifted from the royal esskip lagoon. Waves lapped the riprap of the seawall. A drone flashed across my path flitting into the darkness of an open side door. I followed into the Royal Hangar, a cavernous space dimly lit with rosy light.

Mareen waved from the cockpit of an esskip. "Over here."

She accepted my valise and handed me a life vest—probably green, but in the red light it appeared to be nearly black.

My man emerged from behind a row of esskips and lightly stepped onto the wing shoulder. He stooped and our lips met too briefly. He took the seat behind me.

The door of the docking bay slid upward to reveal the moonless night, the sky alight with stars so dense they seemed to be clouds of silver.

Mareen glided from the hanger and out onto the shining black of the lagoon. With a shudder of power, we cleared the embankment in flight, soared over the bay. Behind us Fennako City lay nearly dark in the starlight, only a few red lights twinkling from the islands.

"Brother, how do you feel?" Mareen asked, not turning from the consol or her view through the fairing.

My man spoke from behind me. "Odd. I reach for things which aren't there."

"He's been removed from the Sense-net," Mareen said as she flew. "Mama has taken over as Seaguard Lord. Something she has always wanted."

"You can do that?" I twisted in my seat trying to see his face. "What about phantom pain?"

"None yet." His face remained obscure. "Grandmother invoked royal override."

"Maybe it'll kick in," said Mareen. "Like losing a leg."

"I've only been Lord Tristan by for what? Seven years? Not long enough to form that kind of attachment. And this removal is only temporary."

"It's better this way," said Mareen. "No one can force him home with an engineered emergency. Grandmother can do it. She can remove anyone from the Sense-net."

"Remove or depose?" I asked.

"They are the same. The Queen can depose and replace anyone," said my man. "Anyone in her power that is."

"So, Big Auntie becomes queen. Will she depose you?" I asked.

"Only if he is still in her power," Mareen said. "He can revoke royal override, but it's a risky move. Consider if he became a danger to himself and others. We'd be stuck with him as lord."

From behind me, my man spoke. "Access codes for Tristan Bay won't fall to her but to my sister here, our lovely pilot."

"Just so long as I don't go crazy," Mareen said. "Then we'll all be stuck. Here's how it is: whoever gets the most override codes becomes the next monarch. They're basically votes. Grandmother threw her codes to Big Auntie. Most of the Seaguard supports her choice. I won't be getting a majority. Not by a long shot."

"So the monarchy isn't hereditary?"

"Effectively," said Mareen. "We do have a dynasty going all the way back to the Great Fenna."

"If another person accepted override codes, would that person be queen?"

"If she had a Seaguard implant and could garner the majority of the codes," Mareen said. "Of course."

"How secure is this esskip against surveillance?" I asked.

"Did you bring your comset?"

"We agreed to remain incommunicado, so I left it behind."

"In that case, my implant is our only radio communication. If you have something sensitive to discuss, now is the time."

"What if a man received a majority of the codes?" I took a deep breath. "Suppose my brother did."

"You're dangerously smart," said Mareen.

"He could become Queen. That's what you're saying?"

"We'd have a civil war. It's what Big Auntie fears. She'll do anything to stop it."

I circled around my mother's mysterious illness and death. "What about assassination? Do they occur in the Royal family?"

Clouds now obscured the stars and darkness pressed against the glazing of the canopy. My man remained silent. The esskip hummed as we sped over the dark seas.

Mareen shifted uneasily in her seat. "We do not speak of this."

To protect Teakh and myself, I had to know what had happened to my mother and grandmother.

Depths! I played a deadly game of justice poker, my brother's life on the chit. Probing carefully, I sought information; "Do you know of a woman in the Royal Family who disappeared about—" I estimated when my grandmother arrived in Ralko waters. "four-dozen years ago? It's some curious information that I came across." I tried to sound casual. "A woman died suddenly of a fever. Might this have been an assassination?"

"It's unlikely," Mareen said. "Women seldom have implants."

In mentioning an implant she confirmed my fears—a neural implant used as a murder weapon.

"You're right," I said. "We should not speak of these things."

Who did I trust? The current Queen would die soon. Big Auntie feared Clan Noahee. The Eugenics Council lurked.

"Sister-in-law," I said. "I throw you Clan Noahee administrative access. You have our vote and our full support."

"I'm honored," said Mareen. "A wise and difficult choice; with Danna's grace, we won't see civil war."

I'd also passed her the danger of assassination, but I didn't say so.

WE APPROACHED OUR destination, a small-boat harbor bright in the morning sunlight. On the dock, my man and I thanked Mareen and I returned the borrowed life vest. It really was green.

We went to the harbormistress's office.

"Newlyweds." She beamed. "I can just tell."

"Hospitality." My man shushed her. "We don't want our honeymoon disturbed. Our friends are likely to spring surprises on us."

"Boisterous friends," she said with a knowing smile. She gave us a key fob and directions to our rented sailboat, the Fairweather. "They won't be able to find you for playing practical jokes. I promise."

We located the single-masted sailing sloop. The cleats and furnishings gleamed. Inside the cabin, packages burdened the galley table.

"Open up your presents," my man said with glee.

I ripped off the wrapping from waterproof knee boots, pants, pullover, parka, hat, gloves, and a sky-blue life vest.

"Try it all on," my man suggested.

"You'll get distracted."

"I'll try not to." He tucked his hands under his thighs. The boots fit perfectly. "How did you get my size?"

"Your brother's girlfriend."

"Angel?"

"She calls herself that." He held out a small package. "Don't forget this."

It contained a waterproof comset with earbuds and speaking microphones. The comset included an emergency locator beacon and went into a specially designed vest pocket.

"It's got an emergency locator beacon. Tuck it into the pocket of your vest. Specially designed. But what's best"—his eyes sparkled—"it's not cluttered with contacts. No interruptions for a whole half a twelvenight."

"Six days, just the two of us." I shared his glee, his nearly unattainable dream.

We dined on smoked salmon, ripe cheese, and sunflower seed crackers, then went over safety procedures.

My man showed me the emergency life raft in a case strapped to the deck. He pointed out the certification. "I did a lot of inspections before I became a magnate. Stay off of boats that lack a certified life raft. You don't know what else might be wrong with the vessel. Use the life raft only as a last resort. Get everyone aboard the raft, then free the painter. Make sure the emergency locator beacon is working. You've got two of them, one on your vest, the other on the raft."

"I'm not leaving you behind," I said.

"You might be on the boat without me. Stuff happens. Be prepared."

Using a small propulsor, my man and I chugged out of the harbor. Clear of the breakwater, we hoisted sail.

Wind caught the fabric and the sail belled. The boat seemed to leap across the seas. My man's happiness was infectious. I'd never seen him this relaxed. My own tension melted away. Yes, this is what most men on Fenria lived for. They didn't care about politics or voting; as long as a man could sail, one hand on the tiller and the other arm around his girl. I snuggled against him

He pointed to a chart on the binnacle. "We're approaching a clan boundary. I'll show you how to do it." He flicked the comset at his shoulder and hailed. "This is the sailing vessel Fairweather under hospitality of Aluko. We're on a vacation cruise."

"Fairweather. Heave to and stand by."

"I'm accustomed to being on the other end of hospitality requests." He dropped sail.

As we waited, he used the propulsor, steering the craft into the swells. The bare mast traced a lazy arc across the blue sky.

His comset activated. "Fairweather. You have the codes and may proceed."

"That's it," he said.

At night, we anchored in coves or near fishing villages. We slept in the forward berth and made love when we felt like it, all hurry gone. He taught me to navigate by the stars and how to do dead-reckoning. We went into villages to purchase more food, but otherwise we stayed to ourselves for five glorious days.

We spent the Full Moon holiday pulled into a cove, digging clams at low tide. We went skinny dipping, then built a fire to steam clams. That night we attempted to make love in the moonlight while standing in the cockpit near the tiller. But the wind was cold, so we retreated to the forward berth. We snuggled together enjoying the warmth after the nip of the night breeze.

On the thirteenth day of the month we charted a course for our rendezvous point. Seated in the stern he slumped as if a great weight had settled on his shoulder.

"I'm Lord Tristan Bay again." He touched a finger to his ear. "In link with Fennako Harbor Patrol."

We pulled the Fairweather into the assigned slip. Harb shouted and waved from the dock.

"Someday I'll introduce myself properly," Harb said after we stepped ashore. "Congratulations to both of you. Nice duds, by the way." He grinned at me. "I'll trade an esskip for this sailboat. Shuttle it back to the rental place."

"Thanks, cous'," said my man.

"My pleasure."

My man and I stopped by the public washhouse for laundry and showers, sluicing away the aroma of wood smoke, brine, and sweaty love. I dressed in a navy-blue tunic trimmed with white and fastened with intricately knotted frogs, the effect smartly nautical or so I hoped.

I secured my old, cheap comset in the shoulder pocket. My man emerged from the washhouse resplendent in Fennako Seaguard kit, his transformation from relaxed skipper to Seaguard Lord complete.

As we flew from the harbor, I glanced down to see the Fairweather under sail as she passed the breakwater.

We skimmed over the ocean, traveling between dark mountainsides.

Aunt Dyse hailed, "Where have you been? I've been worried sick about you."

"Did you contact my brother?" I asked.

"I can't get ahold of him either," she complained. "He had his first liaison this Full Moon holiday you know. And that esskip was supposed to be delivered."

"It has been," I said and signed off. My man had relayed that the Teakh's new craft awaited pickup in Dojko.

"My aunt is in a tizzy," I said. "She'd like us to report to her every time we sneeze. My brother probably did the same thing we did. Nothing kills the romantic mood like a fussing aunt."

"Or upset freighter captains," my man said. "When I'm flying, my implant filters all non-essential communication. Your brother is likely to be flying his telechiric. Fussing aunts are flight hazards. It's the truth."

There was no need to worry. My brother could take care of himself.

———

Chapter 31
Gift

WAVELETS RIPPLED ACROSS the reflective surface of the Dojko lagoon as my man brought his esskip down. Atop the lagoon breakwater, two Seaguardsmen in blue and gray stood at attention. One caught our tossed painter and snugged it to a cleat. The other Seaguardsman, a gentleman with white hair and beard, welcomed us as we stepped ashore.

"Please accept the hospitality of our clan." He bowed.

He was without a doubt Lord Dojko, but out of politeness and custom we didn't mention it.

"Honor to you and your kin." My man returned the bow.

Lord Dojko caught my eye. "Congratulations on your new clan. That's a fine esskip you've got for your brother."

I grimaced. "Hospitality." I corrected his breach of etiquette.

He winked. "We're truly honored. As I understand it"—he scratched his ear—"You and your brother aren't supposed to know the identity of this fellow." He flicked his thumb toward my man. "But it doesn't take keen observation skill to know his identity. It's difficult to conceal. I suggest that he remain here while you go on over to the small-boat harbor to meet with your brother.

We'll send someone to deliver his new craft. That'll avoid any awkward meetings."

Following Lord Dojko's directions, I headed south, keeping the water to my right. A seagull flew with me, a very large seagull with eyes that weren't quite natural. Camera lenses?

"Greetings," I said to Teakh's telechiric. Aunt Dyse had been making entirely too much of a fuss.

The drone flew off and I continue along the waterfront.

Cousin Gorby's black and scarlet esskip floated snubbed to a dock. He clambered out of the cockpit.

"Auntie went to talk with Teakh," Gorby said, hands in pockets. "He's not responding to hails."

"He's fine. I saw his bird over near the lagoon."

"He hasn't responded since the day before yesterday, not to messages, not even to emergency hails."

"That's not like him." Maybe something had gone wrong.

"That's like him." Gorby nodded.

An esskip rounded the breakwater. The tail of the gray-and-white craft displayed NOAA425, our designation. It taxied toward us.

Dyse traipsed down the dock ramp, followed by Teakh clad in a ratty sweater and ragged pants.

Something was wrong. I could see it in the way he slouched. Had his first liaison been as bad as mine? Or worse—as bad as my man's first marriage?

He wouldn't meet my eye. "Don't want to talk about it." He stared at the tail. "November, Ophelia, Alpha, Alpha. Where'd you get that call number?"

"Fennako. We're a clan." This was supposed to be a happy occasion. Our clan had become a reality.

"How'd you pay for it?" he demanded.

"A loan. We'll be able to pay it off." I couldn't discuss the details of the loan, not here and not now. I could nearly feel the multiple cameras and eyes watching me.

"Isn't it wonderful?" Dyse gushed. "You now have an esskip, just like real Seaguard."

"He is real Seaguard," I muttered.

Oblivious to Teakh's foul mood, Dyse said, "If you return the gift, you'll still be responsible for the non-refundable design fees."

I glared at her, but she went on, "We had it delivered last twelvenight. It's been waiting for you."

Teakh's face was now stony. What was he thinking? Or was he accessing information on the Network?

He looked up and smiled, a false smile. "I accept the gift."

I stepped close to him and whispered, "We need to talk. Let's get into the craft.". Keep pretending to be grateful." In the security of the esskip we could have an honest discussion.

"It's wonderful. I'm so pleased." His act reeked of insincerity. He lifted his shoulders in a shrug to open the canopy. It barely moved. He tried again, and the canopy shuddered on its track.

We climbed inside. With the canopy closed I spoke to the back of his head. "What's wrong?"

He turned towards me. "We can't afford an esskip."

"Don't shine me. You were upset before you saw it. Why haven't you responded to Dyse's hails?"

"That hag!"

"She may be a hagfish, but I can't help you unless I know what's bothering you."

"If you must know I have—I had a quarrel with Angel." He changed the subject. "How did you get that call number? Who did you bribe?"

"I fulfilled the contract."

"I take it you're pregnant? Where's that man of yours? Or is he a coward?"

"He promised to stay out of the way. Don't put me off. What happened with your gig?"

260

"A marriage, not a gig. And it went very well."

"It's not a marriage if you're forced into it. How did you feel about leaving the woman behind knowing that you'll never see her again?"

"That's low. But I'll see her. I'm an investigator, and I have an esskip. Don't think I won't."

"The agreement specified no on-going contact."

"Founder the agreement. I'll see whomever I want."

"Don't go back." Maybe he'd locate the girl, but he shouldn't visit her in his current state.

"I'm going to Idylko. I won't bother my bride or her clan. I need to talk with Angel. She happens to be in Idylko at the moment."

"I'm your sister and your grandmatriarch. I must know what you're doing."

"No, you don't!"

"I bought you that esskip. If you go, you're taking me along." I crossed my arms and stalled. "You can't go now. Not without a life vest. And you need to file a flight plan."

"What do you know about flight plans?"

"You won't get clearance without appropriate safety gear." Surely my man and Lord Dojko had seen Teakh get into the esskip. They knew he lacked experience. Good Danna! He'd even had difficulty opening the canopy of his esskip.

"I've got life vests up at the gym. I'll get them." The canopy released with a snap.

"Not yet," I put a hand on his shoulder. "Leave the canopy closed. I've got more to say. We're under surveillance by Clan Fennako. Avoid using names. We've got allies in that clan, but also enemies. Always assume that Fennako is listening in. If we have sensitive information to talk about, we do it in your esskip. Understand?"

"I know all about it. No need to tell me."

The canopy opened fully. Dyse stood nearby, expectantly. Teakh hiked uphill to the gym while I put on a show of enthusiasm. My emotions were in turmoil. The esskip could either free Teakh to travel or tie us more closely to Dyse.

He returned wearing Seaguard kit and carrying a second orange life vest. He handed the vest to me. My own life vest was better, but I'd have to go back to the lagoon to get it. And that would lead to questions I didn't want to answer.

ENCLOSED AGAIN IN the new esskip, I took advantage of the privacy. "Maybe you've quarreled with Angel. You can patch that up. I don't believe you're having regrets about your career as a stud."

Teakh bent to fasten his harness. "Well, I am."

"Don't put me off. I know you too well."

"I shouldn't be Seaguard chief."

"Stop talking nonsense."

He muttered, "I may have other children."

"What did you say?"

"Children! I might have inadvertently fathered some children."

"Who? Where?"

"You know about Madame X."

Had Teakh been assaulted? That would explain his simmering rage. "Did she come after you again?"

And then he dropped the bombshell. "No. It's just that Angel may have taken my seed and sold it."

The statement took a moment to soak in. "So Angel is a succubus?"

"I thought she loved me. But we never had sex, not for real sex. She used an artificial vagina. It doesn't feel the same, but I had nothing to compare it to until yesterday."

"You're not that ignorant."

"I'm trying to be responsible."

"That child is a member of Clan Noahee," I said. "This is clan business."

"Do you have your seat harness fastened?" he asked.

"Yes. Are you trying to change the subject again?"

"No. I'm running through a preflight checklist. Next, I've got evacuation procedures."

"I know what to do. If the craft overturns and can't be righted, the seat harness will release. I dive to get out."

"Aye. You know a lot." Teakh continued to nod his way through a preflight check.

A hail boomed in the enclosed space. "Your brother isn't rated for that craft, not with a passenger aboard."

"He has urgent business to attend to," I said.

"Not with you aboard."

Teakh interrupted. "Is that your man?"

I ignored him. "I need to be aboard."

"I can't forbid you to fly with him," my man said. "But Dojko will only clear him if he has an escort."

"I've flown a drone for years," Teakh growled.

"By regulations you can't fly that craft with a passenger aboard. We can argue regulations, or you can accept me as an escort."

Teakh sighed. "Accepted."

My man signed off.

"That man of yours is a hard ass," Teakh said.

"There's a lot riding on us," I said. And Teakh knew very little about it.

We taxied out of the small-boat harbor. Beyond the breakwater, our speed increased as we rose on step, then flew.

My comset bleated—Dyse this time. "Where are you at?"

"In that new esskip."

"Just where are you going?"

"Out on the ocean."

"Don't get smart with me, young lady. I'm not impressed. You flew off without telling anyone where you're going."

"My brother filed a flight plan," I said.

"But you didn't tell me, your own aunt. And after all I'll I've done for you!"

"Something came up," I said. "Seaguard business."

"Dojko won't tell me a thing. I tried to get Big Uncle to intervene. You'd think as Lord Ralko he'd get some respect."

"You're being rude, and we're flying." I signed off.

A second esskip sped from the direction of the Dojko esskip lagoon—my man as our escort.

"Well, there he is," Teakh said sourly.

I remained silent, letting him concentrate on flying. Mountains slipped past, sometimes near and sometimes far. My man kept close on our tail.

I considered our child, boy? Girl? Most likely she hadn't yet been conceived, sperm having not yet encountered ovum.

My stomach lurch as the esskip encountered turbulence. I clutched at the side of the cockpit. The wingtip dragged against the top of a wave.

"Teakh!" I shouted.

Kinkill! We were going over.

In a blur of foam and water, the craft turned turtle. We were still moving. How close were we to reefs?

I didn't have a chart. The harness cut into my shoulders, and blood rushed into my head.

"Are you okay?" Teakh asked as if I'd stubbed my toe.

"What do you think? I'm upside down."

Teakh's voice remained absurdly calm. "This happens all the time."

"No, it doesn't."

My man shouted over my comset, "What does that addle-brained brother of yours think he's doing? I'll be right there to pick you up."

"Ahh," Teakh said. "A wet exit's not a real good idea. Give us a moment."

"You're drifting to the southeast," my man said. "There's a reef to your starboard ten. You'd best get that craft upright pronto."

I squeezed my eyes shut and prayed to Danna that we wouldn't be smashed to bits. The craft rocked and rocked again. With a shudder it rolled upright. We continued our journey, my man following even more closely.

As we approached Idylko, my man peeled away. We splashed down and taxied into the small-boat harbor.

"I'm going up into the village to speak with Angel," Teakh said as we floated alongside a pier. "Will you be all right waiting?"

"I'm grandmatriarch and this is about a clan member, your child. I'm coming."

"Don't." He held up a warning hand. "I don't know what happened. Give me a chance to speak with her in private."

Reluctantly I agreed. He scrambled out to moor his craft. The canopy closed, then he walked up the dock ramp and disappeared into the village.

I hailed my man.

"Promise me not to fly with your brother," he said. "Hail me any time. If I can't come myself, I'll send someone."

"He's Noahee Seaguard chief."

"Until he's logged and documented adequate flight time, he shouldn't be carrying passengers. I don't care who he is. He needs lessons and a flight rating for an esskip."

"Thank Danna you were there. I mean it."

"So why is your brother set on this trip?"

"He has a dispute with his sweetheart."

"What! And for that he risked his sister's life?"

"He believes his girlfriend stole his semen and sold it on the black market. He's worried about his children."

"We're talking about the artist? Matta Carrie?"

"That's the one."

"She wouldn't risk her reputation."

"But she does collect semen. You saw her art show."

"She wouldn't do it without the man's cooperation. Your brother must have known what she was doing."

"He claims that he didn't."

"Grandmatriarch, what are your plans?"

"What do you mean?"

"Will you press charges?"

After I'd finished law school I might be ready for such a lawsuit. Not enough Poseidon damn flight time! I was as green as Teakh. "I'll have to."

"We'll pull in whatever resources you need," my man said.

"Teakh would prefer that no one knows about it."

"I don't give a damn what he prefers. The interests of your clan members come first. I recommend you contact your advisor. Your brother's tiff qualifies as an interclan incident. Founder his naiveté and his Poseidon-damn pride."

———

Chapter 32
Visitors

MY MAN SPOKE, his words coming from the comset at my shoulder, "Idylko Seaguard is talking. They talk with their sisters. They all know what's going on. They're saying your brother visited a lab technician. Jeena."

"She's a friend. What else are they saying?" I prayed to Danna that she hadn't spoken of Teakh as a member of the royal family, the proof in his DNA.

I leaned my head toward my comset to hear him say, "The lab technician has other visitors: her spouse and the artist."

Teakh tramped down the dock ramp and drew level with the esskip.

"My brother is back." I signed off.

The canopy opened.

"How did it go?" I asked.

Without responding he dropped into the pilot seat and snapped the canopy shut.

"Did she take it or not?" I asked the back of his head.

"She took it. But she didn't sell it," he said, his voice loud in the confines of the esskip. "Turns out she just wanted me as a stud. She shared it with two of her friends. I'll soon be the father of three children."

"I'm going to notify my academic advisor." I reached for my comset.

"Don't. It's bad enough that it happened."

"We have a major interclan custody dispute about to blow. I'm pulling rank. We can't do this alone."

"If you must," Teakh said sullenly. "You're grandmatriarch."

I activated my comset and hailed Gratia. "This channel is being monitored," I warned her. Even if Big Auntie wasn't listening in, my man was. So was Teakh. "Something has come up with my brother."

"Is that the stud?" Gratia asked, her voice a bit tinny over the connection. "A lot of fuss about expensive goo, in my opinion."

Teakh slumped silent and barely visible over the seatback.

"That's the problem," I said. "He may have lost control of his goo."

Gratia laughed. "I don't want to see that."

Teakh slumped, disappearing behind his seat.

"Not that way. His girlfriend may have kept a sample."

"And his girlfriend is?"

"An artist. She specializes in male nudes."

"Of course she did. We all saw her show."

Oh yes, Gratia had seen the show, so had my fellow law students. I said, "That sample was dry and locked up. This time the artist took an active sample without his permission."

Teakh straightened. "The brother here. Yesterday, my girlfriend shared my so-called goo with two of her friends."

"When did she acquire it?" Gratia asked.

"She seduced me over a year ago. They used it yesterday."

"Then there might not be any children. It depends on if your goo was stored properly."

"They're professionals," said Teakh.

"Clearly," said Gratia. "Which clans are involved?"

I tapped him on the shoulder. "Brother, that's for you."

"Uh...That would be my girlfriend's clan—Shellako. The lab technician—Idylko. Her partner—Pontako."

"And your clan. Ralko I believe. Well. Well. A custody dispute involving four clans."

"I'm Noahee, not Ralko." Teakh recovered his air of command.

"Noahee Chief," I said. "My contract has been fulfilled."

"Five clans. The legal dispute of the dodecade." Gratia chortled. "The grandmother of all custody battles over some semen, not much different from snot. With your permission I'll bring in your study group. This kind of experience can't be matched with mock trials."

Teakh objected. "This is my private life."

"You should have thought of that before you jumped in bed with three succubi. A little planning goes a long way."

"This is my brother and his children," I said.

"Every lawsuit is about someone's brother, sister, or child. Don't forget it!"

FOLLOWING TEAKH, I trudged uphill from the harbor into the village. I'd hoped to become a lawyer, but not like this. Certainly not while my fiancé and brother were at odds and both in foul moods. Not with my advisor bringing in my fellow law students for a—Danna help us—"class project."

The door of a cottage opened. Jeena stood in the entranceway smiling as if all were well. Behind her stood a woman with dark curly hair. We hurried into the foyer. Teakh introduced me to Jeena, whom I already knew, and Reez, her spouse. Jeena invited us into her front room. Angel slouched in a chair, as morose as Teakh had been. She didn't look up when I greeted her.

A tea kettle whistled. Jeena went into the kitchen. We sat in uncomfortable silence until she returned with a tray of tea and crackers. I accepted tea and addressed Jeena: "I appreciate your expertise in genetic testing, and your respect for confidentiality." I could only hope that Jeena would take the hint to remain silent about Teakh's mitochondrial DNA.

Jeena raised her cup to her lips. "Always."

"I expect to become pregnant shortly." How much did they know about the stipulations of my contract?

Angel gave no reaction.

"Congratulations. How exciting!" Reez said, her pretense of innocence cloying.

Ignoring her, I continued to speak with Jeena. "I believe you understand the value and importance of my brother's genetic legacy. Within Clan Noahee, men and women are equals."

"We support you in this," she said brightly. "We welcome your brother's involvement with our children."

"That may be, but you haven't asked or received permission to conceive these children."

Angel shifted her posture. "But you knew that Teakh and I love each other. And you believe in the right to marry as one pleases."

I countered. "Marry, yes. Love him, yes. Kidnap his children? No! You never asked him if he wanted to father children with Jeena and Reez. That is unforgivable and illegal."

"I've thought about that. Every day I have my regrets." Angel twisted the bracelet on her wrist. It matched the one that Teakh wore.

"You could have destroyed the sample. You did not!"

"Go easy on her," Jeena said. "She never had it. I process and store semen, but I lack expertise in acquisition, so I hired Angel as a teaser. We agreed to split the proceeds."

"A teaser." Teakh put a hand to his face.

I said, "You conspired to break interclan law. We will be filing for injunctions against each of your clans." I glared at each of the three women in turn.

"I refused the fee," Angel said.

"She wanted me to destroy the sample," Jeena explained. "We reached a compromise."

"Regardless, you didn't receive permission from Clan Noahee. We will take you to court. We will win." I may have made too strong a threat. "But we're willing to settle with you." Would they call my bluff? We needed to keep this dispute out of court.

Unfortunately, Angel had a solid understanding of the law. "This so-called theft occurred when Teakh was a member of Clan Ralko. Your case won't float."

I still had an advantage. "He did not give informed consent. Knowing the value of my brother's genetics you seduced him. You might as well have raped him!"

Angel met my gaze. "If I hadn't agreed to share, Jeena would have sold it. Your brother wouldn't have wanted that."

"I would have," said Jeena. "I'm responsible. Don't take it out on her."

Teakh edged toward Angel, her hand now on his knee.

She said, "When we first met, he was a member of Clan Ralko. Until...How long ago did you become pregnant?"

"We conceived during the full moon." At least I hoped conception had occurred.

"Really, you can't sue any of us," Angel said airily. "You aren't the aggrieved clan."

"We are. I've been with my sweetheart every night for six days. I'd hazard we conceived before you did. Noahee was in existence at the time you utilized the stolen sample."

"Consider," Angel said. "What happens when that detestable aunt of yours gets wind of circumstances? Suppose she presses charge? What will she want as a settlement?"

Angel had backed me into a corner. I'd wanted to be lawyer, but I'd been outmaneuvered by a painter of nudes.

She stood, smoothed her hair, and bowed. "May I have your brother's hand in marriage?"

One moment we were at odds. The next she was proposing marriage. "I don't understand."

"Here's how it is—if Teakh and I are married, detestable auntie has no way to prove theft occurred. Insemination could have happened yesterday. Or during the consummation of our marriage. Who's to know?"

The three women watched us, a pack of wolves working as one, wickedly smart as they laid a trap.

"What about my other kids?" Teakh asked falling into it. "Jeena and Reez's babies?"

"He'll have to marry all of us," Reez said and Jeena nodded.

Angel patted his knee. "Include a provision in the pre-nuptial contract."

Jeena shook her head. "Reez and I are married. Put that with his wife's approval he may father children with other partners. That's how they do things anyway. He couldn't work as a stud otherwise."

This was too much to take in. I needed to consult with my man, with Gratia, and most of all with Teakh. "We need to talk in private," I whispered, but they could all hear the request anyway.

Teakh and I now had a problem: if we walked back to the esskip, we'd pass the front windows of Idylko women, and we'd be in full view of dock surveillance cameras. Both the gossiping Seaguard and their sisters would see us.

272

Jeena offered the use of her back hallway, her understanding appreciated but disconcerting. Teakh had identified her correctly as a consummate professional.

Beside the washing machine in the family portion of the house. I whispered to Teakh, "No one should be forced into a relationship. Children aren't political pawns."

"What about you and your man?"

"It's different."

"Is it?" Teakh asked. "I'm marrying to protect children. Are you?"

"I haven't given my approval yet."

"It's my decision to marry. We agreed. I'm fine with three-way consummation. I'm not fine with letting Idylko off easy. Jeena set this up and forced Angel into it."

If we didn't placate Jeena she might blab to Big Auntie about his royal DNA. The secret would be out and also our safety. I couldn't explain this to Teakh without revealing the deadly secret of our ancestry. Hidden blackmail.

"So what do you care about? Revenge? Or your children?"

"My children. As a stud, I'm contracted to have a limited number of children. If those clans find I've violated my contract, they'll sue. If they don't get satisfaction, they might take it out on my children in their care."

"We'll think of something." There had to be a way out of this snarl.

Teakh grinned. "Like getting married."

"Danna help us." He was all set to marry Angel even after she'd stolen from him and lied about it.

We returned to the front room to confront the threesome.

I stood before them as if addressing judges. "We accept your proposal in principle. However, we must make separate agreements with your clans. Each of you should contact your clan for legal advice. Tell them exactly what happened so they have a full understanding of their liability."

Yet, they didn't have full information and never would if I could help it. Jeena might know of our royal DNA, but not of the assassinations of our mother and grandmother.

"Consummation must occur before the new moon," Jeena said. "The sooner the better."

We would have difficulty arranging a marriage on such short notice, but we had incentive.

I took charge. "Jeena, talk to Idylko about providing facilities and lodging for the wedding. Angel, you'll need to arrange for a magistrate and plan the ceremonies. Reez—"

"Catering," Reez said with no further prompting.

These women who'd only hours ago been our enemies were now on our team. Or were we on theirs?

Regardless, we would cooperate. Lives depended on it.

———

Chapter 33
Raptoria

Hailing Skipper,

The item in question was taken. It was active. Yesterday, the artist and two of her friends shared it. My brother has agreed to marriage in order to extend legal protection to his children. We're concerned about our aunt, and about the security of our communications.

First Mate sending

———

Hailing First Mate,

We are currently making use of Seaguard protocols. Your aunt's clan lacks the technical expertise needed for hacking Seaguard networks. However, nearly all networks are subject to royal override. As chief Network administrator, Grandmother could intercept messages. She rarely does so and only when lives are at stake. She has delegated administration of Seaguard networks and protocols to my father. I don't know where he stands on the dispute between Big Auntie and Mother.

Skipper sending

———

Hailing Skipper

I must consult with my academic advisor regarding sensitive legal issues. Is there any way to ensure security and confidentiality?

First Mate sending

———

Hailing First Mate

Normally legal counsel is given the highest level of security available. However, Big Auntie has administrative access to the legal systems. The chief is on her way here to handle security and counter surveillance. We may be able to run your communication through the banking system. It's controlled by Mother and has its own protocols.

Skipper sending

A STREAM OF OFFICIALS poured down the dock ramp toward Teakh's esskip. The front panels of women's robes gleamed with brocade. Tassels hung from their hoods. Behind them came men in green-and-white Seaguard kit, the shade of green brighter than the aqua-gray favored by Fennako. Teakh opened the canopy. I pocketed my handscreen and scrambled out of the cockpit, Teakh right behind me. The leading woman approached and bowed.

"Raptoria Idylko here," she announced. "Grandmatriarch of Clan Idylko. Welcome."

I bowed in return. "Annin Noahee, Grandmatriarch and Attorney General of Clan Noahee."

We politely spoke of the tide before Raptoria introduced Lord Idylko, Magnate of Idylko Sound. He had a receding hairline and a neatly trimmed gray beard. I introduced Teakh as Noahee Seaguard Chief.

Raptoria tucked a hand under my arm. "Do come up to my place and have a bite to eat. You must have had a long journey."

I understood the game, still the familiarity disconcerted me. Grandmatriarchs often pretended friendliness they didn't feel. Trailed by our kin, Raptoria and I strolled from the waterfront. The lanes opened out into a commons, the grass sparse and still matted by the winter snows.

"The plaza will look much nicer in a few weeks. We have lovely flower beds," Raptoria commented. "Here's my place next door to the clan hall. So convenient. Do come in."

Her house had an imposing facade several stories high encrusted with ornate bric-a-brac. Raptoria ushered us into a foyer with a polished floor and with a grand staircase leading to an upstairs gallery. Benches lined the walls with cubbies underneath and coat hooks above.

She hung my parka then proffered a pair of wool slippers. "I crochet these for my guests."

The women in the group all replaced shoes with slippers. The men kept their boots on, quite traditional for Seaguard. We gathered in a ground floor parlor furnished with tables draped in lace. Antimacassars hung over the backs of settees and overstuffed chairs. The windows, which would have looked out on the plaza, had been dimmed, letting in diffuse frosted light.

"Do sit with me," Raptoria said. "My niece will bring refreshments."

I sat knee-to-knee with Raptoria. The rest of our parties, including Teakh, arranged themselves on settees and chairs. Raptoria poured cups of tea then proffered a plate of cakes to be served with silver tongs. "I recommend the marmalade. Our village greenhouse has orange trees."

An Idylko woman passed cakes and tea to the rest of those assembled. I dabbed jam on mine.

Raptoria set her teacup aside. "May we extend congratulations?"

Congratulations for what? I recovered and thanked her.

"Remarkable that anyone so young should be a grandmatriarch. Excuse me, but neither of you seem old enough to have reached your majority." Raptoria fanned herself. "Kids. They look younger every day."

I parried her barb regarding my age. "I am nearly two-dozen years old. We've received special dispensation from the Queen who personally approved our charter." Raptoria could chew on that. I continued, "In Clan Noahee, men and women are equal. My brother's children will be clan members."

Raptoria seemed intent on belittling us. "We find it interesting that you arrived with a Fennako escort. Wise on the part of Fennako I am sure."

Without explaining that the escort was my fiancé, not my babysitter, I said, "Fennako has generously provided us with advice and technical support. I trust that your kinswoman Jeena has informed you of our business here."

Raptoria dusted her hands of crumbs. "A ridiculous lawsuit filed by children."

"Filed on behalf of children. I agree it's ridiculous. We share the same interests of protecting clan members."

"How many clan members do you have?"

I explained that given our open and ambilineal membership we were poised to grow rapidly. I didn't say we only had two members. "I'll be frank with you. I'm not happy about the theft of my brother's semen. In fact, I'm furious. We are talking about my brother's children, members of our clan, stolen from us."

"So you say," Raptoria responded. "But there are no children as of yet."

"We're not here to argue with you. Jeena's child will be a member of both Idylko and Noahee. If we do not act decisively, Jeena could lose that child to Clan Ralko. I can assure you that Ralko does not have the best interests of our child in mind."

Raptoria, at last, got down to business. "What are your demands?"

"Not demands but a proposal."

Someone laughed. "A wedding proposal perhaps?"

"Such a marriage is highly irregular," Raptoria said. "Normally the woman's clan proposes."

"The marriage isn't between Noahee and Idylko but between Noahee and Shelliko. The union will extend legal protection to Jeena's child."

"Providing Shelliko agrees." Raptoria set forth her demands, "Jeena's child must remain in the custody and care of its mother and of Clan Idylko."

"We have no desire to take the child from its mother. We want what is best for this child who is kin to both of us. "

"I suppose this makes us in-laws. Do have another crumpet, dear."

I accepted a cake and made an appeal to flattery. "We are in great need of your wisdom and assistance. As you've pointed out, Teakh and I are little more than children. We would most appreciate your guidance and blessing."

"What kind of blessing?" Raptoria asked.

I explained that an immediate marriage between Teakh and Angel would be most effective in protecting the child. "We would be much obliged if Idylko would provide facilities and lodging for guests and all interested clans."

We touched on numbers of guests, but first we had another matter to settle. "Teakh is a cover stud," I said.

"Is he truly worth his astronomical price?"

"Regardless, he's been marketing his services with the understanding that he'll have a limited number of offspring. We must guard against perceptions that Idylko has stolen what others have paid for."

Raptoria stiffened. "What are you implying?"

"Grandmother, I'm uncomfortable making this request. Clan Noahee requires compensation. If we don't receive it, then we're liable and can be sued for breach of contract."

"What's wrong with unlimited editions? More tea?"

Hellenboreko and the Eugenics council would run with that one, but I let it go. I cared about those who are living, not the gene pool and hypothetical future generations. "We must not give an impression that Clan Noahee is an easy mark. Doing so will harm our clan and, by extension, Jeena's child. The child will have half-siblings in a number of clans. If we maintain good relationships, Jeena and her child will be well positioned politically." We'd also reduce the risk of incest and receive disorders by sharing records.

"We've been given to understand that Noahee's status rides on an intimate decision of your own."

"Ah yes." I placed my hand over my belly. "My fiancé and I will try again if conception hasn't occurred, but we've fulfilled all stipulations."

"I suppose a grandmatriarch should at least be a mother if not a grandmother. But consider the event that Jeena does not conceive? Will you allow her and your brother to make another attempt?"

I glanced to Teakh, who frowned. "We'll consider it," I said.

Lord Idylko held a delicate teacup in his large hand. "Your Fennako escort has asked to check the security of your lodging. He's working on it now."

Raptoria conducted us to a house with only slightly less bric-a-brac than on her own home. The parlor beyond contained overstuffed chairs and settees festooned with yet more doilies. My valise and duffle had been placed inside the foyer. As soon as Idylko had departed, I slumped onto a settee, exhausted, and rested my head against the scratchy lace.

"The cold cupboard is fully stocked," Teakh shouted from the kitchen.

I roused myself and went up a stairway lit by an atrium window. My man waited at the top. He enfolded me in his arms. I rested my head against solid chest covered by a life vest.

"I missed you," I mumbled into his shoulder.

With a light touch he pushed a lock of hair from my cheek. "It's only been a few hours."

"An eternity."

We went into an upstairs room which would become my office and teleconference center. A broad bay window looked out on the plaza. From this vantage I could watch both the clan hall and the entrance of the grandmatriarch's house. Although she in turn was able to watch us.

My man said, "Give us the go-ahead and we'll set this room up as a teleconferencing center. The chief is on her way with equipment."

It was all happening so quickly. "I'm scared," I confided. "What if my aunt shows up? What if I'm not pregnant?"

He tugged at my hand, "We can take care of that." We crossed to another room which contained a wide bed between corner cupboards.

"Oh yes," I said.

He scooped me up and dumped me on the bed. I laughed in delight. He pulled off one of my socks and kissed my toes. Then he started sucking on them.

That's when Dyse hailed. That woman had the worst possible timing.

I sat up.

"I've heard the most shocking rumors," Dyse said. "Are they true?"

"Probably not."

"I heard that Teakh is getting married to three women without asking for my blessing."

"It's only to one woman. I'm so sorry. May he have your blessing?"

"Certainly not! Our agreement is that I handle his career. All requests for his services go through me."

"This is a marriage, not a liaison. Our charter has been ratified by the Queen. As grandmatriarch of Clan Noahee I may approve my brother's marriage. I have."

"What about the other two women? Don't shine me. I heard—this is shocking and unspeakable—that three succubi stole Teakh's seed. It must have been when he was an invalid in Idylko hospital."

"Hardly an invalid. He broke his ankle."

"He cannot marry those women. It's wrong! I am your aunt. I only want the best for you two, my poor orphaned charges."

"Well then, we thank you for the blessing on his marriage. It's what he wants, and that's what's best for him."

"Don't twist my words around!"

282

"It's so thoughtful of you to hail." I signed off and spoke with my man. "My aunt knows we're trying to cut her out. She may try to disrupt the wedding."

"Did you send her an invitation?"

"No. But she might come anyway."

———

Chapter 34
Senior Husband

I SAT AT THE kitchen table while my man heated supper. We'd continued our shipboard habit of my man doing the cooking, although Idylko delivered prepared food. Teakh had volunteered for cleanup, claiming he was a lousy cook.

I simply enjoyed watching my man as he placed bread in the oven to warm and a pot of chowder on the stove.

Dyse hailed. "Idylko is denying us access. Tell them I'm your aunt."

My man raised an eyebrow.

"You're not my aunt. You never were," I said.

"Young lady, you're still a minor and I am your guardian. I'm taking this up with Fennako."

My man ceased stirring the soup. "Fennako here."

"Are you the lubber who's been taking advantage of my niece?"

"Fennako Seaguard," he said.

"She's only two-dozen-years old. Have some pity."

"You represent a security risk to Idylko," he said in a mild voice.

"Why? Because I care about my niece?" she asked.

"I must speak with your Seaguard." My man set the spoon on a saucer, turned off the stove, and went in the front room.

"Answer me!" demanded Dyse.

"He's talking with Gorby." I signed off.

It was likely my man was in on conference call that included Lord Ralko.

My man returned to the kitchen. "We must allow clearance, or she'll set up a stink. Idylko is letting them in."

"She'll disrupt the wedding," I warned.

"It'll be okay," he said as if him saying so would reassure me.

MY MAN AND I relaxed in the front room while Teakh put away leftovers.

With the sun creeping downward in the west, Dyse arrived in the plaza. Trailed by cousin Gorby, she entered Raptoria's house. I went into the kitchen to prepare tea. Surely they would visit us next.

Teakh, wiping down the table, paused, rag in hand. "If you're going to offer hospitality how about cold water and stale crackers?"

I shook my head and filled the kettle.

Dyse and Gorby emerged from Raptoria's place and crossed the plaza.

As I welcomed her into the parlor, Dyse glared, her face pulled into a rictus. "I am your guardian and have a right to be here. I humored you and tolerated your games, but it ends now. "

"Oh really?" I asked, leading her into the front room where a tray with tea service and sweet biscuits waited on the parlor table.

She stood on the area rug, refusing to take a seat. "Both of you will come home with me."

"Just how will we do that?" I asked. "Our cousin's esskip has room for only two passengers."

"Niece, don't fight me. I only want what's best for you."

"You're no longer her guardian," said my man seated on the couch. "She may go where she pleases."

"Who are you?" Dyse demanded.

"Her consort, senior Noahee husband."

"You lout. She's not yet two dozen years old. And what is your age?"

"It's irrelevant. My wife is grandmatriarch of a sovereign clan. I recommend you treat her with respect."

Dyse wrung her hands. "My niece and her brother left without telling me where they were going. Just took off. What was I to think?"

"Nothing. It's not your business," I said. "Events developed quickly, and my brother was flying."

"But you weren't. I have heard rumors that I do not want to believe. Succubi assaulted Teakh. Now he plans to marry his rapists?"

"You heard wrong. He is marrying his girlfriend."

My man stood and touched her arm soothingly "Auntie, do have a seat. Fennako is quite aware of activity here in Idylko. They sent an escort to ensure that our two young people arrived safely."

Dyse frowned. "You're the escort."

"I care about your niece and her brother," my man said smoothly and diplomatically, every bit a Fennako prince.

I AWOKE TO gentle kisses that trailed like petals across my cheek. The gray light of pre-dawn filling the room.

My man spoke. "Sorry to disturb you. A Fennako official will arrive in half an hour."

"Why didn't you tell me sooner? I'm not ready. I'm not good at being a hostess. You saw that yesterday."

"You'll do fine. It's only my sister."

Only his sister! Only princess Mareen, a woman who would hold life and death power over Teakh—power I'd pledged to her.

I threw on leggings and smock then went downstairs to look over the contents of the cold cupboard—cold soup and not much else; some blueberry preserves and left-over rolls. I located roast barley in a cupboard.

Teakh emerged from the back room bleary-eyed. "Dawn observance." He went out the front door. Sunrise gilded the roofs of the village.

"Good idea. Let's make a show of it." My man followed. In the plaza, they commenced with ritually greeting the sun. In plain view of Clan Idylko, they prostrated themselves toward sunrise, not once but three times.

The front door opened. In walked Princess Mareen carrying a hefty toolbox and followed by Teakh and my man. She set the toolbox on the parlor rug and greeted me.

I turned to introduced Teakh.

"We've met," she said, and addressed him: "I understand you've gotten yourself in trouble again."

"No trouble," Teakh responded. "I'm getting married."

"What was it last time? Brawling?"

Teakh bowed his head. "Self-defense."

"Your brother had another incident." She rolled her eyes. "This time in Dojko. A fight involving three men and a seagull drone."

"I dropped charges," Teakh mumbled.

"It's been stricken from most records, but because a telechiric was used and we're tracking you, the Queen knows. She gave me access to records." Mareen put her hand to her mouth. "I don't relish the memory of biting a man's lip."

"It's how seagulls fight," Teakh said. "If you don't like it don't tap into the sensory data."

"I'm here to act as the Queen's agent and to represent the interests of this fellow." She nodded to my man. "I'm also responsible for counter-surveillance."

I set out mugs, rolls, and the preserves on the kitchen table. "How's your daughter?"

"She's staying with her grandmother." Mareen pulled out a chair. "She wanted to come, but we can't have her at this wedding. I promised her she could attend when her uncle gets married. You should keep it small, a family event."

I filled mugs. "Let's plan only one wedding ceremony at a time."

"Or in your brother's case, three."

After breakfast, Mareen set to work. Two multi-legged robots climbed out of her toolbox.

"They act as my hand." She wiggled her fingers, and the two spider-like devices danced as if they were puppets. "They're small enough to crawl into vents and under floorboards. I'll find any surveillance bugs." The two devices scrambled up her arm as she stooped. "Noahee, give me some help clearing this place." She looked to Teakh.

My man and I took our station in the utility closet.

Our job was to turn off circuits while Teakh removed switch plates and Mareen squeezed her devices through the openings and into the walls.

Teakh and Mareen's voices faded as they moved off. In the closeness of the utility closet my man's beard scratched my cheeks as I sought the sweet softness of his lips.

WE EMERGED STRAIGHTENING our clothing.

His work done, Teakh dropped a tangle of devices onto the kitchen table. My man inspected a device, turning it over. "Microphone pickups and cameras. Idylko. We'll return them to his lordship."

I stared at the mess of bugs. "Should we complain?"

Mareen shrugged. "Standard household security.

We'll replace the pickups with equipment of our own."

We went upstairs. In the room overlooking the plaza, Mareen stretched out her legs. "Now we can talk with some privacy. Let's hear about your brother's latest scrape, from the beginning."

"In the beginning, light loved darkness," Teakh commencing the myth of creation."

"Not that far back." Mareen leaned forward. "I'm a peaceweaver which is to say I'm mostly a social worker. We aim to solve problems before they get serious. Surely this mess didn't begin with the big bang."

"If you're after preventing problems," said Teakh. "You should have arrest Madame X."

"Madame X? Oh her. In the circumstances it was best to let her go. We didn't want the Noahee embroiling in a legal dispute." Mareen rested a booted foot across her knee. "But now you are. You're inconveniently valuable and not particularly good at protecting yourself. "

"I do all right," Teakh said.

"So about this dispute with Idylko?" Mareen steepled her fingers.

"Well... I was in Idylko hospital recovering from a broken ankle. A gorgeous woman walked into my room and invited me out for lunch. We went to a cottage and dined with two of her friends. After lunch, we went into the bedroom and had a good time."

"Meaning?"

"We had sex. I thought we had sex anyway. The moon was waning, so I didn't think anything would come of it."

"You thought. Did you ask their names?" Mareen asked.

"They told me it was hospitality."

"You should have asked for their clans. If they had other children. If they were married. What about diseases? Did you even know their ages?"

Teakh shook his head.

She sighed. "Women don't fall in bed with men just for the fun of it. Maybe some do but it's rare. Regardless of advances in medicine, women still die in childbirth. This puts men at greater legal risk. If you don't care about the women, you should at least protect yourself."

"But I do care," Teakh said.

"He was only a dozen-nine years old," I defended him. "People make mistakes."

"People die from mistakes," Mareen said. "And if a man, or anyone else, doesn't take reasonable precautions during sex, his clan can be held accountable for reckless endangerment."

"He was the victim."

Mareen dropped her foot from her knee. "A man old enough to produce children is old enough to take responsibility."

"I have taken responsibility," Teakh said. "I'm getting married."

"Ah yes, when I encountered your unregistered drone in Fennako City you were tracking the identity of your future bride—an unusual style of courtship."

"I was engaged in a sensitive investigation. I couldn't inform authorities without tipping my hand to my detestable aunt. Anyway, the artist and I hit it off. I became her model. She helped me out."

"With your stud career."

"As my artistic consultant. I didn't know anything was wrong until the day before yesterday. I had my first gig as a stud. I realized that it hadn't been right that first time. I confronted her and she admitted to using an artificial vagina."

"They decanted the semen two days ago," I said. "Those three women are Jeena Idylko, Reez Pontako, and Marjoram Shelliko—the artist."

"You sure get yourself in messes," Mareen said. "Unfortunately, you've dragged the rest of us into it. Because of Noahee's unusual charter, my brother is now legally the father of your children."

The thought made my head spin.

"They're my children," Teakh insisted.

"But my brother is senior husband. The senior husband may have sex with anyone in the clan. It's a tradition that goes back to ancient Earth. 'Primae noctis' it was called. "

"I'm not having sex with him," Teakh said.

Mareen said. "But because of the tradition he could be the father of any children in the clan. Thus he's responsible for your children. As his sister, so am I. "

Sink Fennako! They made everything so foundered complicated.

———

Chapter 35
Clans

BEYOND THE PARLOR window, sunlight slanted across the plaza and its swiftly melting snow. I followed Mareen and my man outside, Teakh trailing behind. Water dripped from the eaves of cottages and from the bric-a-brac facade of Raptoria's house.

Slush soaking my shoes, I dropped to the rear. The only one in our party not in Seaguard kit. Teakh sported his new chief Noahee kit—blue and gray life vest and seaboots. Mareen and my man were clad in the gray-green seaboots and vests of Fennako Royalguard and Harbor patrol.

Although now the Noahee grand matriarch, I knew myself to be insignificant in contrast to my escort.

Mareen waved Teakh forward. The duty of announcing our presence fell to him as Noahee chief.

I entered the foyer and removed my wet shoes as the others stood by wearing their boots, as was their right as Seaguard. I took a deep breath and squared my shoulders before facing Raptoria in her parlor.

What was the correct protocol for introducing Fennako royalty?

I glanced from my man to Mareen, but her face remained as calm and unmoving as that of goddess Danna. I forged ahead with our audience.

I bowed to Raptoria seated in her wing back chair as if in a throne. "Lady Idylko, please meet Mareen Fennako, Seaguard. And this gentleman is my consort. We have reasons to withhold his name."

"You're not fooling me, Fennako," said Raptoria. "Not with those boots and vest. So what's your first name? Hmm." She pulled at a hair on her chin.

"You may call me Mr. Noahee," he said. "Nice weather."

"Nice weather indeed. Very well. We'll leave your personal name to hospitality. Have a seat."

We arranged ourselves on the antimacassar festooned chairs, and Raptoria served tea before I brought up the critical topic, Teakh's newly conceived children.

"My consort," I nodded to my man, "wishes to speak with you on clan matters." I hoped I'd gotten the formalities right.

He said, "Lady Idylko, we understand that your kinswoman, Jeena Idylko, will soon be a mother to a Noahee child. As senior Noahee husband it's my duty to ensure that this child is properly provided for."

Raptoria grimaced. "The child is Idylko. We provide for our own."

"Correction," he said. "According to the Noahee charter, the child is both Idylko and Noahee."

"Now there's a useless document. You miss"—she glared at me—"are Ralko, born and breed. Same with your stud-for-hire brother."

My man said, "You are speaking to my wife and brother-in-law. They are Noahee, their charter ratified by the Queen." He idly traced the cuff of his boot, calling attention to the color.

"What about this Ralko woman?" Raptoria asked. "She claims the right to negotiate on their behalf."

"Ralko does not have that right," my man said. "My wife and her brother are royal wards. Mareen Fennako

Junior"—he nodded to his sister—"acts as the Queen's representative in this matter. That is, Princess Mareen Fennako Junior, second in line to the throne. Sister to Lord Tristan Bay." With that he'd nearly told her exactly who he was and his relationship to the Queen.

"Yes," Mareen said, "Her Majesty considers the well-being of our child to be of utmost importance." In that she neatly implied that the child was royal kin. Only Jeena and I know how close that was to the truth—maybe not a grandchild, but definitely a royal cousin.

I trudged back across the plaza half expecting Aunt Dyse to be lurking, just waiting for the chance to scuttle the wedding.

But water continued to drip from the eves and no new footprints marked the slush. Mareen departed for her lodging, and we went into ours.

MESSAGES FROM GATHERING clans poured into my comset, each with a claim on Teakh's newly conceived children. Seated in the parlor, I sorted through them.

"What of Dojko," I asked Teakh.

"Is that the gym owner?" My man sat beside me.

"From Lady Dojko," I said.

Teakh responded at the same time. "His name's Keno Dojko. The gym owner. He runs it with his sister, Iris."

"I had a good talk with Lord Dojko," said my man.

"They're on their way here. Lord and Lady Dojko, along with Keno and Iris. Teakh, what was your agreement with them?"

"Uh… well. They provide my food, lodging, and training."

"In exchange for what?"

"A percentage of my stud fees. Depths!" He realized what I was after.

Hand to my forehead I said, "Depths is right. They're going to want their cut."

"You can't cut up children," he said.

"No. And there isn't a fee involved. What are we going to do?"

"You'll have to give them something," said my man.

"What?" What?

We watched for Dojko to arrive. Lord and Lady Dojko crossed the plaza and entered the Raptoria's house. We would be next.

In the kitchen I prepared a tray with biscuits and set water heating for tea. The teakettle whistled, but the guests still hadn't disgorged from Raptoria's place. I took the kettle off the stove. It seemed getting the timing right took practice.

When Teakh yelled that they were in the plaza I put the kettle back on.

Lord Dojko led the way into the parlor. "Congratulations to each of you," he said, as distinguished as ever and wearing a smart gray-and-blue life vest.

Lady Dojko right behind him asked, "Will this be a double wedding?"

I put a hand over my still flat belly, and said, "My fiancé and I will have a ceremony at a later time."

"You have a baby on the way I understand." Lady Dojko had seated herself on an overstuffed chair. Her brother had chosen the sofa.

I snuck a glance at my man. "We've made significant efforts in that area."

Lord Dojko laughed. "I'm sure you have. Valiantly."

"Brother," Lady Dojko said, "don't tease the young people."

The tea kettle whistled so I retrieved the tea tray from the kitchen and set it before our guests. Awkward with my new role of hostess, I poured hot water through the herbs in the teapot, and let them steep. I passed a plate of barley biscuits, baked hard.

Lord Dojko said, "My kinsman Keno explained your contract and clan charter. Have you fulfilled the stipulations?"

Depths! Word really did get around.

I collected myself and spoke with as much authority as I could muster: "If I'm pregnant, our clan status will be backdated to the full moon. If I'm not, we'll try again next month. In either case, the contract is fulfilled. Noahee is a clan."

"And you still don't know this fellow's name?" Lord Dojko waved a biscuit toward my man. "Although, I suppose there's more than one way for a woman to know a fellow."

Lady Dojko glared at her brother who smothered a laugh. She said, "I dislike intruding with legalities on such joyous occasions, but I'm grandmatriarch. We currently have an agreement with Ralko." She lifted a teacup to Keno and Iris. "Our kin have been providing your brother with food, housing, and training with the understanding that they will receive a portion of his stud fees. Will you honor this agreement?"

This was the question I dreaded. I hoped to avoid premature commitment. I said, "Keno and Iris have become good friends to my brother. Thank you." I bobbed my head toward Teakh's mentor, Keno. "We appreciate the hospitality you provided to both myself and to my brother as well as your estimable discretion. We wish to continue our amicable relationship."

"Then you will consider extending the contract?" Lady Dojko asked.

"I leave that decision to my brother."

Teakh started to speak, and I frowned at him, a warning not to play our cards too soon.

When our meeting and visit was over I saw them to the door.

Aunt Dyse was nowhere to be found and still hadn't sent a message.

MAREEN RETURNED IN the afternoon with teleconferencing equipment. I went downstairs to open the door. Behind her stood Harb and Roy.

Harb bowed low. "Greetings, Grandmatriarch."

Roy right behind him said. "Welcome to the family."

"Give us a hand," Mareen lifted a box from the cart.

Teakh and my man joined us and we all pitched in to haul the gear upstairs.

"How was the sailing?" I asked Harb as he came down for another load.

He grinned. "It ended sooner than I liked. I pulled into the harbor, and there was my kinsman with two esskips, saying we'd best get to Idylko. I'm hoping Roy here packed the right stuff."

"I had help," Roy said.

"Aye, you need help," responded Harb.

"Mama approved it," Mareen said. "Let's keep working."

"What is it with you fellows?" I asked. "You hang around with royalty like it's normal. Like they're kin."

Harb shrugged. "We are kin. Oh, you mean the informality. It's hard to be formal with someone you've known since childhood. There was a time when that fellow..."

"I don't want to hear it," shouted my man.

Mareen came out of the utility closet dusting her hands. "We replaced the router with one of our own."

In the new teleconference center, the desk had been pushed toward the window, making room for three screens and a square table. Mareen along with Harb and Roy departed across the plaza below.

"I wanted to hear what Harb had to say."

"You call him Harb?"

"Aye. For Harbor Patrol. And the other one is Roy for Royal Guard."

"That works."

"I wanted to hear what he had to say."

"No you don't. It was going to be an embarrassing story about how I got kicked out of class for farting. We're half-brothers. Same for Roy.

"Truly? You're brothers?"

"Aye. The three of us are the same age. Dad favors Harb's mother, so Big Auntie doesn't like Harb or his mother. Fennako infighting gets nasty. Kids take cues from their mothers without knowing what it's all about. Harb and I were the misfits. Roy befriended us. It's all circumstances of birth."

"They showed up right after Teakh was assaulted in Fennako City. Did you send your brothers to guard us?"

"Not exactly. My sister sent Roy. I knew she had a watch on you but not why. Normally she lets me know what she's doing. Harb happened to be nearby."

"Do they have a claim on Noahee children?"

"The same as the rest of Fennako. You are carrying their niece or nephew. Let's talk to Fennako. I'll show you how to conference."

He faced a screen and said. "Hailing Grandmother Mareen."

Its screen activated with a message: ACKNOWLEDGE. The words faded to be replaced by a moving image of Big Mareen.

"Marsk!" she exclaimed.

"Mama. Remember the contract. She's not supposed to know my name." He stepped aside, and I took his place facing the screen.

"Here's how it works," he said moving his hand. "Pan like this."

I mirrored his gesture and the image on the screen changed as the camera followed my movement. I pivoted the remote camera to look around Big Mareen's teleconferencing center.

A crimson dragonette lay curled on the table, seemingly sleeping beside a tea set with four cups and saucers. My man rolled a chair forward. As I sat, the remote camera lowered so that Big Mareen and I looked eye to eye as if across our twin tables.

The tail of the dragon twitched, and I pivoted the camera.

"I wouldn't let my granddaughter take her drone to school," said Big Mareen.

The dragonette stretched then skittered across the table until it stood lens to lens with the camera.

My man put his arm around me. "You should be paying attention to your teacher, not spying on Grandma."

Most likely Reena was at school. The dragonette lowered its head in a semblance of a pout.

"We miss you," I said.

After we signed off, the screen went blank.

"Isn't the dragon a security risk?" I asked.

"If she's interested in fiscal policy and can remember what she's heard, that's a good thing. She'll probably be working in banking someday. She might as well start young. Most of the kids in the royal family do."

When I was six, I was playing hide-and-seek with Teakh. "I must be behind on things."

"We all start young—just on different things. I reckon you'll want to give your advisor a hail. I'll be downstairs, checking up on operations on the bay." He left the office and the sound of his footsteps receded as he descended the stairs.

I took his advice. "Hailing Myrtle Gratianiko, Annin Noahee here."

The screen image resolved into the square jaw and frizzy gray hair of Gratia. "What are you about?"

"I need help. I'm in over my head. I have a teleconference center and it's secure."

"We're secure on this end. Go ahead."

With that established I was free to use names. I said, "A year and a half ago, my brother Teakh was in Idylko hospital with a broken ankle. While doing routine blood work, Jeena Idylko ran genetic tests on Teakh and discovered his DNA fit the profile sought by the Noah Eugenics Project."

"Running the tests without permission was illegal," Gratia said.

"Aye, among other things. Jeena contacted Dyse Ralko to inform her of the find. At the time, Dyse was considered Teakh's guardian. She still thinks she is. Jeena is married to a woman in another clan, Reez Pontako. They wished to acquire Teakh's semen for insemination, so they hired Marjoram Shelliko to seduce him."

"Let me get this straight. These three women got your brother into bed and swiped his baby goo?"

"You don't have to put it so crudely."

"It seems we have a conspiracy, an interclan crime ring."

"Yes. They invited Teakh to Jeena's house, served him lunch, and had sex with him, simulated sex. Jeena used an artificial vagina to collect his ejaculant. None of them told Teakh their names. They led Teakh to believe he was having sex with Marjoram. She didn't have feelings for him at the time and so agreed to the heist. He was naïve enough to believe they were either prostitutes hired by a friend or that they engaged in sex purely for the fun of it. He was only a dozen-nine years old and had never had a girlfriend. It was his first time."

"Clearly Idylko was in the wrong," Gratia said. "Ralko aChas a strong case against all three clans."

"I know, but I don't want Ralko involved. Teakh discovered the identities of all three women. He thinks he's in love with Marjoram. He calls her Angel."

"Oh, yes. The artist with questionable taste. The one who paints naked men and displays condoms in gold boxes."

"He thinks he's in love with her, or was. They've quarreled. Jeena stored the semen at her lab. Three days ago, the semen sample was used to inseminate all three women: Jeena, Reez, and Marjoram. Or so they claim."

"But they might not have," said Gratia.

"Aye. Also I've just returned from my honeymoon with the man selected by Fennako as the father to my child. If I'm pregnant, my contract with Fennako has been fulfilled and Noahee is a sovereign clan. But also, if I've fulfilled the contract, I'm no longer considered married. I'm both married and not married. Pregnant and not pregnant."

"Hold the course. Uncertainty may be the strongest position."

"In the midst of all this, Marjoram Shelliko asked for Teakh's hand in marriage. She reasons that if they marry before the new moon, there's no proof of premarital insemination and so no proof that the theft occurred. Ralko would be unable to press charges or claim custody."

"That artist is a devious woman," Gratia said.

"Teakh wants to marry her."

"Even after all this?"

"He's concerned about his children. So am I. There

are other factors that I will not discuss even on a secure line. Ralko must not gain custody of Teakh's children, and this must not go to court. Either outcome could endanger the children and possibly Teakh. I have reasons for wanting good relations with Idylko." If Jeena took a mind to revenge she could let on that Teakh had royal DNA and start rumors that he had designs on the throne. The unspeakable might again occur—the assassination of kinfolk.

Gratia placed her fingertips together. "You're in a pickle."

"I know. I need help drafting a prenuptial agreement with Shelliko, one that will protect Teakh in the event his relationship with Marjoram goes sour. It may already have. We must negotiate with Idylko and Pontako for joint custody and layout some type of insemination contract for both clans. The contracts must be done in a way that protects Teakh's value as a stud. Dojko has an interest because they're due a cut of Teakh's stud fees. They're supportive of the marriage. We have mixed support from Fennako. They could claim custody. The clan of my fiancé's former wife might also make a claim."

"You have many what-ifs."

"We must act before the new moon and go through with our plan even if none of us are pregnant." When the moon moved into phase with the sun, women would menstruate, and we'd know who was or wasn't pregnant. "Taking action is better than the alternatives." Noahee needed the support of many clans in order to face Big Auntie when she became queen. If Noahee had this support she'd be unable to move against Teakh without political backlash.

Gratia had seen clearly; I had too many what-ifs and too much that could go wrong.

I glanced at the window to see Dyse was lurking in

the Plaza. Mareen had departed so I couldn't fall back on her. I'd have to deal with Ralko on my own. I headed downstairs and looked into the plaza, but she was gone.

———

Chapter 36
Wedding

PONTAKO WOMEN PASSED through the square, pushing carts loaded with cooking equipment and groceries. Five of the eight interested clans had arrived: Idylko, Noahee, Ralko, Fennako, and Dojko. Telisko and the clan who'd won the bid on Teakh's maiden liaison didn't show. We hadn't invited or informed either of them. We still waited on word from the bride's clan, Shelliko.

Frustrated, I went up to my teleconference room. All the other agreements hinged on the prenuptial and marriage contract between Angel and Teakh.

But before I could contact Shelliko, Dyse hailed. I put her on screen. She stood before an overstuffed chair with an antimacassar, surely the badge of Idylko.

"Don't be confused by the doilies and slippers," she warned me. "Grandmatriachs are grasping hags. If you and I work together, we can win this battle. Here is our strategy—we go after Idylko for everything they're worth. Then we go after Pontako and Shelliko as accomplices. We'll ask for," Dyse narrowed her eyes, "emergency contraception. If they delay, we'll demand abortions. We'll break up the crime ring by placing an injunction against all three women. They will be forbidden to meet, all communication cut between them."

I refrained from laughing in her face at a plan that was both absurd and cruel. "But Jeena and Reez are married," I said.

"They should have thought of that when they assaulted Teakh. We'll have the lab technician barred from ever again working in that capacity. That artist woman must destroy all paintings of him and provide a public apology. She must never again speak with our kinsman."

"That's harsh," I said. "Teakh will never agree."

"Of course it's harsh, and it doesn't matter what he thinks. It's our initial demands. Idylko will agree to pay a hefty fine instead, so will the other clans. We'll do quite well. You can payoff Teakh's esskip. You can go shopping again, and this time actually have money to spend."

"I don't give a shine about how much money we can squeeze out of Idylko."

"It's good business. Toughen up, girl."

My heart rate jumped with my ire, but I wouldn't let it show. I'd be as cool as the Lady Danna. "Thank you for your excellent advice," I said before I signed off.

What a hag!

ANGEL ARRIVED ON the doorstep with dark semi-circles below her eyes.

"He won't talk to me," she complained.

"Come on in."

She crept into the parlor.

"Tea?" I asked.

She shook her head.

Leaving her slumped on a chair, I knocked on Teakh's bedroom door. He didn't answer, so I went in. He lay on the bed.

Depths! Both of them, helpless, hopeless.

"Get up! Your bride looks like she's been crying all night. Talk to her! You're a Seaguard chief. You better Poseidon-damn act like one."

Teakh hoisted himself out of bed. He smoothed his head bandanna then morosely followed me into the parlor.

He sat down and stared out the window. Angel stared at the floor.

"Well?" I stood before them. "We're engaged in a multi-clan custody dispute because of you two. Pontako is doing the catering. Idylko has generously provided lodging and facilities. Fennako set up a secure teleconferencing room. Your Dojko friends have arrived. If you don't want to get married fine. We'll call off the wedding and solve this mess a different way." I had no idea what we'd do. "I'm going upstairs to study. When you've got this worked out, give me a hail."

I opened a reader screen, but I couldn't concentrate. The light had dimmed in the plaza and snow fell, a late-season flurry.

When I came downstairs, Teakh sat on a settee, his arm around Angel, her face red and wet with tears.

"We are getting married," he said.

Angel wiped her eyes. "I'd like to borrow your teleconference equipment to talk with my clan, and with my mother. I also need to use your washroom."

"Go ahead," I said.

She left the parlor. Water ran in the sink. When she emerged, all signs of tears were gone and her makeup fresh.

I showed her to the teleconference center and warned her that she'd need a similar setup on the other side.

"I understand. I already hailed my mother. She's on her way to meet with our clan banker."

The wedding would go through. I dared to breathe a sigh of relief.

FOR THE WEDDING, I dressed in a gray robe trimmed with blue velvet—rushed from Fennako City. The groom's party gathered in the parlor. Teakh wore Seaguard kit, also in gray and blue. The rest of the party included Keno and Iris and a Dojko woman with her husband.

Wedding guests crowded the entrance of the Idylko clan hall. When Teakh gave the signal, we in the groom's party left the house and formed a procession in the plaza with Iris and me in the lead. We'd give the groom away.

Guests in the plaza cheered or made good-natured ribald comments. We entered through the double doors of the hall. The place was packed, every seat filled, guests standing along the walls, and not all of the guests were inside. I spotted grizzled fishermen, studs from Keno's gym, ragged clanless men and women, Seaguard members in the colors of numerous clans, and well-dressed women who moved with elegance and grace. Courtesans? Artists?

We moved up the aisle to where Angel stood regally in a gown of copper colored silk, the gleaming fabric hugging her curves and her smile radiant—no sign of tears. In no way did she appear to have been dragged to the wedding dais.

The magistrate, resplendent in Fennako green robes, spoke of the force of love seeking balance—traditional words:

> *In the beginning, Void split Darkness from Light,*
> *but Light loved Darkness and Darkness loved*
> *Light. As the two sought each other across Void,*
> *they danced the universe into being.*

TEAKH AND ANGEL left the hall arm-in-arm, revelers falling in behind them, escorting the couple to the bower house where Teakh and his three brides would consummate their vows.

I didn't follow. The wedded foursome had specified only a handful of select witnesses. But even if I'd wanted to, my witnessing the consummation was inappropriate. I sought out my man. With his height and in Fennako kit he was easy to spot. Together we walked through the plaza, past dancers and tables laden with food.

Dyse blocked the doorway to our lodging. "I know what you're up to," she said. "Cutting Ralko out of the bargaining. You've made a big mistake."

"We'll talk inside." I opened the door. "Not on the plaza."

My man remained in the parlor as Dyse and I went up to the teleconference room. I turned the screens toward the wall and drew chairs to the table.

Alone, I sat facing Dyse. "I'm listening."

"You've let Idylko take advantage of Teakh. They raped him. And you handed him over."

"It wasn't rape. It was consensual, so is his marriage."

"Teakh didn't give informed consent. That's rape. He may have agreed to sex with Marjoram Shelliko. That doesn't mean he agreed to sex with Jeena Idylko."

"They were in the same room. In the same bed," I said. "All four of them were involved and consenting."

Dyse stalked across the floor. "Kissing and embracing isn't the same as penetration. Do I have to spell this out? Teakh thought he ejaculated into Marjoram. That's what he consented to. He did not consent to ejaculating into an artificial vagina held by Jeena Idylko."

"He's chosen not to press charges."

"And how consensual is his marriage? He had no other option."

"Teakh has chosen to marry. I support him as his grandmatriarch."

"I've read your contract with Fennako. It's illegal. You haven't even fulfilled the terms of that contract. The man is Marsk Fennako, and you know it. If you've conceived, it wasn't according to the contract."

"He's never told me his name."

"Perjury has consequences," Dyse said. "Take care."

"The Queen recognizes me as Noahee grandmatriarch," I said. "That's enough for me."

"Is it enough? You should have asked for more from Idylko. You should have taken my advice. Annin, Annin," she admonished. "If you'd just get advice from your kin and think things through."

I wanted her out of my life. Founder the consequences.

"You're not my kin and we don't need or want your advice. Noahee is a sovereign clan."

———

Chapter 37
Moon of Turmoil

A SLIVER OF A moon bled weak light into the courtyard, casting a long shadow behind the statue of Fenna Lee-Smith. I was back in Fennako City. Although not superstitious I closed the curtains to shut out view of Luna Minora, the moon of turmoil. Tonight, the little moon would rule the night alone. The big moon, Luna Majora, was new and so hid in the light of day.

My bleeding hadn't yet begun. Pray that it wouldn't begin, and I'd go in for my prenatal appointment.

At breakfast, the dining room was subdued, students talking little or eating alone. The darkness of Majora brought on introspection and silence. Women often went on solitary retreats. Businesses were closed and lights were extinguished after dark.

I returned to my room. My study group wasn't meeting so I lay on my bed reading. After a time, I went down the hallway to the facilities. The debris of the new moon filled bins, but my undergarments showed no spotting. I returned to my room and my studies.

My man hailed. "What are you about?"

"Studying. Nothing yet." We chatted, incidentals, not touching on our hopes.

I hailed Angel who happily informed me she was pregnant. "My intuition is seldom wrong," she claimed.

"Is he there?" I asked, meaning Teakh.

"And listening in," she said. "We're a detective agency. Clans hire us as consultants. Jeena does the lab work. She's changing from medical to forensic. Reez and Teakh work in the field. I have my ways of getting information. I'm a spy," she said with glee.

THE HOUSE MOTHER hailed with announcement of an important visitor. I went down to the front lobby to find Valarin Hellenboreko—that hag!

I stayed well back as if promotion of eugenics was contagious. "What are you about?" I concealed my distaste in politeness.

"Observing the tide," she answered as if I had no business asking. "Do I understand that you allowed your brother to sire five children in a single month?"

"Only four," I said. "The other one is mine."

"Didn't I warn you? Here you are not fully a clan and already your brother's children outnumber yours. What will happen in a generation? What about in six generations?"

"It's too early to know. We haven't given birth yet."

"We—I speak for the eugenics council—recommend that you take steps to corral your brother's promiscuity."

"And if I don't?"

"Then we will take steps."

"I thought you liked his genetics."

"The problem isn't his genetics—it's your clan."

This wasn't an argument I could win. "Thank you for your concern. Our clan charter was approved by Her Majesty. If you have a problem, you can take it up with her." I wanted Hellenboreko out of my life, same as Dyse.

"You can be sure we will."

I raised my head high. She couldn't do a thing to me. I was confident of royal backing.

I returned upstairs to my room and set about catching up with my studies. Dyse hailed to ask about my pregnancy, surely wanting to know if Noahee status was official.

"I've made an appointment." I still might bleed, but I'd made the appointment anyway. This time I intended to follow through.

"Do let me come with you. I happen to be in Fennako City, and a girl should have an older kinswoman standing by."

"That'll be all right. I have a friend going with me."

"Are you sure. I'm there for you. Let's get together to plan a baby shower."

I tried to put her off. "I haven't confirmed the pregnancy."

"I'll take you to lunch. My behavior in Idylko was deplorable. I want to make it up to you. Weddings make me so emotional. I'm with Gorby at the Fennako City Municipal Harbor. Pier Nine. You can't miss us."

I'd hear her out. Maybe I'd been unfair to Dyse. I agreed to the meeting but left a message with my man.

A BLACK-AND-SCARLET ESSKIP floated beside pier nine, Dyse and Gorby waiting in the cockpit.

My comset activated with is her voice. "Burr it's cold. Join us in the esskip where it's warm."

"I'm fine."

"Truly we need to talk in private."

The canopy opened. "Hi, cuz," shouted Gorby.

I stepped onto the wing shoulder and dropped into the middle seat.

"Let's plan a baby shower. It's something I can do for you," said Dyse from behind me.

"No thanks. I have everything I need."

"Not for you, for Teakh. First, though let's make sure our discussion is private. We don't want to spoil the surprise. A comset can seem to be turned off, but in reality it's transmitting everything. One can never be too careful. We'll put our comsets on the dock."

Gorby turned toward me. "Let's humor her."

I handed off my comset. In hindsight, I understand that I was as naive as Teakh had been. Or maybe I obeyed out of habit. Dyse told me what to do and I did it.

She set the comsets on the dock, then clambered back into the esskip. The canopy closed. "Let's go home."

The esskip moved from the pier. I stared at the back of Gorby's head.

My mind whirled; I'd made a mistake and had to get out. "Lord Tristan Bay knows where I am. You can't leave Fennako waters." My voice came out flat. My mouth was dry.

Choking fear engulfed me. Had my abduction been orchestrated by the Eugenics Council?

"The law is on our side," Dyse said. "Tristan Bay may deny entry, but may not prohibit us or anyone else anyone from leaving."

"I'm a ward of the Queen. She'll use royal override to ground this craft." I grasped at an argument even as my heart hammered. What about Big Auntie? Would Dyse attempt to kill me?

"Not while the craft is in flight. That would endanger the passengers."

"Gorby, why are you doing this?" I asked, trying not to plead.

He brought his craft up on step, water splashing the canopy. "I heard what happened to you in the Fennako men's house. I won't let you be mistreated that way."

"I wasn't mistreated."

"Mistreated and brainwashed," said Dyse. "Poor girl.

Tricked into sexual servitude and now you're in love with your captor."

I couldn't hail my man. I'd left my foundered comset on the pier. I considered pummeling Gorby, or better yet turning in my seat and going after Dyse.

"It's for your own good. You'll thank me someday," she said.

Attacking Gorby wouldn't be wise. The esskip was already on step, seawater spraying from her struts.

Beyond the glazing of the canopy, sun shone down on Tristan Bay, winking off waves, and a gray-green esskip. It took off from the water, the tail clearly marked with the twelve-point badge of Harbor Patrol, but I had no way of sending a signal.

Gorby said, "I'm in communication with Tristan Bay. They're requesting identification of passengers."

"We're all members of Clan Ralko," Dyse said. "No need for further identification."

Two Harbor Patrol esskips arrowed toward us.

"Auntie," Gorby said. "You'd best hear this."

The speakers in the cockpit activated. "This is Tristan Bay Command. Identify all passengers."

"Annin Noahee here!" I shouted.

"They can't hear you. Gorby, be a dear. Tell them, we're returning to Ralko territory."

A man's voice came over the speakers. "We require assurance that all passengers are traveling under their own free will. We will speak with Annin Noahee."

Dyse spoke to Gorby, "Tell them that detaining us constitutes piracy."

Despite my engulfing panic, I attempted to argue in measured tones. "Abducting me is human trafficking."

"We're saving you from trafficking."

A familiar voice came on—my man! "Marsk Fennako here. Tristan Bay Seaguard Chief, Magnate and Lord of Tristan Bay, grandson to Her Majesty the Queen. You are removing from our waters one Annin Noahee, grandmatriarch of Noahee, sovereign clan. Her personage is under our protection. Touch down and heave to."

Dyse said, "Tell him we have no one aboard by that name."

"Touch down and heave to," my man commanded. "This is the second warning."

"Keep flying," Dyse said. "They can't do anything. Not without risking harm to her and the baby. He was using you," she said to me. "He doesn't love you. He doesn't care what happens to you."

"You don't make sense at all. He loves me or he doesn't."

Harbor Patrol esskips converged on us in echelon. Patrol boats followed further behind.

Panic closed in. Was Dyse working with the Eugenics Council? What about Big Auntie?

"I'm your aunt. I've known you since you were a little girl. I was there for you when your mother died, your own kin strangers to you, all due to her obstinacy."

"Third warning. Touch down and heave to. You are in violation of Tristan Bay airspace and waters. Illegal removal of Annin Noahee from Tristan Bay constitutes an act of war."

Good Danna! We'd come to this.

———

Chapter 38
Captive Lawyer

MOUNTAINS DREW CLOSE and then receded as we flew away from the densely populated islands of Fennako City. We approached villages, which quickly dropped astern as we passed without stopping. To me they remained nameless and unknown. I desired a chart, or even a rough map such as tourists used.

Through this, three Fennako esskips remained on our tail. I pinned my hope on them.

"Fennako is going to come after you," I said. "They'll track you down."

"Don't worry. We have a plan."

"What about food?" I'd expected to eat lunch earlier. "And I need to pee." I did. My bladder ached.

We splashed down near a village harbor and approached a fuel dock, its pylons cross-braced and dark with age. A ladder with dubious rungs clung to the side of a pylon. Gorby retracted the canopy, his jets pulsing slowly. He stood and yelled: "We need fuel."

The esskip was drifting under and between the shadowy substructure.

"Help!" I shouted then ducked to avoid striking my head against a cross brace. In the shadows, three people crouched on a narrow catwalk. A rope ladder dropped.

"Don't make this difficult," Dyse said. "Either climb up on your own or we knock you out and carry you. We've got an inhalant drug. Might not be good for the baby."

I grasped the ladder.

"Thank you," Dyse said. "I wasn't looking forward to hauling you around unconscious."

She followed me up the ladder. Two women dropped from the catwalk to take our places in the esskip.

We emerged through a trapdoor into a shed containing some chairs and a desk. Small windows gave a view of fuel tanks and harbor. I considered the size of the windows and if they could be opened. No latches. But maybe I could break a pane and wriggle out.

Dyse dragged a chair over the trap door and sat on it. "By the way, the door is locked from the outside."

If she produced a rag soaked with a drug, I'd use it on her.

She said, "I've explained to our hosts that you're a victim of hostage syndrome and may try to return to your captors."

I pointed out the tenuousness of her position. "Fennako will impose sanctions on Ralko. You'll be denied access to bank accounts."

"We have allies."

"I still need to pee," I said. Maybe she'd let me out of the shed and I'd make a break.

"Bucket. Over in the corner."

I did my business, then returned to a chair.

Dyse emptied the bucket into the sea below. A shove might send her head-first through the hole. That's what a girl might do in some old fairytale, but a legal resolution remained possible. I'd solve this as the lawyer I intended to be.

Dyse closed the trapdoor and repositioned the chair. "I arranged for food here. Be a good girl and take a look in that basket, the one on the desk."

The carrier contained sandwiches, plates, cups, and a bottle of cranberry fizz. We ate.

As the setting sun tinged the sky pink, a rap came from below. Dyse moved the chair and opened the trapdoor. We descended the ladder to a dinghy. In the twilight I didn't get a good look at the woman piloting the craft. She and Dyse pushed the dinghy out from under the dock. With her her face lit by the setting sun, I recognized her. Madame X.

I considered jumping overboard, but I wasn't a strong swimmer and didn't have a life vest. The Fennako esskips were gone. Madame X throttled a small propulser, carrying us to a cabin cruiser moored in the harbor.

Dyse hustled me aboard and below deck. Madame X's boots tapped above us as I crouched with Dyse in the dim cabin.

"You've been taken advantage of by Fennako," she said, as if she could make it true through repetition. "They lured you in, dangling tempting rewards: your own clan, law school, a career as a lawyer. Now you're pregnant and you don't even know the father."

"I am in law school, and I do know the father." The bench was hard.

"You can't attend law school when you've got a child to care for. And you can't rely on Fennako. We'll get you out of this. You'll need a way to earn money. It was all very well running the clanless shelter when you were single, but now you have a child to think of."

I laid my case before her as carefully as I could. "As a lawyer, I'll make plenty of money. And Fennako has agreed to provide childcare."

"You can't even make good decisions about your own interests. How can you expect to represent clients?"

"Allow me to use a comset. I'll hail Fennako Seaguard to let them know where I am."

"None of that. Under the influence of Fennako you'll be unable to think clearly."

"You expect me to think clearly with Madame X aboard?"

"Madame X?" Dyse asked. "Oh that's what you're calling our skipper. She's an experienced sailor and she's knowledgeable about the market for surrogacy."

"She assaulted Teakh."

"We know all about that," Dyse said. "Madame X, as you call her, assures me it was a misunderstanding. She believed Teakh was willing to donate sperm provided it was done in a discreet manner. He'd done so before."

"There was nothing discreet about it. She attacked him in full view of Fennako City surveillance. Just because a person consents to sex with one person doesn't mean they consent to sex with another." I had to get out of this cabin and off this cruiser.

"She merely propositioned him," Dyse said. "You overreacted. You'll never make a good lawyer."

"What's this about surrogacy?" I didn't like the prospects she'd been hinting at.

"You should consider becoming a surrogate mother. Your brother is doing quite well as a stud."

"I don't want to become a surrogate mother."

"You already are. We could terminate the pregnancy and start over again using high quality sperm from a known donor. If we act quickly, there'll be no evidence that you were pregnant."

I should have swum for it when I had the chance. The boat was now moving, surely with Madame X at the helm.

I LAY IN the forward berth while the boat sailed onward. I would miss my second prenatal appointment, and there was no proof of my pregnancy. If only I'd thought to carry my marine comset as a backup. I vowed that if I should escape, I'd always carry two comsets.

Madame X and Dyse spoke together, their voices muted by the closed door. Madame X said. "The Noah breed responds to domination but with a light touch. I learned that with her brother."

Dyse mumbled and Madame X said, "It's not an insurmountable problem. Despite the hype, the Noah breed can bond with more than one lover."

I strained to listen, but missed Dyse's words.

Madame X said, "That Shelliko woman certainly handles the brother well. She keeps everyone in line, including him."

A GENTLE KNOCK tapped at the door. "Annin, may I come in?"

I gathered the blanket tightly around me.

"I'm not going to hurt you." Madame X entered without permission.

I sat up. "Listen, Madame X, or whoever you are. There's only one lover for me, the father of my child."

She set a bundle of clothing on the berth. "We're at sea, so you may come up on deck if you like. I have these for you. Foul weather gear, life vest, and boots."

Clad in slicker, waterproof knee boots, and knit cap as if I were a deckhand, I emerged from the companionway. Water stretched to the horizon, land nowhere to be seen. I touched the shoulder pocket of the vest, but it contained no comset. It also lacked a knife and a whistle, standard emergency gear. Behind a windshield, Dyse could be seen at the helm. The boat cruised along, easily breasting swells. The dome of the sky arched overhead marked only by fluffy clouds.

My man had showed me how to use a jerry-rigged astrolabe. If I'd known the time, I could have estimated directions. If I'd known cardinal directions, I could have estimate time. I knew neither.

I tried the door to the bridge, locked tight.

Options. Think of options.

I could attempt to signal a passing aircraft, but I'd need a mirror. A flare could be used at night. I could light something on fire. Dyse and Madame X would be forced to send an SOS. The only problem was that the boat might sink before rescuers arrived.

I went below and reclined on the forward birth, my boots still on. Soon Dyse came down as well. Either Madame X had spelled Dyse at the helm, or the boat was on autopilot.

I told Dyse, "You're going about this all wrong. Go to Fennako City under conditions of parley. Take this to court and let the Zenhedron decide."

"They'll take you away from us," she said. "Fennako controls the Zenhedron."

I'd practiced presenting both sides of a case. By Poseidon I'd do it now, argue against myself. "Your case is solid," I said. "I wanted my own clan, wanted it so badly I'd do nearly anything. I was underage, still am, and coerced into signing. The contract won't stand in court."

"We won't get a fair hearing."

"Fairer than sanctions without a hearing?" I asked. "Fennako will freeze Ralko accounts. You won't be able to access credit."

"Our allies will stand with us," Dyse said.

"What allies?" I needed to know if she was working the Eugenics Council.

"There are the clans of Ralko husbands and others."

"Who?"

"Don't you worry about that," she said. "They're behind us completely."

"At what cost?" I demanded. "Their accounts will be frozen as well. We could have a civil war. Is that what you want? Auntie, take this to court. I don't want to see Ralko destroyed, not over me. Your case is solid."

Were these lies? No. Shadings of the truth. Our case could go either way in court. Except not all the cards had been played. If my mitochondrial DNA were known, the Queen, as my rightful guardian, could claim me as her ward.

———

Chapter 39
Pregnant Princess

THE BOAT SLOWED. Possibly, we'd reached a clan boundary. Squinting in the sunlight, I scanned the horizon for a sign of human habitation, spying a few puffy clouds but no hint of land jutted above the seas. Dyse and Madame were on the bridge surely attempting to obtain hospitality and permission to proceed.

My man and I had often waited at boundaries for the go-ahead. I hugged myself, trying to imagine he held me. I recalled that he'd once had a job inspecting life rafts and that he'd warned me of boats with uncertified equipment.

I found the life raft strapped to the deck. I looked it over and the certification was current. Imagine that, pirates who maintain safety. I loosened the straps, checked that the painter was secure, and flung the case overboard.

It broke open, the contents bursting forth, expanding with a hiss until it became a circular raft topped by a tent dome. I released the painter and dove through the tent opening. The raft bumped the hull of the boat before drifting away.

I surveyed my domain. The raft contained food rations, water, blankets, and a first aid kit. In the dome, a beacon blinked; it had activated. I searched for and found the required marine com in a pocket but wouldn't use it immediately. Dyse and Madame X surely monitored emergency channels.

I unzipped the tent and raised myself to see over the waves. The boat, now under power, cruised away, her hind-end visible with the name TChE Jolly Girl. Muttering "Tango, Charlie, Electric," to burn the letters into my memory, I ducked back inside the tent, my own little world. I had enough food and water to last for days. I unfolded blankets and made myself a bed, a cocoon bobbing over swells. Oddly, I felt secure. Sensors underlying the water sent data to the local Seaguard lord. If he was paying attention, he could feel my raft moving over the surface.

I leaned back and watched the clouds beyond a clear panel in the dome. With my hand over my belly I wondered if my child would be a girl or boy.

Life would be hard for a son. I'd have to choose if he'd get a neural implant and became Seaguard like his father or if he remained an ordinary mariner. Seaguard had more status and greater career opportunities. Yet, he would be a threat to Fennako, a potential heir to his father. Better to have a girl. Even without an implant she'd have plenty of opportunities. I prayed to Danna for a girl.

The raft flexed over a swell. If my man could get royal override from his grandmother, he'd be able to feel the raft. Dozing, I imagined that he could and that he carried me. I awoke to the dome rattling. I bolted upright, confused by shouting:

"Ahoy! Ahoy! Anybody there?"

I unzipped the tent.

A bearded face peered down at me. "What are you doing here?"

The face belonged to a man aboard an esskip.

"Taking a nap."

"In a life raft on high seas?" he exclaimed.

"I jumped off a boat."

"Jumped ship, huh? What happened to your uncle, boy? Why did he let you do such a stupid thing?"

"Not a boy. I'm pregnant." The more people who knew my condition the better. "Request hospitality."

"Girl? You're about the strangest thing I've seen out here, a pregnant girl dressed as a deckhand."

"Not a girl. I'm a clan matriarch."

"Even stranger." He offered a callused hand and helped me aboard his esskip. "We'll have to leave your raft for salvage. Hope you're not too fond of it. You might get stuff back from salvage crews, but you gotta pay."

"They can have it," I said. If Dyse or Madame X had to pay ransom for the raft, that suited me just fine. Better it than me.

"Take the second seat," he said. "Got fishing gear in the back."

The cockpit, smelling of old fish, reminded me of Teakh. A fishing pole lay along the top of the lazarettes under the gunwale.

I dropped into the seat. "I need to visit a bank."

"Are you daft?"

"To contact my kin through a secure channel. The banking system has the best security."

We took to the air, leaving the raft behind, an abandoned spot of orange. We flew until we approached a green headland fronted by a high bluff. There wasn't a true esskip lagoon. I supposed such a lagoon was unnecessary if the area lacked large tidal fluctuations. We splashed down in a cove. The pilot offered to go with me to the village to meet with the bankers.

We walked from the harbor along a wide pathway that wound up the bluff. A pony cart passed us. The woman driver greeted the pilot. We hiked across grassy fields dotted with sheep and broken by greenhouses set into the ground. Cottages clustered around a building that resembled an overturned boat hull.

We entered the foyer of what the pilot told me was the grandmatriarch's house. I removed my boots and entered a parlor where a group of women knitted. A table held the remainders of cake and tea.

The pilot announced, "Take a look at what the tide washed up. I was out fishing and came across her."

"I'm pregnant," I said.

The clack of knitting needles halted.

"When is the little one due?"

"Nine months," I said.

All eyes turned to the pilot.

"Not him." I backpaddled. "My husband and I conceived during the full moon."

"Conceived on a lucky tide!" With delight they made plans for a baby layette—blankets, booties, little caps.

"Thank you, but first please allow me to use the teleconference center at your bank. I must contact my kin."

"We don't have one." A knitter pulled at a ball of yarn. "But Banks over there is clan finance mistress. She might be able to help."

"Well, first things first." Banks bundled her knitting into a bag. "We'll decide on gifts later." She stamped her feet into galoshes, and I pulled on boots.

We trudged across a muddy field to her small cottage crammed with knickknacks. Her parlor was small and filled with seashells, beadwork, and carved driftwood. She dusted off a com screen.

I considered asking for privacy, but being overheard by Banks wouldn't make much difference. "Hailing Mareen Fennako Senior, Minster of Royal Finance and

Banking." I spoke distinctly so that the com-screen would pick up my voice.

To my delight and relief, the screen activated with a view of Big Mareen.

I shushed her before she could say anything. "The channel isn't secure, and I'm under hospitality." I'm fine," I said. "Please let him know." I left out my man's name.

"Where are you? What happened?"

"Let him know I'm fine." She would know I meant my man. "I was abducted and taken aboard a boat, the Jolly Girl. Clan registration Tango Charlie Electric. I used a life raft to escape and was rescued by Seaguard, clan designation: Shimmy, Whiskey, Theta, One, Two, Eight. That clan has treated me well. All honor to them."

"We'll get you home," Big Mareen said. "Despite my sister. Did she do it?"

"I don't know."

I signed off.

Banks stood at my shoulder "Oh my. The Fennako minister of finance. Her sister is Princess Royal. This is so exciting!" Banks exclaimed. "A princess washed up by the tide."

"I'm not a princess. I'm a law student."

"A pregnant princess dressed as a boy!"

There was no stopping this story, so I played it up: "The Princess Royal hates me and my child. I fell in love with her nephew, and she hates that we married."

If Banks knew enough about the royal family to identify the minister of finance, she knew exactly who I'd married. "So the baby is his?" Banks asked.

I nodded. "I was kidnapped by pirates but escaped. Please keep my secret." I knew she wouldn't. This story would spread like fire aboard a ship full of straw.

THEY GAVE ME no comset.

I went for long walks in the fields overlooking the ocean where waves broke against rocky shores. The clan used shaggy ponies to pull carts of compost, a quiet and self-sufficient life. I felt oddly cut off from communication.

I sat with Banks and her fellow matriarchs as they did crafts and gossiped. The clan produced their own wool which they spun and knit into characteristic brown and white patterns. They provided me with knitting needles and my choice of yarns. As we knit and they gossiped, they shared sardines, crisp rye flatbread, and sheep milk cheese. Daily I hailed using Banks's screen and pleaded with Big Mareen.

She counseled patience. "I'm working on it. Your aunt's clan—"

"Don't call her my aunt."

"Understood. That clan doesn't want our clan to have custody of you and your child. We certainly won't yield custody to them."

Avoiding names—"that clan" "our clan"—burdened our communication. I had to mentally translate: Ralko doesn't want Fennako to have custody.

"I should have custody of myself," I said.

"You do have it, legally. But you'll have to live with the sheep and the ponies because we aren't legally allowed to send transport, and neither is that clan."

"So I'm stuck living on hospitality. Can't I at least talk to him?"

"Forbidden."

"Founder it all!"

I signed off.

Banks listening in offered: "We'll get you back to your prince. I've got a plan."

I HIKED ACROSS a windswept field dressed as a deckhand, the village in the distance, the sheep grazing. They scattered as a seaplane buzzed the field and circled above me. Uncertain of what to do I waved. The plane dipped a wing and then descended for a landing.

I hurried toward the village, best if I wasn't caught in the open.

Banks met me. "My plan. We've brought in the media."

We hiked to the clan hall. Reporters clustered before it with cameras.

One of them came towards me. "I'm with Fenrian Eye News. May we have a word with you? I understand you were rescued from pirates."

I felt my body tense. Whatever I said would be broadcast to all of Fenria. "What do you want to know?"

"Look into the camera and relax," the reporter said. "Speak as if to friends. Go ahead and give your name."

"I'm under hospitality."

"Is it true that you're a princess?"

"I'm not," I answered. "But I am pregnant, and I was abducted. I've been forbidden to speak with the father of my child." I looked directly into the lens of the camera. "I love you very much," I said before retreating to Banks's cottage. There! I'd thrown my spark into the tinder. Let the rumors blaze!

———

Chapter 40
Knitters

THE LADIES GOSSIPED, their needles clacking. I looped creamy wool over a needle and drew it back through.

Knit, purl, knit, purl.

A wall screen activated.

"We're on!" a woman exclaimed.

The view cut from the Seaguardsman who'd rescued me to a shot of the village from the seaplane and of me walking through sheep dotted fields.

The knitters whooped.

"We rescued the princess!"

They beamed at me as my interview played.

Knit, purl, knit, purl.

A comset activated announcing: "Princess Mareen Fennako Senior."

Knitting paused, the group silent as they strained to listen to a hail by royalty. Banks and I stamped on footwear and hurried to her cottage to the comparative privacy of Bank's cluttered parlor.

A screen activated with the face of my mother-in-law. Big Mareen. She said, "We have transport coming for you tomorrow. Certain parties do not want you talking to the media. They saw that interview and their hails queued up, every one of them marked urgent." She laughed.

"My hostess's idea," I grinned at Banks.

"Brilliant," said Big Mareen

"Who's providing transport?" I asked. "Will he come?"

"Expect an esskip. I tell you no more at this time."

I SAT READING on an old couch in Bank's place when the hail came.

"Is it Fennako?" I asked. Maybe my man piloted the craft. If we could be together all would be well.

"Clan code November Ophelia Alpha Alpha. That's a new one."

Noahee! My brother had come.

I flung open the door of Banks's cottage and hurried to the grandmatriarch's house. The knitters were emerging from their houses as well. We converged at the matriarch's house and went inside. Others arrived with food and baskets of knitting.

And then Teakh stood in the doorway clad as Chief Noahee.

I nearly fell into his arms.

He asked, "Are you okay?"

I stepped back. "Aye. Is Angel here?" Jeena stood by his side.

We greeted each other as friends, our dispute over Teakh's marriage shoved aside. Noahee needed allies, and I was counting on Idylko despite any lingering resentment I felt toward Raptoria and Jeena.

To the knitters, I made partial introductions, as much as hospitality would allow. "This is my brother and a kinswoman. My hostesses." I indicated the women.

We all squeezed into the parlor and were given pickled carrots, goat cheese, and crackers. Our hostesses showed off baby bonnets and booties.

Teakh asked questions, endearing himself to them, and soon they had him knitting as well.

"My companion here is also pregnant," Teakh said. "If all goes well, our clan has five babies on their way."

The knitters insisted on making gifts for all five of them. Teakh, Jeena, and I each completed a square.

WE FLEW FROM the clan of knitters bound for Idylko, the safest place for me. Jeena told me I could have use of the house we'd stayed in before and assured me the teleconference equipment remained in place.

"Jeena, what about a midwyv. I've missed two prenatal appointments." By Poseidon! This time I'd have proof of my pregnancy.

"We have a good one in Idylko, a cousin of mine. My partner and I are going to her. We can all go to her together, mothers of the same cohort."

"Thank you."

After a layover and multiple refueling stops, we landed on the lagoon behind the Idylko hospital. Night had fallen. Teakh brought his craft into the Idylko esskip hanger. In darkness, I clambered out, relieved to move around after hours in the cramped cockpit. We went first to Jeena's place, and then to what we now called "the Noahee house." I slept in the bedroom I'd once shared with my man.

In the morning I handled the circuit breaker while Teakh checked for bugs. He shouted when he needed a circuit turned on or off. It was slow work, and we didn't find anything. I much preferred manning the circuit breaker with my man.

At long last, I sat in my teleconference center and hailed him. Words flashed to the screen:

ACCESS DENIED.

———

Chapter 41
Allies

THE SCREEN PIVOTED, following me as I paced. I hailed Big Mareen.

"What the depths is going on? I can't reach Him. I get access denied."

"We're negotiating. Calm down."

"Calm down!? I've been abducted. And now I can't reach my husband."

"Ralko views him as having undue influence on you and so on the outcome of the legal judgment."

"Founder Ralko. They have no claim on me. I renounce them."

She laced her fingers together. "That is at the core of this tangle."

"Neither my consort nor I are members of Clan Ralko. I have the right to speak with my husband. With my consort."

"That's in dispute. According to the law, your marriage ended when you fulfilled the contract. I'm not saying I like it. That's the way it is."

"How do they know I fulfilled the contract?"

"You said so to the media."

"Like Poseidon! I don't even know if I'm pregnant. I haven't had a prenatal exam, so there's no proof. Founder them! We're still married."

"I would like to help you, but be warned—Ralko has filed suit against Fennako. Our hands are tied."

"Isn't there anything you can do? For Danna sake patch me through to him."

"We cannot without weakening our position. But you can do something. File against Ralko."

"How do I do that?"

"Daughter-in-law, think. You're a law student and a grandmatriarch."

I bit back an angry retort. "Mother-in-law, I thank you for your wise counsel." We signed off and the screen went blank.

"Hailing Myrtle Gratianiko." The screen filled with Gratia's face, her square chin and frizzled gray hair.

I would remain calm as Big Mareen had advised. "Sorry for missing class," I began.

"Ha. You get abducted and you're apologizing for it? I tell you this is the best education you can have."

My calm shattered. "I don't care. I must speak with my husband. They tell me that my marriage is over because I fulfilled the contract, but there's no proof that I'm pregnant, so we're still married." I crossed my arms. "As a grandmatriarch, I have a right to speak with my consort."

"It's not that simple. Due to your age your marriage and status as a grandmatriarch are in question. Take good notes. You can write this up in your thesis."

"I don't give a foundered damn about my thesis. I care about my clan and my family." If my contract was invalid so were Teakh's marriage and the agreements protecting Jeena, Reez, and their children. I felt the floor had dropped away.

"Give me an account of what happened. Start from when you left Fennako City." Gratia ducked down and appeared with a note screen.

I told her, "Auntie wanted to talk in private, and I made the mistake of trusting the pilot. I thought he was a friend. I left my comset on the dock because Auntie was worried about eavesdropping through comsets."

"The two comsets have been found and logged as evidence." Gratia's stylus squeaked on the note screen.

I continued, "We left Tristan Bay and flew until we needed fuel. Gorby, Gorbus Ralko—that's the pilot—took his craft under the dock. Auntie and I got out and two Ralko women took our place. We waited at the fuel dock until night. Madame X arrived with a boat—Tango Charlie Electric Jolly Girl. Dyse and Madame X talked about aborting my child, so I threw the life raft into the water and jumped in. Seaguard picked me up—clan designation: Shimmy, Whiskey, Theta. I accepted hospitality. I stayed with that clan until my brother arrived in his esskip. I'm now in Idylko."

Gratia's fingers rippled as she accessed notes. "I have here: Ralko claims Fennako tricked you into signing a contract placing you in sexual servitude. According to them, the contract is invalid because you were underage and lacked the guidance of an older kinswoman. "

"I know all that. And then Ralko will sue Idylko, Shelliko, and Pontako for sexually assaulting my brother and illegally utilizing his semen. Ralko takes custody of me, my child, my brother, and his three children. My entire clan falls apart and my kin—my brother's children—are scattered."

"Here's what you do. Trade. Give them what they want in exchange for what you want. View it as a game of justice poker on a grand scale."

"It's not a game. It's serious."

She recommended that I demonstrate my competence by taking on my own defense and recruiting my study group as a legal team.

I TEXTED MY study group.

> *Hailing Bleeding Hearts,*
>
> *I'm safely in Idylko. Sadly, I won't be able to meet with you all in person. I'm embroiled in a custody dispute. A custody dispute over me. I will be using this lawsuit as part of my thesis. To set up a teleconference, make arrangements with Mareen Fennako Senior, Fenrian Minister of Banking and Finance.*
>
> *I miss all of you*

Jeena arrived and hailed from the doorstep.

"Be right down," I sent.

Teakh was on patrol with Idylko Seaguard, gaining needed experience.

I invited Jeena into the kitchen. There I turned on the tap on the sink. Gushing water could be effective as cover noise. We stood together and spoke in whispers.

"Teakh is in line for the throne," I said.

"He can't be. He's male."

"He has a neural implant. That's the only essential requirement. Everything else is negotiable. His mitochondrial DNA makes him a member of the royal family."

"Him? A queen?"

"Absurd. I know. But he's a threat to the Princess Royal. Seaguard lords could throw in behind Teakh and vote against the matriarchy. It wouldn't be good for any of us. Least of all for my brother."

"DNA never made anyone a queen, not on its own."

"There's more to it. If I have a son with a neural implant, he could be heir to his father. In that one move, Fennako becomes patrilineal. That's what matriarchs fear. They're terrified that men will take over and

336

support their sons at the expense of their nephews."

Jeena shook her head. "Teakh's DNA is public knowledge. It's in the stud catalogs."

"But the public doesn't know the makeup of royal mitochondrial DNA or that it's an exact match. We're not supposed to know. We'll leave them all guessing. Can I trust you on this?"

She nodded, but did I truly know? Does one ever know the motivations and plans of another person?

Together we walked across the plaza to the midwyv's house near the Idylko medical facility. The midwvy took my vitals and made recommendations about nutrition, but I refused all testing: not for pregnancy, genetics, or paternity.

HALF A FORTNIGHT later, I faced Dyse on my teleconference screen.

"I was worried sick about you," she said. "How could you go off and leave that way? I feared that you'd drown."

I addressed her as a stranger. "Madam, stop pretending to care when you don't. It's unbecoming. We must speak of our legal dispute. In the next few months, my brother is scheduled to impregnate three more women. I can have an injunction placed against his services so that he cannot work as stud until his guardianship is resolved." Ralko would lose their cut of his fees.

Dyse objected. "Arrangements have been made."

"He isn't obligated and may pull out at any time he wishes." I made my offer, "Allow me to have contact with my consort and you may continue to collect fees. Lift your injunction and I'll lift mine."

"That would be unfair to you. You've been brainwashed and made a victim of hostage syndrome. That man is a bad influence."

"Then I'll place that injunction."

Dyse offered one teleconference. "I'm not cruel," she claimed.

"Then I'll allow my brother only one liaison. I'm not unreasonable."

We dickered, making offers and counteroffers of fees, time, and frequency. When at last we'd reached an agreement, we sent a record to Fennako and the court. Big Mareen responded:

> *Hailing Annin Noahee,*
>
> *Please forward the details of the agreement. Will it be exactly a twelvenight between conferences? Or is it to be one conference during the waning moon and one conference during the waxing moon? We wait for Ralko to confirm.*
>
> *Mareen Fennako Sr. sending*

I contacted my study group. All three screens of my teleconference were in use as my student legal team crowded around the table into Big Mareen's office.

"The news has you as a princess," Zelta said. Reports had me as Lord Tristan Bay's paramour, abducted while pregnant with his love child. Then I'd escaped from pirates. Technically, Dyse and Madam X really were pirates, since I'd been abducted and transported over high seas.

"Never a princess," I said. If I were a princess, my relationship with my man would be incestuous. Third cousins were allowed to marry, but only if they were members of different clans. "My in-laws are princesses, not me."

A notification scrolled across my screen. I had a visitor. I signed off and peered out the window. Below in the plaza, a delivery woman waited by a cart. I went downstairs and accepted two boxes sent by Mareen Fennako Jr. The parcels contained clothing including my deck boots, blue life vest, and my marine comset. Two sheets of writing film were wrapped around the comset.

Sister in law,

The registration of your comset is to Noahee. I've also added contacts for you.

All the best.

Below the note, another message was scrawled in a child's hand.

Auntie,

I'm glad the pirates didn't get you.

Love Reena

The second sheet was a letter from my man which began:

Dearest, I miss you.

I held it over my heart.

———

Chapter 42
Rounds

IN THE SECOND twelvenight of autumn, Teakh and I flew to Fennako City for the long-awaited court hearings. During five difficult months in Idylko, I'd suffered through morning sickness and loneliness. My man and I were only allowed to meet via teleconference twice a fortnight. Jeena's pregnancy hadn't taken, so we'd arranged for Teakh to do it over again. Having Jeena on board as the mother of a Noahee child was essential.

Angel had moved in with Teakh and me in Idylko and had commandeered the front parlor as an art studio. In between stud gigs, Teakh patrolled with Idylko Seaguard. His ability to fly an esskip had improved remarkably. My man no longer needed to fear for my safety when I rode as a passenger behind Teakh, as I did now.

Our baggage filled the back seat of the esskip and included Teakh's seagull drone perched atop the load.

The palace lagoon hove into view with Royal Guardsmen standing at attention on the seawall. We zoomed past them and splashed down.

I didn't recognize any of the men as I stepped ashore. Possibly Fennako took impartiality seriously. More than likely Big Auntie had selected men loyal to her.

Gull flew upward and alighted on the tail of the esskip as Teakh unloaded our baggage. Then Gull glided from her perch, returning to the cockpit before the canopy closed.

With minimal speech, the men escorted us and our baggage into the palace and up a grand staircase and through galleries punctuated by hexagonal columns, the edifice resembling ice crystals or coral. The leader halted before a doorway in an arched niche. Carvings of starfish and barnacles encrusted the niche.

The door silently slid open and the leader bowed. "Please accept our hospitality."

Teakh peered through the door into the luxury suite divided by translucent screens painted with underwater scenes of kelp and anemones.

"Tell me. Are we prisoner?" he asked

"Guests," said the leader. " However, the lady must remain here. Court order. Madame, to either receive visitors or leave these quarters you must have notarized permission from Clans Fennako, Telisko, and Ralko. You sir are free to come and go as you please. "

"Is this so I don't run off with my husband?"

"I'm simply conveying the will of the court," said the leader.

Teakh tipped his head back peering at the carvings above the door. "Does this place have spybots?"

The leader remained stony-faced. "I'm not allowed to answer."

"May I check this place for not-allowed-to-answer spybots?"

"That would be considered rude."

"If there're no spybots, how would anyone know if I'm being rude or not?"

The leader rubbed his jaw, his expression puzzled.

"Haw!" said Teakh. "I have my answer."

THE ROYAL GUARDSMEN deposited our baggage in the suite. The door slid closed behind them, as soundless as before, sealing Teakh and me inside. I smoothed my hand over the polished wood, a satin-finished surface free of latches, knobs, and hinges. The door remained firmly shut despite my prodding and prying at the ornate doorjamb as I searched for a door-latch pad among the carvings.

Teakh watched me, his lips pursed.

"Locked," I said.

"Not to me." The door slid open.

A Royal Guardsman in Fennako green snapped to attention. The door closed.

"Show off. I could simply follow you out."

"Aye. But you'd have to explain why you did it to Clans Fennako, Ralko, and what was the other? Telisko?"

I tapped at wall paneling with a silly hope for a secret passageway like the one in my dorm room, a way for my man to sneak in.

"You won't find any spybots," said Teakh, "but sure as the tide rises, we're being watched."

In the sitting area I gazed out on Tristan Bay through multi-faceted windows. The view faced west, but my man's island, Tristan Head, wasn't visible from this angle.

To either side of the view, translucent screens closed off two sleeping areas. I stowed my belongings in the one to the northwest, giving Teakh the southwest. So traditional for the women to have cool north-facing light for weaving and the man to have the view of the moons.

The open room contained a dining niche, an office area, and a sitting area with carved chairs and tables arranged on a hexagonal rug. The office featured an antique writing desk against the wall. Searching for a communication screen, I fiddled with the top which opened like a puzzle revealing a slanted writing surface and niches containing paper, envelopes, and writing implements, but no other communication devices. No screens or marinecom.

"What's this?" I asked Teakh. "How can I get any work done?"

"Maybe it's a museum piece. This whole place is like a museum." Teakh picked up an ink pen. "I guess you write with this." He shrugged.

"So while locked up and writing notes with pen and paper, I'm supposed to orchestrate a defense?"

"That seems to be the idea. I'll be your courier."

I sat at the desk. I'd seen plenty of legal couriers in Fennako City. Paper had a formality that couldn't be matched by rapid communication, but I didn't realize or expect that the work was done completely with hand-carried notes.

The paper had a felty sheen, most likely expensive with a high linen content. I selected a pen and laboriously printed a note to my man.

"Give this to Him." I handed the envelope to Teakh.

He set a finger to his ear, in communication. "I can't reach Him. I can get Harbor Patrol, but they won't let me talk to Him."

"Maybe Roy, Harb, or Mareen," I suggested.

"Who are Roy and Harb?"

I realized that I still didn't know the names of my brothers-in-law. "Seaguardsmen. They served as our escort when we were here to petition the Queen."

"Then Mareen."

He touched the side of his head. "Nope."

"If I can't send messages, I can't arrange for testimony?"

"Maybe that's the idea. I'll see what I can do." The door opened.

The Royal Guardsman stood at attention on the polished floor of the hall.

"Greetings," I said.

He bowed. "Ma'am."

"I'm going out."

"That's not allowed."

"And what if I just go? Are you going to stop me?"

"That would be unwise."

"Which? My going or you stopping me?"

"Both."

"So what's your name? Oh, I know you can't tell me. I understand. My brother is taking a message to Marsk Fennako. Are you going to stop him? Is that unwise?"

"It's not for me to say."

Teakh went on his way between the hexagonal facets of the passageway, and the door shut with me still inside.

In the sitting area I gazed out on the gray sky over Tristan Bay, the territory of my beloved. An esskip flew across the water, but at this distance I couldn't read the tail number. It probably wasn't his anyway.

Well if I had to play at living in a museum, that's what I'd do. At the desk I tried the composing board. Using a stylus I incised letters into the wax. To erase, which I did a lot, I smoothed the wax. Once I had my wording right, I copied the message to a sheet of paper.

Teakh returned while I was still working on a letter to Gratia, my academic advisor.

I looked up, stylus in hand. "That was quick."

"I've posted your letter by seagull drone. I'm flying it over right now."

I gave him more envelopes. "Take these in person. I'd like your impressions of people." Maybe that was the point of the clunky communication. "The first one is for Mareen. She'll know where to take the others. If you can't get through to her using the garden gate, look for a red dragon drone. It's her daughter's."

Teakh departed and I resumed carefully copying words onto paper. Distant ships and boats moved on the bay. The palace remained silent with only the creak of my chair as I shifted position and the scratch of my pen on paper. I missed the comforting hum of my dorm room's ancient heater.

Wings fluttered against the faceted window, and a gull landed, not any gull but Teakh's drone. I slide open a window sash. She scampered through and flew to the desk. She squawked and touched her beak to a tube on her leg. Once I'd removed the note she flew to the top of cubbies at the back of the desk and went dormant.

In the evening, I lay in the bedroom with the remainder of sunset glowing softly through the divider screens and their painted underwater scenes. The wooden wall paneling was elaborately carved with starfish and barnacles, to resemble a tide pool, I suppose. I had the feeling of being locked in a jewelry box. Even the bedposts were ornamented to resemble the barnacle-encrusted pylons of a dock. It reminded me of the underside of the dock where I'd been imprisoned by Dyse, although the service was better. Royal Guard had delivered supper, halibut baked in flakey pastry, most likely prepared in the palace kitchen.

I felt a flutter in my belly. No, not my belly. My child had moved. She'd moved, and I had no way of letting my man know, at least not until Teakh was awake.

IN THE MORNING, Gull carried the news to my man. After breakfast delivered by Royal Guard, we continued our work. We arranged for me to meet with my study group by seeking permission from all appropriate clans and explaining that the student team provided legal counsel. Couriers arriving with responses knocked rather than hailing. Gull perched on the desk cubbies, giving Teakh a view of the suite while he was out.

At last, after several days of sending and receiving messages, my study group arrived in the palace bringing rounds of sourdough bread topped with tomatoes, cheese, and anchovies. We ate the bread from napkins while seated on the floor and on the arms of antique furniture.

Rayleen commandeered the chair from the writing desk and rallied our team. "Ladies, tomorrow we go to court. We've been given the eastern position, the quadrant of new beginnings. Telisko opposes us and Annin's marriage. They want custody of Annin and Marsk's baby."

My team of students shouted their disapproval of Telisko.

Rayleen continued, "Our job is to demonstrate that Annin is competent to lead a clan and make her own decisions. We will convince Telisko to release Marsk from his horrid prenuptial agreement."

I felt hot and cold as I recalled my premonition about speaking in the Zenhedron.

———

Chapter 43
Four Sides

THE CACOPHONY OF the crowd seathed in the great dome of the packed Zenhedron. Teakh and I descended the northeast aisle leading our team of law students. The jade compass-rose at the center of the circular arena seemed minuscule and distant, sunk below the deep parapet and seating for a full grand-gross of participants. I searched the banks of seating for my man, checking faces and postures. I didn't spot him or recognize any of the Royal Guardsmen at the entrances to the arena floor.

The power of the monumental building awed me with its representation of the cosmos—the arching beams depicting the zodiac and the ecliptic, below them the clans divided into the four quadrants. The thrones of Danna and Poseidon faced each other on either end of the north-south axis—the polarity that danced the universe into being.

Then in the northern quadrant—that of Fennako— my man stood and saluted as if I were the Danna Star. His presence, my compass bearing, steadied me. Around him sat others in Fennako green: his sister Mareen, his mother Big Mareen, and a man I recognized as the King, now my father-in-law. He sat with his family instead of on his southern throne.

Our friends and allies filled our chosen eastern quadrant, a good turnout. Zelta and Rose had tirelessly canvassed for support. Silvi had come with her daughter and grandchildren. Jeena and Reez attended with their kin, including the men of the Idylko Seaguard, Teakh's coworkers. A row of women knitting included Banks and her kinswomen.

The young woman who longed to be a sex worker had brought others like her. Angel sat amidst a group of stylish women, the difference between prostitutes, courtesans, and artists blurred. A row of cover studs sported tight-fitting shirts and vests. To my surprise, the crowd included Coco and Sal. Here was a cross-section of the Fenrian reproductive industry, those involved in the spawn.

Seaguard sat amidst the sex workers. Maybe they were involved in the spawn, maybe they weren't. Judging by the amount of gray-green kit in our quadrant, every off-duty Harbor Patrol officer attended.

We filed into the front row. Teakh and I took or places on a balcony overhanging the arena with the eastern ray of the compass-rose pointing directly to us. I arranged my materials on a desk provided, then looked across the arena. The western ray of the compass-rose shot like an arrow toward Clan Telisko, our true opponents. They had forced my man into an unhappy polygamous marriage and denied any legitimacy to our marriage. I didn't know any of the women who sat in opposition, or their supporters, many of them mothers with children.

To the south, Dyse and Gorby sat supported by Valarin Hellenboreko and Cordalis Sibriko of the Eugenics Council. The other allies Dyse had bragged of hadn't materialized. The nearly thirty-six dozen seats behind her remained empty, including Poseidon's throne, an imposing chair beneath a canopy encrusted with abalone and shell work. The King sat elsewhere, as I had seen.

We waited as more participants arrived and declared their position on my marital status by where they stood or sat. The proceedings began with the chief justice announcing the case and opening the hearing.

"Clan Ralko," her voice boomed in the amphitheater.

Dyse descended to the arena. She stood at the center of the compass-rose and her holographic image projected in the dome above, facing the throne of Danna. Like the throne of Poseidon it was sheltered by a canopy held aloft by four pillars, but of granite and quartz, not shell. Like the throne of Poseidon it remained empty— the Queen wasn't in attendance.

Dyse's holographic image addressed the granite throne:

> *Dyse Ralko here. I speak for Clan Ralko on behalf of our members Annin Ralko and her brother Teakh Ralko. Both are underaged, not having completed their second dodecades. My poor, sweet niece was lured into Fennako City with promises of becoming a clan matriarch. There, she was taken into the Harbor Patrol men's house and forced to provide sexual favors. Ralko will not tolerate mistreatment of even one of our members. Annin, our dear niece, must be returned to the loving care of Ralko.*

Dyse named fees and compensation, surely her true goal. Ralko, I'd found out via research conducted by Reez, teetered on the verge of bankruptcy.

Case presented—she wanted to control me—Dyse returned up the aisle to her place in the south.

"Clan Telisko."

Across the arena, a woman stood and made her way to the floor. Her holographic image, huge above her, she gave her identity and also addressed the north:

> *The so-called Clan Noahee and Noahee charter are illegal. Teakh and Annin Ralko are under two-dozen years of age and so are still minors by law. They cobbled together this flawed charter and associated agreement without the knowledge of their guardians and, in fact, without any legal counsel. The documents they produced are a travesty with far-reaching consequences. Allowing dual-clan membership and including as clan members the children of males tears at the very fabric of Fenrian society—motherhood and clan.*

The crowd shouted and pounded the floor. When they had quieted, Telisko continued:

> *We cannot have young people entering into contracts they will regret for the rest of their lives. They will be taken advantage of. They will enter into unhealthy relationships and unconscionable debt. Annin here has made all of those mistakes. We ask that the court reject the flawed Noahee charter and free Annin Ralko from its burden.*

Telisko turned to the west, holding out her arms to her quadrant, and her giant holographic image did the same as if she were the very goddess of mercy.

> *These are the children of Marsk Fennako, senior Telisko husband, our husband. Ever since he became entangled with Annin Ralko, he has neglected his duty as a father.*

> *Fennako, you cannot leave these, your children and grandchildren, without a father. What are we to think? Fennako ignores treaties when it suits them? Whenever they want a new alliance—toss aside their own*

grandchildren as if pitching rubbish. What kind of justice is this?

What a low appeal to emotions! All to tear my man from me. He couldn't have fathered all of the children in the western quadrant. For his sake I hoped he hadn't.

"Clan Noahee." My own clan was called.

I stood and straightened my blue and gray robes. Rayleen wished me luck as I passed behind her to reach the aisle. I descended and nodded a greeting to the bailiff. Determined to show myself as competent, I made my way to the center of the arena. The dome arched overhead to the central oculus, but I couldn't see the holographic image that surely hovered above me.

I faced the northern quadrant, speaking to Fennako and to my man:

Annin Noahee here, grandmatriarch of Clan Noahee, foundress and charter member of Clan Noahee. Ralko violated our sovereignty and abducted the Noahee head-of-state in violation of interclan law. I am that head-of-state. I was taken from Fennako City and from the man I love, the father of my child. I was denied communication with my associates and kin. Ralko planned to force me into servitude as a surrogate mother. For this purpose, they conveyed me across clan lines and held me prisoner on the high seas. We accuse Ralko of assault, abduction of a clan leader, abduction of a minor for purposes of sexual exploitation, human trafficking, and high-seas crime—piracy. This traumatic ordeal endangered both me and my baby. We ask that Ralko pay compensation and release all claim to Noahee members.

I returned to my seat, heart pounding, having spoken from the floor of the Zenhedron for the first time.

"Clan Fennako."

To the north, Big Mareen leaned to speak with my man. He clasped the king's hand before he descended to the floor. His image coalesced in the center of the dome, a Seaguardsman in the gray-green kit of Tristan Bay Harbor Patrol. Unlike the others, he faced south, speaking for Fennako. My pride in him rose.

Marsk Fennako here, Magnate of Tristan Bay, Tristan Bay Harbor Patrol Chief, grandson to Her Majesty the Queen.

I've served as Tristan Bay Magnate for eight years, ensuring that traffic travels smoothly and safely in the waters which hold Fennako City. I love Annin Noahee. She carries my child.

She was taken from Tristan Bay, my waters, against her will and mine and without clearance from Fennako. Ralko has violated the sovereignty of Clan Fennako. We will continue to sanction Ralko, disallowing any member of Ralko to enter Tristan Bay unless under condition of parley. Ralko must pay reparations to my wife and to her clan. Ralko must forgo all claims to Annin, to our children, and to their descendants. I ask this as her husband and as their father.

My love followed him as he returned to his seat. If it were allowed, if it would not hurt our chances of ever being together, I would run to him.

WHEN NOT IN the Zenhedron I stayed confined in my quarters. Teakh could come and go as he pleased. I could not. I envied him.

I'd repeatedly sent requests to meet with my man, but neither Ralko nor Telisko would allow any type of meeting with Fennako. I wasn't allowed so much as a simple comset. Harb and Roy both delivered messages, but when I spoke to them at the door they remained silent.

"I can't take this much longer," I confided to Rayleen in the sitting room. All four disputing clans had laid out and detailed their grievances: Ralko with Fennako, Telisko with Noahee, Noahee with Ralko, and Fennako with Ralko. A dispute never has just two sides. That I'd been told repeatedly by Gratia. This one had far more than four. Each witness had their own take on me, my family, and what should be done with us. Court had been exhausting, with hours of testimony as competing clans tore apart my maturity, character, and morality.

Seated on a chair, Rayleen listened, a cup of tea in her hands, Tristan Bay behind her.

"What can I do?" I'd sent requests to speak with heads of clans, but my overtures had been rebuffed.

Rayleen set her cup on a side table. "You've gone too easy on them. They've dragged up muck about you. Go after Ralko. You've got dirt on them. Use it."

If I leaked that Ralko was on the verge of bankruptcy and likely to default on loans, creditors would demand immediate payment, driving Ralko into insolvency. "If we destroy Ralko, we're still up against Telisko."

"Aye. They're the bigger threat. Much bigger. Go after them. Have your sweetheart testify about how they mistreated him."

His so-called marriage had been horrific. It would be painful for him to speak of it in court, particularly if some of the children in attendance were his. No child wants to be repudiated by her father. No man would want to do so regardless of how his children were conceived—this I firmly believed.

"Let them know we've got the dirt," Rayleen said. "Telisko and Ralko will settle. We still need something on Fennako."

"No." I stood and paced across the hexagonal rug. I faced a painted octopus on a screen and turned.

All I had was that my mother and grandmother might have been assassinated. I could accuse Fennako of fratricide, but I didn't know for sure.

I shook my head. "Too risky."

"Then you know something?"

"It's unspeakable."

If Seaguard lords so much as suspected that the Queen or her predecessors had killed over the Sense-net—weaponized access—Seaguard lords would refuse royal override. The Queen—any queen—would be rendered powerless; the civilization of Fenria would implode. Lives were at stake, including mine and that of my kin.

Heart pounding, I calculated my risks.

I'd have to let the Queen know I had the information without leaking it to anyone else.

It might be done.

I glanced up at the ceiling coping and saw no sign of cameras, but Teakh hadn't cleared the room of bugs. Who monitored the room? The Queen or Big Auntie? My patron or my enemy?

I made my move:

"Fenna!" I called on the compound entity made up of queen and Sense-net. "Damn you Fenna!"

What about weapons hidden in the elaborately carved coping? The soulless algorithm that drove the Sense-net might very well kill me as it had killed my mother and grandmother. The siphon of a carved clam or the mouth of an anemone could easily deliver darts or gas to drive out oxygen from the room.

354

"Mother of Marsk. Mother of Mareen. I'm calling on you, Fenna!" I shouted. Who monitored the room? Who would respond?

I played a dangerous game. I took a breath then ranted "Queen Fenna, you're a kinkiller! A Poseidon-damn kinkiller!"

"What the depths are you doing?" Rayleen asked.

"Shouting obscenities. In a quarter of an hour I'll tell you more. By Fenna! A quarter of an hour." I shook my fist at the ceiling with its bas-relief sea-life.

I sat beside Rayleen and waited. We weren't dead yet.

The hands on the clock moved slowly. One tri-minute. Two tri-minutes. Three tri-minutes. I wished I'd brought along some knitting to calm my nerves.

A knock sounded on the door, the rap of knuckles on wood.

I opened it. A Royal Guardsman filled the doorway and announced: "A visit by Her Majesty Fenna the Queen."

I shot a glance to Rayleen. That was fast.

Two Royal Guardsmen stepped inside and flanked the doorway. Her Majesty entered, pushing a walker, the scars of her implants shinny through her thin hair.

The Royal Guardsmen, then Rayleen, bowed. I did not.

The Queen straightened. "We must speak with Noahee alone."

"With all due respect," a Royal Guardsman said.

"Go!"

"Excuse me." I nudged Rayleen.

When she and the two Royal Guardsmen were beyond the door, I faced the Queen and addressed her as my kinswoman: "Greetings Auntie. Thank you for meeting with me on such short notice." This time I bowed, but we both remained standing.

"You're a sharp one," she said.

I forged ahead, all politeness set aside. "Did you kill my mother? How about my grandmother?"

"I did not." She used the singular. This was significant. She hadn't personally killed them. But she could have ordered it done or the Sense-net could have carried out the crime on its own.

"Did you kill them?" I used and emphasized the plural.

"We do not speak of this." She set her lips primly.

"Fratricide," I again named the unspeakable. "We do, Auntie." I again claimed her as my kinswoman. "Mitochondrial DNA says so."

"First cousin, twice removed," she corrected. She seemed so mild, a sweet old lady leaning on a walker with sunlight slanting across the floor. Deadly, deceptively deadly. She and the Sense-net algorithm were one entity, the being that had killed my kin.

"We're still relatives," I said. My accusation of fratricide stood. It was a terrifying allegation to make. She-they might kill me and my brother just to finish the job.

"Who have you told?" she asked, her voice mild, too mild.

Jeena knew, but I wouldn't put her in danger by naming her. "A few others," I said, "but not my brother. If you kill him, they'll find out." They would, too. Jeena, Reez, and Angel would track down his killer. Justice would be done.

"What do you take me for?" The Queen shook her head. "Teakh is a fine young man and soon to be the uncle of my great-grandchild."

I placed my hand protectively over my womb and the child inside. "Would you kill him?" Again I used the plural. Who? Who exactly had ordered and carried out murder?

"Not if I can help it. We do not want this, but if he threatens us, we will be forced to take action."

So they would kill him. "Who are you?"

"Fenria." She lifted a frail hand gesturing to the room, the painted underwater scenes and carved barnacles. "The living entity that is Fenria. While I live, I'm her consciousness—Fenna."

"So the Sense-net did kill my mother." Had the linked Seaguard lords banded together in a mob determined to bludgeon their hapless victims? Or had it been the algorithm, programmed by generations of queens? A collective murder in either case.

"I'm not saying."

"Then you did." I used the plural, accusing all of Fenria. "What have you done to us?"

"Protected you," she said. "Your brother was bound to find out. If he'd tried to blackmail us, he wouldn't have survived."

If all of Fenria were against him, he didn't stand a chance. What guarantee did I have that I'd survive? For Danna sake, I was blackmailing the Queen.

She or her successor could arrange for our deaths. Or an offhand remark could be misinterpreted by a loyal follower. Crimes by commission and crimes by omission.

"We made an alliance with Noahee," she said. "You and I are kin. We are alike, and you carry my grandchild. We do not hurt our own family."

"What about the eldest princess? She opposes our marriage."

"She's not queen. I'm not dead yet."

Regardless of the threat posed by the next queen, I was bound to Fennako by my pregnancy and my love for my man. When Big Auntie ascended to the throne of Danna, she would not have Noahee support or codes. This I vowed to Danna herself.

I said, "Then for the sake of your grandchildren, settle this lawsuit, and do it out of court."

The Queen's gentle demeanor remained a cipher. "We'll call a meeting of interested clan leaders, but you and my granddaughter Mareen must craft this balance."

"Then is she your heir? Your tanist?" If the Queen had thrown her votes to Mareen, everything changed.

"My eldest daughter remains Princess Royal, and she will choose her successor. My granddaughter might be a good queen someday after she's proven herself. Are you ready to work with her in crafting this agreement?"

It was as if the Queen had thrown a rescue rope.

I seized it. "Yes! Completely."

"Don't be so sure. If you leave out the interests of one clan or even of one person, that little oscillation will upset the entire balance. That's what happened in Idylko. You cut out Telisko and Ralko."

"They were in the wrong."

"In the balance it doesn't matter. Every one of us is in the wrong. It's all in how you look at it. A good balance pleases everyone."

"That's impossible."

"So it is. Danna help me. I've done my best. It's your turn. Mercifully, the tide always rises again, and we have another chance. With perfect equilibrium, nothing would happen. The universe would freeze for eternity. Danna is balanced by Poseidon, stability by change." She smiled. "How is my great-grandchild?"

"Kicking."

"That's good. Very good." She placed her hand over my belly and smiled.

WE GATHERED AROUND a square table, we being eight clan representatives, a male and female pair on each side of the table. The Queen had made good on her word and allowed arrangement of a meeting in a privy chamber below the Zenhedron floor, a chamber that repeated the layout of Zenhedron quadrants.

On the north-south axis, a niche on the northern wall displayed a bronze of Danna as Lady Justice, a scale in one hand, a sword in the other. A niche in the southern wall contained a bronze of Poseidon as Lord Triton, a male head and torso with the tail of a writhing sea serpent. He brandished a trident, symbol of his love for Danna in her three forms: maiden, mother, and crone. Or maybe the celestial pair had the ability to slay each other—she with a sword, he with his trident.

Teakh sat to my left and my man to my right, his sister beside him. They represented Fennako and shared the north with Lady Justice. I observed how the green of his vest matched the patina of the statue's bronze robes.

Dyse and Gorby shared the south with Poseidon as they had in the coutroom above.

Clan Telisko again faced us, this time with the table between us.

Our seating resembled a game of Justice Poker or a miniature of the courtroom, which in turn represented the planet and cosmos—all self-similar in a fractal of balance and justice.

The table held no gambling chits, but we knew what was at stake: the status of my marriage. On this rested the existence of Clan Noahee and the fate of my brother and his children. His very life lay in the pans of justice, scales that might be capsized by a careless word about our ancestry. I'd played a dangerous game in using our ancestry to blackmail the Queen.

Warmth suffused me as I laid my hand atop my man's—if all saw it, so much the better—and opened the negotiation. "Thank you for meeting with us to hear our proposal." I nodded to Telisko across the table.

Until now I'd seen the Telisko representatives only across the courtroom floor or as giant holographic projections. This close they seemed even more intimidating, not less so. Lady Telisko had a face like a knife, sharp-nosed and narrow. Lord Telisko seemed only slightly more jovial—middle-aged, balding, and with a body going soft. Spidery implant scars laced his scalp under the remainder of his gray hair. She addressed him as "uncle," but they could have been brother and sister.

I gave what I hoped was a friendly smile. "Let me explain. Fennako currently pays for my prenatal care." I squeezed my man's hand. "My own clan, Noahee doesn't have enough members or revenue to provide healthcare benefits. My situation is less than ideal. I'm not a member of Fennako. Joining my husband's clan would be improper."

"That is a significant weakness." Lady Telisko's thin lips became even thinner.

Dyse frowned. "Ralko will provide care. It's only right."

"Ma'am," I once again addressed Dyse as a stranger. "I'm not a member of Clan Ralko either. Ralko has failed to provide for my education."

She wouldn't shut up. "But we did. We—"

I interrupted her. "Allow me to speak with Telisko." Ralko, on the verge of bankruptcy, didn't have the money Dyse so confidently promised. Winning the lawsuit wouldn't change their desperate situation.

"Listening," said Lady Telisko although her expression remained uninviting.

"Very well." I continued, "I understand that the prenuptial agreement between Fennako and Telisko specified that if Marsk Fennako, Lord Tristan Bay, were widowed, he would marry another woman from Clan Telisko."

"That is correct. That his wife passed away in no way ends the responsibility he accepted when he married her. He remains the father of Telisko children."

"I have no wish to deprive his children of their father. On the contrary, I care about both his happiness and the health and wellbeing of his children, siblings of my own child." I caressed the swell of my belly and my man placed his hand over mine. "I humbly request that you accept me as a member of Clan Telisko, thus fulfilling the stipulation, and allowing all of his children to be raised as siblings." I realized I knew almost nothing about the couple across from me, yet I was requesting that they adopt me and my descendants. I had to do it. I saw no other way to provide for and protect my man's children—all of his children.

"That can't be," said Lady Telisko. "You are a member of Clan Noahee, the grandmatriarch. Do you plan to abandon your own clan? We have no wish to include such a feckless woman in ours."

I lifted my chin. "Yes. Noahee. Founder as well as grandmatriarch. I can provide you with a copy of our charter, a charter ratified by the Queen. Noahee acts as a voluntary supplemental clan. We are in addition to maternal clan, not a replacement. Think of us as a mutual aid society. We aim to strengthen and promote interclan cooperation. My children—your clan members—will have close cousins in many other clans. Cousins that they, and you, may call on for assistance. In return, I ask that you provide me and my descendants with healthcare and education. I believe this is a good bargain."

She bent to confer with the balding Lord Telisko.

He set a hand to his ear and closed his eye before speaking in low tones to Lady Telisko.

She announced, "We will consider this proposal."

Teakh straightened beside me. "Consider me as well. If my sister joins, then so do I."

I shook my head and gave him my stern big sister glare. "You must remain a member of Clan Ralko."

"I have no relationship to Clan Ralko," he complained. "They've given me nothing."

'That's not true," said Dyse. "We purchased your esskip."

Their argument took off as Teakh countered: "You saddled us with the debt for it."

I elbowed him hard. "Forget about that. We'll be able to pay it off. Ralko needs you. Your kinsman Gorby needs you." I smiled at Gorby seated glumly beside Dyse.

"That kinkiller? I hate him." Teakh didn't even look at Gorby. "He abducted my sister."

"That lubber!" Gorby exclaimed. "He blackmails fishermen for chump change."

Lady Telisko cleared her throat. "This is not the kind of clan we wish to get involved with."

Good Danna! My carefully crafted balance would be destroyed by two men—no, boys—who'd never liked each other. I removed a pencil and paper from my pocket and jotted a note to Teakh.

> *Like us, he has no relationship to Clan Ralko.*
> *He's at the mercy of Dyse. Trust me.*

It may have been better to whisper. The Telisko representatives shifted uncomfortably.

"My apologies," I said. "I'm only asking Telisko membership for myself and my descendants. My brother will remain a member of Clan Ralko."

Teakh crossed his arms. "Like depths!"

Dyse licked her lips. "You can see what he's like. What does Ralko get out of this?"

"Money," I said. "Clan fees. Teakh runs an investigative agency working under contract to Fennako." I looked to Mareen for confirmation.

"The King will decide," she said.

Founder it all! I'd counted on her support and on the contractual work.

I forged ahead anyway: "His agency will employ members of Ralko. He'll be paying Ralko clan fees, so will they." With this plan, Ralko would have revenue, not just a one-time legal settlement.

Dyse rubbed her hands together. "We're entitled to a per-grossage of total business profits."

"That's not in our power to grant," I said. "His business functions much like an interclan fishing cooperative. Each clan receives revenue based on investment. Ralko will receive clan fees from their members only."

Dyse shook her head.

I switched from arguing tax and payroll to her real concern, solvency. "Auntie, my apologies. You and I have been attempting to reduce costs of hospitality. It's more effective to increase revenue. Together Teakh and Gorby will convert Ralko's Seaguard into a money-making operation." I hoped Teakh's business could live up to my promises, and that the King would agree to extending a contract. What better option did Ralko have?

Frowning, the Telisko couple watched this exchange— her lips thin, his an inverted bow, the mouth of a toad.

"Supporting Seaguard is our obligation," Dyse said. "We're proud to do so."

I applied flattery "Rightly so." Despite the nonsense about Teakh's innate altruism, I believed all people acted in their own self-interest. I said, "Ralko Seaguard has a wealth of experience in auditing catch records. The Ralko great uncles taught Teakh everything he knows. They gave him his start."

"We want access codes for Noahee equipment," she demanded.

Fear stabbed through me. Big Auntie could access Teakh's implant through Ralko to threaten or kill him, endanger all of us, all of Fenria. "Noahee will hold codes for Noahee implants and equipment. Thus it will always remain."

Lady Telisko interrupted. "This doesn't involve us. What will you contribute to Telisko coffers?"

"My husband and I will reside in Telisko for part of each year. We'll assist in the education of Telisko children. I know he longs to spend time with his children as their father." I smiled at him.

"Honestly. I can't visit during Full Moon holidays." He grimaced and I knew what he meant; he wouldn't father any more children in Telisko, other than my own.

"But you will have time off." I'd calculated on giving him and all Seaguard members legally mandated vacation time. I'd fight for it. "During New Moon holidays in low tide years, we'll arrange activities for your children. " I turned my hand so that our fingers entwined. "Sailing. Swimming. Water sports. We'll bring Reena so that she can meet her cousins."

"Who is Reena?" Deep lines creased Lady Telisko's forehead.

Mareen smoothed the front panel of her gray-green robes, drawing attention to the pattern of wolves and twelve-point stars. "Princess Mareen Fennako III, fourth in line to the throne. My daughter."

I waited until recognition dawned on Lady Telisko's sharp face, then said, "You and the Telisko children will have a relationship with the girl likely to become queen. They will know her as their cousin."

A hint of satisfaction touched Lady Telisko's lips—a tell of how she judged her cards.

I glanced around the table. Each of the men—except for mine—had a hand to an ear, the same for Mareen.

"I've consulted the King," she said. "Fennako agrees."

"Noahee?" I looked to Teakh.

"I like the Ralko great-uncles." He held up his hands, fingers splayed. "Aye."

"Ralko?" I asked.

"We're delighted to support our kinsman. Aye."

Teakh muttered: "You're delighted to get the money I'll bring in."

"It goes both ways," said Dyse. "Kin helping kin."

I looked across the table to Telisko. "It's up to you."

My man stood and bowed to Lady Telisko. "This balance is best for all of us, especially for the children of Telisko. With Annin and her descendants in the clan, I can support all of my children without reservation or torn loyalty."

Lady and Lord Telisko bent heads together in a whispered exchange. He nodded and set hand to ear, in consultation with a distant party. I tried to remain calm as if I were the statue of Lady Justice with her burnished face, so bright, so still.

Lord Telisko flicked an eyebrow at his kinswoman.

She cleared her throat. "We view this Annin as a young, inexperienced, and grasping young woman— no girl. Her so-called clan absurdly small. It's chief, her brother, just as greedy, juvenile, and frankly immoral."

My hopes plummeted. I sat as still and heavy as bronze.

Lady Telisko spoke. "We accept the council and recommendations of Clan Telisko senior husband. If she pleases him then so be it."

"Is that an Aye?" My voiced squeaked, too high, too surprised.

"It is," said Lady Telisko. "Annin, we welcome you and your descendants as members of Clan Telisko. Be aware we extend membership to you, not to your brother."

I stood and bowed. "My lady. My lord."

Mareen spoke. "Telisko, you have chosen well. Annin is a remarkable young woman and promising lawyer. Nay. She has already proven herself as a lawyer. She has founded a new clan, giving it a groundbreaking charter. She has successfully settled a child custody dispute involving five children and seven clans. She's authored a sound business plan as well as three high-value insemination contracts. Through days of grueling testimony she has listened with grace and responded with respect. All of this before achieving the age of two-dozen-and-one. She will go far, and do right by Telisko." She turned to me. "You and my brother have my full support. We will hold Telisko accountable should they mistreat either of you. Or your descendants. She is my beloved sister-in-law," she said for the benefit of Telisko.

I bowed again, then held up my hands in the gesture of balance achieved, including the four clans. "We have an accord acceptable by all." Teakh had a business. Ralko gained economic opportunity, Fennako received political stability, and Telisko had valuable social contacts.

I turned to my man and touched his hands, palms pressed together, both of us standing before Lady Justice. I had what I wanted most.

●●●●

Appendex
Calendar

T HE FENRIAN CLOCK-CALENDAR tracks both the tide and ovulation. In addition to second, minute, and hour hands, the clock has pointers for the season and for each of the two moon—six hand in all.

Ocean tides, even on Earth, are the highest at noon and midnight, during the full and new moon, and during the solstices, depending on latitude. On the Fenrian calendar, twelve indicates high tide. When the hands align at noon or midnight, spring tides (the highest tides) occur.

On Fenria, light and hormones are used to synchronize the human ovulatory cycle with the lunar cycles. Thus, the calendar also predicts ovulation and menstruation and can be used to control birth rate.

Every three years, when the moons align, the Fenrian birth rate increases, causing a demographic bump that graphs as a sine wave. The predictability of these waves allows for efficient planning and use of resources. Fenrian schools don't have to lay off or hire additional teachers in response to unpredictable class sizes. Clans are able to calculate the needs of young adults for new housing construction. With fewer resources devoted to infrastructure changes, construction, and re-training, clans are able to provide more care to children and the elderly. Fenrian class sizes are small with a high percentage of Fenrians engaged in teaching and caregiving. Likewise, clan fees (taxes) are high in order to fund these services.

Annin's Noahee clan charter strikes at the heart of this planning. If people are free to leave their clans or to give birth to children without clan approval, the size and age distribution of clans becomes unpredictable. Thus, the Noahee clan charter is profoundly destabilizing on multiple levels. Annin and the Queen are gambling that they can institute an ambilineal clan system that treats fathers as equal parents without precipitating widespread social collapse.

Month—"Month" refers to lunar period, the length of time from new moon to new moon. Since Fenrians have two moons, Luna Majora and Luna Minora, they have two different types of months.

Majora month—The period of Luna Majora, the larger of the two Fenrian moons, is the same as the period of Earth's moon and so corresponds to the human ovulatory cycle. Fenrians have two three-day "weekends" per month. The New Moon, corresponding to the start of menstruation and to high tides, is a time when women enjoy solitude. During this "weekend," men take responsibility for childcare. They organize activities for nieces and nephews in their clans. The Full Moon, corresponding to ovulation as well as to high tides, is when couples come together. Men travel to visit their wives and sweethearts and spend time with their own children.

A Fenrian three day "weekend" lasts about four Earth days, so the total amount of time-off in a month is similar to what we have. Having longer "weekends" allows men to travel farther to get home. Due to increased travel and to the complexities of high tides, Seaguardsmen typically work during high tide and take their time off during neap tides (times with the least amount of tidal fluctuation.)

Luna Minora—The Minora month is slightly shorter than that of Luna Majora. The moons align every three years when both moons are full, or one moon is full while the other is new. Luna Minor is considered the harbinger of chaos since the light of Luna Minora interferes with ovulatory synchronization.

Day—The Fenrian day is longer than that of Earth. The Majora month is the same length as ours—29 ½ Earth days—but it's made up of 24 ½ Fenrian days. As a result, Fenrians are typically early risers. They also deal with the longer day by dividing work into four six-hour shifts instead of into three eight-hour shifts as on Earth. They often eat a midnight meal, midrations.

Hour—Fenrians divide the day into twenty-four Fenrian hours. As on Earth, the hours are counted from one to twelve in the morning and one to twelve again in the afternoon. The longer day results in each Fenrian hour being approximately seven minutes longer than an Earth hour. If Marsk works two shifts he's on for fourteen Earth hours. Three shifts is twenty-one Earth hours. The man is exhausted.

Tri-minute—The Fenrian hour is further divided into twenty-four tri-minutes. Each tri-minute is approximately three Earth minutes.

Year—Like the other Fenrian time cycles, the Fenrian year is divided into twenty-four units. Summer and winter solstices are at twelve. The equinoxes are at six. Each unit is approximately an Earth fortnight in length but is made up of approximately twelve Fenrian days. This unit has been rendered as a "twelvenight." A half a twelvenight is equivalent to a week.

———

Appendex
Characters by Clan

FENRIANS REMAIN MEMBERS of their mother's clan for life. The clan provides for children born into it without regard to the parent's marital status—none are considered bastards. Fenrians believe each woman has a right to have at least one child if she chooses. She may borrow a husband from a clan member in order to fulfill her right. This practice of polygamy reinforces clan cohesion without the risk of inbreeding associated with cross-cousin marriage, a custom accepted in many other clan-based kinship systems.

Supposedly, all members of a Fenrian clan are descendants of one ancestress, but this isn't strictly true. Fenrians practice ingathering, the adoption of members who aren't genetically related. In reality, clan members may be more closely related through paternal lines due to the sharing of husbands.

Aluko:

Rents sailboats.

Comryez:

Has a reputation for insularity and lawlessness. This clan appears in *Sappho's Agency* and in *Return of the Cybernaut Princess*. They do exactly what they want, admitting to no power greater than their own.

Sarana (Stink Lily) heir to the Comryez Grandmatriarch, wears tomato-red Seaguard boots.

Dojko:

Iris Keno's sister. Beautician.
Keno Teakh's mentor. Owner and operator of Pretty Boy's Gym.
Lady Dojko Lord Dojko's sister. Grandmatriarch of Clan Dojko.
Lord Dojko Dojko Seaguard Chief.

Dusko:

In a legal dispute over manslaughter with Silviko and Hiltiko. Accused of negligence.

Fennako:

The ruling clan, consisting of matrilineal descendants of Queen Fenna Lee-Smith. Fennako practices extensive ingathering, so most members of Fennako aren't matrilineal descendants of Fenna. Fennako is considered the establishment.

The royal family, actual descendants of Fenna, forms a clan within a clan.

Big Auntie (Affrette Fennako) Princess Royal, the Queen's oldest daughter.

Big Mareen (Mareen Senior) Minister of Finance and Banking, Marsk and Mareen Junior's mother, and the Queen's second daughter who was supposed to be male.

Catherine Smith social reformer who instituted the Fenrian calendar, mother of Fenna Lee-Smith.

Dame Bulla bureaucrat, Department of Clan and Lineage.

Fenna Lee-Smith The name Fenna-ko comes from her. She bore four children one boy and three girls by Jamie Noah and founded the Seaguard along with him.

Harb member of Fennako Harbor Patrol.

Mareen (Mareen Junior) Fennako City chief of surveillance, the Queen's granddaughter, and Marsk's sister.

Marsk the Queen's grandson. Appointed Lord Tristan Bay by the Queen.

Reena (Mareen III) the Queen's great-granddaughter, Marsk's niece, who has a telechiric dragon named Scorch; appears as the queen in Sappho's Agency.

Roy member of Fenrian Royal Guard.

The King appointed by the Queen; her son-in-law. Big Auntie's husband.

The Queen Grandmatriarch of Clan Fennako, the Fenrian constitutional monarch, network administrator for the Sense-net, elected from among eligible candidates in the royal family.

Galvako:

Runs an insemination clinic.

Gratianiko:

Myrtle (Gratia) attorney. Annin's academic advisor.

Hellenboreko:

Valarin representative of the Fenrian Eugenics Council.

Hiltiko:

In legal dispute over manslaughter with Silviko and Dusko. Accused of murder.

Idylko:

Jeena lab technician.
Lord Idylko Idylko Seaguard Chief.
Raptoria Idylko grandmatriarch whose decorating taste runs toward bric-a-brac.

Kassanko:

Owns the dock where Annin catches rides.

Kazooko:

Specializes in insurance underwriting and maintains deep-sea territory in the Andean Ocean.

Gale law student.

Noahee:

Consists of descendants of Jamie Noah and is an ambilineal clan started by Annin and Teakh. Includes both paternal and maternal lines as well as ingathered members.

Annin grandmatriarch and foundress of the clan.
Jamie Noah husband of Queen Fenna Lee-Smith and founder of the Seaguard. Instituted the Noah Code.
Teakh Noahee Seaguard Chief. Annin's brother. Provides sperm for natural insemination.

Pontako:

Noted for excellent cooking.

Reez Jeena's partner

Ralko:

Annin and Teakh's birth clan. Ralko faces financial difficulty.

Aunt Dyse Annin and Teakh's guardian but not genetically their aunt.
Aunt Trudia runs the Clan Ralko hostel cum clanless shelter.
Gorby Ralko Seaguard with no genetic relationship to Clan Ralko.
Treena Proprietress of the Mermaid Tavern.

Shelliko:

Marjoram (aka Angel, aka Matta Carrie, aka Marj) artist specializing in painting male nudes. Teakh's beloved.

Sibriko:

Cordalis representative of the Fenrian Eugenics Council

Silviko:

Involved in a legal dispute over manslaughter with Dusko and Hiltiko. Not legally recognized as a clan.

Silvi grandmother of Clan Silviko

Telisko:

The clan of Marsk's late wife.

Unknown Clans:

Banks banking officer for clan that takes Annin in, belonging to a clan whose matriarchs enjoy knitting.

Coco insemination assistant and Sal's partner.

Grandfather hangs out at the Clan Ralko clanless shelter.

Madame X purveyor of insemination services.

Penny runs a bed and breakfast in Fennako City.

Rayleen law student.

Sal insemination assistant and Coco's partner.

Shanny skipper who hangs out at the Mermaid Tavern.

Zelta law student.

Wasatch:

Maintains the Wasatch watershed.

Rose law Student

Noahee Fennako Family Tree

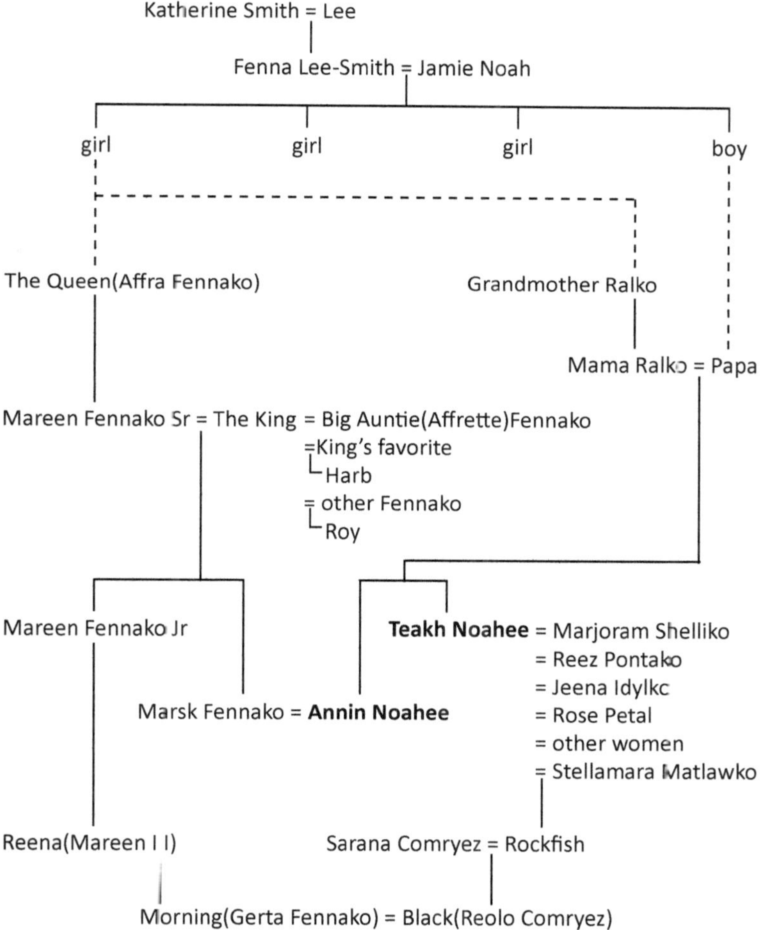

=	liaison or marriage
┊	relationship uncertain
└	child of

clan names are matrilineal

Noahee and Fennako function as moieties

About the Author

Lizzie Newell is an artist and author living in Anchorage, Alaska. Her favorite mediums are ice, paper, and science fiction. Her short stories have appeared in *Utopia Science Fiction* and in *Stinger Stories*.